Circo del Herrero

Learn more at: circodelherreroseries.com

CIP data pending.

Cover design by SOBpublishing. See end for credits.

Special thanks to Aeroplane Media and Julie Wallace for their help during the production of this manuscript.

Print Paperback:
ISBN-10: 0692259716
ISBN-13: 978-0-692-25971-9
Ebook:
ISBN-10: 0692250409
ISBN-13: 978-0-692-25040-2

Distributed by/through/from SOBpublishing.
Author's Dedication: "For no one in particular."

[BLA and GB GABBLER are characters in this story.
This novel was written by one person, not two.
This was just a disclaimer.]

Circo del Herrero

Contents:

The Annotated Manuscript: The Automation: BOOK ONE

Vol. 1 of the Circo del Herrero Series

By B.L.A., the Narrator, Storyteller, Omnipresent One

&

G.B. Gabbler, the Editor, Annotator, Reason This Is Seeing the Light of Day...

Acknowledgments (more like admissions):

I, the author of this story (who prefers the title "The Narrator"), would like to thank my "Editor" for the revisions and annotations associated with this account—even though said Editor took the liberty of chopping up my work and was quite insistent on making things "less embarrassing" (my Editor finds me shameful on many levels—especially when I claim this story is true). Though sometimes overzealous, there's no one else I'd let touch this work but dearest *Gabbler*.[1]

---

[1] Yes, I'm the Editor—the fourth wall-breaker. You might even call me another character in this story. At the very least, I'd like to think I'm its muse. My name is G.B. Gabbler (gender unimportant). The footnotes are all mine. I mention it only because the Narrator thinks it necessary to constantly remind you whose story this is and that I've *edited* it. I've changed various names, locations, and facts within this story—for more than one reason.

Chapter the first,

Too many freaks, too few circuses:

Please share my umbrella?[2]

Gabbler told me to start my story in a more interesting place (where I *had* started it wasn't "entertaining enough"). So, *in medias res,* here you have it:

As Odys walked down the sidewalk he saw the man—the man standing at the crossroad. The man just stood there, even though he didn't have to. The light was green and he was free to walk across. But he didn't. He simply stared at the traffic flowing past him. He even waved on the car waiting for him. *Come along, motorcar. I'm in no hurry. Have a good day.*

Odys noticed the man carried the absolute *longest* black umbrella, the fascinating kind that adapts into a perfectly fine walking cane. But there wasn't a chance of rain today. Not even sprinkles. Mildly overcast, perhaps, but nothing to deserve something *that* drastic.

And goshwow was that a top hat the old man was patting on?

As far as Odys could tell from the man's backside, this giddily-suited gentleman had time travelled from the 1800s—give or take a hundred years (Odys was no good at history). Not that Odys judged people by their appearance. No, Odys didn't judge, though he was mature enough (as a twentysomething) to know that elders didn't usually go about playing dress up. Not on days other than Halloween. And even then...

Odys avoided eye contact when he eventually caught up to the stranger. Normally, he would have given a curious grin to someone so done up, but not today. Today was different. Today Odys was one. Not two.

His broken-down car had not only forced him to walk but his runaway sister had forced him to walk *alone.* Okay—fine—she hadn't really run away but she *had*

---

[2] An obligatory epigraph for you: "There were golden handmaids also who worked for him, and were like real young women, with sense and reason, voice also and strength, and all the learning of the immortals; these busied themselves as the king [Vulcan] bade them, while he drew near..." —Homer's *The Iliad*, Book XVIII (Samuel Butler's 1925 prose translation).

abandoned him this morning. Now Odys was forced to brood and sulk and not know what to do with himself.

The older fellow didn't bother to glance at our aimless-Odys, who arrived just as the light turned red. The orange hand. That's no high-five it's asking for. Don't walk. Don't talk.

As he waited for the next green light, Odys stared straight ahead—watched his wakeful downtown settle into its afternoon place—refused to gawk at the probably-charming old chap. Gawking was rude anyway, right? Right.

Odys was much too depressed to spark a civil greeting. Or smile. Or even acknowledge the fellow's existence, for that matter. *I don't see this*, Odys thought to himself.

Yes, just stand still, Odys. You can't see him, he can't see you.

He'd just ignore the man until that light turned green. *Green, green, green. Turn green already, damn it.*

"You look like you've lost something, Odys Odelyn."

Odys made eye contact.

The old man adjusted his white-gloved hands on the umbrella's handle. *A swanky circus ringmaster, this man!* No, scratch that. Odys had always pictured a ringmaster with elaborate facial hair—a curled handle-bar mustache and devilish beard. This man was too clean-shaven to be a ringmaster, though he reminded Odys of one nonetheless.

LADIES AND GENTLEMEN, BOYS AND GIRLS, CHILDREN OF ALL AGES...

"Pardon?" Odys said with a frown (he refused to enjoy this unwelcome human interaction). And had he heard his name? What had the old man said? In his resentfulness, Odys had already forgotten. But *we* haven't, have we, Reader?

The man smiled—a warm and sophisticated grin. His jauntily-angled top hat half-amused Odys, who tried to hate it (he would enjoy nothing today).

...Was he some sort of immaculate butler?

"I said," (no longer lending Odys his eyes), "you seem lost."

...*Was he on his way to a steampunk convention?*

Odys realized he should respond. "Do I know you?" Hadn't the man said his name? Hadn't he? Hadn't he?

"Afraid not." The older fellow cracked another knowing smile. The man's confidence made Odys's eyes shift.

Odys gave himself a shake. Maybe he'd misunderstood.

The light turned green. Walk. Walk faster.

As they walked, the old man swung his umbrella—tapped it on the ground between his paces. These two characters fell into step, neither one walking too fast or too slow. Odys kept his hands in his pockets (defensively) while he tried to out-walk the man. But the man kept up with Odys's stride, his fancy coattails floating behind him. The tap, tap, tap of the umbrella's metal tip echoed off the cement. It reverberated in Odys's feet.

The sound annoyed Odys—so much he couldn't help but count the times it hit the ground—*eleven, twelve, thirteen*...

The tapping stopped and Odys sighed with relief. They both stepped up onto the sidewalk. A few more steps, then: "So, where *are* you headed this morning?" The man turned to Odys at last.

Blue eyes. Tiny little dots of sky. They peered at Odys as if looking at an old friend...an old friend he had dirt on.

"Just walking." Odys shrugged off the man's interest.

"Ah, me too." The man nodded. He tucked the umbrella under his arm.

Odys didn't know how to respond, so he didn't.

The traffic light turned red. Don't walk.[3]

"Have you a *reason*, boy? For walking, that is?"

Odys wanted to yell, *YES, MY STUPID CAR WOULDN'T START*. But it's a story full of curse words and violence (we'll save it for another chapter).

---

[3] Can I suggest jaywalking at this point, Odys?

"Well, it's not really any of your business is it?" He felt bad instantly, so tacked on a nervous laugh.

"I suppose you're right, yes!" The man tapped his umbrella point on the ground—too jovially. "Forgive me for prying. I get carried away."

Odys cut his eyes at the man. Had this man escaped from some loony bin, and did Odys need to alert someone? He seemed harmless enough, yet there was a mischievous purposefulness behind his every action.

"…I see you're admiring my outfit?"

No, actually. Odys had just blotted it from memory, looked ahead, prepared to forget everything so he could concentrate on the important matter: his traitorous sister.

"Yes, you *are* dressed up," Odys forced a smile. All the man needed was a monkey on his shoulder or a few pins to juggle.

"I'd like to tell you I don't normally dress like this, but I do. I look nice, don't I?"

That statement deserved a chuckle. "Yes, you do," Odys consented. He frowned at his own laughter.

…Was this some candid camera prank?

"I met my wife, you see, wearing a suit like this. She's dead now. I made a promise that when I met her again, I'd be wearing a fancy suit." No chuckle from Odys this time. Had the man met his wife at some historical reenactment? Had he expected to die for a while now if he dressed like this all the time?

"As they say," the man continued, rocking to and fro until the light turned green, "you never know when you're going to go. You can't plan for it. Unless, of course, you commit suicide. Then you *know* to dress for the worst."

Wait. What?

Odys was about to be confused when (ohthankgod): Green. Walk.

WALK QUICKLY, ODYS.

The man turned left as they stepped onto the curb; Odys went straight. One, two, three four, five uneven steps before: "Oh, Odys Odelyn!" he heard the man call. He made a half-trumpet with one hand, "You dropped this."

This?

Odys paused and turned in the alleyway's threshold, right beside a giant green waste bin and a loading-dock. Another chill ran down his spine. That was definitely his name. He wasn't mistaken, was he? He *had* heard his name, hadn't he?

Oh, hadn't he!

Like a magician performing slight-of-hand, the old man concealed something in the palm of his glove. His fingers opened like a magical bloom. He presented a shiny, round…quarter?

Well, it was the about the same *size* as a quarter, anyway. It reflected a spectacular amount of light—amber light. The showy presentation enchanted Odys. He had to *force* himself say, "No, it's not mine."

(Once again, he'd already forgotten the man said his name).

"Oh, but I'm sure it is, *Odys Odelyn*," the man insisted with slim bantering flair, a twinkle in his blue-blue eyes.

Third time's a charm. Odys Odelyn. No mistake.

"How'd you know my name?" Odys demanded, jaw clenching. Who'd want to harass him like this? He didn't have the energy or the time—

"Are you so sure it's *your* name?" the old man said, walking forward and seizing Odys's hand from his pocket. He inserted the warm coin in Odys's hand. "There's bound to be more than *one* Odys around. The name's not *that* original. After all, every time someone says Odysseus, they're saying *part* of your name—"

"My name's not Odysseus—"

"No one said it was." The man gestured with a nod to the coin.

Odys couldn't help but look at it. He realized its tarnished spots didn't stop it from shining.

"It's a penny," the old man said. "Penny for your thoughts." He tapped the ground with the umbrella again. He tucked in his chin and stared at the cement as if wishing he had kept his findings.

Odys examined the coin to appease him (Odys was in no *real* hurry this morning and perhaps this would lead somewhere).

"The date, there, says 1793," the man pointed, although Odys had already read it. "They only minted them that year. A collectable, for sure. Only seven known in existence, and that *isn't* one of them. You'll not want to give her away or sell her— no matter the price!" His polished voice was unexpectedly grave, more warning than advice.

Odys rotated the side that read "One Cent"—the side with the intricate wreath. He turned it over to the head: the profile of a woman with flowing hair.

Odys looked up. The man removed his hat. Odys felt like Frodo taking on the burden of Bilbo's ring, though he had no idea why. (But don't get ahead of yourself, Odys. Who said you're the hero of this story?).

"Why're you giving this to me?" His cold lips could barely form the words.

"Giving it? My boy, you dropped it!" *Silly young man!* "Did you know, Odys Odelyn, that many would like to do away with the penny altogether? They say they cost the government more to make than what they're worth. Many would rather have us round to the nearest nickel and be done with it. A disappointing thought, for sure. I always *did* like picking homeless ones up from the ground. In fact, that's how I discovered that one, there. People drop them like trash and simply let them be—as if it costs more to bend down than to leave it. But for me, I liked to save money. I valued little nothings, you see." He nodded, trying to make himself believe his memory. He smoothed back his hair one more time, tapped his hat down. "As they say, 'Find a penny, pick it up, and all your days you'll have great luck.' Don't forget that, Odys Odelyn. Today's your lucky day."

Before Odys could question that statement—

"Many would say that the girl on that coin is Lady Liberty. To a point, they're right. But that specific girl, there, is *not* the lovely lady Libertas! Not really. You may call her that, but ironically…that penny is anything but *free*. Not only is she *trapped* in that metal, but *bound* to be spent. That woman, there, is just the right sum for the ferryman."

What the hell was this, his catechism?

The old man lifted his umbrella and swished it toward Odys, tip inches from his face. Odys jumped back, almost bumping into a tiny woman with her dog. The dog didn't mind, but the woman glared.

"Let's just say, Mr. Odelyn, that the penny is my debt—my *obligation*—paid in full. I'll owe nothing else to you since you now have the funds. The rest is up to you."

Enough with the money puns, man.

Odys put up his hands. "Er—all right, then." Anything to shut this man up. People were staring as they tried to make their way into one of the building's entrances. *Is this man putting on a street show? Why's he dressed up? Is this a film production? Are we on camera?*

The man lowered his umbrella, fixed the hat on his head, smoothed down his breast. "Will you hold this, Odelyn?" The man presented the umbrella's curved handle.

"*How* do you know my name?"

"Take the umbrella and maybe I'll tell you." The man raised a brow.

To move this show along, "Fine."

Hands free, the old man reached into his suit pocket. Odys froze in place when he heard the click and saw the barrel—the barrel pointed *directly* at his face.

Holyshit.

"Sorry to do this, here and now, but I'm crunched for time. You walk very slowly, Odys." The mad man's voice was so rushed it whispered—Odys could

9

barely hear it. The onlookers (debating whether or not to record this on their phones) were too preoccupied to hear.

"I'm being followed, you see. I'll need you to put that coin in your pocket. Quickly, now, boy! Don't spend my time—I've paid enough, dealing with you. That's it. Put it away. Don't you drop her either, boy. She's small enough to fall through that drain, there. Or even an unsuspecting pocket hole. She's very important. Now, open the umbrella."

"What?"

"I said open the umbrella!"

Obediently, Odys fumbled with the binding strap's button, hands shaking.

The black webbing popped out like a monstrous bat wing.

"Hold it up. That's it, yes." The man's eyes darted about. The few in the area were clearing out, ducking and rushing from this antiquated man with his antiquated gun.

Odys rested the umbrella on his shoulder, noticing the man was going to speak once more. Odys swallowed hard, bracing himself.

"Now, Odys Odelyn, that's my last cent, there. I've spent the rest. It's up to you to buy more time. Spend wisely."

The man drew back the gun and held the nose upward, as if finished with his prestigious show. But no. That wasn't the end of his haywire session:

The man shoved the gun in his mouth and gave an encouraging wink—a wink!—right before Odys heard the echoing BANG.

The pigeons flapped up.

As the blood, hat, and brains showered from the sky, Odys half-noticed the shiny name carved on the umbrella's handle: *Pepin J. Pound.*

PEPIN: Willing to share his umbrella.

WALKING: Because he knew Odys would be walking.

HOW DID HE KNOW?: Because he's the reason Odys's car didn't start.

CHARM: 100%[4]

Chapter the second,

A penny for a pound:

Is this story just a Trojan horse?

Bang/boom/splat. Odys hadn't just witnessed a suicide. He'd witnessed an obliteration of unearthly proportions.

Pellets of warm fluid and gooey chunks fell from the heavens—Odys stooped and shielded himself with the umbrella.

…Could *that* little gun have caused *that* much damage?

When the blood-rain finally stopped (not that it was *excessively* gory—PG-13, I would say. Nothing *Kill Bill*), Odys straightened from his cowering stance and lowered the umbrella. The decapitated corpse was mostly-neckless. The (practically) toy gun hadn't done *that* to *this* corpse. Hell, no.

…Had it—had the head—*exploded?*[5]

Odys covered his mouth with the back of his sleeve. His eyes darted around— *Maybe someone else had actually shot him with a—a—a freaking bazooka or something?*

When the cops arrived Odys was still standing there. Odys dropped the nasty umbrella eventually, because a policeman led him to a warm car.

He was shaking. Shaking. Shaking as he noticed the shocked onlookers off in the distance, giving their various testimonies to surrounding officers. The news reporters would be here soon. There was a man in one of those trash-sack suits—the poncho

---

[4] Our chapters will always end in lists. Why? What do lists have to do with this story? I asked that same question. Our Narrator replied that, because this is a "Prose Epic" paralleling Epic Poetry (supposedly), these lists are a transmuted throwback to the "Epic Catalogue." I guess I liked the excuse, so I kept them. After all, lists are one of the essential elements of an Epic, no matter the content of said lists. And, yes, this does mean you should expect other elements of the Epic to appear in this novel, actual poetry excluded. Invocation of the Muse to appear momentarily.

[5] A bit of a messy finish, but it certainly wasn't anti-climactic…

kind that keep the gooey evidence off your clean clothes. He held a writing tablet. Someone called in more assistance.

Odys tried to read the other witnesses' lips as they gestured to the scene. He looked to his right where they were bagging the headless body and scraping off the remains from brick walls.

"A bullet did *this*?" The question full of doubt.

"Yep, we found it. There's no other weapon, no traces of anything else…"

No wallet, no ID, no nothing. Have fun identifying THAT decapitated body.

"He never met the man before?"

"Said he didn't."

"Where'd he get the umbrella?"

"Haven't asked, sir."

"Where did you get the umbrella, kid? Kid?"

Odys felt eyes on him from above. He had looked up—up at the sky as if expecting to see God pointing and laughing. Instead, he noticed a man watching from the rooftop on the building across the street. Odys touched his pocket to make sure he wasn't going mad—yes, the coin was still there.

The man was crouched low, like a monkey. His hair could have been red or orange or…

And he was tossing something—flipping it up in the air with his thumb and catching it. Maybe a rock? No. It was a coin—an omen. Each time was a perfect catch, even though he wasn't looking at the coin and his eyes were *most definitely* on Odys.

The man was mocking him. Flip, flip. A coin for a coin. He had *wanted* Odys to see him. He dashed off before the officer tried to see what Odys saw.

"Sir? Sir, can you hear me?"

The question registered. Odys gave a languid nod, eyes flickering back to the roof-spot. He was just being paranoid. The man was only some curious roofer who had heard the commotion. That's all. God, *please*, let that be all. No more of this, *please*.

"Is this his umbrella?"

Another nod.

"Why do you have it?"

"He gave it to me," Odys answered.

"Do you know his name?"

Odys shook his head.

They examined the umbrella, asked someone on the other end of their cop-radio to punch in "Pepin J. Pound," to search under aliases. Nothing came up. "Might be the brand," the officer said. "Or his stage name?" They all chuckled at the thought. "Is there anything else you should tell us? Did he give you anything else, Mr. Odelyn?"

How did *they* know his name? Is there no such thing as *anonymous* anymore? Oh, that's right—he'd given them his driver's license, his information. "Yes," Odys answered. He reached into his pocket, dug for the coin, watched their expectant faces.

He hadn't had his hands in his pockets for a while, so they were chilled—numb. He felt the coin—but what was that? His fumbling fingers cornered something sharp and jerked back.

He shook his hand, putting his finger to his mouth, expecting it to bleed. But nothing.

Perhaps it was all in his head. His fingers were just cold. Too cold. Everything felt like a bite or a sting when cold.

But no. The coin he had reached for felt heavier—it weighed down his pocket. He was becoming lighter than the coin. He leaned to the side, inclining like a catatonic drunkard. The *coin* was drawing him down.

Falling out of the open car, an officer caught him. Odys realized he couldn't feel his feet or hands—was he having a heart attack? Hardly. He's much too in-shape and good looking to be killed off just yet. Sorry, Odys, you'll live through this.

"The hell's the matter with him?"

"The sight must be getting to him. Put him back in the car, will you?"

But blood hardly bothered Odys—he wasn't squeamish. He could watch whole episodes of documentary surgical procedures and never have to look away! He wasn't some wimp!! He loved gore—blood and guts!!!

"Goddamnit, the kid threw up on me…" The man grumbled, jumping back too late, a look of pity upon his ugly face.

Odys mumbled a sincere apology, resting on his knees.

A female officer bent down, examining him. A concerned interest haunted her expression. "Mr. Odelyn, you all right?"

No, actually. He's just about to black out. And you, lady, are about to load him onto the parked ambulance that, after having seen the scene, hadn't planned on taking anyone *alive* to the hospital. So let's get this over with:

An agonizing pain pulsated though Odys's torso; they saw his blue-web veins push to their pale surface. He crumpled to the grey pavement. Over and out.

Stanza: Even a "Prose Epic" needs a break every now and then.

He woke up in a hospital bed.

He touched the blanket, looked at his hands. He wasn't hooked up to anything— no IV, no heart monitor. So why was he here? There were smears of brown on his arms—places the nurses hadn't given their all in cleaning off the blood. He touched his nose, realizing he didn't have his glasses. Deep in thought, he let his fingers slide down his bare face. It was times like this when it would suit to have a beard to stroke—something for his long fingers to do.

But what he lacked in facial hair he made up for in ponytail.

An attendant noticed him fretting with his messy hair and called someone— someone wanted to talk with him, so just sit tight.

More like sleep tight. He wasn't sure he could stay awake.

A few minutes ticked by. The other person was taking their time. As Odys waited for the doctor or officer or *whoever* who needed to talk with him, he replayed the morning through his mind—he replayed every second to be sure he wasn't going mad:

Why did he meet Pepin? *Because I was walking.* But why was he walking? *Because my car didn't start.* But where was he going? *Fuck.*

That's something he couldn't tell the cops if they asked.

Stanza: We interrupt your normal programming to...

...Deflate the tension I've worked so hard to build and flood you with back story.

And what that means is this next part *should* have been Chapter One. But, because Gabbler said I had to *kill* someone first to get your attention, we moved it. Beware the lengths Gabbler goes to, to keep you interested.[6]

Stanza: On the same morning Pepin offed himself.[7]

The cat was heave-hiccupping on the rug, tongue out as it tried to oust the thing gagging it. Vomit, you see, is the proper way to start this story. Vomit is the metaphor.[8]

Though you may cringe now, do remember, the cat—the stupid cat—is a main character. Not only had this stupid cat upchucked a slimy landmine, but Odys had just stepped in it.

---

[6] Says the one who asked for my help! I may be the one who cut and pasted this here, but the Narrator *did* approve it. But, to justify my action: this coming section is no flashback. I know we all hate them in novels—so tedious to break from the structural narrative! No, no, it's not a flashback. It's an *insert*. The Narrator would want me to be very clear about this. Yet, in defense of flashbacks, all novels have them (it seems). So it's only fair that this Prose Epic doesn't escape the same treatment.

[7] In other words:
Chapter the first,
A mad alchemist:
Not a mad scientist?
(As cut by me)

[8] Vomit of the Epic genre, that is. Word-vomit, on the other hand, is why B.L.A. needed an Editor.

"Odissa!" he shouted. "Can't you clean this crap up?"

"It's not crap. It's vomit!" she shouted from the kitchen.

He mumbled under his breath. Then, "So you *know* it's here?"

No response.

"Your stupid cat hairball'd the freaking hallway, Odissa. Don't just leave it!"

"If you don't want it there, then clean it!" his sister snapped back. Her "stupid cat" had started a new diet recently; he was having some trouble adjusting.

"You're disgusting." Odys grouched.

"You're the one who won't clean it!"

(Even if she *did* clean it, it wouldn't be good enough. Odys had a very specific method for cleaning such things).

Odys rolled his eyes. Then rubbed them. Where were his glasses? Everything in the apartment was a blur. Speaking of their apartment:

Though they could have afforded something bigger—much bigger—the quaintness suited their tastes. The bigger the place, the more stuff you'd need to fill it. And they already had *enough* stuff. They wanted to escape it—escape the *stuff* they could so easily acquire.

They had money. They'd always had money. And money had them.

In rejection of their privileged backgrounds, they'd embraced minimalism— though it could never minimize their past. That was something they could not escape. Even if they gave away all their savings, the act couldn't rewrite history.

They've been written down in ink. Not pencil. (Cue serious music).

He put his still-dirty foot on the carpet reluctantly. When he reached the kitchen counter, he took out a clean mug. "I'm not going to clean it," he lied. He'd clean up the hairball eventually. They both knew this. Even though it wasn't his cat, he'd clean up after it (hell, he'd likely deep-clean the entire apartment because of it).

It had always been *her* cat. Never his. The very second they'd moved into this apartment, she'd picked up the stray. God, that was a while ago, their "freedom" (as he called it). Now he was in his twenties and had a young-old face. The smoking didn't help with that.

He cut his eyes at his sister. Odissa took a humble sip from her coffee, flicked open their morning newspaper. She tossed away the green rubber band and headed straight for the arts section (where the book reviews are). Such a pretentious nerd she is.

He poured his own cup of instant-life, watching her. Her brown eyes rolled over the words behind her glasses, those old-school frames.[9]

Odys thought the style suited her, but that they were ridiculous. She was often outrageous to scare people away. They needed no one else…

BUT SO ANYWAY.

Done staring at her glasses, he soon realized she was already dressed—ready for the day. But it wasn't even noon yet. She was never dressed (let alone fully awake) this time on Fridays. Usually they were freewheeling slobs together. She would stay in her pajamas, not put on makeup, not do her hair. They looked even more like twins that way (he smiled at the thought). But now she was dressed, all prim and proper—makeup, hair, outfit.

He took a swig from his mug, a little dribbling down his chin.

Hot, hot! How the hell can she stand it this hot? Dabbing his face, he pretended it didn't faze him. He put down his mug and cleared his throat, about to interrupt her concentration. "You're dressed early."

"Yep," she replied, walking over to their wooden table. She plopped the paper down with a soft smack. She didn't look up from her news.

Odys took up his mug and followed her restlessly, a little puppy. He pulled at his junkyard-worthy undershirt to dry the coffee stain. He gave up and reached for a half-empty cigarette carton.

---

[9] This, Dear Reader, is what we millennials called a "fucking hipster." But, I love her despite this.

17

Just as he lit one, she was holding two fingers out, expectant. Her precocious eyes never left the crisp newspaper. Impatient, her fingers cut the air like scissors. *Chop, chop!* He removed the cigarette from his lips—which he hardly ever did unless the "drag was dragged," but Odissa was the exception. He placed it between her slender fingers. "Thanks," she said, bringing it to her lips. Doing so, "We *really* should consider using matches only."

He raised an eyebrow. "Yeah?"

"Yes. It'd not only facilitate our toxic habit's bio-degradable nature, but it's also more stylish." (There's probably a more pompous way of saying it).

"I told you that last week. Those *exact* words."

Plagiarism! And what next? Would she say they should roll their own too? She'd become so snooty.

"But now I agree with you." And she just kept smoking, as if this hackneyed tangent never happened.

She was actually too much of a "good girl" to look like a professional smoker. But don't let appearances deceive you. She could drag harder than…well, she could drag, anyway. Nothing more than that. She's a modest girl.

After lighting a cigarette for himself, Odys could *now* have his "breakfast," as he called it.

He drummed the table with his restless fingers. His cigarette burned away like a horizontal chimneystack. His right hand flicked on and off his Zippo lighter. He hoped the annoying sounds would redirect her attention. But her eyes kept reading. She was so austere. Was a book review more interesting than him?

Puff, puff, puff from the corner of his mouth.

The warm cigarette never left his lips. Once it was lit, it was permanent. Not even when he talked would he take it out. He would speak through the sides of his mouth rather than wave it between his willowy fingers for attention. Besides, he didn't talk much anyway. Not when he was smoking—which usually meant he was alone or with others who didn't talk much either (case in point: his sister).

Only when he was eating or drinking or didn't want the ash to fall on him would he *occasionally* remove it. Most times, however, he cared very little. His smoking habit wasn't for looks, no. Cigarettes were a purpose—a means of shortening/enlivening his dull existence. So no, he wouldn't remove it.

His fingers drummed faster on the wooden table. He snapped the metal lighter shut. Aha! There were his glasses. He reached across the table, past the fancy ashtray. Ah, he could see.

But sight was his foe.

The apartment overwhelmed him. Now that he could see it properly, he felt the need to "tidy up." But he resisted the urge and settled for fidgeting in his seat.

He would clean things and count things and align things and straighten things and smooth out that rug when Odissa wasn't looking.

(I bet you thought they were slobs, right, because of the remaining cat hairball? No, no. Don't jump to conclusions!)

Odissa was lucky to live with Odys. That meant the only place she had to clean was her own room (which she still didn't clean regardless). What's more, she made it a point to give her brother more work—like the time she bought that hideous silver lamp with five bendable fixtures for the living room. *He* had to drive all the way back into town, return it, and pick out a style with an even number of bulb-holders. His eyes flickered to that very lamp. With six bendable heads, it looked like a fucking hydra. Almost gave him a heart attack the first few nights they had it.

He tore his eyes from it.

Some might say those eyes, fairly sunken in their molds, were too detached—and that just might be true. They were brown. Just like his hair. Brown. It may or may not be his favorite color; his preferences shifted. Brown like his sister's.

And why was she dressed, again?

Her brown eyes, however, were nearly black—black like that cup of non-froufroued coffee she was just about to finish. Though so dark, they made her ordinary face yieldingly simpler.

And since we're comparing them, notice his face is bolder. Everything about his sister is nothing more than a softer and more ordinary version of himself. Softer eyes, softer complexion, softer smile, softer voice, softer…

Identical twins look alike, but fraternal can be yin and yang. Contrasting similarities. Distorted effigies of each other. But by now you get the picture. MOVING ON.

He brushed sterile ash off the table to the floor he'd sweep later. "You look very nice in that outfit." (He wasn't going to let it go).

She exhaled before answering, "Why, thank you, Odys." Her eyes froze under their lids. Wait for it…wait for it…

"But you only have three rings. You need another."

"I know, Odys. Did it just to piss you off." She smirked up at him, folding her paper. She rested her hands atop each other, that cigarette burning in the right. Her spare fingers fiddled with the ring on her left hand—the ring-finger's ring—a silver band—a wedding ring to those who didn't know better.

"You know what Travis told me yesterday? 'Librarians should devour books, not smokes.'" She marveled at her burning leaves. She'd meant to change the subject.

He took the bait. He corrected her, "We aren't librarians, just library assistants."

"Same thing," she shrugged, waving him off with her smoking hand; don't be nit-picky.

That's that.

It was pleasurably hard to breathe (which was Odys's only mindless action for the time being). The room was full of tantalizing smoke—wonderful, lingering, suffocating smoke. The smoke swirled around them like dancing phantoms. They were soon on their third round of cigarettes (insisting on advancing their inevitable lung cancer), before he realized he *still* had a cup of coffee. Ah, it was nice and cool, too. He wouldn't have to nurse it. Yes, sir.

His square-framed glasses slid down his nose. He didn't push them up. The glasses are deceptive, they make him seem placid and introverted. He's not. Not really. He doesn't hide behind them as some do, but he does use them to mislead. If either of them hid behind spectacles, it was his sister—but it was hardly a disguise upon her dainty face. Or maybe it was. Bookish by nature, she fit the librarian stereotype perfectly. Except the smoker bit, perhaps.

She was elegant when she smoked, unlike him—though not on purpose. He liked to watch her smoke; it comforted him. He enjoyed her tapering hand bringing it up to those lace-thin lips. Every interval between intakes was unique, and he observed each with revived curiosity.

She'd pretend not to notice his overly entertained eyes tracing from (one) the whirling smoke to (two) white cigarette to (three) pale face to (four) curved neck to...One, two, three, four. He would count her. On and on in an infinite sum that somehow always ended in an even number. She was even. Always even. Always balanced.

...Their mutually parasitic nature was (for lack of a better explanation) the reason I wanted to start my story here. Don't feel uncomfortable, my prudish readers; don't convict them just yet. Yes, you might already suspect an unorthodox sibling relationship, but don't let me prick your conservative bubbles. I haven't earned that power yet. Just ignore this erotic needle as I wave it in your face. It's not going to hurt. Much.

Honestly, you're just like everyone else familiar with the pair—guessing, predicting, and judging right from the start. Strangers often mistook them for a married couple; or, for those more familiar with the pair, to assume incest. Sometimes Odys even introduced her as his missus to ward off the curious stares and sly questions. *Just who was that girl he brought with him, and—more importantly— what was she to him?* Dear Odissa would play along buoyantly, bless her heart, and together they'd make a grand time of it. It was easier to pretend.

Thus, at parties (Odys was unusually popular despite his efforts; Odissa usually came off as the reclusive sort who scared away inviters), they would say things like,

"Let me introduce you to my wife," or, "Have you met my husband?" when speaking about each other.

Odd phrasing of that nature.

It not only kept things (such as their clinginess) smooth and simple, but it also kept them from, as they say nowadays, being "hit on." And the plain rings they both wore on their fingers added to the effective repelling. Their make-believe marriage proved they needed no one else. They *wanted* no one else. So please go away.

To Odissa, they were Cleopatra and Ptolemy. Their solitude was their Egyptian throne. They were gods among men. No Caesar would overthrow them. But historical parallels aside:

He couldn't stand not knowing what the special occasion was—the reason she was dressed. "What would you like to do today, Odissa?" he asked, leaning towards her.

"Have you, dear brother," she said in her most pompous (and fake) British accent, "forgotten what today is?"

His eyes narrowed.

She rested her head in her palm. "Well, you must've suppressed it. I'm going to see him today. Our *father*."

"Oh." Odys mouthed the sound. "It's *that* time of year."

"Hm," she answered, no emotion in her sound.

He evened out her newspaper, putting the pages in a nice stack parallel to the table's dull edge. He liked even lines. He counted to an even number before taking his next step. One, two, three, four, five, six, seven, eight:

"Don't."

"Don't?"

"Don't go." It was almost a command. "Please."

She laughed, a feigned noise, and put out her unfinished cigarette. He counted the number of times she smashed the tip into the tray. Onetwothreefour…five. He hated odd numbers!

She saw him cringe. She knew *exactly* what he counted.

"I have to, Odys. We need the money. That's how it works." She slouched back in her chair, waiting for his unavoidable reaction. She always used tender unpleasantness to control him.

"You don't have to go anymore, you know." Quietly, "We don't need *him*."

"Yes, we do. If I didn't go, we wouldn't live comfortably. Gourmet coffee has its price tag." She attempted a smile at her own humor.

He put out his own cigarette—onetwothreefourfivesix (see, Odissa? *That's* how it's done)—and proceeded to space out the butts in a symmetrical arrangement. Just as he liked it. There was nothing else on the table to perfect. Nothing else to distract him. His brow wrinkled once more, the corners of his mouth declining. Though he had a naturally somber semblance, it was even more depressing with the topic of *their father* on the table.

"This will be the last of it, I promise. I'm going to ask him for more than usual. He won't mind. We're almost done with school anyway, and so I might—"

"If you ask for more, he'll ask more from you," Odys interrupted.

She frowned, disapproving. He could be so childish when it came to her. He didn't like others stealing her attention—attention that was his. She answered him, "Then I'll do more."

He didn't like that answer. One, two, three, four. The seconds ticked by like a clock in his mind. "C-can I go with you?" He faltered the question. He didn't want to go, but he wished to express his willingness to suffer. "I don't even have to show my face—"

"You know he wouldn't like that, and I'm not supposed to ask. And if he found out—"

"Then how long will you be this time? You have work Monday."

"Tuesday, actually. You've got Monday by yourself, babe. However, I should be back by Monday. That's his estimate."

Odys's jaw clenched. That was too long. Longer than usual.

23

"I'm also going to ask him about it." She was trying to justify her visit.

"It?"

"Well," her voice lowered, "who our mother was. Or *is*, whatever. I think he's willing to tell me now. Now that we're about to graduate. I can get *something* from him."

"I don't care to know. Any woman insane enough to—"

"Maybe we're adopted, then," she admonished him.

"That's likely," he laughed. It was too much to hope for.

"Maybe we killed her at birth," Odissa stated, as if this was normal breakfast conversation. "Maybe that's *why*."

That shut Odys up. He never thought she'd speak her mind so flippantly. Or that she'd speak that theory aloud. Sure, even he'd wondered about it, but...

"Never mind," Odissa said, waving her hand.

Truth be told, she had very little interest in mothers. Which was why they had never spoken about this before. At least, not like this.

Odissa stood up. "I'm already packed. See me out?"

He walked her to her car. He shook off the cold and his thought about dragging her back to their apartment and tying her to a chair.

He tossed her bags in her trunk and slammed the lid. She waited for him to come back and face her. He didn't meet her eyes as she stood there in her cute little scarf and jacket and mittens. Her petite, tip-tilted nose was pink. Her breath turned to fog. "Don't do anything stupid, Odys, okay?"

He nodded, lying. As soon as he returned to the apartment, he'd have his fit.

"And don't forget to feed—"

"I won't, I won't." he grumbled. "I won't forget to feed your stupid cat."

She put on a prepared smile and reached up to pat his cheek with her mitten. *Good boy, Odys.* He leaned away from her, a scowl on his poignant face. She expected this reaction. She could deal with his melancholia now, just as he'd deal with hers upon her return. She was always *affected* after "seeing their father." Odys always had to fix her afterwards.

Sighing, she entered her silver car, closed the door and drove out of the apartment lot. When he could no longer see her down the street, the separation had begun.

Our maverick stood still in the cold. All alone. One. He hated that number. He wished he hadn't shrugged off her touch. She hardly ever offered affection. And when she did, it was only to him. How dare he deny her that?

Blowing through his nose like a provoked bull, he cocked his head. He debated something:

See, he might have gotten dressed in a rush to walk her down here, but he was *still* dressed. He shouldn't waste his reasonable effort. He tapped his pocket—yup, wallet and keys. In a solid beeline, he went to his car. He'd go driving; he might even follow her (just a little ways). Nothing weird about that. Nothing that would surprise her.

He shut his car door and put the key in the ignition.

But wait.

…What the hell? Car won't start. Won't start. Start. START!

He must have tried ten times. Ten thousand fucking times.

As he hit the steering wheel—teaching it a lesson—he threatened to set it on fire. He settled for a dent in the car door, compliments of his foot.

He wasn't normally a violent person.[10]

Not about to pop the hood and let some know-it-all, car-savvy guy tell him he needed to do *this and that and that and this* to get it running, he decided just to walk. Just walk. Walk it off. Besides, he deserved this bad luck—to treat his sister like that. Walking was his punishment.

---

[10] Don't defend him, Narrator. He's actually very violent, in my opinion.

He rummaged through his deep pocket as he stepped onto the sidewalk. His shaky hand searched for his extra lighter as the other pulled out the cigarettes from his back pocket.

He smoked the fuck out of that cigarette.

His glasses glinted as he looked left and right before crossing. January was cold in these parts—though it doesn't matter *where* he is right now, so I'll not say the place. Locations are unsubstantial (as my Editor tells me). Just focus on the storyline. He'll not be staying here much longer anyway.

His feet made shuffle-sounds that helped him feel pathetic. It was a relatively dull walk, sparse traffic and people. A few morning joggers here and there, plugs in their ears. The genial cigarette smoke blew back in his bare face, thawing his sharp nose. He usually had those dark circles under his ever-scowling eyes, though today they were especially dark. Shady circles came with the complexion, you see. Oh, and that reminds me—I meant to mention that *complexion*.

It was rumored his father was Turkish or Russian or Armenian or Siberian or something.

Something.

But Odys didn't care. Rumors concerning his father (interestingly enough) were often more entertaining than the man himself. Odys should know. He'd suffered them both. Rumors *and* the man.

His father—a hieratical-looking man in memory, but not in person—had sometimes spoken with a deliberately veiled burr that, at times, sounded like a sick blending of all Indo-European language branches—the kind of generalized accent that had broken down and only escaped accidentally. Or, as was also likely, his father had merely acquired it. How, though? Do not ask. He never answered.

So, despite my best efforts within this whitewashed genre, in sum we have two white rich kids. Trite upon trite. *But* who said Odys and Odissa were even the main characters? Not I![11]

...If anything, Odys often looked in the mirror and thought he looked nothing like his father. The fact he couldn't grow real facial-scruff led him to wonder...

Actually, forget I mentioned that.[12]

...The light had turned green. The pixilated man appeared in the light-box-thing. Walk. Walk. Walk. Don't walk. Run before that crazy driver hits you. Geez, what an asshole! A human can only walk so fast.

In his rush, his hair fell in his face. He tucked it back. He wore it down to his shoulders and tied in a limp tail-knot creature. His tangled mane was always pulled back, though wavy-scribble strands somehow found their way over his forehead. Like an earthy curtain, today those loose locks helped veil his building insanity.

More ash fell onto his messy front—his shabby and somewhat-threadbare style was his only outward means of conveying his aforementioned minimalism (minimal use of the hairbrush and fashion sense). His unkempt air made him proud. He was good at being hygienically slovenly. "Hobo-grunge" might be the proper term, though I'm no authority on the matter. Odissa always held her tongue on this issue. He chuckled at the thought, smoke wafting from his lips. (He caught this sudden outburst and corrected the impropriety. He was, after all, supposed to be brooding).

As Odys walked up the sidewalk steps, not grabbing the frosty rail, he realized he was near his favorite used bookstore—ah, so that's where he was going. Subconsciously, of course. He rounded the corner, planning to pass it off. He knew it wasn't right to visit a place that isn't *solely* yours. Odissa's absence weighed him down...

He blew smoke out his nose, a deprived dragon.

---

[11] Our Narrator tries very hard to be progressive—with the best of intentions. But it seems the story they need to tell won't "let" them. (What an excuse, am I right?).

[12] You should not.

All his depression might seem uncalled for—a very silly reaction to his sister visiting their father. But perhaps you don't know the half of it. Not yet. I haven't even told you *the man's* name—not that names tell you much about a person, really.[13]

When Odys and Odissa were children, they imagined what their father must be doing all those days, weeks, months he would disappear. They wished he would never reappear. "Business trips," he'd called them.

As slightly older children, they envisaged the man as possibly a con artist, a spy handler, or government mercenary—his black-market character surely fit the profile. Turns out, it was worse than they feared.

He was none of those.

During their lax childhood, the twins had watched many a gangster film and noted that the mobsters had to go *somewhere* for their medical aid; they couldn't just check into a hospital every time they got in a gun fight. That's the first place the cops look. There had to be a doctor on hand—for special cases and such.

That's where their father would fit into their make-believe beliefs.

He did not *make* them believe otherwise.

All they knew for sure was that his study was packed with medical textbooks—some in different languages. They doubted their father could read them all, but they took up slack on the shelf.

Many of their father's rooms were locked. The study was the only "secret" place they'd managed to enter. This was (most likely) because there were few secrets in that dusty room a child could understand. The eye-level volumes were the ones you were *supposed* to notice—the ones distracting you from the plain, more important books high up. Their little eyes couldn't see into the towering shelves where the good stuff (no doubt) was tucked away. They hadn't dared go up the winding

---

[13] Oh, they tell you enough all right. Especially if the person chooses their own name—which is what their father did.

staircase or use the rolling ladder; if they had, not only would it have been riskier, but they might have learned their father's true profession.

And they already knew too many secrets.

Their father, when at home, would lock himself in his rooms. He'd stay in there for days and leave the children to their aloof nannies—plural. Yes, they had several over the years.

Odys wondered why their father even bothered coming home. It's not as if the twins wanted to see his face—his face with that scraggily beard (their father's facial hair added to his sophistic undercurrent, and Odys hated it. If he could ever grow such a monstrosity, he wouldn't. He feared he might actually look like his father, then. One time, he took his sister's hair up to his chin as she tried to touch up her face in a mirror. It was no real comparison). But why are we talking about beards? Let's get back to our hero twins' upbringing.[14]

They were very well off, and it seemed likely their father acquired the wealth from somewhere—or, possibly, *someone*. Little did they know how close their guesses came. A pomegranate isn't a carrot, but it's still just as edible—and Mr. Odelyn Sr. enjoyed the company of many a *delectable* character.

Perhaps the yummiest of his contemporaries was Mr. Augury, a man who had made frequent visits.[15] As the family's lawyer and oldest friend, every time his derby shoe stepped through their childhood threshold, their father would drop what he was doing and leave his off-limit rooms. No one could delight their father quite like Mr. Augury.

And no one consumed more of his time.

---

[14] "Receive your guest the bearded men" —*Chilam Balam*, Mayan book. It is a supposed prophecy and relates to Cortés and his welcoming. The beard, in my opinion, eerily foreshadows something about Odys. The beard (or lack thereof) is most important. The Narrator wants you to notice this...And then quickly forget it.

[15] And yes, I (the Editor) changed Augury's name (as I have changed/edited others) to OBVIOUSLY represent someone of ominous importance. Our Narrator had a laugh at the name I picked. An approving laugh.

29

Mr. Augury had a much older air and frame than their father, though he wasn't *ancient*. Only distinguished. Odissa called him Guglielmo Marconi. Her father, on the other hand, was Grigori Rasputin. "Though I think that's only when he's around us," she had added. She could be so forgiving.

Odys didn't know why she always compared people historically, but she usually got it right. Like Hegel with his spiritual manifestations in history, Odissa pursued this timeless principal in her own life. She was a sibyl who knew the past foretold the future.

But back to *Marconi* and *Rasputin*:

The twins didn't know how the two had met and never cared to learn. Why learn about a subject you hate? Such knowledge was useless to them even if they knew it. It could never rid them of their father. Even though their father had died, Mr. Augury was still alive. Thriving. Doing their father's will beyond the grave.

That's right, kiddos, their father is *dead*. You didn't read that wrong. I never said he was alive, did I? Go back and check, if you don't believe me (even Gabbler, my Editor, called this twist "mindfuckery." I disagreed.). I'll admit I meant to mislead you a little, but I never said he still lived.

See, to the twins, their father and Mr. Augury are as one. Their father had been a regal man and Augury preserved his regal wishes.

Their father no longer had a voice of his own.

Augury was that voice.

Though Odissa had gone to "see their father," the stone monument he'd become was hardly the worst part of her ritual reverence. Mr. Augury was sure to stick to the will and its *multifarious* rules for their inheritance. He did control it, after all. That's why Odys couldn't go with Odissa. It was against the rules. Their father hadn't wanted it—and still didn't. That's what Mr. Augury said. His words might as well be their father's. His word was law.

Even though their father was nothing but a skeleton in the closet, Augury could still hear him. Mr. Augury, in more ways than one, was *Odi Odelyn*.

ODYS ODELYN: Son of a trickster; named after him too.

SEASON: Winter—perfect for brooding.

ADDICTIONS: Cigarettes, coffee, and maintaining even numbers—not in that order. He's actually on the lookout for a fourth addiction, to make the number even.

TYPE: Byronic hero, theoretically.

Chapter the third,[16]

Alchemic principals:

What's the *matter*?

Odi Odelyn. Yes, that was their father's name. Odi, short for Odysseus. A heroic name.

Odys hated that name—he couldn't read Homer because of it. The twins strongly suspected it wasn't their father's birth name, because if it was one thing they *did* know about their father, it was his profound adoration of pagan myths. And if there was another, they knew people rarely liked their parent-bestowed birth-names. They were evidence of this (teachers always spelled Odys's name as Otis, and Odissa's as Odessa).

...Not that Odys cared about his stupid name.

Odys flicked his finished cigarette at the pavement and stepped on it. When he looked back up, he noticed someone stopped at the far-off crosswalk—the crosswalk he was headed towards.

It was a blurred silhouette in the morning glow. The figure just stood there...even though the light was green and he was free to walk. The man simply stared at the traffic flowing past him. He even waved on the car waiting for him to cross.

Come along, motorcar. He was in no hurry. *Have a good day.*

Stanza: And that's where we began, didn't we?

Yes. Yes, it is. We've come full circle.

"Fucking shit, it really happened," Odys muttered to himself in his hospital bed.

---

[16] Or, **Chapter the second**, if our Narrator had their way.

Stanza: Ch. 1 insert is DONE—let's get back to the real Ch. 3.

The officers asked him more questions—questions after questions. He signed his witness statement after recounting the whole ordeal and refused further conversations with social workers (who were very concerned about his mental stability). Cup after cup of coffee was proffered, because he looked so "terrible." Coffee was the only thing his nauseated body desired, though it was hard to take in.

The doctor had told him they didn't know what was *exactly* amiss with him, but his heart rate was low—below average—probably just nerves—here, take some of this.

The doctor had told the officers (who were surprised Odys wasn't on drugs): he should be fine—nothing in his system—shock manifests in different ways.

A cop who had just arrived wanted to know why the suicide had been so *messy*. A nosey nurse (who had overheard other doctors and nurses from the morgue) explained that if the bullet hits the right vein—the right angle—maybe—case closed.

The cops told Odys an officer would drive him home—thanks for cooperating.

"Whu-whaat time is it?" Odys asked as someone helped him into his coat. It was irritating how *slurred* his voice came out, how much energy it cost to emanate only four words, how they looked on him with concern and then skepticism.

"Just now ten."

"A.M.?"

"P.M. You were out quite a while."

Thanks, Pepin, for ruining my day and making me look like a weakling—if Pepin's who you really were. He put on his glasses, took back his wallet. His fingers also felt the coin. It was still there, eerily warm.

He fell asleep on the way home. The driving officer woke him up.

"I think we're here, kid." Pause. "You need help getting out?" No, thanks. "Call if you need anything, right? Not that you will, but." Pause. "People kill themselves every day. You just got lucky enough to be part of their attention-seeking. Don't let it get to you."

More like, *don't be such a little girl.*

"We'll send someone tomorrow to check up on you, likely." Shouting before the car door closed, "Just be glad you slept through the news crew. They had a fucking field day."

Stanza: Lady Liberty isn't so Greco-Roman.

Odys made his way up the apartment building, holding the rail for dear life. The yellow streetlights let him see his breath, though it felt more like his soul escaping than warm oxygen.

He rested his forehead on the doorframe and fumbled for the right key. He noticed his hands in the hall light. They bore a sickly, lavender tint—shades away from a bruise-colored plum. It was like his body knew he was alone now and, without the eyes of others, was willing to turn on him. His desperate, cadaverous fingers managed to turn the cold knob.

He found his bed. His face hit the inviting pillow...

A few hours later, he heard a thud from his twin sister's room—a drawer closing perhaps? A sniffle? A hum? Was Odissa home?!

He rallied himself out of bed, looking for his glasses. Where had he put them? They were probably in the covers. He realized he still wore his blood-splattered jacket. He was too unwell to bother removing it. Besides, it had nice pockets to rest his limp hands in. He always did appreciate pockets—never mind Pepin's blood.

He shuffled onward, hands nice and cozy. Wait, where was the coin, that ominous penny? *Must have fallen out as I tossed in bed,* he assumed. *Good riddance. May you be lost under the bed forever.*

...On his wobbly-way to greet Odissa (and beg her to care for him), he noticed the cat's hairball crime-scene from *THAT MORNING* had been cleansed of evidence. Odissa must have done it. But, uncharacteristically, it seemed clean *enough* (which was a rare feat for anyone—Odys had high standards). Was he sure he hadn't cleaned it?

He leaned on his sister's bedroom doorframe, flipped on the light. An exhausted smile spread across his too-white face—

But the sides of his expression quickly fell.

She wasn't there. Must've been the cat... "Merow?" He lifted his flickering eyes from mid-floor.

Thanks, cat, for waking him. He'd gotten up for nothing.

The cat looked back down and continued his operation—batting at something between his fuzzy mittens. Odys, about to swoop down and scoop it up (the cat was notorious for eating random artifacts from the carpet), drew back. It was the coin. *Howthefuck* did it get in here?

No doubt, it must have been the cat. That's the only logical way it could have traveled. The pesky creature was always helping himself to their stuff. Little thief.

Odys would have been angry if he hadn't become dizzy again. He could feel the blood rushing through his shriveling veins. The cat screamed at him. He'd forgotten to feed him dinner, but the beast was fat anyway and could miss a meal or two. Odys himself hadn't eaten all day. Even now he felt too weak to eat. The cat could suffer with him. So there.

...Never mind. That was mean. He'd go feed him.

He turned from the cat and coin with a glare, leaving it and heading to the cat food in the kitchen. But: *sniff, sniff.* Was that...*coffee*? He heard the pot begin to squirt out newly-hot contents.

Walking to the counter to inspect the pot, the rich scent flooded his shallow senses. He leaned down, watching the murky-brown droplets fall. He realized he was watching it like someone on LSD and adjusted his countenance accordingly. He blinked past his disheveled fringe, blowing the hair out of his way so he could inspect.

...This was no programmable machine set to a clock (they were still shopping for a fancier one), so *how* was it making coffee for him? He must be dreaming. Sleep walking. Yes, that was it.

He felt like a stranger in his own home...*alone*. He couldn't even trust himself anymore...*all alone*. The cat was there, yes, but the cat couldn't make coffee. No thumbs.

Perhaps he should take a stroll outside—to wake himself up? The crisp air might do him good. Or make it worse, whichever. He paused in the living room, deciding. It was a bad idea, but he thought about it anyway. If he was going insane, better to be *outside* where someone might stop him. He wanted to escape this unusual happenstance—this place where nothing was quite right—this place where he was *alone*.

The exhausting walk to the door had made it impossible to reach his bed again. He couldn't change his mind now (as if he could make it out the door) but he couldn't stand his own restlessness. He moaned, holding back the rippling, undulating soreness. He wanted to crumple over. But he stood for an eternity.

Stanza: The genie skulking in the bottle.

Eventually (thank God) that eternity ended. His unsteady hand was already turning the knob—twisting and wringing out his dubious fate. Odys was just about to pull when:

"Don't leave, Odys," a voice pleaded.

The hairs on the back of his neck stood on end. The voice was quaking bronze gongs—a song calling his body. Though his senses were dulled and fatigued, this metallic sound was sharp and clear. Had he died? Was this a heavenly undertaker sent to collect him?

Heaven or hell, he'd be saved from this tortuous weariness. He turned. He could see a girl's gleaming outline—a thin, polished delineation. He gave a sigh of relief; it was just a girl. Just a girl. A girl?

Not what he expected.

She was like syncopation—softer than predicted. Just from her few words, he had *almost* been sure she was anything but human. But now? Now he wasn't so sure.

She stood paces away from Odissa's room—had she just left it?

The dress she was wearing—Odys knew that dress. It was Odissa's. But this girl wasn't Odissa. "It isn't safe, Odys Odelyn," she told him, her voice like tiny brass bells now. "Not until we're both fully stable." Her posture was reserved yet poised.

"How—how'd you get in here?" Odys managed to say. Each hoarse word felt like slime leaving his tongue. She'd given him a heavy jolt, his senses galvanized—though he still wanted to puke and pass out simultaneously.

The dark apartment kept him from perceiving her face entirely, but he could sense she softly smiled—a smile like the glint of copper, quickly gone.

"How'd I get in? Well, now. You let me in." She spoke as if reminding a sleepy child.

He licked his lips in thought and tasted metal—metal in the air. Her body swayed in place—she was a sinuous cobra half-moving to the snake-charmer's tune in his head. "You let me in," she insisted. She tucked her hair behind her ear, waiting for response.

"Did I?" He almost didn't doubt it at this point.

She nodded.

Clearing the clot in his throat, "Why are you wearing my—my sister's dress?"

She strode up to him. Her every footstep consecrated the floor. "So two girls can't wear the same dress?" She stretched out her arm, flipped on the light with a kiss of her fingers. Those beckoning fingers took their time to coil back to her serpentine hand—the action exact, like a temple girl's ritual.

The simple fixture above them illuminated her once-suppressed face. Odys sunk back. She was *too* attractive. Like a human knows an android isn't real, he felt there was something unnatural about her "realness." Her auburn hair fell in docile coil-waves around her pointed features; those thick locks reflected too much light and compelled his barely-open eyes to squint.

Her complexion was bronze-tinged. Her eyes—lids large as cloak hoods—crowded her face. If he had to guess, he'd call her Indian or Middle Eastern—no, let's compromise: Pakistani.[17]

In the light, she was a living sculpture—copper-casted. Any moment now she'd sprout multiple arms and assume a goddess's holy pose.

"You should be in bed, Odys," she suggested, at ease in coaxing him. He wished he could obey. But it wouldn't be that easy.

"You know my name too? How come everyone seems to know that? And *why* are you wearing my sister's clothes?" He actually wanted an answer to this one.

"Simple, Odys," she replied with a forced—almost malevolent—grin, "I needed something to wear." At least she was honest. She pulled up the falling strap from Odissa's oversized sundress.

His questions were getting him nowhere. He leaned against the door, closing her off from escape and helping support his drained body. "How the hell did you get into this apartment?"

She straightened her posture. He'd already asked that. The girl—almost angrily—bit her lip. "I told you, Odys. *You* let me in."

His brow furrowed. "Why don't I remember?"

She stared at him with those huge eyes—eyes with irises like tiny, glinting pennies at the bottom of two wide, clear wells. "I'm not lying to you. I can't lie—not to you. There's a difference, you know, between being *invited* in and being *let* in. I was let in, but *not* necessarily invited. Do listen, Odys, for I'm enervated too." She put a sensitive hand upon her chest—that bursting chest was the only thing the tiny girl-woman filled in Odissa's dress.

"How—how did I 'let' you in?"

"Well, plainly stated," she paused. "I was in your pocket."

He laughed. "What now?"

---

[17] Gandhi wouldn't think it was a compromise.

"The penny—the one that Pepin gave you. *I'm* the penny." She gestured to herself with her delicate hand—up and down. Ah, it's not every day someone tells you they're coinage. "Your cat tried to eat me, back there. Frisky little thing doesn't know to it play cool. I swear, I've nothing against cats, as long as they don't swallow. I've been swallowed before—by a dog, see. Not a very pretty way to pass the time, I tell you. Can't turn humanoid in a dog, no. Not unless you want the damn animal to explode."

Odys shook his head, trying to understand—a cold sweat formed upon his wrinkled brow—his hair stuck to his face—he couldn't keep up with her. So he decided to slow her down: "Who—who's Pepin?"

"Oh, come! I know you're smarter than that, Odys. He made it very obvious for you. Pepin! Pepin—the man with the umbrella. Pepin—the man whose head exploded. Pepin—the man who set all this"—she gestured to Odys and herself—"up. I suppose he arranged it very nicely, every detail perfect. I *should* know. He made me enact parts of it, no doubt. It's always hard to remember first off. I'm still getting used to you. I'm too busy to remember my own past—if I can remember it at all. Gods only know what Pepin made me do. And what he made me forget."

She rubbed her forehead. Her gaze didn't meet his, though the twinkling eyes noted his reaction.

Odys slouched lower on the door, legs about to give way. This young girl—probably somewhere between seventeen and twenty—was rambling on about things he'd rather not hear. The sad part was that he felt he could believe every word.

Odys looked up through his brown hair. "Why'd his head *explode*? Was it a bomb? It wasn't some sort of—of murder was it?"

"Oh, that's simple," she shrugged it off. She noticed the cat down at her feet. "Pepin's head exploded because *he* killed *himself*."

"What are you even saying?" *Of course he killed himself, woman!*

She snapped her fingers—she had perfect nails—the kind of nails he saw on Asian salon windows, on posters with sun-washed color and feminine hands posing in awkward positions around hideous flowers or retro orbs. Everything about her was perfect—proportionate, symmetrical, idealized.[18]

"Pepin's head didn't explode *because* a bullet went through his brain. A normal shot wouldn't have bruised him. The bullet only worked because *he* was the one that shot it." She bent down to pet the cat. The cat usually hated visitors—just like his owners. "With a man like Pepin—a man with no soul to hold him back—anything he does to himself is amplified and injected into the action."

"*What?*" It was seriously hard to follow.

"Never mind," she sighed. "I'm overwhelming you. Can you give me a cigarette? It'll make us both feel better."

"Excuse me?"

She didn't even wait for the OK. Reaching in his pocket for his pack and lighter, she was smoking away before Odys could count to five (which he wouldn't want to do, even if he could spare the energy).

She sucked on the paper so deeply that the tip transformed to ash in one robust inhalation. He could almost experience the sultry smoke entering her lungs, feel its exalted warmth, imagine its texture. Was she even old enough to smoke?

The smoke drifted from her tiny nostrils. She closed her eyes and sighed.

"Exactly what I needed to go with my coffee. Some say that your addictions stem from what your soul craves," she mused, examining the deteriorating cigarette. "Chocolate, I hear, can produce the feeling of being in love. Those with a jones for chocolate therefore crave love." She walked over and smothered it in the coffee table's ashtray. Now there were an odd number of butts.

She rubbed her acute chin. Each time Odys blinked to clear his vision, her skin tone shifted into phosphorescent tints and hues, like dazzling tricks on the eye—just subtle enough to make you disbelieve.

She had a second cigarette going when she asked: "I wonder what coffee, cigarettes, and *even numbers* say about your soul, Odys?"

---

[18] Idealized by who, though?

He found it hard to breathe, especially when she glanced at him with that too-knowledgeable visage. How did she know? The coffee and cigarettes were obvious; physical proof of those addictions were scattered through the apartment. But his compulsion? That was less palpable.

To provoke further confusion, she began an improvised list of metaphysical traits Odys carried: "You like paperback books because you can fold the cover around, making the book easier to hold with one hand. You've never smoked pot, nor had any desire to. You also hate the idea of alcohol—anything that can make your mind less guarded and allow someone to discover your inner secrets. And boy, you have a few, don't you? You hate board games—though you tolerate chess. You dress like a slob to counteract your regal upbringing. You hated gym class. In high school, most of the guys thought you were a homosexual, but you actually—never mind I won't go there. You also have a thing for Asian girls, though you've never truly pictured yourself with one."

She gestured to herself as if the situation were somehow ironic.[19]

Odys slid down the door—ass hitting the floor. He watched her brandish the smoke-trailing cigarette. The ash-air smothered him as it swirled around her, a sacred aura. He couldn't swallow his spit. His body couldn't process this cathartic assault—this looking-glass reflection of his innate self.

"Who the fuck are you? Did—did Pepin know all this? Did he—did he tell you?"

Taking out another cigarette, she silently snickered. It reminded Odys of his own smugness at things he knew better than others.

"No, Pepin didn't tell me. Granted, Pepin knew a lot about you, but he could never *know* you like I do. Oh, don't look at me like I'm crazy. You didn't tell the cops about me. You realized I was more than just a penny. Right after Pepin's brain scatter, when you touched me in your pocket, I *know* you felt it…"

Her voice trailed off, recalling the ordeal—as if she had been there.

---

[19] Isn't it, though?

She walked back over to him. "I *know* you felt me draining you." She bent down in front of him, balancing on her toes—her heels gracefully in the air! She placed the cigarette effects next to her. "I still am."

Still sucking the life out of him.

Cigarette smoke glided into his face. "I can tell you're going to like me, Odys. Eventually." She pointed at him with her pretty cigarette-clasping fingers. "I'm sorry I'm taking so much of your energy all at once to revive myself. It can't be helped." She frowned. "You do look like shit."

With unhurried approach, she reached out and touched his chin. Her white-hot touch agitated his tessellated brain. The world reversed into negative. He closed his eyes—drifting in and out.

He melted into her palm.

If you could see through the girl's eyes, you would see his face flush with color—healthy once more.

He realized her action and drew back, eyes sinking into his pallor skull, a shadow overtaking his attenuated body. "What'd you just do to me?"

She smiled—teeth so perfect. She withdrew her limb from him. "I cut the distance between us." She blew smoke in his face. It was almost as soothing as her touch. She cradled his chin and mantra-chanted, "*Nephesh, nephesh, nephesh.* The soul is breath. Your body's having a hard time adjusting to losing its soul. In fact, I don't think I've ever seen a Master look so godawful. Maybe it's because you haven't eaten in a while. Or perhaps it's because you're fighting against me."

"My soul? What do you mean I don't have a soul?"

She shook her head. "No, it's not that you *don't* have one. I have it now. I'm the shell that encases it—the lock and door that keeps the world from it. Your soul manifest, perhaps. I *am* you, Odys. An extension of your body. We're the same *person.* Your soul's my windup key."

She put a hand on his knee and leaned into him, looking him straight in his eyes. There it was again—that nervousness surfacing to her face. And there it went, tucked away. Her self-control scared Odys.

"Forgive me," she smiled broadly—never blinking. "It's usually the Master who has more control of their bodies—never as equal as this. You're letting your soul run itself. How strange. How scary."

She smoothed his hair. The caress belied his independence; it seemed inappropriate—someone so beautiful couldn't be alone with him. This was a dream. That's all. He'd wake up and find Odissa still at home. She never would have left. He never would have tried to start his car. He never would have met the suicidal stranger. And he certainly wouldn't have an anthropomorphic penny.

He gripped his stomach as nausea struck him. She quickly put her hand back on his face.

"Whatever you're doing to me…stop it." *Reverse it. Make it all better. And then go away.*

"You have every right to be angry. But this is how it works."

"It?"

He saw through his half-shut eyes that she struggled.

"There's a name for what I am, Odys. I'm your Automaton. You're my new Master. When Pepin, my old Master, killed himself, he canceled the bond I shared with him. I became functionless—stagnant—inanimate. I couldn't change from my object-form until you touched me—until I took your soul. I need a soul to fuel me— to wind me up. We're like machines—your soul is the rechargeable battery. But I'm far from wires, gears, and bolts."

Her expression became sullen. She tore her attention from him. "I don't know why Pepin planned for you to 'reactivate' me,"—she flinched at her own word choice—"But I know he had his reasons." She paused. "In his last years, Pepin wore great unrest and would hardly let me see his thoughts—let alone remember them after his death. All his plans—all of them—were clandestine. He hid his true self from our shared brains. He was a good Master—one of my favorites—you already like him, you just don't know it." She began to smile, then her face dimmed. "Yet, it's unsettling that we don't know his plans for you."

With one free hand, she reached behind her, as if digging in a pant pocket. She retrieved something. "I'm as clueless as you," she said, unfolding his glasses (Oh, so that's where they were—but where did she pull them from? She was wearing a dress!). "Statistically speaking, I had to *happen* to someone. But the ratio's tweaked, since Pepin *chose* you. He meant for you to touch me before anyone else could. He cheated."

She placed his glasses on his nose and tucked them in. Her hands lingered. The frames were warm, as well as the glass. They fogged up, making the moment more awkward.

Odys blushed.

She cupped his cheeks like one does a puppy. "Admit it, you prude; it feels better when we're close."

Yes, yes, fine. It did. By her strange witchery, he no longer felt as if he might die. This time he embraced the rushing palliation.

"Don't worry, it won't always feel this taxing. You should be better in a few hours, *if* you get some rest. Now, promise me you won't try to leave, all right? Don't open this door." She pointed behind him.

"Why not?" He forced himself to acknowledge her request, even though he wanted nothing more than to evaporate through her hand.

"They'll know you're well again, and then they'll come."

"They?"

"No one to fear, Odys," she soothed, outlining his features with her fingertips until he closed his eyes once more. "Though we must be cautious. There are other humans with Automata out there—but only a few. They are a group. A family. Pepin wasn't part of it. But that doesn't mean you can't be. I can't remember why Pepin left them, but I don't think you'll have to avoid them like he did—oh, why was it that he left them? I can't remember!" She was talking to herself.

She remembered Odys and looked down at him. "Under my aegis, you are safe." She continued to brush his spectral face. Her touch became unnoticeable as he drifted farther away.

It was almost like she was Odissa, if he stared at the hem of the dress—*the dress!*—yes, of course, the dress. His eyes shot open—the girl felt the sudden tension. He wished she didn't wear it.

As if reading his thoughts, the girl said, "If that's what you want. But first take this." She forced her cigarette between his lips. Before he'd even attempted the first intake of smoke, the dress glided to the ground.

But she hadn't withdrawn her hands from him—her hands were there—right there! She hadn't taken *off* the dress—she hadn't *touched* her dress.

And that glint in her eyes—that proud glint.

The girl was clearly not intangible, though the dress had fallen through her like a coin in water. Even Odys, in his sickened state, could tell she was completely solid. Solid as something non-air could be. It had been her body—her limbs, torso, legs— that had reshaped itself around the falling dress. Like quicksilver, she had reformed around it as it reached the ground. It took Odys a moment—a long moment—to realize she was crouching before him *nude*. The dress wrinkled around her feet. Her bare legs pushed together. Her arms didn't even bother to cover anything—

Because she had no navel. No nipples. No...

Stanza: Faux skin of the golem of metals.

He quickly shut his eyes.

Careful what you ask for, Odys.

"It's okay, you can open them now. I'm covered."

What what what? *No longer naked?* Well, if she could take the dress off that quickly, she might be able to put it *back on* in the same amount of time.

Odys opened one eye and lowered his defensive hand. He swallowed hard, though nothing but mortification went down.

She smoothed out a tube-like dress as she stood and tugged at the hem—a snake pulling at her second layer of skin. The dress was a metallic material that complimented her complexion. It glinted like a newly-removed cicada husk.

"Took me longer than anticipated. Like I said, I'm tired too."

"Took you longer?" Odys questioned, his voice a little higher than usual.

"It's a part of me; it's my skin, if you will." She attempted to keep said "skin" down to her knees. "I can—to a point—shift my skin around a bit. It makes me use a lot of our energy, though—oh, forget it." She gave one last ineffectual tug at her hemline. "Anyway, didn't want to waste more of you, you see."

She bent back down and tried to keep her legs close together; the hem was rolling up despite her efforts. "It takes a lot of concentration just to create something this scanty. Later on, once you get more sleep, I can create something more modest, of course. Not that you should care about modesty." She took the cigarette back from his lips, just for one more good suck then, "I'm going to get us some coffee." She jostled the butt back between his lips.

"But I thought I was supposed to sleep?" His lids clamped down. This wasn't happening, this wasn't happening, this wasn't happening.

She patted his cheek. "Decaff, babe."

When she took a step back, he could feel an airy yank starting from the pit of his chest. Part of him departed with her. He knew it like a compass knows north.

"Come, up you go. On the couch." She gave him her hand; he clutched it like a blind man pleading to Christ. If it would make him feel better, he'd do anything she said—would believe anything she told him. Her arms lifted him like iron levers. She helped him to the couch and left him there like a rag doll.

She was back in a flash, handing him his mug. She removed the finished cigarette from his compliant lips. He no longer cared if there were an even number of butts—how many had she smoked again?

45

She crossed her legs. Her foot bobbed. She toasted the air with her own mug. "Your addictions are now mine."

Stanza: Pinocchio wants to be a real puppet.

Odys hadn't started drinking yet, he was too busy glaring at her and feeling exposed.

"You still don't believe your eyes, Odys?" she asked. "Not even my comforting touch has swayed you to belief? Not even my tricks?" She pinched her dress. "Jesus, you're still praying this is just a dream."

More like nightmare, but whatevs.

"Well, what else can I do?" She placed her mug on a coaster. "I guess I could tell you that I have only two forms. Sorry to disappoint, but I'm far from a real shape-shifter. I'm more of a shape-*tweaker*. For example."

She elevated her left hand and, with her right, began to pull at each left finger as if removing a snug, veneer glove. "I have my coin state, which may come in handy when I need to be hidden from, say, your sister." Odys watched her peel something off her hand. "Then, I have my human-esque form, to make you feel more comfortable when talking to your soul."

Comfortable? Ha! It was much easier to talk to a soul he wasn't sure he had.

She gave one last tug on her middle finger and withdrew a diaphanous skin in the shape of her hand. As it left the hand, it turned to a golden gauze-glove. Between two fingers, she dangled the limp material—never letting go.

"Those are my only two forms, though they can be slightly manipulated."[20]

She rolled the material into a ball between her lithe hands and, like a magician, pulled her fists apart. Her upturned palms revealed empty hands.

"Notice, I didn't let go of the glove as it exchanged hands. That's because it was still a part of me, Odys. Just as you can add melted metal to melted metal, I can

---

[20] By "manipulation," she does not mean she can assume completely different human appearances (i.e. look like more than one person). There's a difference between dying your hair and having facial reconstruction surgery. She seems to carry consistent traits that cannot be entirely manipulated. It probably takes too much concentration and/or energy.

move my body parts—so long as they're always attached to me. Manipulation has its limits, as does hylomorphism. What else might I do to prove you're not dreaming?"

Her candor made him hide an anxious smile. He supposed if this didn't turn out to be a hallucination, he'd owe her some apology.

"You should drink your coffee, it's getting cold."

"I like it a bit cold."

She surveyed him with a sidelong glance, self-assured. She'd already *known* how he took his coffee. She was just pretending she hadn't, to make him feel more comfortable…

He took an obligatory sip and observed her satisfied grin. Trying to swallow the hot liquid, "What's your name?"

"Thought you'd never ask, Odys." She pushed back her falling bangs; the glossy fringe grew longer as it left her fingers.

Freak, Odys thought. *I'm in a freak show.*

"If you don't know my name, I'm not as real as I could be, isn't that right?" She sighed. "Nevertheless, if you want to know what to call your newest, quintessential body part, it's *Maud*."

MAUD: The machine prosthetic.

CREATOR: A god.

SIBLINGS: Eight.

GASOLINE: The soul.

Chapter the fourth,

The jinn in the coin:

Can you trust the Midas touch?[21]

---

[21] "Yet which of our gowned masters will give a tempered hearing to a man trained in their own schools who cries out and says: 'These were Homer's fictions; he transfers things human to the gods. I could have wished that he would transfer divine things to us.' But it would have been more true if he said, 'These are, indeed, his fictions, but he attributed divine attributes to sinful men, that crimes, and that whoever committed such crimes might appear to imitate the celestial gods and not abandoned men.'" —Saint Augustine, *The Confessions*. Beware of the traits gods give *you*.

"Maud," Odys repeated. He liked that name—as if he'd known it all along. "No last name?"

"You really think something like *me* has a last name? Sometimes I don't have a first." She helped herself to yet another cigarette. "Want one?" she offered (his own pack, no less).

He shook his head.

She ensconced herself in the seat. "Masters call me what they want. Maud's the default name. You *can* change it. Though Masters never really do. Not entirely. They're afraid of offending The One who made me." She pointed up and blew the smoke through her nose like a divine bull—a bull misplaced in a matador's arena. "Maud's a strange name for me, isn't it? When someone says 'Maud,' no one pictures, well, this." She motioned to herself. "If *you'd* made me, you would've gone with a more *exotic* name. Or the complete opposite—something simple and clever. Like 'Penny.'" She snorted. "But then again, that's the point. I'm not supposed to make sense or be clever. I break stereotypes. I'm an *American* coin after all—yet I wasn't crafted here. My creator gave me traits that were to *His* fancy—not anyone else's. But I'll stop talking about myself—even though it's the only thing we *should* be talking about because, let's face it, I already know everything about *you*."

"…I get the feeling I'm supposed to ask more questions now?"

"Well, it would be better than me monologue-ing all the time."

Stanza: The dialogue is quite the monologue—in more ways than ONE.

He said the first thing that came to mind, "What are you? I mean, how do you exist?"

She raised an eyebrow—as if she could ask *him* the same question. "A god made me. The blacksmith one—the god of metallurgy—sometimes associated with volcanoes—yes, *that* one. Ah, I see that light bulb going off. I make more sense now, don't I?" She gave another condescending arch to her eyebrows and sipped her coffee.

"Vulcan?" he asked—as if to be sure he was getting his mythology right. He wasn't about to say *Hephaestus*, because he wasn't sure how to pronounce it.

She nodded.

"See, reading *The Iliad* in grade school wasn't a total waste of time, now, was it?"

Before thinking, he blurted, "Is there no way to—"

"Undo this? No. You can't take it back, Odys. There's no way to be rid of me. If I could, believe me, I'd give you back what's yours. This is no sweet cupcake for me, either. I feel what you feel. What's done is done. The only way Pepin could get rid of me was to die by his *own* hand. The only way to break it is for *you* to die. I can't."

"Then put me out of my fucking misery. I don't know what you're doing to me. But it hurts." He pressed his eyes under his glasses.

"I'm in pain too. You just can't tell because I'm an Automaton."

They observed each other for some time. Odys may have even dozed off. He wasn't sure.

The cat jumped upon the armrest beside her with a sweet, ruffling cat-noise, starling him.

"He's too comfortable with you," Odys mentioned, eyes just open enough to notice.

"Ah, well, I did feed him these past few days, so I'm no stranger." She gave the cat a good chin-scratch.

"Past few what?" He was alert once more.

"Days, Odys," Maud repeated. "You've been asleep—off and on—for days. Even on the floor, there, was the span of hours."

"It was? What day is it, then?" He tried to glance at a clock but his hair fell in his eyes.

"Tomorrow—which is in a few minutes—will be Monday. But don't worry. No one but your boss has called, asking if you could work an extra shift on Saturday. And I quit for you."

"What? What do you mean?" Odys would have stood up (to further express his shock), but that little outburst cost him. He dabbed at the new coffee stain on his pants.

"I had to, Odys. It's not like you could work for them now. Not with what's going on."

"What're you saying? I need that job!" he shouted at her between pants-drying actions.

"No, you *don't* need it. Besides, why's Odissa going to see Old Money Bags if you really *need* a job? Yes. I know what you fought about that morning. I know where she went."

All he could do was glare at her in shock.

"Listen, Odys, if I say you don't need something, you don't. I can't lie to you. Let me show you *why* you don't need a job."

She retracted her hand and raised an inveigling forefinger. Her eyes searched around the room, pinpointing his hallowed ashtray. "Observe, please." She gestured to the somewhat-filthy thing. She placed her finger on the dimpled rim and traced it. When her finger left, it was no longer just a plastic, black ashtray. It was a *golden* ashtray.

"Solid as can be," she added, handing it to him for corroboration. He took it, his hand falling from the unexpected weight. His jaw dropped. He didn't even care about the butts falling to his lap.

She shrugged it off as if to say, *Meh, it pays the bills*. "Every atom—molecule—whatever-the-hell—equivalently changed. Don't ask me how it works. Moreover, don't expect me to *always* be able to do it. I have to use energy for this sort of thing—like forming clothes. Just look at me, panting. Also, when we pawn it they'll ask where you got it. If they don't the first time, they will the second. I can turn things into any metal you like, but selling the stuff can get tricky. But don't worry, we'll find ways. Welders love my work." She watched Odys place the tray back on the coffee table, as if it was an explosive device. "Just be thankful I didn't turn the couch solid gold, Odys. Would've fallen through the floor."

Odys leaned back in his seat and held his mug for comfort. "Okay. But what now? What am I supposed to do with you? You have to leave—you can't stay here."

"If I don't stay near you, you'll die. You can't live without a soul, Odys. Your body will shut down. You'll feel worse than you do now—"

"If that's what it takes to get rid of you."

"You'd leave Odissa here, without you?"

He pouted—no, *glowered*—at her.

Speaking of his sister: "She said she would be back on Monday. She—she didn't call?"

"No, she didn't call." Maud put her cigarette out in the now-gold ashtray. "The only other activity you've missed is the officer stopping by. He couldn't wake you. I pretended to be fifteen and without ID, just so I could convince him I was a family friend come to care for you. They mostly bought the lie, especially since I can flatten my chest if need be." She examined that bosom. "However, while we're on the topic of *Monday*, you have school, yes? I don't think you should be going to school any longer. Just as work would be unsafe, so will school. You have little reason to rush learning. While I have your soul, you're immune to so much as a paper cut—unless, of course, you wanted one. You have a few hundred years ahead of you, most likely—give or take the *internal* forces." She frowned at the ashtray. "I slow the aging process, but from the looks of things, lung cancer might've set in."

The cat curled himself in her lap. As she stroked its back, Odys felt envious, then ashamed.

"But how'll I explain this to my sister?"

Maud shrugged. That was the least of their worries. "I have a *feeling*, Odys, that your sister's just as symbiotic to you as I am. She won't question you if you play your cards right. However, I'm not saying you *should* tell her about me." He wasn't planning on it. "For the time being, I'll be the spare change in your pocket. Literally."

Odys leaned forward, face in his palms. He was feeling much more assured, yes. Assured that this was madness.

When would this hallucination end? And just what—what!—would his sister think? She'd probably be excited. She was all about the fantasy shit...

And speaking of his sister, he wondered why his sister hadn't come home yet. He was hoping for an arrival sooner than Monday. Why was it taking her so long?

"I would say you should call her, but..." Maud said, as if she knew he was thinking of Odissa. "She doesn't have a cell phone. Neither do you. You both hate them. You don't want them, because you don't need them."

"We're never apart," he defended himself.

"Save for these *visits* she goes on."

As if it justified his anti-cell phone behavior, "She said this would be the last time she'd go to him."

"Speaking of *him*—no cell phones means it's also one less way for *him* to find you—and to find Odissa. Let's not pretend your 'no cell phones' rule is about simplicity. As they say, the nose knows all." She tapped her nose.

Did they say that? If so, who was *they*?

"*Stop* talking about him," Odys said.

"If Odissa's not home tomorrow, we must do something. It's important we locate her." With her eyes averted in thought, "If Masters like Pepin are out there blowing their heads off, you can be sure something bad is going on. We don't know why you've been involved. Your sister's unsafe until we do. They no doubt know you have liabilities."

"What does my sister have to do with this? Are we in danger?"

"I don't know, Odys," she responded, leaning forward. "But there's certainly the possibility. Other Masters might feel threatened by you. They're watching. They'll know you have a sister. Remember that your sister's more mortal than you, therefore making her life much more precious, correct? No doubt others like us will realize this."

He didn't like the connotations. "Should we find her? Right now?"

"No, Odys. That's not what I meant." She rested her elbows on her bare knees. "I'm not going to pretend we're entirely safe. The others won't like that they had no say in Pepin's plans. They didn't choose you. And they don't know why Pepin broke the rules for you…"

She talked as if Odys now held some position or title in a council of other "rare coin collectors"—if you will.

"These others with—" *whatever you are.*

"Automatons, yes. Or Automata—however you want to pluralize it."[22]

"They were watching—from the roof. Weren't they?"

"Yes. And they always will be. They tend to keep tabs on one another. For personal safety and so forth. We aren't coeternal, Masters and Automatons. Precautions are necessary."

"Precautions?" Odys repeated.

"Don't worry. If they didn't want you in the picture, you'd be dead already. They'll want to know why Pepin killed himself for you. They'll not waste his death. Oh, don't look as if we should be hiding in bunkers, Odys. You're not dead yet. They're only making sure they've nothing to fear from you."

He glowered again.

"Tomorrow. We'll talk more about this tomorrow. Let's get some sleep. You're already looking better than you did on Friday night." She took away his mug.

He wanted to offer her Odissa's bed, though he wasn't fond of the idea.

"No, thank you," she said, grasping his arm to pull him to his feet. "I won't need it."

"You don't sleep?"

---

[22] We're inconsistent ourselves.

53

"That's not what I said," she replied, her face unreadable as he straightened. "Automatons eat and drink and sleep. We need such things…to keep our Masters healthy, too. Not as much as Masters do but…" She shrugged. "Even the soul needs a sojourn from the physical world."

"Then where will you sleep?" He didn't budge.

"Why, with you, Odys. Ah, I hope that doesn't upset you."

Hope? But she knew it did! It was clear by her expression.

She snapped to obdurate. "It's not as if I haven't been next to you, these past days. You wanted it. How else do you think you're alive, if I hadn't been so near? If you're apart from me for too long, you—"

"Die?"

"You might. But let's not test it." She narrowed her eyes. "As I said, I've never experienced this type of slow recuperation from a Master. It's a slight rejection of me—you're strong-willed, Master." Her eyes snapped to him minatorialy.

Master, Master, Master. She sounded like the actress from *I Dream of Jeannie*. She certainly looked more like a genie/jinn than the pale Barbara Eden.

Maud patted his arm with patronizing force, "Don't think that we can't make this nightmare easier on us both, Odys. Don't you remember I can turn into a penny?" She took his hand in hers—cold yet burning. Then, as if his own were a black hole sucking her entirety, her body was drawn into the crevice of his sweaty palm. In the blink of an eye, the woman was gone and the penny was there, inert.

Observing the tarnished coin, he wondered if it had all been a vision. What if he'd only dreamed this Lady Liberty had spoken to him?

"I'm going insane."

"I think you should go to bed, Odys. You're starting to doubt reality."

Damn.

He squeezed the talking coin (to muffle any further communication) and went to his bed. He kept her in his fist, pressed to his soul-hungry veins.

Stanza: Let's fast forward through sleepy-time, shall we?

So, because I hate dream sequences and respect you enough as a reader NOT to force you through someone else's incoherent, speculative thought, I'll tell it to you straight.

Odys got pretty comfy that night.[23]

Well, eventually anyway. Mostly, he was too sick to bother with being anxious/worried about the implications of owning a MOTHER. FUCKING. AUTOMATON. Let's just say that when you're in a coma-like state you tend to forget what made you so comatose.

Thus, against his will, he let himself carry out his "normal bedtime routine" under those flannel sheets all the way to morning. Which means he tossed and he turned and he reached out and—

Wait a second.

His eyes shot open. He realized what he clutched—and what clutched him back.

Releasing a spew of unrepeatable words, he jumped out of his rickety bed, mattress wobbling and making the girl stir with its quaking. The *naked* girl, I should add.

Shielding his eyes—while continuing to curse—Odys dashed from his room. The girl raised her head. What was wrong? She looked down. Oh. *That's* what's wrong.

"Shit, shit, shit," she hissed as a second-skin formed.

Opening the previously-slammed door, she followed him out, repentance consuming her.

Odys stopped his pacing and mumbling and slouched over the kitchen counter.

"Odys—"

"What. Fucking. Happened?" He didn't turn to her.

"Oh, come on! You remember. It wasn't a dream, last night." *Stop wishing for that.* "It's me, *Maud.* Your Automaton. Your penny. Nothing happened. We didn't do anything in there. Trust yourself."

---

[23] A reader's discretion is advised. (Cough, cough).

She leaned against the kitchen doorframe. She was a guardian pillar-statue before some grand temple, supporting its structure with her celestial weight.

"Are you covered, then?" he snapped.

"Yes, I am. I'm so sorry—we Automatons dream too, you see. Sometimes I dream myself into my humanoid form. We all do it. I didn't *mean* to. Clothes take concentration. And how else would you get better, if we weren't touching?"

His hands formed bridling fists. "My life is some—some divine *porno* now? That what this is?"

(I agree with Odys, here, that the forced sexual tension is a bit cliché and caters to a specific sexual fantasy, but don't blame me. I'm not the one that made Maud as she is).[24]

"I didn't mean to do it," she continued. He could feel her take a step from the threshold. "*You* didn't mean to do it. You didn't *make* me do it. It's not our fault. I tried to stay a coin, I promise—"

"You should've warned me *that* could happen." He pointed to his room.

"Then you wouldn't have gotten any sleep. You'd be dead!"

That's right, Maud. Completely ignore the fact your boobs were pressed up against him, your bare leg wrapped around him, your hand tangled in his bed-head hair (that was still standing up, btw).

"Hey, now, you were quite clingy too, thank you very much," she chided his thoughts.

"Stop it!" he snapped over his shoulder. *Stop getting in my head.*

She walked past him. She now wore a less-than-chaste metallic tank-top and short-shorts—the best "clothes" she could manage. It came with the voluptuous territory.

"You'd better get used to me, Odys." Maud found a half-used pack of cigarettes in a drawer. "No need for modesty. It's not like you're *really* attracted to me, though

---

[24] Sure you're not.

I *know* I'm attractive. Gods know I'm not 'attracted' to you. We're the goddamned same person, Odys. Get that through your head."

He stepped toward her. "If you know so much about me, then you should know I don't like this conversation. *And* you should know it's not about you in my bed. It's about how the *fuck* am I going to hide a naked woman every night from Odissa? Huh? You're no fucking coin!" He gestured closer and closer to her face, hysteria pulling his lips. "What's the fucking point of being able to turn into a coin if you can't stay that way?"

She didn't bother to respond, because he paled and had to grip the kitchen counter, becoming dizzy and out of breath. He took a seat at the table, barely making it there before his legs started to shake.

Triumphant, she lit the cigarette. "You should have breakfast."

"How can you talk about *breakfast* at a time like this?"

"Um, maybe because you're fucking hungry? Eat something."

"No. I might throw it up."

"But you must eat, Odys. Just because you don't eat doesn't mean this isn't happening."

She went to feed the cat first.

"Give me coffee, if you must give me something." He put his head in his arms, needing a pillow.

"Make your own damn coffee. Show some initiative. I've been taking care of you enough. You're better than you were. You've gotten plenty of sleep, at least."

Moaning, "If something like you is possible, then why isn't it possible to *undo* you? To free you from me?"

"This is fate. Everyone falls victim to it one way or another—and other platitudes like that—blahblahblah." She picked off tobacco leaves from her tongue, watching the cat eat.

"This wasn't the Universe's fault. It's *Pepin's*." He realized he was drooling on his hand and grimaced. He was disgusting. But he was too lazy to wipe it off.

"This could've happened to someone else, yes. But it didn't. The gods planned for *you* to deal with Pepin's plans. Otherwise, they'd rearrange this situation. But they haven't. They obviously like where this is going. And speaking of *destiny*," she said as she put the cat food back up, "is that supposed to be blinking?"

Maud pointed to the answering machine. She knew—because Odys knew—that it shouldn't have that RED. BLINKING. LIGHT.

Odys forgot his sickness. He rushed over to the machine and hit the tiny play button. In its robotic voice it spoke, "Monday, 6:30 a.m."

He'd never even heard the phone ring. He glanced at the clock. He'd slept in late. He'd been out cold. He narrowed his eyes at Maud, as if maybe she had ignored the ringing. But something told him she was just as ill as he and had needed her sleep too.

"Odys, babe, I'm leaving the hotel now—using their phone. Probably will stop for food soon. Sorry I took longer than I'd hoped..." Blah, blah, blah. Odissa would see him soon and they could talk about *"what happened."*

Odys drooped. "I hate when it takes long. I'd hoped he'd let her leave sooner."

His rising panic made Maud shift her footing. "She's fine, Odys. She always is."

"Fine isn't good enough," he grumbled, rubbing his face. He looked around the apartment. He hated the emptiness.

"I need to get out." He paced a few steps this and that way. "Perhaps go to the store, or have breakfast out. I don't want to stay in here. I can't stay in here—not with you. I must get out."

(I applaud you myself, Reader, for being cooped up with him this long. You deserve an outing!)

"All right, then," Maud said, though hesitant. "But I must warn you. *They* will see us leave. When we get back, things may not be the same. An active Master is scariest of all to them. Activity always invites the chance for things to go wrong."

"What would you have me do, then? They're bound to barge in now—that's how you make it seem."

"I'm just telling you it's about to get more complicated. The only reason they haven't come in yet is because they're summing you up first. They don't know what's going on, either. They don't know why Pepin killed himself. That much I remember. That was his whole fucking point. But, certainly, leave if you need fresh air."

"Can—can you make yourself a penny?" He felt it rude to ask. "It would make things *less* complicated." He didn't want the neighbors to see this beautiful girl perambulating with him. They might get the wrong idea. They might tell Odissa.

She slipped a smile. "Of course." Her body fell to the ground, her second-form rolling in uneven circles until ringing to a stop. He scooped her up (with only slight hesitation) and was halfway through the apartment parking lot when:

He remembered his car wasn't working.

He cursed under his breath and looked down at Maud. "Why didn't you remind me?" As if it was her job.

"You were so excited, even I forgot. I'm not feeling too well myself, you know. You're a lot to keep up with. And I wanted out, too."

He spoke to void, "I guess we'll stay inside. I would walk, but I remember what happened to me last time I tried that. Unless, of course, you know what's wrong with my car?"

Do Automatons fix cars?

"I do know, actually. Let's just say you're going to need some new parts for her. And they could take weeks to get in. Pepin *wanted* you to walk, Odys."

"Home it is then."

Mrs. Firth-from-Down-the-Hall was coming out of her apartment, curlers in her hair, about to toss out a few trash bags. She caught Odys's last words to the coin in his palm. She did a double take.

Odys retrieved his keys, pretending he was sane, mumbling a song to make it seem like he'd been singing.

Stanza: No man is an island.

59

Closing the door behind him, he went to flip on the lights.

But they were already on.

Two unfamiliar heads peaked out from the kitchen.

Odys goggled. Maud fell from his hand and reshaped herself to stand in front of him. She placed a hand upon him, telling him not to move. "I told you, didn't I?" she hissed.

One of the two strangers was leaning against the kitchen counter. His head had rotated in their direction, unworried. His eyes were indiscernible behind dark sunglasses—the kind so dark you can see your own reflection; a reflection that distracts you with your own warped image. He had been blowing a huge, globular bubble from a piece of bright blue gum.

It popped.

He sucked it back in and continued chewing, indifferent.

The other man, however, had to step around the kitchen wall to espy what his overly-relaxed comrade had noticed; he was carrying Odys's carton of soy milk, wiping his chin clean of newly-slurped dribble.

Odys's heart shot to his ears. It was that one—the one helping himself—the one with red-red hair—the one with the scraggly beard—the one with the cavalier gawk—that looked familiar.

The man from the roof.

How the hell had they gotten in here? And so quickly too. Hadn't Odys locked the door behind him? It wasn't even damaged.

Though Odys froze, it wasn't out of fear. They weren't looking for a fight.

Odys's eyes flickered to Maud. Her posture was defensive, arms crossed but unafraid. "They wait for us to leave before they sneak in. Too afraid to knock, are we, boys?"

The redheaded one almost smiled. "Why knock when you have a key, Maud?" He raised a single finger; it turned into a key until it he tucked it back into his palm.

He twisted the cap back on the soymilk unhurriedly. He snapped the carton down upon the counter beside his friend, the man with shaggy jet-black hair.

That black hair was too long and too short. Too in-between. The black-haired man had an aloof and remote bearing, his jaw chewing away at the bubble gum, arms across his chest. It was hard to tell his expression, or the direction of his gaze, because those huge sunglasses covered a great portion of his drawn-out face. His blanketed eyes might as well be closed—taking a nap.

Both men looked about the same age. No more than thirty. Probably.

The redheaded one was in a suit—an abnormally close-fitting and flattering white suit.

If Odys hadn't been uncertain about their intentions, he would have found time to feel bland compared to these dandified hoodlums.

"We thought you were going out." The redhead gestured to the door. "You know the drill, Maud. We were just going to do a quick run-through before we came over for an *official* visit. Getting to know the territory, that's all." Like it was the most reasonable excuse in the world.

The man with glasses turned his head away, staring off into the kitchen as if Odys bored him. Like a cow, he kept chewing away on that too-bright, too-fruity gum.

Chomp, chomp, chomp.

Familiar-looking Ginger, however, walked forward. A too-wide smile pulled his lips like an exaggerated Greek theatre mask. His scraggly chin-strap beard helped embellish the lunatic expression all the more.

With each show-offy step he seemed to stand taller and taller. He was maybe two or three feet away from brushing the low ceiling. Maybe less. Yes, less. With cocky disapproval, "So. This is him, the other face of the coin?" His body seemed to shrink back down to their eye-level as he scrutinized Odys. "A bit grungy for a rich kid, no?"

61

He had asked the question of Maud, pointing at Odys as if Odys was her new pet fish—uninteresting and, well, a fish.

But she didn't answer him; her chilled silence was response enough. Her lips stiffened. She didn't like how the Automaton had asked *her* as if her Master wasn't there.

When Maud didn't respond, the apathetic sunglasses-man (still in the kitchen) finally began to emerge from ennui and act alive. There was a histrionic quality to his movement. Something told Odys the man had to *embellish* every action. Otherwise there was no point in moving. With a wave of his hand and a tilt of his body, "What's he look like, *Fletcher?*"

FLETCHER: someonething very tall.

MASTER: Likes fruity stuff.

GLITCH: He sometimes blacks out/passes out when he's bored or unneeded. But I wouldn't call it narcolepsy. It's more like a computer's screensaver going up. He knows how to tune out the world. He was designed that way. And his Master finds use of it.

SEEING EYE DOG: For Dorian (who's here to chew gum and keep bitches in line).

Chapter the fifth,

Metempsychosis:

A pair of eyes for a pair of twins?

The sedate-souled man (still in the kitchen) had not turned his head to inspect Odys himself when he had asked his question. His disinterested, drowsy speech was *almost* free of any accent—a Spanish cadence flamenco-danced behind those teeth (something I'll just point out but won't force you to read). *"What's he look like, Fletcher?"* he had asked. It echoed through Odys's skull.

Fletcher, as we can now call him, looked back at his Master. His thick, knotted dreadlocks clung about his shoulders as he did so. The red hair—hair such a deep blood-red it sparkled like the paint-job of a flashy red car—was tied off with a lock somewhere between his neck and lower back. They looked more like limp spikes than actual hair. His made Maud's hair look red-brown.[25]

Fletcher rubbed his fuzzy chin as he answered his Master, "What's he look like? Well, Dorian, darling, he's average, I guess. Very average."

"Wonderful. What's his *color*?" the black-haired man (ostensibly called Dorian) asked. He adjusted his sunglasses. "Tell him so he knows we know."

"Brown," Fletcher nodded, agreeing with himself. "A pale-brown nature. Brown hair, brown eyes. Just like we guessed from the photos."[26]

Fletcher cut his pinprick eyes at Odys, letting him know they already *knew* him. The Automaton chuckled at Odys's confusion, shoulders rolling. Speaking of those shoulders, Fletcher had a purposeful slouch. His slim body bent forward and back, slumped against an invisible wall. He was lanky—rather, willowy—reaching at least a head taller than the rest of them.

"Charming. And how is he taking to Maud?" Dorian asked.

Couldn't he see for himself?

"He seems—"

But Maud cut him off. "Stop pretending you can't see him through Fletcher, you blind bastard."

"Fantastic alliteration, Maud!" Fletcher smirked, wiggling in place. That smile showed off one hell of a jaw line.

"You can ask me these questions about *my* Master. Better yet, talk to him yourself."

---

[25] I cut this bit from the actual text, but thought some of you might actually enjoy the Narrator's further description: "This new Automaton (as Odys had assumed because of its bare feet; not even Maud thought to wear shoes—too much effort) was far from freckled-fair. His complexion was one smooth surface of light olive, like some muted tin can—a man who should have owned black hair. For example, if this were a black and white noir film, that red hair would *translate* as black. Yes, yes, under the right circumstances, Automata can look completely natural. Completely normal. Completely no cause to stare. But the world is not always black and white, and Odys couldn't help but stare."

[26] At first I thought this little "color" bit was weird. But it is explained later. I won't ruin the buildup for once.

Razzle-Dazzle Dorian raised his brows in disapproval. "Can I, Maud?" Straightening up, he was taller than he first appeared—though not so tall as his Automaton (no one was). He would have looked better with height—less platitudinous—though he wasn't *exactly* short. Fletcher was just freakishly tall, which made everyone else wee-little afterthoughts.

Despite his height, Dorian was quite eye-catching in his worn jean jacket, the sleeve cuffs pulled back like stiff wings on his forearms, hands in the pockets of his tight pants. Underneath that jacket was a bright turquoise shirt, blinding Odys's feeble eyes as it contrasted with those loud—nay, screaming—bright-purple pants. He looked like a goddamned peacock. And seemed proud of it.

Dorian walked past them, as if to take a look around. But he did no looking.

He had a nonchalant and buoyant walk for a sightless man. With his hands in his pockets, he had no way of guarding himself from undetected objects.

"*Can* I ask you, Maud? Can I really? I mean," Dorian expounded, "he can make the puppet talk but can he make her tell the truth? *No se.* You've been in here for days. *Days.* Pepin's dead, and you don't even have the courtesy to call and tell us why he fucking killed himself—why he gave you to someone we didn't even know. If you *knew* something, then you'd tell us. *Por qué no* haven't you told us? You should've told your new Master the rules. He needs to understand the way we do things."

"Why, so you could just barge in anyway? I knew you were watching this whole time, Dorian."

"*Sí*, and he knew it too, didn't he? He should've made a peace offering to get on our good side if he wanted to be treated nicely. Now we can't treat him nicely, Maud."

"You weren't going to treat him nicely, Dorian."

"That's kind of true. See, even if Pepin erased things in your brain we'd like to know—which we all know he did—that doesn't necessarily make you innocent. What Odys doesn't know can hurt *us*. That's why we're here, after all."

"But does that automatically make us your enemy?" Maud snapped, her feral eyes darting from Dorian to Fletcher.

Dorian shook his head, hair ruffling. "No, Maud." He had an almost inconspicuous way of talking from the side of his mouth, probably because of all the gum stuffed in it. "But you certainly aren't in the clear. Odys Odelyn, you know who I am? Recognize me? Think long and hard. If Maud remembers me, so do you."

Odys didn't understand.

"Playing stupid, are we?" Dorian shrugged. "Not that we didn't see this coming."

"He doesn't know who you are!" Maud insisted. Her passion redirected their attention.

Fletcher stepped closer to her, lowering his face to meet hers. He took her chin like a doctor examining a patient—clinically. She didn't fuss.

Though he was perfectly clean, there was a rusty, grubby nature to Fletcher's fingernails. In fact, anything worth outlining on his person had a dark, tarnished discoloration. It reminded Odys of a corroded antique—no, no!—a relic or artifact—something you'd find in the bottom of the ocean or in an ancient burial chamber; old and sacred, something with character...

Odys noticed several silver-like rings on Fletcher's fingers. They pressed into Maud's skin. What's more were those six—maybe seven—earrings framing his ear. God only knows how many were on the other side. He had details. Maud didn't. She was too tired to create them—no ornamentation.

Fletcher leaned close—closer than Odys liked—and took a sniff of her. A long sniff. His upper lip lifted as his nostrils widened. He closed his eyes as if it helped mull over the scent. Fletcher concluded, "She's not well."

"As if she couldn't pretend," Dorian said, as if to himself. (Granted, Fletcher *was* his self).

"She's conserving energy," Fletcher supposed, frowning. He opened his eyes. "If I didn't know any better, I'd say they're not even synced yet." He was talking aloud for Odys's benefit. Dorian *wanted* Odys to hear.

"Conserving energy, Maud," Dorian tsked. "Just what've you two been up to, to waste so much of it? Why must you conserve?"

"He *hasn't* synced with me, actually," Maud admitted for Odys. She waited for Fletcher to release her—not about to make any quick movement.

Dorian snorted. "Impossible. He'd be dead by now."

"Maybe he'll do our job for us, then. All we have to do is give it time." Fletcher flashed his pearly teeth down at Maud.

Odys licked his lips, building up courage to speak.

"He's afraid of me," she insisted.

Fletcher opined, "If you wanted us to take you seriously, you wouldn't've hid in here for days." He released her from his examination.

"We weren't *hiding*," Maud corrected. "You knew where we were. He was ill—very ill—until today. What was he supposed to do? Just look at him, Fletcher."

"Oh, no doubt he *is* ill," Dorian put up a hand. He had many rings, too. "But *why* is he ill? Each human reacts differently to an Automaton. Every human has their personal weaknesses." He walked over to the couch, taking cautious steps. "Maybe this is just Odys's weakness. It's good to see you, by the way, Maud. Or," with a self-deprecating smirk, "at least it would be, if I could *really* see you."

He sat down on the couch with a laugh-sigh. As if he weren't blind, he put his scuff-free kicks on Odys's coffee table—like he'd known the table was there all along. "It *has* been a while." Dorian stared off into space, watching the blank TV screen in front of him. "I'm sorry for your loss, also. Pepin was a good man, despite everything he's put us through."

"Pepin was a shut-in," Fletcher grumbled, expressing how Dorian really felt.

Dorian smiled—at the TV. The blank TV. "No harm in that, as long as he wasn't planning something too upsetting for us. And just what *was* Pepin planning, Maud?"

Fletcher stared at Maud when his Master asked it, tongue in his cheek.

"She can't remember," Odys finally spoke.

"Yes, yes, Mr. Messyhair. I'm sure she can't. Pepin was no fool. It's all *muy* convenient to wipe a hard drive. But what about you? What do *you* know about Pepin?"

"You were there," Odys pointed to Fletcher. "That's the first time I'd ever seen him."

"No need for nervousness, Odys," Dorian said. "As long as you cooperate, we'll not kill you." He frowned, playing with his rings. "No sense in killing you before we assess your usefulness. But if you're not useful, well, we'll have to make something out of this shit pile."

"If you touch him, I will kill you," Maud said—all seriousness.

Dorian's head tilted to Maud's direction, a creepy smile on his face. "Ah, Maud. Pretty face, tiny frame, metallic aura. Automatons never change. Neither does their color. It's the Masters that change—that still grow old. *Elixir vitae!* You know what that means, Mr. Odelyn?"

He didn't turn to address Odys. The TV was Odys. "Of course you do. Maud knows what it is. Maud knows she's the elixir. But me, well, I'm the antidote to that poison. I'll put you out of your misery if you're not careful about your Automaton's threats, there. But I digress."

"He can't read my thoughts." Maud was begging him to play nice. "He doesn't know what's going on here, Dorian. We're not well."

"He's well enough to be a bother, Maud. More of a bother than he's already been..." He slapped his knee. "And you've absolutely *no* idea how boring it was, waiting for you two to come out. We've been waiting and waiting just to get inside here safely. But that plan was foiled." He gestured to the foilers. "Fletch, search the apartment. We've wasted enough time."

"What?" Odys burst out. "Wait a second, I don't—" Maud turned and put a hand on his forearm, drawing his attention.

"Just let them. They need to know they can trust you."

"Trust me? They're the ones who broke into my place!"

"Hey, now, we didn't *break* anything," Fletcher retorted. He paused from his movement toward Odys's bedroom.

Odys ignored Maud and moved to defend his territory. "You'll search this fucking apartment over my dead body."

…Perhaps that trite phrase *wasn't* the smartest thing say (but he wasn't feeling a hundred percent, so we won't judge him too harshly), because Fletcher faced him in an instant, one hand in his pocket, the other pointing two fingers at Odys's head like a gun.

"Gladly," Fletcher accepted, slouching into the word. His sickle-smile widened as his fingers morphed into a darker, more metallic matter. Right before his eyes, Odys saw Fletcher's hand produce—manifest!—a sleek handgun from its own fractions.

Handy, to have a body that could grow weapons faster than a human could grow hair.

Odys went cross-eyed just looking at it.

Fletcher stepped even closer. "Have something you don't want us to see?"

But Fletcher's eyes darted away from Odys, distracted. His Master was in pain—crumpled over. He saw Maud standing over Dorian—her eyes met his with a flint-like spark.

…Dorian sat back up as if Maud hadn't just given him a blow that could have knocked the lights off of San Francisco. He drew out a new pair of glasses to replace the ones she'd just cracked on his face. Somewhere between point A and B, she'd knocked Dorian silly.

"Don't you dare point a gun at him—I'm not pointing one at you!" she barked at Dorian.[27]

Dorian smoothed his hair, smiling. It wasn't often a Master got to experience pain unless another Master/Automaton gave it.

---

[27] Gun = Fletcher's fingers

"Well, I can't say that's the first pair she's broken," Dorian forgave, not bothering to pick up the previous pair's pieces. Odys wished Dorian's hair hadn't been so disheveled from the impact. Maybe he would have seen the rest of his mysterious face.

"I didn't ask for her—for this," Odys stated, pointing at the ground. Apparently the ground represented "this."

It was the only defensive thing he could come up with. His eyes were still watching Fletcher's hand. Maud's reaction to the (literal) *hand*gun made him assume it *would* work.

Odys's statement seemed to upset the Automaton even more. "*He didn't ask for this? Does he think any* of them did?"

Odys saw Fletcher's dreadlocks stiffen like angry snakes. Maud was quickly between them. Fletcher was so close it looked as if he might bite her. "Disrespectful little—"

But Maud pushed Fletcher back. Though it was nothing but a blockade, Odys sensed a rumbling in his chest when she shoved Fletcher—felt the two souls colliding.

Odys noticed Dorian's head perk up. He'd felt it too, maybe even more sharply. Maud had meant to *shock* him.

Fletcher took a few guarded paces back, out of respect for the other Automaton. The gun sunk back into his palm, leaving only five dangerous fingers. His hand wiggled its finger-limbs, itching an invisible irritant at his side.

"We're innocent until proven guilty." Maud reminded them. "Now do what your Master told you. Search the place. You won't find anything."

Fletcher walked off, entering Odys's room. He glanced over his shoulder before closing the door defiantly.

Odys found it odd Fletcher would leave his Master all alone. If they didn't trust Odys, why would Dorian leave himself unprotected? Something told him Dorian liked to play with fire, to test its warmth.

"Please, Odys, Maud, sit down," Dorian invited them.

"Odys wants to stand," Maud said, crossing her arms. It was then that Odys noticed what she'd chosen to "put on": basically little more than underwear. Conserving their energy didn't conserve her modesty. But Odys was too troubled with these intruders to care. Odys rubbed the back of his neck, trying to keep himself calm.

Dorian chuckled to himself, as if he were the scariest thing on the planet. "Odys, Odys. Don't act so scared. It's not like we've decided your fate yet. I see Maud's shown you her gilded finesse." He pointed to the golden ashtray.

How did he know it was there? How did he see it? Because Fletcher had noticed it, some time ago. "Be careful not to be too greedy too soon. Gold is costly, when you're tired. Also, it makes you look more suspicious. You're supposed to be sick, after all."

He crossed his legs and leaned forward on his elbows—a physical representation of his shift: "Now down to business, Odys. I may not respect you because you have no fashion sense, but you're still a pretty face I don't want to ruin. I also don't want the trouble of giving Maud to some other poor soul. She's already *happened* to you, so we'll try to deal with it."

He steepled his fingers under his slight chin. "You see our dilemma here, no? We aren't unreasonable people." He laughed as if that wasn't true. He leaned back on the sofa, spreading his arms wide. His wingspan almost reached the tips of the couch, just short of where Odys's fingers could wrap around. "I find it odd that it's taken you so long to stabilize, Odys. When, exactly, did you touch Maud?"

"Near the alleyway, like he told you," Fletcher mumbled from in the kitchen. They heard a squeaky cabinet door close—hadn't he been in Odys's room? They'd never seen him pass!

Dorian laughed, proud of the distraction he had been for his Automaton. *This kid really is sick—too sick to pay attention.* He pulled out another pair of glasses from his pocket (this pair aviator style). "Yes, Fletcher, I know what we *think* you saw."

Dorian put the extra pair on his head, making it seem like he had two sets of eyes. Like a headband, it pushed back his straight bangs. "You were quite far away when you spotted Odys, Fletcher. And Maud *did* stay in his pocket the entire time...How good of an actor are you, Odys?"

Odys didn't dignify his question with a response.

"Just so you know, we received a call from Pepin—the evening before the incident. That's how we were able to locate you. Pepin told us how to find him. We had no fucking idea what the bastard was up to," Dorian laughed. "But, when you get a strange message from someone you haven't heard from in a while, you can expect *something* to happen. Especially from Pepin. But as I was saying. Wait, what was I saying? Oh, yes. Odys, you don't have a reason to be *pretending* now, do you?"

Dorian reached into the same pocket he'd retrieved the glasses from and pulled out a pack of gum—the way-too-fruity kind with the flavor that lasts maybe five good chews. It was the last piece. Before he took it out he offered, "Gum? Let me guess: no, thanks?"

Odys got them back on-topic, "You've already made it clear you don't trust me or anything I might say. Perhaps I—I touched her just now, before I left the apartment? Maybe that's why I'm still sick."

Geez, Odys, don't try to play mind games before you even know the rules.

Dorian chuckled as he put the fresh stick in his mouth. He used the remaining wrapper for the old piece. He needed a good gum-to-teeth ratio. "If that were so, you'd still be out cold. Plus, Fletcher's been watching you. Maud's walked by that kitchen window. She's been animated for some time now. It does take weeks to *fully* adapt, though most Masters don't have health problems as you still do. It's not every day you're forced to interact with your soul, comprendes?"

He continued with conversational air, "I'm *concerned* about you, Odys. Having an Automaton is draining. Some might say having one is like being pregnant for eternity,"—Dorian giggled to himself—"though it's hard to know, since there are few Masters who ever give birth, given our lifestyle…" Chew, chew, chew. "I only bring this up because I think it may be a small clue as to who you really are." He waited for a reaction.

"…Who I am? But I thought you already knew." Odys listened for Fletcher. Where was he now? He couldn't hear him ratting around.

"Well, we *know* you are Odys Odelyn, but that hardly tells us anything. We need to know why—of all people—Pepin chose you."

"Is he the evil twin or the good twin?" Fletcher asked with a gradient laugh.

Odys jolted. How *dare* they know Odys was a twin. "I don't see what my current sickness has to do with Pepin randomly picking me."

"I don't think it was random at all. You see, methinks there's a reason you don't want Maud. And I think I see that reason." That was ironic, coming from a blind man. "Ah, I *knew* there'd be a day when we'd have someone who didn't want their own soul. The masochistic sort. Though you know the key to your full recovery, you retain a considerable degree of detachment from your Automaton—from *yourself*. I find this odd on two accounts, Mr. Sickypoo. The first would be that, well, look at her. Why wouldn't you accept such a tempting gift—especially if you're a straight man? Second, Odys, the pills to cure you are right there,"—he pointed at Maud—"and you refuse to swallow. You like the pain. Tell me, Odys, you ever been suicidal?"

"That's hardly your business," Odys replied, somewhat distracted when Fletcher sprayed some of his sister's perfume in the bathroom. Liking the smell, he gave himself a squirt. *Must they touch everything?*

"Fair enough, then." Dorian lifted his hand in apology. Odys noticed his thumb ring. Odys would never wear a thumb ring. "But I'll speak my point. Pepin might have picked you because he knew you'd be a willing scapegoat—a scapegoat for his bigger plans. Tell me Odys, do you have a *cause* to die for?"

Odys was sure there was a clear difference between not wanting Maud and not wanting to live. "I don't want to die," Odys stated, just for future reference.

"But do you want to *live*?"

"Isn't that what I just said?"

"Whatever you say, boss." Dorian pushed the sunglasses up. "You don't want to die? Sure, sure. Me, though, I don't ever want to go to Singapore. They ban gum there." He flashed his gum between his teeth. "That's what I don't want."

"So your sister sleeps here?" Fletcher asked, motioning with his thumb to the room he left behind. He was a quick little bugger.

"Yes," Odys answered through clenched teeth.

"Then why's there stuff piled on her bed? Boxes, books, and shit—it's the biggest *shelf* in there. Where the hell does she sleep?"—as if she were a messy slob, which was slightly untrue. "Does she not sleep at all? Insomniac or something? We *know* she lives here."

"Just what exactly are you looking for? Why not search Pepin's house? Even *I* would like to know what you'd find there!"

"Oh, we've searched his place all right—more like *places*," Fletcher chuckled, picking up the small trash bin in the corner and turning it upside down. He prodded through their garbage with his monkey foot. It turned up disappointing.

Odys shivered, imagining what messes he'd made in the other rooms.

Fletcher dropped the bin. "We found exactly what we expected there: nothing."

Odys shifted his footing. "Just leave Odissa out of this. She doesn't know anything and she *won't* know anything. Your secrets are safe—I'm no threat to you."

"Oh, now, it's not so simple," Fletcher laughed as he walked up to his Master. He jumped up like a weightless sprite onto the couch's arm—squatted like some bony orangutan. The Automaton's "fabric" clung to him as he balanced, threatening to be re-absorbed into his well-sculpted frame. "You can't just shoo us away that easily. Even if we trust you, you aren't off the hook." He removed Dorian's extra pair of glasses and slid them on. He cocked his head and stared at Odys, a creepy fashion mannequin too real to overlook. "You're one of us now. We won't let you ruin everything we've worked so hard to keep secret."

"That's right, Fletcher. He has something of ours, doesn't he? He has Maud. We have to make sure he won't misuse her."

"I already told you I won't."

"Easier said than done, Mr. Browneyes." Dorian tucked his hair behind his ears, though it was too short to stay tucked for long. "You may not want your sister to find out about Maud, but humans are too curious for their own good. And speaking of your sister, we'd rather like to know where Odissa is at the moment, and why she hasn't been back since the incident. We know you two don't have cell phones, we've checked up on it. Otherwise we would have found her by now. It's odd to find someone this day and age without a cell phone, isn't it Fletcher?"

"Yes, Dorian, it is," Fletcher nodded. "Almost seems fishy." He tapped Dorian's cheek affectionately with the back of his hand. Dorian took out his piece of gum. Like a bird feeding from his hand, Fletcher peeled off the tacky blob and popped it in his own mouth.

Dorian re-tucked his hair behind his ear and re-crossed his legs. "No cell phone *is* fishy." He itched his chin. He was clean-shaven, though the faintest shadow threatened to darken his shy chin. "You see, Odys, we happen to know you and your sister have lived together for some time now. She usually *is* here. Right here. Can you tell us why she *isn't* she here?"

"Why do I get the feeling you already know where she went?"

"'Know' is such a precise term, Odys. We only have a *guess*. You going to confirm my guess or no?"

"Odissa left on Friday. For a business trip," Odys lied. Anything concerning their father and/or his lawyer was just business. Family business. "She's supposed to come home today."

"Should—should we send someone to look for her?" Maud asked. Her tone made Odys's ears perk—as if she were requesting.

Dorian to Maud, "You sound worried. Do we have a *reason* to send someone out?"

"When common humans are involved—"

"I'll talk to Mother about it," Dorian raised a few fingers and turned back to stare at the television. "But, if *we're* just learning about Odissa, Leeland's bound to know zip. Unless—" His eyebrow shot up over his frames, "Leeland knew about Pepin's setup already?"

"Who the fuck is Leeland, and why do you have to ask your mother for permission to protect my sister?"

Fletcher rolled his eyes at Maud. "So he's going to pretend like he doesn't know who Mother and Leeland are?"

Dorian huffed. "My, how their names always come up together, though."

Fletcher glared at the other Automaton, waiting for her to say *how much* Odys might know about them. But she only pursed her lips, allowing them to do the damage.

"I'll take Mother if you take dick-wad," Fletcher mumbled to his Master.

"Sure. Leave me with the hard part!"

"You know I can't talk about *that* part. It sounds too silly coming from me. I never do it justice. I'm not serious enough."

Dorian prompted Fletcher to get on with it.

Fletcher snarled at Odys. "Fine, I'll give you a fucking history lesson. Take notes. Mother's the one who sent us to watch you. *And* the reason Dorian's accent keeps slipping to Spanish." He glanced down at Dorian. "You can tell how much they've talked by the times he reverts."

"And, my God, I've been slipping a lot lately," Dorian grumbled.

"She's the Big Boss. And, since Pepin blew himself up, she's the oldest of all Automaton Masters now. Runner up is Leeland. She's the one Leeland hates the most."

"And loves the most," Dorian said in aside.

"Can you not wait your turn?" Fletcher clucked at his Master.

"I think that's enough about Mother." Dorian shifted in his seat, suddenly uncomfortable. "This boy is suppressing things for a reason. And it's not because of Mother. Leeland, though." Dorian crossed his arms. "Leeland is an old Master—a Master of Coraza. His *second* Automaton."

Fletcher tilted his head, judging their reactions. In a sing-song voice, "Someone had to die for him to gain herrr…"

"This is why he doesn't talk about Leeland," Dorian waved to his Automaton, exhibit A. Dorian tucked away a bitter-looking smile behind his lips and tossed aside a pillow. "We Masters can't die very easily, Odys, but Leeland wants to change all that. He's succeeding in many ways. Leeland's first Automaton was Admund, the first-made of Automatons—the one who 'knows' the most—the Automaton who has lived a little longer than the rest. Maybe by a few seconds, maybe by a few years. Who fucking cares? The point is, he saw things his siblings didn't."[28]

Dorian was off-topic but didn't seem to care. He was trying to get comfortable on their damn couch once more—this topic made his sweetness sour. Made him squirm. Fletcher frowned at Dorian, knowing his Master was stalling. So he intervened.

"The fact of the matter is, Mr. I-don't-know-who-Leeland-is, we lost track of him."

"Pepin isn't the only one we couldn't keep tabs on," Dorian added.

"But what does Leeland have to do with me?" Odys demanded. "Or my sister?"

"Leeland, Leeland Lafayette," Dorian mouthed, a sadness invading his throat as he fought against melting into the couch.

"*Monsieur Lafayette*," Fletcher spat. "Name ring any bells?" He shot a dramatic glance at Maud. "Do *you* even remember, Maud? Or is that something Pepin erased too?"

"He's not ready to know who Leeland really is," she warned.

Odys might not be ready, but you are, Dear Reader. In fact, you've been (informally) introduced to him before.

---

[28] Admund the Automaton saw his siblings being made, for one.

Stanza: Allow me this moment to set up the Dramatic Irony.

Leeland Lafayette—double Ls—such alliterative flow! Gabbler chose it, as Gabbler chooses all names to replace the real ones.

Odys Odelyn. Odissa Odelyn. Odi Odelyn.

I can tell you Dorian's last name starts with a D, too, if you hadn't already guessed.[29]

Do note, Admund (Leeland's first Automaton), had no alliteration to his name. Automatons have no last names. They need no last names.

Need them? No. Have them? Sometimes.

And *what if* we gave him—Admund—a last name? What would it be? Hmm...

How much more can I prompt you?

The alliteration gives them *anonymousness*. Yet it also gives them *identity*. What "A" last name has my Editor written in? What "A" name has been given? Come on, I know you haven't forgotten! Who, besides his father, does Odys hate?

I'm tapping my chin in thought.

Hmm...Doesn't "Admund Augury" have a nice *ring* to it? Indeed it does. The first created of all Automata would certainly make for a very fine lawyer, I assume. For no reason in particular.

Stanza: Now that we know what Dorian and Fletcher know...

Dorian stretched—stretched away the tension this topic was giving him. "He's not ready to know who Leeland is? But, dear Maud, he already knows."

"I do?" Odys asked Maud.

"Fletcher, show him that he knows."

Fletcher whipped out his hand, fingers forming a sheet-like film. An image upon his paper-skin slowly formed. Like a photograph—a thin computer screen—Fletcher created an image between his fingertips. Easy as designs on fabric, Odys supposed. 2D not 3D. Like a tattoo to a human.

"You recognize him?" Fletcher asked.

---

[29] Such like a comic book.

Odys took a step back. Yes. Yes, in fact, he did recognize *him*—that image on the sheet.

"This, Mr. Odelyn," Fletcher stated flatly, "is Leeland. Your sister might be in danger if he is involved. Leeland has more than one Automaton. And, if we're not mistaken, he'll want yours as well—whether or not you had *arrangements* with him. Understand? Best to confess right now if you made a deal with him and or Pepin so we can help you."

"Define help!" Maud spat.

Fletcher ignored her. "You'll be nothing but a device for his bigger plans. Don't play dumb, boy. No, don't look to her. She can't help you. She hasn't so far, has she?"

Maud waned, chin lowering.

Dorian grew impatient with Odys's silence. The boy continued to stare at the photo as if still confused. But how much simpler could they make it for him? "Is this Master your father?"

"My father is dead."

"Are you so sure about that? Because last I checked, Leeland is alive and well, and, quite frankly, pretty damn near immortal. Think about it. Didn't your father hang around another man—a strange man like Fletcher and Maud—he maybe couldn't be separated from him? That sounds *un poco* like a Master-Automaton bond, no? No? Maud, why is he not answering me? Odys, just say it. Is Leeland the man you knew as Odi Odelyn?"—angrier—"*Is* this man your father?"

"*No.*"

The tension snapped.

…Ah, Reader, I bet you thought Odys would say *yes?* Of course you would. I led you to it. But don't expect to be fucking clever, got it? Just because I let Gabbler edit the names to obscurity doesn't mean I'd let anyone fuck with my plot twists. Never.[30]

---

[30] Geez, Narrator. Lesson learned.

Fletcher's face fell. "He's not? But you recognize him."

"I know him." He shot a nervous glance to Maud. Why hadn't she told him? Why hadn't she *said* something? "I—I think my sister's in danger."

"Of course she is, you fucking idiot! Now who is he, Odelyn?" Dorian pressed. "Who's Leeland to you?"

"That's—that's *Mr. Augury*."

DORIAN: In-between stagnant and transitioning.

FACT: He thought Leeland would turn out to be Odi Odelyn. Guess not. [31]

BITTERNESS: Not caused by coffee.

SEXUAL ORIENATION?: About to be straightened out.

Chapter the sixth,

A curious case:

Isn't that what killed the cat?[32]

"Mr. Augury?" Dorian repeated, screwing up his face.

"Yes," Odys answered.

"And who is that?"

"So you *don't* know about my father?"

"You just said this *wasn't* your father, Odys. Seriously, get your stories straight."

"It's not. That's not my father. But—but what do you know about my father?"

---

[31]Talk about a red herring! Yeah, so the Narrator misled you on that one. And, to a point, so did I (sorry). But this probably isn't surprising. The Narrator is trying too hard, I know—I know! But we can't let my "editing" get in the way of the story, you see. This is just how my Narrator reminds me who's boss. So petty.

If it's any consolation to you, Reader, there will be no more hateful twists like this one (if you even care to call it a plot twist, pitiful as it is). This one was done for a point (a point directed toward me, not you). Our Narrator is the real god in the machine.

Yet what a discovery! If Leeland isn't Odi Odelyn then that means Odys and Odissa were raised by an Automaton. Not Leeland himself. (Crisscross!). But, what's worse/interesting is...Odissa just visited Leeland, our story's quintessential bad guy.

(Dun, dun, dun!).

[32] I've found another relevant quote for you: "My name is Nobody. My mother, father, friends, everyone calls me Nobody." —Odysseus to the Cyclops, Homer, *The Odyssey*, book IX.

"I know he's dead—supposedly—and that his name is Odysseus—Odi, for short. Other than that, our evidence suggests you didn't care much for him. After all, your sister handled everything with the lawyer, Mr. Augury—who's *also* just as hard to match a face to." He frowned at the picture Fletcher had concocted. "Granted, we had a fifty percent chance."

"So you *do* know who he is?" Odys was exasperated.

"'Know' is such a precise term." Dorian repeated himself. He enjoyed confusing Odys.

"Does this have something to do with why you're not afraid of me?" Odys asked. "You already know everything about me, don't you? Everything!"

Dorian shrugged. "We clearly don't know enough, because our first guess was that Leeland was your daddy dearest. But yeah, I'm not *afraid* of you. I pity you. It's not just Pepin who involved you in our mess. You've always been involved. Leeland had *plans* for you, Odys."

"Odys has a part in two plays." Fletcher studied Odys for his Master. "Pepin's and Leeland's."

"Sí, sí, you've got Pepin's destiny written all over you. We just can't read his handwriting. But Leeland's, well, his handwriting is very *neat*. Much more readable."

Fletcher "put away" his faux-photo, the image he'd conjured from memory—an unflattering image, at that. He crumpled it into his hand, the paper wad disappearing like a magician's trick, reabsorbed into his body.

"I must say, Dorian, this *is* unexpected," the Automaton stated to his Master, hands on his hips. "If Leeland isn't his father, then…who is?" His black eyebrows jumped up and down, inviting Odys to guess the secret.

Dorian frowned at his Automaton's eagerness—the same kind of frown you give when disappointed with your reflection in a mirror. "Well, Fletcher, since we opened the grave and no body was there …"[33]

"You did something to his body?" Odys asked, slightly appalled.

"No!" Fletcher snapped. "Didn't you hear us? There wasn't a body TO do something to. Stupid boy—listen! Besides, it wasn't us—per se." He pointed between himself and his Master. "We were busy watching you."

Dorian sat back down. He thought aloud for their benefit, "It is nothing for an Automaton to fake a death. I mean, depending on how long the Master and Automaton stayed apart for their whole *act*, it might put a strain on the Master…But once the casket was closed, no problem; an Automaton needn't breathe. It's also nothing for an Automaton to break free from the ground—dirt, wood, cement. That's nothing. *Nada y nadie.* Your father—who wasn't your father—easily faked his death at his Master's behest—in whatever way. Obviously."

This all made perfect sense to Dorian.

The only unnerving thing about Dorian's acceptance was that he seemed to welcome it—as if this, perhaps, was the resolution he had wanted all along from this encounter. He even gracefully itched his groin, at home and so comfortable with his surroundings.

He clapped his hands together, the mystery solved. "Also, though you're putting on a good show, the fact Maud wouldn't recognize Leeland or Admund from your childhood memories—and therefore didn't *clue you in* before we mentioned it— makes this all seem *suspicious*." He scrunched his nose and made circular motions with those same hands he had clapped.

Odys couldn't help but agree.

Maud huffed. "Of course I knew. But look at him! He didn't *want* me to say it. He didn't want me to *know.* Can't you see he doesn't want this? He doesn't

---

[33] Pun from epigraph-footnote intended. (I don't care if I'm the only one laughing here—I have to make this editing job fun SOMEHOW).

understand what all this really means. I can't speak unless he *allows* me. Do you think I've been given the chance to tell him so much as the time of day, let alone everything I know? You think this is how he wanted to break it to himself? No. He wanted me to do it *gently*. Now I can't. Fuck you both for making this so hard on him!"

She stepped in front of Odys, as if defending him instead of herself.

Fletcher and Dorian shared a side-moment: "Do we believe her?" "Of course it's a logical excuse." "I'd suppress it to, if I were him." "I wouldn't want to be an orphan, either—to start from scratch."

"You know we can hear every word you're saying right?" Maud said.

Dorian shushed her. "Don't interrupt me while I'm talking with myself." A few more mumbled word with Fletcher, then: "Fine, Odys," Dorian announced. "We'll pretend you didn't know your 'father' was an Automaton."

"But I saw his body. He was dead." (Odys still refused to believe). "He *died*."

Maud looked at Odys, as if she wished she could have told him sooner—in a different way. She made him feel like he'd been holding her back. Admittedly, he *didn't* want to know all this. He didn't want this to be happening at all.

"He couldn't die, Odys," Maud said, turning to him. "Automatons *don't* die. You only viewed the body once, didn't you? Leeland likely bought off the funeral home, the cemetery—to make things run smoothly. Leeland isn't stupid. He arranged everything. For about eighteen years he had to pretend as you grew up. With his Automaton no longer needing to stay away with you twins, it could be less stressful—less stressful on his body. And, less complicated in terms of keeping up the act. At least on one end. He's still pretending a little, though, isn't he?"

Odys's mind darted to Odissa and her *visit*. "I don't understand why he would fake his own death!" Odys shouted, denial oozing from his every twitchy movement. "It makes no sense. We were about to move out anyway when it happened. We wouldn't have been in his way—"

"He didn't want to give you the chance to come back to him and force the act on again. And he knew you hated him," Maud stressed.

"So you think he was doing me some sort of favor?" he barked at her.

She stepped closer to him, as if about to comfort him. But thought better of it. "Masters and Automatons can't be apart for long. That's why Augury was always there—*Leeland* was always there. Always visiting your father; your father always visiting him. He wanted to *insure* the act was over, Odys. But he also didn't want to ruin everything he'd built up. He kept ties to you and Odissa for a reason."

Dorian nodded as if things were adding up. "After his fake death, the distance was absolved. He could pull the strings from afar as Augury."

Odys shook his head, panic rising. Not only was his father non-human but was—worse still!—alive. "No. No," was all he could say.

"My God, he really *isn't* synced with Maud," Fletcher gaped. Fletcher cleared his throat. "Just look at his face."

Odys tried not to sound stupid but he just had to be sure: "Does that mean I'm—I'm potentially—I'm half—?"

"Automaton?" Fletcher sniggered. "Weren't you listening to us, boy? You hear him, Dori? He thinks he's half Automaton! Hell, no. If you were, that'd be a miracle. An *unnatural* miracle. Automatons can no more make babies than a…Well, we *can't*. You must have noticed Maud's unapparent, well, you know." He whistled and pointed between his nipple areas.

"*Everyone* has noticed, from time to time," Dorian stated through his pensive stance. He rubbed his chin roughly.

"We're not reproductive beings," Fletcher went on, wanting to be clear. "Though still very sexual." He gave a soft thrust.

Dorian ignored his Automaton's joke, realizing something. "This still doesn't make any sense. What's Pepin's motive?"

"Fuck Pepin's motive," Maud said, "I want to know why Leeland made an Automaton raise his 'adopted' kids." She used bunny ears when she said "adopted."

"This means I'm an orphan?" Odys said to himself.

Fletcher gave a laugh of pity. "Nothing gets past you, huh?"

"You know, don't you?" Odys realized. "You know who I am!"

"No, *you* know who you are but apparently you won't let *Maud* say!" Fletcher shouted at him. He realized his excitement and took a deep breath.

Dorian tried to explain himself, his Automaton, "I think we're almost on the same page."

"But the question now is, where in the world did Leeland find a pair of twins?" Fletcher asked.

"You're saying there's no way he adopted me legally?" Odys interrupted the conversation.

Fletcher chuckled. "Our kind can't do anything *legally*, dear. We're off the grid."

"Legal or not, you hated him anyway, right?" Dorian asked.

"What makes you say that?"

"As I've already implied, Odys, we have many sources. Most proved what kind of relationship you had with your father."

"And those sources would be?"

Fletcher tucked his hands into his armpits. "Your school records mentioned you had a father, but the little box you checked said never to contact him. Always a nanny or a 'guardian.' And the angsty blog you dabbled with for less than two weeks when you were sixteen?—that clued us in too. You do know how to leave a trail, Odys Odelyn. But don't worry, we can clean it up."

"Now, Odys." Dorian put a finger to his lips in thought, "Let's not beat around the bush any longer. We need to help your sister. Leeland wouldn't let go of something he's invested so much into, right? And that's just what you twins are— investments. Big investments. He has a lot of stock in all of us. He puts us on the shelf like a piggy bank until he needs some *change*." He shook the metaphorical piggy bank. "Now, this Mr. Augury. He's a secretive man, right? Just *how* does Odissa know where and when to meet him?"

Knowing it would sound cliché, "He contacts her."

"Of course he does," Dorian laughed. "And she believes, of course, that he's *retired*. So that's why he has no offices and work number? Plus, he's 'old school,' so he doesn't have a cell phone of his own, right? And because he lives in, perhaps, say, Guatemala, it's no use for him to give you a *real* working number because international calls are a bitch. Am I getting warmer?"

Odys's silence told him he was.

"I swear to the gods," Dorian chuckled. "He's played every trick in the book. And he's played them so well. No wonder you didn't see through it, Odys. I don't blame you."

"Don't patronize me."

"I wasn't. I sincerely pity you. I pity your sister more, because she's with him now, right? Is that why you wanted me to send someone to escort her safely home, Maud? Is that why Odys is so worried? Is this why you worry *for* him, Maud? Poor boy didn't realize *why* he was so worried. But it all makes sense now, doesn't it Odys?"

"She's on her way home." Maud reminded them. "Leeland *let her go*. Even you know that by now. I saw you tapping the wires when Odys was ill." She pointed out the window.

"Leeland probably doesn't know Pepin's dead yet," Dorian supposed. "He doesn't know he shouldn't have let her go."

Fletcher shrugged. "Maybe he forced her to call and give a fake update."

That sent a chill down Odys's spine.

"Or," Dorian mused, "if Leeland *does* know that Pepin's dead." He paused. "Maybe letting Odissa go will just be part of some *bigger* plan?"

"Oh my God! Enough with the conspiracy theories," Maud said. "Whatever the case, Odissa needs to be found."

Dorian straightened and walked to the door. "I doubt Leeland will be right at her heels when he finds out Pep is dead. Leeland has had his plans for the twins all along. Lee's never been chomping at the bit." He said it as if he *knew*. "It's not as simple as *helping* you, Odys. You've always needed help. After all, we would've helped you a long time ago had we known about you."

"Don't try to flatter him!" Maud barked. "You only help yourselves."

"Speaking of helping yourself," Fletcher noted, "Odys has done a bang-up job of it already." He pointed to her. "Touching our things."

Maud glared up at him, body mimicking his crossed arms. Fletcher towered over her, twice her size. He seemed to delight in her attention—even though so negative. Dorian didn't move, letting his Automaton have this moment. "You really should get dressed, Maud." Eyes moving up and down on her barely-clothed body.

"Your chin-strap is hideous," she said.

"But you do like the dreads?" Fletcher peeked over Dorian's sunglasses.

"I can tolerate them," she told Fletcher, her bright eyes narrowing.

"I'll have to change them, then." Keeping his chin-strap beard, the dreads disappeared, his hair morphed into a spiky mohawk with spikes reaching *at least* six inches. Maud scoffed, turning away; she had known precisely what he was going to do.

...Odys grimaced at the playful tension and wondered if Dorian was trying to lighten the mood through Fletcher. Dorian needed Odys compliant, not defensive.

"Put it back, Fletcher." Dorian opened the door. "I liked the dreadlocks. But Maud's right, you're too pretty to cover that face with hair. Doesn't suit you." With a too-pleased smile, "Odys, our souls critique each other. That's a sign we're growing comfortable. Come, Fletcher, let's go."

Spikes falling and twisting back into their previously freakishly-long dreads, Fletcher put his sunglasses on his head like a tiara and followed Dorian, putting a gentle hand on his Master's back.

"You'll hear from us again soon, Odys Odelyn," Dorian said. His hand twisted the door knob excessively. "Very soon. Don't leave your apartment. We'll be observing. I'll tell you what Mother has to say in regards to your status among us *and* how we'll handle your sister. Adios."

"'Handle' my sister?"

Dorian ignored the question, about to step out. But he remembered something. "By the way, what is the cat's name?"

"The cat?" Odys repeated.

"Yes, the cat." Dorian turned around in Fletcher's protective arm. "Fletcher noticed him in Odissa's room. The fluffy brown tabby. Not very friendly."

"Not to strangers, no," Maud informed, her voice piqued.

Odys raised a hand, telling her *quiet.*

Fletcher's eyes widened, thrilled in their interaction—as if Odys had just told himself to shut up.

Odys asked, "What does the cat have to do with this?"

It was ludicrous to include the cat as some sort of problem to their operation.

"He's another liability to you—and, potentially, to us. We need to have inventory of our *valuables.* Any life can be worth something, depending on what you're willing to pay for it. Leeland picks only the *choicest* liabilities, to save time and effort. He knows you'll care nothing for the bum on the park bench compared to something you've invested in."

There was that word again. *Invested.*

"Your sister has a fucking photo of him on her dresser, man," Fletcher stated, creating a baggy sweater to make it look like he was ready to brace the outside air (barely-clothed people tend to stand out in winter). Imagine what metallic sheen the sweater had—be creative.[34] "He's a liability by default."

Fletcher propped the door open with his bum, waiting for Odys to tell them the cat's name so they could leave.

---

[34] The Narrator seems to already tire of describing the ever-changing outfits of Automatons. For future reference, if clothing is not described to your satisfaction, feel free to concoct your own fashion for the volatile characters. I do.

But Dorian would wait no more. "No matter, Fletcher. Not everything needs a proper name in order for us to take account. Besides, we don't want to get too attached. Although"—a smile came to his lips between gum-chews—"we already have a good guess from the vet records that his name is *Bulfinch*."

BULFINCH: Named by Odissa (it was either that or Lancelyn Green).

FOOD: Canned food, dummy. What's with this dry shit?

BATH: What are tongues for?

PETS: Are a major plot device, so don't laugh because a cat gets his own list, stupid human. And stop wiping your muddy shoes on that rug! That's where he throws up. And sleeps in the afternoon.

Chapter the seventh,

The immortal Hand or Eye:

In what furnace was thy brain?

Fletcher bowed—*Adieu*.

As the door shut behind the unwelcome visitors, Odys turned on Maud.

"My cat's vet records? Seriously? What else do they know that they shouldn't?" (As if the cat needed such privacy).

Maud huff-sighed. "Don't underestimate what they *don't* know. They were more afraid of us before we found them in our kitchen."

"*My* kitchen. Not ours. I may need you like some sort of goddamned IV, but you're no welcomed guest, either!"

She ignored his shouting. "You haven't eaten in three days, you need some food. I can't eat for the two of us." She put up the soy milk carton Fletcher had left out, its sides moist with condensation. Odys hoped it was still good after being left out for so long.

"Don't change the subject."

"What subject, Odys?" She picked up a rag.

"They came into my home!"

"Look, under their 'rules,' I'm their property. They're only *letting* you 'rent' me. You're a storage unit for them. I have no say what the other Masters do with us. Neither do you. The gods give, but Mother can take away."

"They seriously take orders from someone they call 'Mother'? They're fucking freaks, Maud."

"And what does that make you?" She bit her lip and stopped her tidying—tidying for Odys. Like Master, like soul. "Mother has to protect what she's built up. You can't blame her for that."

"'Built up,' is it?"

Another huff-sigh. "She and Pepin set up the network—the group. A few decades later, Pepin wanted out. Mother took over. He left and we (more or less) retired. Until now."

"That the abridged version?"

"Any time I have to talk to my Master *aloud* is the abridged version."

"Yeah, like I want to read *your* thoughts. Who knows what's in that hard drive of yours? Viruses? Spyware?" He noticed his antagonizing didn't bother her. "If Mother and Leeland are the oldest Masters now, how old does that make Dorian? How old is he?" He looked twenty-five, no more than thirty.

"Dorian's about sixty—maybe sixty-five—if he didn't lie to us about his age."[35]

She saw he wanted more—more dirt on this Dorian fellow. Finally! He was interested. Dorian was the bridge Odys needed to bring himself across.

"He's the newest Master, after you. No longer the baby. He was [around twenty][36] when Fletcher came into the picture. He didn't know Pepin well."

"But he seems to know 'Leeland' well." He used finger quotations around the name—as if *Leeland* were somehow a phonier name than *Augury*.

"They could say the same about you."

---

[35] Never ask a lady her age.

[36] I am also responsible for the brackets/omitting clear identifiers. Think of them as me turning up the music whenever our Narrator starts to sound too insane. Pay no attention to the man/facts behind the curtain.

"And they hate him because he wants to kill the other Masters?"

"Is that not a good enough reason?" She laughed. "But yes. That and the fact he doesn't play by their rules." She saw he didn't understand. "They try to keep tabs on each other so if a Master dies they can get the Automaton *before* an innocent civilian accidentally picks them up; also, that way they can choose who gets to reactivate the Automaton—someone they all like, of course. After all, they have to live with each other—for a *long* time, right?

"Off and on, Leeland's created quite a stir for the others. His last attack—as they would call it—was on Dorian a few years after Dorian became a Master. Let's just say Leeland found some of Dorian's 'liabilities.' Other than that, Leeland's been quiet. That's scariest of all."

"Why does Leeland do it? I mean, why does he want to kill all the Masters?"

She wouldn't look at him. She knew he didn't want to know. "Not the other Masters, Odys, just *Mother*. If you want the simplest answer, you might just say that all the other Masters are Mother's liability. They all love her dearly and she loves them. That's why it's important they find out if you're worth the trouble of keeping. You'll need to love her, too." Maud found another cigarette. She'd found nothing she wanted to eat. "Everyone needs a mother."

"What's her real name?"

"You think anyone really knows that?" Maud laughed. "Nah, no one knows. Pepin wasn't even sure—and he knew her the longest. You and Dorian here are the only two Masters alive with *real* names—names that can be fact-checked. You didn't get the opportunity to hide yours; and Dorian, well, he didn't know to. Names are such strange things." She could tell he wasn't about to start calling Mother "Mother," though. "When we aren't calling her 'Mother,' we're calling her '*Gwen*.'"[37]

MOTHER: A.K.A. Gwendolyn Gwendy.

---

[37] "Then all went on their knees, and holding out their arms, cried, 'O Wendy lady, be our mother.' 'Ought I?' Wendy said, all shining. 'Of course it's frightfully fascinating, but you see I am only a little girl. I have no real experience.'" —J.M. Barrie, *Peter Pan* (novel). I was quite proud of the fake name I picked for Mother's fake name.

NEED-TO-KNOW: She has many children.

HER INTERNET MEME?: Pedo-Mother-Bear.

ALWAYS: In need of a good cry.

Chapter the eighth,

Occult Science:

Is it easier than Occult Mathematics?

"That's as real a name as we know for her." She gave a bitter smile. "Pepin had a few names of his own." She sucked her cigarette to stop smiling.

"...You want to know what Fletcher's inanimate form is?"

"Is it not some sort of coin like you?"

"No. A rusty, red paperclip. The kind you see in college parking lots. You know they could have been useful at one point, but you walked over them too late and it's already rained and the red-brown will look unattractive on your crisp homework papers, so they're not worth picking up."

"Why would a god make him a paperclip? It's too simple. And modern."

"Why am *I* a U.S. coin? I certainly wasn't minted the year my coin says. I was modern once. Vulcan knew our forms would eventually fit into a time frame. He *planned* for it." Maud tapped her nose.

"But your timeframe has passed."

She shook her head. "No. What I'm saying is the Automaton forms are all starting to catch up with the present. All our forms have proper context now. *Now* is the time Vulcan planned for us to be relevant most of all—"

Before she could properly punctuate her sentence, the apartment door opened. Waltzing in, Fletcher threw down a large duffle bag near the couch. Dorian floated in behind him.

"You're back sooner than expected," Maud stated.

"Mother does have a phone, you know. All we had to do was call to give her our update," Fletcher said.

"Well, then, I retract my statement. You took your time."

"Had to collect our things from the car, Maud," Dorian said, leaning against the back of the couch. "Besides, we weren't sure we were going to let Odys live, on our first visit. We didn't know if luggage was—how do I put it?—necessary. Plus, we had to get a fresh pack of gum, see?" He held it up.

"Excuse me?" Odys questioned.

"Well, we do like gum," Dorian grinned—his fake grin reaching the bottom of his glasses and exposing his wad.

"He doesn't care about your gum!" Maud snapped. "Just what do you think you're doing?"

"Sorry, chap," Dorian said, turning his head in Odys's direction—a courtesy for Odys, "but we're moving in."

Stanza: Are they at least paying rent?

"House arrest," Dorian expounded. "To protect our interests as much as yours."

Fletcher waltzed into the kitchen. Opening the fridge, he took out the milk Maud had just put back. He grimaced, noticing its warmth. "Don't you people ever put back your spoilables?"

"I have a sister, you know," Odys stated, wondering how they planned to hide from her. How would he hide Maud, let alone two more strangers?

"Your sister is all the more reason to have us around," Dorian gesticulated. "Without us, this place'll be a hotspot for hell."

"So you expect Augury to pull something?"

"Leeland, you mean. And eventually, yes."

"And what about Odissa? What are Mother's orders?" Maud asked. "Odissa may have left Leeland, but Leeland still knows her whereabouts. Send someone to her area. Then if something bad happens, someone will be able to reach her quickly."

Dorian raised a hand. "Yes, yes, I talked to her; Mother's willing to send scouts out for your sister, though that doesn't mean they'll find her. She drives a silver Honda, right?"

No answer from Odys. He knew he didn't *have* to answer.

So Dorian went on: "If you can inform us where she's heading from, we'll update them."

"From the cemetery-mausoleum park in [redacted]."

"Well, yes, but how *far in* do you suppose?" Dorian leaned forward, as if talking to a little child.

Odys guesstimated her location.

"Very well, then. Fletcher, please make the phone call before Odys has a panic attack."

"Why do I have to do it?" He said, still rummaging through Odys's fridge. He picked up a log of cheese and sniffed it. He put it back and checked out their yogurt selection. If they'd had whipped cream, it would have already been swirled in his wide mouth. *Blah! These people eat too healthy.*

"You must make the call because you have my phone."

"That's no good reason," Fletcher grumbled as he closed the fridge door and pulled out a phone from his back "pocket." "Can I also order a pizza? These kids got nothin'."

"If you must."

"And Chinese for dinner?" Fletcher turned to Odys, eyebrows asking if he was interested in takeout.

"Whatever gets you to make the goddamned phone call," Odys growled.

Fletcher glared at him, his fingers punching away at the cell phone as he glided to the bathroom for quiet.

"I suppose," Dorian stated, standing up from his leaning position, "when your sister arrives, we'll need to get our stories straight." No duh. "Mother has asked we not tell her anything. Understood?"

Of course that was understood. But did Dorian *understand*? "I wonder how we'll do that, since you probably won't let her go to school, work, or out of the apartment?" Odys pointed out.

Dorian chuckled, taking off his jacket. He was well built for a blind man (who should have found it hard to walk straight, let alone work out). He tossed his jacket perfectly on the back of the couch, as if he could see it. Fletcher not only saw for him but reminded him where everything was, didn't even have to be in the same room for the whereabouts of things to be clear, if he tried.

"You've gotten crankier, Odys." Dorian said, tucking his straight hair behind his ear. He seemed genuinely concerned. "Something the matter?"

Yes, being a prisoner in his own home is *exactly* how Odys wanted this day to play out, Dorian. "I don't see what good can come of this, even if this makes things safer."

"Sorry, can you repeat that?" Dorian put a hand to his ear. It was hard for him to concentrate on two conversations going at once (for he could "hear" Fletcher's current one in the bathroom as well as his own). Dorian didn't like his distance and so walked over to the table to sit with them.

Odys saw his hand reach out—for the first time—to guard against unexpected collision with its edge. With Fletcher away, it was more dangerous for him.

"He said get the fuck out, Dorian," Maud mumbled.

Dorian crossed his arms and legs. He sighed despite pushing a smile. "So, Maud, what's this new Master's addiction, hm? Anything we should worry about?"

He "looked" at Maud when he asked it. Well, in her direction, anyway. Dorian remembered facial cues were important, even if they landed like a bad joke.

"Why do you care?" Odys asked, a bit nastily. It was, after all, *his* addiction.

"Well, you may not realize it, but addictions—"

"I know, I know. She's given that speech already."

Maud glanced at Odys. "He's coffee and cigarettes."

"Ah, the two that blacken you from the inside," Dorian stated, tapping his chest. "But, speaking of coffee..." He motioned to the empty table. *Be a good host, Odys.*

Maud's lip twitched. "I'll put a fresh pot on."

Odys found nothing to resent there.

Dorian remained quiet for a time, probably retreating to his own thoughts that Fletcher's current phone conversation clouded. Odys took the opportunity to stare/glare at him (since Dorian would never know the difference).

Dorian raised a finger. "Mother just told Fletcher that you'll be meeting her tomorrow—and that she's sent out one Automaton and Master to try and track down Odissa."

(Because Odissa is the damsel in distress—something every story needs).[38]

"Tell her thank you for us, Dorian," Maud said.

"Don't thank her just yet. Your sister's vague whereabouts kind of make things pointless. But, if Leeland *does* make a move, we'll have someone on their way to clean up the mess."

"That's a nice way of putting it," Maud hissed, starting the coffee pot.

"Well, Maudy," Dorian defended, "when you have *all the time in the world,* you can waste it by looking for little girls." He frowned. "We're good at tracking people, but we're not omnipresent."

"But you and I both know that if fate wants you to find her, you will. We can all smell the gods on this one. Every domino falling into place."

Fletcher came out of the bathroom, wad of tissues in hand. "If I were you, I'd worry more about Bulfinch," he grumbled as he looked over his shoulder, dabbing his nose with the tissues. "If he pees on our bag, I swear I'll make his innards into violin strings."

Bulfinch was sniffing the unfamiliar bag cautiously, whiskers rowing with every new smell. He noticed their attention and became self-conscious, darting away when Fletcher blew his nose.

"Must you blow so hard?" Maud growled, annoyed.

"Gold?" Dorian asked him, curious.

"No. More coppery than anything," Fletcher replied, scrunching his nose and examining the goods. It hardened in the tissue.

---

[38] I wonder how Odissa would feel about that.

Maud rolled her eyes.

"Just be glad Automatons needn't use the restroom," Dorian chuckled. From the corner of his mouth, "Flushing metals. It's not good for pipes."

"Unless, of course, we want to," Fletcher added, dabbing his nose. The sticky coppery-stuff clung from his nostril to tissue.

"He *needn't* blow his nose, either," Maud stated, annoyed with their prattle.

"But it tickled. The cat hair got up my nose." He pointed to the non-existent cat (likely in Odissa's room now). "An Automaton must keep his bellow clean!"[39]

Maud took out some mugs, gave Dorian a handful of sugar packets (just as he liked it).

And they waited on the coffee.

Fletcher, who realized the sudden lull in this plot,[40] strutted into the living room and turned on the television, plopping himself on the couch.

"You don't mind do you?" Dorian asked, like a parent for a child.

"No," Odys answered, glad to be rid of Fletcher.

...

They listened to the hum of the television and drank their coffee. Every so often Fletcher would laugh, and so would Dorian. Maud and Odys exchanged uncomfortable glances, feeling trapped and in a dream. A bad dream.

Though Fletcher sat in the other room and Dorian's back was turned to the television, Dorian enjoyed the same scenes as Fletcher, laughing aloud as if his eyes were watching.

Fletcher began sniffing loudly—snorting as if he had something else stuck in his nose. He was doing everything but picking it.

"Fletcher, dear, you still remember the bathroom?" Dorian asked, standing up. He could tolerate his own sounds no longer.

---

[39] Fletcher seems to be comparing his nose to a bellow, which is quite interesting since blacksmiths and smelters use bellows—which fall under the reign of Vulcan himself.
[40] He's not the only one who noticed.

"Yes, boss," Fletcher replied as his Master walked in. Dorian didn't shut the door behind him. Merely needed a tissue. He delivered it to Fletcher.

"Couldn't have gotten it himself, huh?" Maud said as she pulled at her shorts. She was having trouble keeping her always-metallic clothes at a suitable length.

"He's watching my show for me, isn't he?" Dorian stated, as if Maud weren't making sense. "It's not a *commercial*."

They heard Fletcher blow. It sounded like a faltering foghorn.

"Geezus, I told you, Dorian!" he exclaimed. "I told you Caffar put that pet tracker inside me when we were sleeping—back in June!" Fletcher shouted at the tissue, "I told you she was experimenting with me again! The fucking thing's all corroded too!" He tossed the wad away from him, appalled.

The pet ID tag had made its way through his body—rejected it through one of the few available Automata-openings. Fletcher shivered. "You *have* to tell Mother about this! It's unacceptable. We feel violated!"

"Who's Caffar?" Odys whispered to Maud.

"Another Automaton on 'Team Mother.' Her Master likes to *try* things."

Dorian sighed. "Who knows, Mother likely told her to put it in you. At least you know your body got rid of it."

"I'm not some cell phone Mother can bug whenever she wants to." Fletcher turned back to his TV show. "And you all made fun of me for sneezing!"

Speaking of noses—Maud had a tickle of her own, though it had nothing to do with cat hair. "Talking about noses makes it itch," she laughed for Odys's sake.

Odys noticed Dorian's ear turn toward her as if this talk of noses were too, too fateful.

With the same hand she had scratched with, Maud covered a gapping yawn. Her body seemed relaxed—too relaxed. Come to think of it, she looked as if she hadn't slept all night. Odys, however, felt better—better than last night, anyway. Maybe this was the stabilizing balance she'd mentioned—the synchronizing? He noticed that they were starting to look alike. (Like shit, in other words).

He realized she was wearing an even scantier outfit—had her shirt shrunk and her short shorts become…? Well never mind, he didn't want to look under the table to properly check.

"I wish you'd eat something, Odys. I'm getting weaker."

"Oh, yes, forgot to tell you that the pizza Fletcher ordered in the bathroom will be here in twenty minutes," Dorian said.

"Pizzas? As in…more than one?"

"He can eat a lot," Dorian elaborated.

"Doesn't mean he needs to," Maud added, just as Fletcher snorted yet again.

She rolled her eyes for Odys's benefit. He almost smiled. Odys observed these two intruders with curiosity and trepidation—to the point he forgot Maud was an intruder herself. She was his only ally now, and he found himself leaning toward her.

Fletcher flipped through the channels with the remote. "Boring, boring, beneath me, boring," he mumbled to himself each time he pressed the button. He only stopped when his (Dorian's, actually) cell phone vibrated. He whipped it out of his "pocket." Froze in place.

Dorian frowned as his Automaton read the text message. "Change of plans, Odys."

"What?" Maud said, itching her nose again.

"You're seeing Mother *today*. Waiting on more info."

Maud was about to scream, *"But Odissa could be here soon!"* but her words were interrupted by a spastic series of stress-related nose twitches.

Like someone gripping their chest during a heart attack, Maud covered her nose with great passion. Her face pinched—her head shook and made her copper curls quake. (Odys became aware that nose-issues were as contagious as yawning). Before she could clothespin it to a stop:

"Achoo!"

Maud's issue, however, was a bit more severe than Fletcher's nose blowing. Right when she sneezed, she disappeared.

Well, not *really*. She was just no longer in her human form. Odys bolted up, looking over the table corner, down into her seat. There, on the chair:

A pretty penny.

"What happened?" Dorian asked—acting truly blind.

Fletcher's head shot up. Leaping over the couch to get to them, he arrived in a matter of seconds. "She sneezed out."

They heard Maud release a soft moan—a sound from nowhere. Nowhere but the penny.

Fletcher leaned in, his long back hunched over. Extended out so, his loose dreads fell over his face, making him look like a weeping willow. "Pick her up, man!" he ordered Odys.

Odys obeyed. "What happened? I—I didn't make her do this."

"Of course you didn't, you anorexic Euro-grungie!" Fletcher snapped in the air, fingers sending (what looked like) sparks as he tried to redirect Odys's attention. "She's tired. No—that's the wrong way to put it. When tired, Automatons can sleep, but this is more along the lines of pooping-out. Exhaustion, stress, trauma!"

"It happens, sometimes," Dorian clarified, more calmly than his Automaton. "When a Master doesn't properly take care of his Automaton or body."

"He tuckered her out. Made her work too hard. Made her hard-drive crash!" Fletcher threw his hands in the air, as if Odys had just broken his new Christmas toy. *Why we can't have nice things!*

"She's unwillingly conserving energy—so she doesn't have to keep up the clothes-act," Dorian reported. "You haven't synced yet, Odys. That's what pushed her over the edge,"—too many programs running at once. "Sneezing out might be the equivalent of a catatonic fit. They vary in size and style, but they can *always* be prevented."

"The nose always warns you," Fletcher said. "Isn't that what I was saying? Nobody ever listens to me."

Odys glared at him. He'll check the nose all right, right after he punches this Automaton in the face.

"How can we not listen to you?" Dorian mumbled. "You never shut up." (Dorian sometimes hated himself, you see).

"This wouldn't have happened if you'd eaten something," Fletcher scolded. Speaking of eating, Dorian was hungry. His eyes darted to the fridge.

"But you told me there was pizza coming!" Odys got the feeling Dorian was playing good cop/bad cop with him all at the same time.

"Boys, boys!" Dorian raised two hands, a strange grin on his face. "It's not that big of a deal—this time. She'll be fine."

Fletcher scoffed and went into the kitchen.

Odys cradled Maud in his palm. "Maud—you okay?" Now that he thought about it, she was acting far different than the scandalously-confident Maud from last night.

"Yes, Odys. Was just a tickle."

"Can you turn back?"

"Best not to."

"Dumb question," Fletcher said, coming out of the kitchen (once again). He was licking a spoon full of coffee ice cream, the tub in his left hand. He made a face as if it tasted better than expected.

"Just hold on to me for now. Not sure how well I can keep clothes on."

Dorian laughed. "He'd best get used to that. If I weren't blind, I'd swear I'd have seen Fletcher naked more times than dressed. Odys, why don't you eat a little something, sí?"

"But not this." Fletcher babied the ice cream. "This is mine." His voice was muffled, because of the spoon.

Odys was about to obey but he remembered the cause of Maud's sneeze-out—the tipping point of her/their stress:

"Wait," he said. "You just said I was seeing Mother. *Today*. But when? I want to be here when Odissa returns—I don't want you two messing with her."

"Relax, dear," Dorian said, waving a hand. "That's part of why Mother will see you now. Your sister's at [such-and-such a place] having lunch."

"There? You mean you've found her?" Odys questioned. He looked at Fletcher who was going through the phone again—likely deleting any evidence of a text message in case Odys demanded to see it. "But that's—that's still *hours* away from here. I thought she left sooner than that. How did they get to her so fast?" Something told Odys they'd planned to spy on his sister since the beginning. "You're sure it's her?"

"Perhaps she made more stops along the way," Maud said from his hand. "She might be shopping. You hate shopping."

"She usually calls if she's going to do that," he said to the air, forgetting she was in his hand.

"Usually is not all the time," Dorian said, smacking his gum. "And with no cell phone, it'd be hard to find a payphone these days."

Odys ignored the condescending comment. "We've got a good three or—maybe—four hours ahead of us, depending on traffic. That's how long it will take if she's coming from there."

"Just enough time for an interview with Mother Dearest," Dorian supplemented, sitting down on the couch beside Fletcher. "Now quiet! I'm trying to watch this."

But Dorian wouldn't get to watch his show after all. There was a knock at the door. "Pizza!" Fletcher exclaimed. He rushed to it, looked through the peep-hole. He gasped, dropping the ice cream tub. Odys cringed at the mess it left. "Dorian, darling, is it just me or did Mother *really* change her plans?"

"Who's there?" Maud asked—a fear in her (muffled) tone.

"Not the pizza delivery man. Fucking hell," Dorian sighed. He put his forehead in his hand, cursing something in Spanish about *la Madre.*

Another forceful knock—

Fletcher put his back to the door, as if to barricade it. To Odys, "She sent the big dogs. Fucking Mother planned on changing her plans all along!" He didn't really seem surprised so much as entertained.

Another knock; Fletcher jumped.

His phone buzzed. He whipped it out.

"In fact," he said, "Mother's escort for Odys got here fast—even before her text to prep us!" He giggled and bit his nails, reading. His eyes danced.

The door shook again. It rattled the walls.

"Who is it?" Fletcher asked, his voice too high and too mischievous as he put away the phone.

"You should open the door before Mother's dog gets angry," Dorian said—as if he had no control over Fletcher whatsoever.

"Open up!" the commanding voice shouted between the *bang bang bangs*.

"Just a minute!" Fletcher said back, still chewing on his nails. To himself, "I—I have to think of something good, Dori. I wasn't prepared for this!" Fletcher flipped back around, peeking through the peep hole again (he had to stoop low to use it).

"Open the damn door, Fletcher!" the woman's voice demanded again. The voice sounded ready to invade. "You can't bide your time forever, coward!" She rattled the locked knob, seeing if were even locked. Mumbling, "Fuck's sake, I didn't die in Vietnam for this." (Not even I know what she means by that).

Odys felt his hand being forced open. Maud fell from it and reformed—though she probably shouldn't have. She wobbled in place and used his arm to steady herself.

She had formed because she wanted whoever was on the other side of that door to see her when they came in. "Don't be scared, Odys."

Odys raised a brow. Should he be?

"Prepare yourself, Odys," Dorian said, his ambivalent tone missing the same caution of his words. "You're going to meet *Bob*."

BOB: More like BYOB.

DOG: More like Mother's b*tch.

LAP DOG?: After she has a few beers.

ESCORT: More like SWAT raid.

Chapter the ninth,

Oh, did I say pizza? Because I meant kidnapping:

Who's fibbing the most?

"I've got it!" Fletcher exclaimed to Dorian—as if he'd just come up with some necessary solution. He had the perfect trick up his sleeve. (Fletcher hadn't seen Bob in quite a while, and he needed to make up for lost time). He cleared his throat. "Password?" he insisted, knowing it was the *worst* thing to say.

A muffled grunt and then, "You're dead!"

The knob twisted to no avail.

Fletcher jumped back from the door. Crouching low in the corner, he tensed with anticipation. He hadn't been given this much opportune fun in weeks.

Most likely, there was no password. And Fletcher was about to die. (Odys certainly wouldn't miss him).

That wicked grin on Fletcher's face met "death" with merry expectation.

Pew, pew.

A silenced gun blew off the knob. The metal parts dropped to the floor, smoking from the heat.

Dorian seemed blasé (as usual) with the commotion and went to top off his coffee (which he did not actually like). Odys was nervous the neighbors were going to hear—or worse, *see*—the hubbub.

"That's my fucking door!" Odys cried.

Maud ate her lips, signaling to shut up about it.

Assuming a butler outfit, Fletcher shooed them away with two hands—*don't mess this up for me*. Maud pulled Odys back.

There was one more shot—a shot to take out the bolt. *Peeeew.* The doorframe was busted, wood-splinters springing to the air. Someone tapped the door open.

The woman who owned the rough voice stepped forth, her hunky boots thudding against the floor. She looked behind her—left and right—to make sure no one had seen her. The curvy female tucked the huge, smoking gun back into her holster and paused in the door way. She crossed her arms, squishing a too-loose camouflage jacket against her chest.

Her Chola-esque aesthetic made it almost hard to tell she was Asian. She had the hard-core makeup: the outlined lips, over-shadowed eyes, packed-on foundation. All that was missing were the drawn-on eyebrows. *Ay caramba.*

Her icy-black hair was slicked back in a loose, low bun. That bun unintentionally exposed the tattoos trailing up her neck; but they weren't your normal, every-day hard-core tats. Not some cheesy dragon, Asian symbol, pinup girl, cameo, or girly rose. Nope. She was more interesting than that.

They were blobs. That's right, *blobs*. Blobs like spots on a cow, dog, or oil-stained driveway. Misshapen, tiny spots with waves, curves, varying sizes—green-black dots as if she were a document with retractions.

"Bob's blobs," as they were called in others' whispered conversations.

Though this drill-sergeant's hair was held down with a bandana, a large portion of her fringe fell over her right eye and trailed down to her full, prodigious lips. Her uncovered eye, however darted to Fletcher—still in his butler suit.

"Still see you make *him* do all your childish bullshit," she chided Dorian.

Dorian sipped his coffee—as deaf as he was blind.

"I only open doors for ladies, sir," Fletcher said, giving the visitor a little bow.

Without giving so much as a second glance, she said, "You look like a damn Raggedy Anne doll, Fletcher, with that damn hideous hair."

In the blink of an eye, he had assumed a full fencing uniform (foil and all), just so he might use them as props while saying: "Touché! Why, thank you, Madame. And, my, my! Is that another spot? I can't wait until you finally decide to dot your face. God knows you should have covered the hideous thing ages ago." Swish, swish with his sword.

"Speaking of faces, might I borrow yours? My damn ass needs a break."

"Your Filipino ass? Or your American one? What ass-hat have you decided to wear today?"

"You want to talk about ass-hats? Let's go back to that hair of yours."

"I'll put that on my to-*don't* list, you crap-burper." He stood at attention.

"As if you even know how to write to *make* lists."

"At least I don't keep lists of all the people I killed in active duty."

"That's not a list, dumbass. It's a tally sheet. Like FUCK I want to know their names."[41]

"That's right, you have a thing about names. That's why yours is so short and simple."

"Your stupid red hair will go well with Dorian's stupid red blood when I spill it."

He rolled his eyes. "Honestly, calling you a bitch would be an insult to all female dogs!" He bit his lip to keep from laughing.

She caught his momentary weakness and began to circle her prey. "...So your butler and fencing suits are for me? Why didn't you slip into something more comfortable, like a freaking coma?"

"Seriously, I can always tell when you're bitchy. Your lips move."

"You don't know the damn meaning of bitchy—but then again, you don't know the meaning of most words."

"There was something about you I used to like...but then, you came through the door."

"I'm searching for a damn fuck to give—"

"AHEM!" It was a voice from the apartment entrance—a polite but reprimanding sound that brought an unexpected end to the flying stichomythia.

This was when Odys realized Bob and Fletcher's engrossing "duel" had lasted only a matter of nanoseconds.

---

[41] Our Narrator said that it's also safe to assume she has a tally sheet for those killed in *inactive* duty.

Bob bowed her head. "You barely giggled this time." She'd let Fletcher win this round—though she still had a *few* more feckless insults at the ready. (Little did she know Fletcher was on his last limbs, ready to pull out the weaker/default "I know you are but what am I?" insults. She could have pulled through). She cracked her neck.

Her Automaton—the one who'd just stopped the madness—followed her in. Ducking to make sure he missed the door frame, he glanced down at Fletcher.

Fletcher frowned, "He's a little tall right now, isn't he?" said Fletcher (usually the tallest one in the room).

"First impressions, Fletcher," Bob said. "First impressions."

"You can't just let him stomp around like that," Fletcher grumbled. "We're weird enough as it is."

And so the other Automaton (with a heavy sigh) began to shrink—shrink like someone lowering a car they had just jacked—until he stood just under Fletcher.

"Better?" Bob growled.

"More natural," Fletcher replied, examining him. "But then again, you two are usually so full of hot air, it's hard to tell."

What this new Automaton now lacked in height he made up for in weight. His vest half-covered nothing but pure, ripped manbod. That well-toned core had pecs the size of dinner plates—dinner plates for giants.

Fletcher made his shirt disappear into his skin and his muscles swell to slightly unnatural proportions, mocking the newcomer.

Bob and Maud rolled their eyes (well, Bob rolled her *eye*—singular. Who knows what the other one was doing underneath all that hair).

[Want to read this new Automaton's full profile? Read this footnote:[42] Or don't. It's your dime.]

---

[42] Our Narrator's description of Bob's Automaton got a little out of hand, so I cut it down— but didn't delete it. (I suspect there's a reason our Narrator went into full-description mode):

"This Automaton held his head high, his back very straight, feet solid on the ground. Bob had dressed him in what Odys classified as 'Motorcycle Attire'—the kind worn

Bob waltzed up to Odys. "So you're the new one, huh? Guess Automatons are like assholes now, everybody has one. You're skinnier than I thought you would be. Grungier, too. Thought Pepin had more class. What're you supposed to be, some damn urban sub-hipster? At least you're not as fucking *prissy* as Dorian. Maud, slutty as ever, I see."

---

by biker gangs for an extra notch of badassery. Like all Automatons, he had a chameleonic appearance, though it stayed within the range of his six-foot framework and dense casing. But don't let my description deceive you.

See, if you could get past that bestial mustache that looked like a cross between an unintentional Fu Man Chu and a Hungarian (perhaps just a Hungarian that severely needed trimmed), past the huge, round nose (like a glob of clay), past the constantly-squinting eyes (narrowed in either anger or smile—the polar opposites not helping his case), past the huge arms that looked like they could snap you in two (bear arms with less hair), past the long tail of braided, hafnium-grey hair (though the color didn't age him), past the bushy furrowed brow (more like a unibrow), he actually had an adorable mug.

The only uncoordinated aspect of his otherwise symmetrical face was his minor under-bite. It made his mouth-line waver between German Cyborg and King Kong. If he were to smile, it would not only be the scariest thing but also the sweetest.

Oh, and had you not been so preoccupied with looking up (and feeling small), you would have noticed the Automaton's almost-bare feet. He, unlike other Automatons, *always* thought to 'wear' shoes (well, they were flip-flops that looked more like heavy getas, but he'd *still* thought to make them. He did, after all, have manners).

Speaking of manners, he was quite the clean-feen, you see. He usually did all of his Master's laundry, sweeping, dusting, cooking, grocery shopping, and etc.

And in a frilly apron most times.

And if this didn't temper him enough, he also liked knitting (though he sometimes miscounted), quilt making (though he was never satisfied with the finished product), and scrapbooking (though he had few moments worth documenting). He loved to exhibit his (quite presentable) creations for any poor soul willing to look—or, even better, he'd give his crafts to you.

The only thing he was positively excellent at (and therefore proud of) was *baking*. The man had a way with sugar and breads, I'll tell you! Vulcan had blessed him with the powers of the oven, some internal timer that got things *just* right.

...But it was Bob who completed Cestus's character.

Bob, who looked maybe thirty-five to (and don't tell her I said this) forty years old, seemed like the perfect, age-appropriate ~~wife~~ HUSBAND for Cestus. That was their IRL ploy— what they used in social situations as their excuse for being together.

...But enough of me telling and not showing. Back to the story."

This woman was a cup full of sunshine. Damn fucking good sunshine. Odys tried to hide behind Maud.

Bob turned away to take in the room with her single eye, hands on her curvaceous hips. She didn't even bother to flick back her bangs to view the world properly. One eye showed too much anyway.

"She's in a good mood," Maud whispered to Odys, her expression shifting. She rested her arm on Odys's shoulder to relax and also hide the fact she was shaky. She couldn't fetter a toothy smile, "Good to see you too, Bob."

"Bullshit," the prehistoric rockabilly snapped (this was actually one of her more cordial greetings). "You both ruined my evening. I had a pool game I was going to win. Everything last minute! Being a chaperone is *not* my idea of fun. Believe me, you're going to make up for it." She pointed at Odys; her leather gloves made a stretching sound.

"Another night of no drinking, Bob?" Dorian said from the couch. "Too bad you can't drown those voices out tonight."

"At least I don't *listen* to the voices like you, you sulky bastard," she said. She peeked into the kitchen. She peeled off her leather gloves as if they restrained her hands (they certainly make it harder to give someone the finger; she was an expert at it). She slapped the gloves in her hand, "You don't fucking see me moping around, do you? No. God knows I fucking get out. The only reason you're not fucking 'hermit-ing' right now is because Gwen made you come here."

Her curse-word collection was *fantastically* arranged. Odys was in awe.

"And just why are you here so early, Bob?" Dorian asked.

She took two sniffs of the air. "Holy Mother of Jesus Christ, how many packs a day are you up to? I'm suffocating in this smoke shop. You and your sister must be on respirators by now."

"I thought you were about to leave, Bob," Fletcher said. "No hurry or anything."

She turned away from Odys, her fringe waving to expose her second eye. That slight little thing glared at the world with continual bitterness and disapproval.

"Believe me, I can't wait to leave," Bob replied. "Let me just set some ground rules for this newbie, here, before we head out. Rumor has it he hasn't synced with Maud, so he'll need to be informed about how I do things." She glanced once at Odys. "I thought not syncing was impossible, but his fuckedup face is proof enough. Don't look at Dorian like he's betrayed you, boy. You want us to trust you, right? Then there can't be any secrets—no bullshit. Which is why you better listen to my rules." She paced to and fro with small range. "I'll give him a good orientation, Dorian, because, hell, I'll never speak to him again after this, God willing."

Fletcher snorted. "Leave no mystery between you that will keep him coming back for more."

"The most intelligent thing you've said all evening," she said over her shoulder. "Now, the ground rules. Odys, I'm the fourth oldest Automaton Master in this crap pile and plan to stay that way. If Pepin were still alive, I'd be number five. I've moved up in the line, though that doesn't mean much since *you* have, too. It's best for the newbies to know their status in this damn order, ain't that right, Dorian?" She clicked her heels.

"Sure is, Bob."

"So that means you do what I say. When I say it. No questions."

SIR YES SIR!

"In fact, it's better if you just don't say anything. Keep it zipped." She leaned into her action of zipping up her mouth. "Number two, you may have noticed this jacket I'm wearing. Yes, I served this country. But don't you dare ask me about my pre-Automaton history. Don't ask me if I'm a veteran. Because that makes me sound old. Veterans are over and done with their shit, and I still wake up to it every fucking day. I wake up to shit. Just like what I'm doing now—cleaning up Mother's shit. You're the shit, Odys. Understood?"

Odys nodded, unsure if she knew the pun she'd just made.

"And yes, these *are* tattoos—not birth marks." She pointed to her neck. "But don't you dare let me catch you staring at them. Because staring is fucking rude and I will blind you. You want to be like Dorian over there? Keep staring."

Odys quickly looked at her lone eye, avoiding the spots. She huffed at his fearful face, turning away in disgust.

Odys thought, *Is that how Dorian...?*

"No!" Maud whispered back, disappointed he would think so.

"Oh, and number three, unless you want your balls chopped off, don't make fun of my name. Yes, goddamn it, it *is* my real name—as real as you'll ever need to know. It's Bob. Just Bob. Not Bobbie, Bobbers, and Godfuckinghelpyou if you call me Robyn."

Odys hadn't planned on it, but okay. In fact, Odys was kind of hoping there'd never be another instance when he'd need to address her at all.

"She likes long walks on the beach, classical music, and her favorite color is black—just like her heart," Dorian said, sliding in a new piece of gum. "What else is there to know?"

"So have we figured out if he's gay too?" Bob asked, her lone eyebrow rose in conflagrated curiosity for any revised intel.

"Why? I didn't think the closet was enemy territory for you," Maud spat.

"He's not gay, Bob," Dorian sighed.

"Then why's his hair so long?"

Something told Odys that Bob didn't really care about his hair or sexuality. It was all a test—a test in how you'd react.

"It's like no one knows what a haircut is anymore!" She pointed to Dorian's hair as well, as if it weren't always that length. "We could give you a haircut, you know."

"Does that mean this colossus is gay, you fag hag?" Fletcher gestured to her Automaton with the biker-braid nearly reaching the floor. Fletcher leaned over to Dorian, whispering, "She'll make him a drag queen yet, Dori. The ugliest one I've ever seen."

She cracked her neck. He had her there. "At least he brushes his."

Bob's Automaton glanced over at Fletcher, expecting a comeback—his poor head had been darting everywhichway as the group exchanged rude discourse. Quarreling was standard procedure with this lot, and he recorded every minute of it.[43]

"But, oh!" Bob cried, remembering she had an Automaton. "I forgot! I'm so sorry," she apologized to the Automaton (so sweetly it was shocking) and beckoned to him. Grabbing him by an arm like a gentleman displaying his arm-candy, "He does deserve a formal introduction." Her head snapped to Fletcher. "Fletcher? Where are your fucking manners?"

Fletcher rolled his eyes as he reclined on the back of the couch, knowing what she wanted (introductions were "standard procedure"). With a wave of his hand, "Odys, meet Bob, her royal bitchiness, and her wife, *Cestus*."[44]

CESTUS: Not Aphrodite's girdle.[45]

HOBBIES: What Bob *used* to do.

FAVORITE HARRY POTTER CHARACTER: Hagrid.

BAKES: A really mean cookie. Seriously. Dey da bomb.

Chapter the tenth,

Screams = curses:

We all curse for ice cream?

"Cestus and Bob, meet Mr. INeedAShower," Fletcher gestured to Odys. "No, no, wait. Our own Mr. *SNAFU*. That's a better one." He saw Bob's lip twitch and eye roll, the closest he could get to her impenetrable approval.

---

[43] I'm assuming he "records" it for later analyzing. Bob must keep her skills in top shape, going up against an Automaton.

[44] Can I just applaud his *mold*? Finally! An Automaton that fits the notorious hype, right? After all, shouldn't this story's Automata live up to the connotation as something god-forged and mighty? Maud (a frail *femme fatale*) and Fletcher (a skinny telephone pole) do nothing at first glance to live up to any menacing bequest. I was getting worried this book was about sex toys rather than war machines... On second thought, that's not much better.

[45] Aphrodite had a girdle named Cestus that had the power to inspire love. This Cestus, on the other hand, inspires us to question who Bob really is inside (let's go ahead and look up the definition of "bipolar").

"And beside him," he went on, "is his version of Maud. Maud 2.0, if you will." He put his hand upon Dorian's head. Dorian didn't seem to care if the Automaton messed up his hair. Fletcher's long fingers pulled through it like a comb, as if considering for Dorian the haircut Bob offered.

"Good to meet you, Cestus," Odys said, extending his hand to the ginormous being. In the middle of his action, he started to regret it.

The Herculean Automaton didn't take his hand, but frowned. Like some towering, sluggish, topiary creature, he held up a beefy finger (one moment, Odys) and retrieved something from his back pocket.

"Something for you," he stated in a rumbling voice. It took a lot of work for his big mouth to form that simple phrase—the sounds more like malapropisms. He handed Odys a knitted beanie cap—one with a giant poof on top. "A welcoming gift," Cestus added, "to start us out on the right foot."

Rather, to make up for his Master's *wrong* foot.

Without asking, he slipped it on Odys's head, a fashion designer making sure the clothes looked right. A finger to his lips, he nodded to himself. That would do.

"And Maud,"—he clomped over to her—"I thought we should make up for all the holidays we've missed. This is for you." And he plopped a too-baggy shawl over her head, arranging it on her tiny shoulders. "Made them myself, of course."

Bob: "We assumed it'd be hard for you to keep your clothes on."

"Thank you very much," Maud said, shifting in the giant blanket now restricting arm movement.

"At least you're decent now," Bob grumbled.

Cestus twirled the end of his mustache, pleased.

"Thank you," Odys remembered his thanks. He was sure he looked like an idiot with his poof.

"Odys is particularly fond of hats," Maud said to assure them.

"Good. But don't be a brown-noser, now." Bob cleared her throat.

"And where's *our* presents?" Fletcher whined has he adjusted a new bow-tie he'd just formed. This one was bigger and more Victorianly-frilled (he'd put on his butler suit once more). As he tugged on his sleeve ruffles, "You can't just give presents to total strangers and neglect the people you know, Cestus! You *know* Dorian needs socks."

Bob pursed her outlined lips. "Don't you have Fletcher to masturbate into?"

"I'd rather have a scarf," Dorian corrected.

"Don't give them *reasons* to call you a fag," Fletcher said. "At least not bad ones." He turned to Odys. "Don't feel special just because Santa here brings you presents. He does nothing but knit all day and can't find enough people to give them to. It's the only way Bob doesn't explode."

Bob changed the subject. "Let's get a move on. It will take us approximately thirty-six minutes to get to Mother's location, and heaven above knows how long we spent trying to open the damn door. Oh, and that brings me to my next damn point." Her eye narrowed at Odys as she put on her gloves. "In the event that you manage to pull something on us, I'm not afraid to pull you down with me—if you know what I mean? Mother may *think* we know enough about you to prove you're just an innocent little victim, but." She paused. "Even the Masters we personally approved started out as innocent and look where that's gotten us."

Bob started out the door, beckoning them with a curt wave.

Cestus waited for Maud and Odys to trickle out, making sure Odys grabbed his coat and scarf before out the door. With a nod, he bid Dorian and Fletcher, "Good evening, boys. Behave yourselves."

"Yessir, Mrs. Bob!" Fletcher saluted. "And for God's sake put a shirt on!" He went to assess the door's damage. To Dorian, "I think my insults are getting better." He examined the blown-off knob. Not much hope for the little thing.

"I'd say so," Dorian nodded. "As well as your composure. You used to giggle so much when she insulted you."

"I didn't giggle," Fletcher said, tossing the knob. "And if I did, it's because *you* couldn't control me well enough. Maybe if you did a bit more laughing around her yourself I wouldn't have to."

Stanza: You're a soul with a body; Masters, with two.

Walking through the parking lot, Odys felt like a prisoner being handed over for transfer.

The day was barely half over, but the sun was behind the clouds. Rain tried to form. It made it seem like evening. The car windows outside wouldn't see the remaining ice melt from their windows. The cold was doing nothing for Odys's health.

He kept glancing at Maud.

Odys didn't so much mind the fact he was having his day interrupted as he did being seen with an overly attractive female, some tattooed freak, and a conspicuous monster. At least Maud was wearing some shoes now, so she didn't look like some abducted street prostitute.

Those shoes looked more like bare feet with dangerously tall spikes sprouting from the heals. The lace-up threads made them appear more legit. He didn't know how she walked in them. So poised.

He counted the times her heals tapped on the pavement.

Odissa never wore heals. She couldn't stand them—or stand *in* them. The poor girl could only wear pretty flats, which Odys liked anyway. His sister was already tall enough...

Walking, walking, walking. Just *where* had they parked? There weren't cars this far out. Only some driverless ice cream...truck.

Odys looked at Maud. *Are you kidding me?*

"That's it there. That's right, the damn piece of junk right there," Bob pointed, seeing Odys's expression. Her voice turned to white clouds in the winter air.

Odys thought they would have driven something, well, less *obvious*. "Standard procedure, boy, so don't give any lip. Standard fucking procedure." Putting her hands on her hips she mumbled, "I swear, this shitty eyesore's a metaphor for my life. Go on. Get in."

"The back opens like so," Cestus said, swinging the hind-end open with ease. The latch had an open lock dangling from it. "This isn't our first choice of transportation. We usually drive our motorcycle, of course."

"We?" Bob said. "You mean me, right?" She didn't want to give them the wrong impression. She wanted it perfectly clear who was *the man* around here.

Odys wondered if Cestus rode in the cramped sidecar or right behind her. Either way, it was an odd picture.

The truck, completely empty, had its serving-windows bolted down from the inside—not like Odys actually expected it to be full of frozen delights, but it was a bit...how shall I put it?

Like a cell.

"What'd you expect, first class armored truck? Hell, no," Bob said. "We only need a damn cage to keep *you* in and *directions* out. Not that you couldn't break out if you wanted to. But if you do, well, I'd *love* to shoot something today. And we can't have you knowing where we're headed, you see, so that's why the windows are bolted. Standard fucking procedure." She pointed into the truck again, telling them to get on in. Don't make her repeat herself.

With a sigh, Maud went up, taking Cestus's hand. Easy does it.

Odys climbed on in and watched Cestus roll down the door. In the darkness, he heard the latch shut and the lock click. A part of him wanted someone to have seen those two stuff him in here. Someone call the cops! Open the door! He'd suffocate!

"Don't be silly, Odys," Maud said, putting a hand on him. "If anyone did see, it's not like you were struggling, right? Besides, if anything bad happens, I can easily break us out of here. Don't freak out so much. We can trust them. Bob's bark is worse than her...well, no, it's not but... Just sit down."

She felt her way to the corner of the truck and sat down, next to the built-in (but empty) icebox. He followed her. He could just make out her outline because of a crack emerging from the bolted window.

It's so cold. Upon thinking that, Maud snuggled in closer to him, just as the modified ice cream truck started.

"Is it always an ice cream truck?"

"Could be. I've never had to be kept from knowing where Mother is before, though. Mother never hid from Pepin. It was Pepin who hid from her. Mother's hiding from Leeland now—as always."

"Well, at least they found my sister."

"Yes." Something in Maud's voice was doubtful.

"Must have hawk eyes if they could spot her while driving."

"That or they're lying to get you to cooperate."

"I wish you hadn't said that."

"I'm sorry," she said. "But you were also thinking it. I just don't want to lie to you."

Odys breathed uncomfortably as Maud took his hand. They were alone now, so he didn't complain about it. He needed her touch and didn't want her to sneeze out again (like an owner embarrassed by an untrained puppy, he didn't want Maud to act up).

The rickety ice cream truck turned. Was that a melody? Oh God, what would they do if a child shouted out "ICE CREAM!" Would they really stop? He prayed not. One look at Bob and any parent would call the cops.

Oh, wait, that's what he wanted, wasn't it?

Maud changed the subject. "I put some cigarettes in your pocket. They'll warm us up."

The lighter illuminated their faces.

"Maud?"

"Yes?"

The truck hit a bump. "Of all people, why me? Why would Pepin give me something that I don't want and that others don't want me to have?"

Cigarette bobbing between her lips, "You and I both know your fate's been tied to Vulcan's game since childhood."

"It's not fair. I'm part of Pepin's game within Vulcan's game. A game in a game—"

She laughed at his dramatics. "Whatever *Pepin's* game, Vulcan's going along with it. You don't see him here, taking me away from you, do you? You can't have made too much chaos for the gods by having me. Maybe you're more important than you think."

"I don't want to be important."

"Everyone can see that," Maud scolded him. "And you're not *that* important. If you were so *important* then you'd fix everything with the snap of your fingers. Don't start acting like a messiah just yet. Just because you have a role in this game doesn't mean yours is the biggest part. Don't let this go to your head. You're just another hand that makes up Vulcan's body. He has many hands—just like every other god."

"What're you talking about?" Odys sighed.

Stanza: Not that you'll have no other gods.[46]

Her eyebrows came together. "There've been many hands, in the past. Hands of hands. Hands always have a *hand* in doing what's meant to be done all along. Hands make up the body of the Universe—God. Whatever you want to call it."

He pursed his lips. "Is this the part where you deconstruct my religious beliefs and blow my mind?" He was willing to let her talk him into it, at the very least. Partly to keep himself from falling asleep.

She blew out some smoke. "Exactly. You're catching on. Of course you would. If you didn't, then you wouldn't have me. Pepin wouldn't leave me to a *complete* idiot."

"…Did I just insult myself?"

---

[46] Not that you'll have no other gods, but that you'll have no other gods *before* me.

"You knew this was coming. You were just waiting for the right time to tell yourself. Not that you'll find it necessarily hard to believe what I'm about to say—"

"Vulcan is a god. There's more to it than that?"

"Be patient! I'm getting to my point—this is a point you've wanted all your life, Odys. A point most humans never get. Don't ruin the buildup. Now, where were we? Hands. Body parts. The Universe is everything, all that jazz."

[...][47]

---

[47] This part was omitted because it probably only makes sense to certain pseudo-intellectuals. Pseudos like Odys with too much reading time on their hands—like someone else I know (cough, cough). Besides, let's admit it, some of you aren't reading these footnotes anyway, and it's my job to edit things down:

"Maud waved a hand. 'Take Prometheus, for example. His limited-yet-significant role in man's creation story begins with clay—no matter if it was the Neanderthal, Denisovan, or Homo Sapien creation. Whatever. He shaped "man" from the ground—a clod of dirt, as the myth goes. Long story short, from dirt man was made and to dirt he shall return. The god that created man was part of the capital-G God. The gods make up the heavenly body—whatever that may be.*

'The hand of God may or may not be a literal hand, just like the hand which molded the Biblical Adam may or may not have been a literal hand. It's all a metaphor. Doesn't God have a merely nominal body anyways?

'Not even the Muslims or Jews will depict Him, for that limits God to man-made characteristics, and God shouldn't be restricted. Jesus is okay to depict, for Christians, but do you think they ever got it right? There were no cameras, back then. I should know. I'm older than the church! Jews weren't blonde,' she laughed to herself, knowing Odys (on any other day) would be loving this conversation. 'And besides, do you really think God is Michelangelo's pull-my-finger Grandpa? Hell, no. But I digress. Prometheus and the like are the hand of the Universe—of God. Anyone can be the hand of God. Even Hitler.'

He narrowed his eyes. 'So you're calling me Vulcan's Hitler now?'

She huffed, rubbed her forehead. 'Good and bad guys play their part, Odys. Prometheus was *punished* for giving man fire—for sympathizing with man. How can the hand of God be punished for what it was meant to do? Why was Prometheus able to do it in the first place, if it wasn't meant to be done? Just think of His poor liver, pecked out every day! Perhaps Prometheus had, in the end, stepped out of line. Fire became the method to make weaponry and thus made way for atomic bombs and shit. It gave man too much power, some could say. But it also helped man survive. We can't really know if Zeus was justified for wanting to keep fire from man, but whatever *happened* was allowed to happen. The Universe still made use of it all. The world still spins on its axis, no? And men got to keep their fires. Same with Hitler. Even when Hitler was alive, the world kept on spinning. The Universe *allowed* him to be born in the first place, right? And It allowed poor Prometheus to be punished. The Universe is never fair. But It always allows you to play your part.'"**

* For an interesting Western hand-of-God reference, see Exodus 33:17-23.

"In short," Maud said, "no matter who you are and what you do, life goes on. The gods don't give a fuck who you are, as long as you carry out Their will, you understand? Messiah or Hitler, you're unimportant. You're a tool—a device. Your plot in this story—this game—is all arranged. You might as well stop fighting it."

What a round-about way of belittling a person.

He blinked past her, taking in her gusty speech-making. What was he trying to tell himself? He looked back at her as he lit another cigarette. The light showed her well enough.

"That's—that's why Leeland's still alive, isn't it?" Odys asked her, his cigarette-rough voice hiccupped the question. He understood why she'd just ranted. She'd ranted because he needed her to. "Vulcan lets him play the 'game' only because he's using him; Vulcan let my father—no, I mean Augury or Leeland or *whoever*—kidnap me and my sister as children. But for what end?"

She shrugged, no inertia in her parlance: "What gives you the right to ask that question over anyone else?"

"But I'm being used like Augury—or Leeland, whatever. He and I are on the same fucking playing field. I don't like being compared to him—don't like that my life is being used against me. That's what this means, doesn't it? I mean, isn't this supposed to be some good guy versus bad guy shit? But how can that be when Vulcan's not choosing sides—when he's an asshole? He let Augury ruin my life—and now he's let Pepin."

There were too many Hands everywhere.

She reached out to him, offering her hand like a cold press to soothe his head. He was so exhausted that he tried to ignore what she was doing. "Maybe the way to feel free is to accept your cage. If your cage becomes your home, then the gods have no power, do They? Not if you like where They've put you."

He mumbled, "I'll never like where They put me."

They rode in silence for a minute or two or twenty.

**Look! A footnote in a footnote! It's a feetnote!

119

"Did Pepin have a family?"

"Didn't he tell you about his wife, when he first spoke? He always dressed like that, you know. Wasn't an act," she laughed. "He had a wife, yes, but when I came along...things got weird. She left him, in the end. At first I was their 'maid,' who stayed in the guesthouse. Because of me, they became very rich. At first Mrs. Pound knew nothing about me. Pepin kept me hidden. Later, it became harder to hide me. Within two years of my bond with Pepin, she'd grown suspicious. She guessed an affair. Pepin tried pretending he was having trouble sleeping so he could lounge in the study with me. But of course I would dream and wake up naked beside him. It's only natural. The first time Mrs. Pound walked in on us...Pepin hated himself. Of course you know what it looked like. And yeah, it's only a matter of time before Odissa finds us like that..."

She took in a shaky breath as the truck made a large turn, pushing them against the wall. "After she left Pepin, she remarried and had children. Pepin was alone. With me. But he loved her until her dying day. But, with a face like his, he had a few affairs. Even with ex-Mrs. Pound a few times."

"And with you?"

"No. Pepin did not love me like that. He was too...racist to. At best I think I he thought of me as his daughter. He *wanted* to, anyway. That was the most elegant way to think of me."

"Maybe it's good he didn't have children, then," Odys said with disgust.

Maud just sucked on her paper.

"Even with all those affairs, he had no children?"

"I see what you're getting at. But he often checked up on that sort of thing. He and Mrs. Pound had been trying for, oh, say, a year before I came into the picture. Nothing happened, if you get my meaning. I think that was probably a good thing. A blessing."[48]

"I see."

---

[48] And very convenient narratively, I might add.

"Besides, being a Master makes it hard to fit children in the picture. They're not something you want painted in. Everyone in your life becomes a liability. In fact, I wouldn't be surprised if you're the only Master *with* liabilities now."

"Without liabilities, though, what's there to live for? Masters obviously don't live for each other. Dorian and Fletcher don't seem to like Bob. If Masters can't tolerate their own, then what's the point?"

"They're *stuck* with each other. You also don't know what I know about them, so you are judging before you understand. They tolerate one another enough to reach their goals."

"Goals?"

"Yes. They've got nothing left to lose. Leeland took everything. They don't have to tolerate each other to still be family. They have no choice now."

Odys chuckled. "I'm surprised they didn't tie our hands. They must not be too afraid of us, you know?"

"You still look like shit, that's why. And it's no use tying mine." He could hear the smile in her voice. "No doubt Dorian's spread the word you're a fucking martyr for your innocence, trying to disown me and all. They know you're complacent. On top of it, they pretty much have your sister hostage—so of course we'll behave. But yeah, I have to give it to them. They are being nice—nicer than I expected…"

Stanza: Ice cream sandwiches.

Cestus and Bob rode in relative silence, the jingle of the truck the only sound they needed. Bob scowled a lot when she drove. Cestus had retrieved his knitting bag and was counting away. This was how Bob multitasked. This was how Bob survived.

"He seems like a nice boy. Nervous-like, but kind," Cestus said as he looped his yarn.

"I'd be nervous too, if I didn't know what the fuck was going on. At least we normal Masters got prepped beforehand. Pepin just trapped this boy into it," Bob grumbled. She turned her blinker on. "Goddamned maniac! Can't you read the sign on my ass? 'SLOW: CHILDREN!'" she pointed behind her. "Damn people, never caring for anything…"

"Well, I think he's a nice boy," Cestus added.

"You would, wouldn't you?"

"Yes, I would, Robyn."

"Sorry. I just have a lot on my mind, you know."

"Yes, I do." He knew best of all.

Silence.

Driving, driving, driving.

"Fletcher's getting pretty good at pissing you off," Cestus grinned down at his tiny Master.

"Yeah, but Dorian's still not reacting enough to me. He always uses that damned Fletcher."

"At least he still acknowledges you through Fletcher. He didn't always do that."

"It's not healthy for Dorian to hold it in. Fletcher can't be his only means of emotion. That stoic bastard isn't going to get better if he won't let us in."

"He'll come around with time."

"Time, ha!" Bob mock-laughed. "Time! All we have is time. How long has it been though? Twenty-plus years that bastard's been like this? So gloomy. He should be happier."

And you're such a ray of sunshine yourself, Bob.

Cestus sighed. "Maybe trying to *provoke* him isn't the way to bring him out of it."

"You always say that, but it's not like other methods have worked. Mother babies him and he just keeps growing more and more distant. Pepin, for a while there, tried to be a father figure. What other methods are left?" she grumbled, honking her horn at a little old lady in the car in front of them. "It's green!" Bob shouted at the windshield.

…

"But you have to admit, Dorian was quick to take on this assignment."

"No, Mother was quick to offer it to him."

"Yes, but Gwen knows what she's doing," Cestus gave a sly look.

Bob turned her head away from him to smile. She was attractive when she smiled. Even when she showed no teeth, the smallest upward lip-arch made all the difference. She only smiled for Cestus, though.

"But yes," she admitted, "Fletcher *was* pissing me off. He and Dorian are a nasty combination for me."

Too many bitches in one room.

"He knows just how to push my buttons. I was about to play dirty."

"And I knew you didn't want to do that."

"No, I didn't."

"Because Dorian—and Fletcher—would never play dirty."

"Though they *did* mention my spots." She squeezed the wheel and hunched forward.

Road rage was the least of Cestus's worries. "Have we not reclaimed the spots, though? Made them our own? Don't they know and respect that? They only make fun of things they respect."

"I know!" Bob growled. "But that was a first. It was mean. Not like that wasn't his point, but..." She cracked her neck.

Cestus said nothing, knowing that she needed to talk—to get things off her chest:

"It's not like him to acknowledge my spots. I just feel so sorry for the kid—for Dorian. He has it worse than me, you know?"

"More or less."

"No. Not more or less!" She snapped at him, swerving a little as she glared. "I get off with these—these tattooed 'scars' and what does Dorian get?"

Bob didn't cry. She just got angry. At herself.

"We lost loved ones too, though," Cestus reminded her. He had to recount his loops after watching the road for her.

"Yes," she huffed. "But I'm not blind on top of it."

Driving, Driving, Driving. SPEEDING. Honk! Honk! Get out of her way, motherfucker.

"...Can you hear that?" Cestus said, leaning in. He pointed with his thumb behind their torn leather seats. "I think they're chatting."

"Why does that make you so happy?"

(Happiness? NO! There'll be no happiness in Bob's ice cream truck).

He chuckled. "It's only that Odys seemed so, well, *removed* from her."

Bob rolled her eyes. "I bet some*thing* like Maud embarrasses him. It's the equivalent of having a porn magazine under your arm all the time. The world knows what you've been doing." WHAT YOU COULD BE DOING.

Stanza: All around the mulberry bush the monkey chased the weasel.

"Fletch, *must* you eat them out of house and home? We just ordered pizza," Dorian said, reluctantly opening his mouth so Fletcher could spoon-feed him.

"But it's coffee-flavored."

"As if I've never had coffee ice cream before." Licking his lips, "Not too terrible. Despite you dropping it on the floor earlier."

"I know, right?"

"You're going to feel bad for abusing their house if they turn out to be clean."

"No. Not really."

"It's so strange," Dorian said, recalling his interactions with Odys, "He only gets excited for news of his sister."

"You don't get excited about *anything* anymore," Fletcher mumbled under his breath as he gathered the last bit of expensive ice cream. He'd finish off the peanut butter next.

"This job's too boring to show excitement. I'm surprised you haven't blacked out from the boredom—you usually put your screensaver up."

"You make me seem like I'm narcoleptic."

"Aren't you? I swear, if you were a computer you'd have a screensaver up in two seconds of no activity. No other Masters have that problem with their Automatons."

"Other Masters have lives, that's why," Fletcher said, draping one of his long legs over Dorian's lap.

"Don't put the tub there. Throw it away. This isn't your house, is it?"

"Fine, I'll throw it away. But later. I'm too tired to get up." He gave a wide yawn and snuggled in. "Besides, if this isn't my house, means I don't have to clean it."

"See what I mean? The moment I let you run yourself, you sink like the *Titanic*." His soul could be so lazy.

"I'm just doing what you won't let yourself do." He put his head on his Master's shoulder, an awkward giraffe.

Dorian nudged him. "Keep your eyes open. I'm watching this show!"

"I can't help it if you're not even going to put an *effort* into helping me wake up. Just because the juke box is on, don't mean it'll play without a quarter."

"So you're a juke box now?"

"Better than the *Titanic*. Not as tragic."

"Well, how much more do you want me to take over, huh? You know I don't like turning you into a mind-controlled zombie."

"Ew, bad analogy. I hate brains."

"Funny you should say that, since you don't have one."

"Burn. However, doesn't hurt as much since you're practically joking with yourself and already know the punch lines."

"Ditto, then." Dorian said, itching his chin. He wanted to shave.

"How bored *are* we, if we have to keep talking to ourself like this?"

"I don't know. What's sadder: the fact we're babysitting a cat right now or the fact conversations with myself always turn out the way I want them to?"

"They're tantamount."

"Want to stop, then?"

"I think that'd save time, since we both know the ending."

125

They both gently nodded to themselves in unison.

...

Fletcher whispered in his ear, "I could wank you off in their shower. That would be fun."

Dorian cracked a half-smile. "Maybe once the show is over."

After the pizza came (and quickly went), Fletcher decided to fix the door. However, his idea of fixing the door was to take off the old and exchange it for someone else's. He was a very clever worker, Fletcher.

"Aren't you going to change the apartment numbers?"

"I'd like to see if Odys notices," Fletcher said, putting on his finishing touches. Duct tape stolen from the kitchen's miscellaneous drawer helped hold the splintered doorframe pieces in place.

"The *neighbors* are sure to notice."

Fletcher half-ignored him. "I'd say they'd need new keys, but it's not like they'll be here much longer."

And an Automaton needed no keys. They *were* keys.

Fletcher spotted Bulfinch sticking his nose out of Odissa's room, sniffing the pizza aroma. Fletcher hissed at him, scaring him back into his hiding spot.

"He hasn't had lunch, has he?" Dorian asked.

"Nope. But speaking of pests, do you think it's wise that Mother sent the you-know-whos to track down Odissa? When Odys finds out who we let near his sister...Well, let's just pray he *doesn't* sync with Maud anytime soon. He doesn't need to know what *she* knows about **them**."

"Was thinking that myself."

Of course you were, silly Dorian.

"...You really think **he** found Odissa?"

"I don't see why **he'd** lie—especially about something Mother told **him** to do. Besides, the stars are aligning far too well for me to doubt fate at this point."

Dorian put his feet down from the coffee table. "Mother knows what she's doing. Besides, she had to give **him** something to do. You know how **he** can't sit still. That's why you and I got the babysitting job. At least **he's** not bugging *us* for once."

Fletcher cringed. "Even so, I'm not going to be the one to tell Odys that Mother sent out our lecherous little *Mecca Makepeace*."

MECCA MAKEPEACE: A feral stray.

MUSLIM?: He *does* identify as a Trekkie.

AGE (ACTUAL, NOT PHYSICAL) AND TYPE: Middle-aged delinquent.

HEIGHT: Just short enough to suffer little-man syndrome, justifiably.

Chapter the eleventh,

The youngest are the elders:

This kinda has the whole *Interview with the Vampire* thing going on, doesn't it?

Mecca Makepeace and his Automaton, Q (short for Quarrel), had been sent on a mission. They were watching for a silver Honda in the opposite lane. Calm-Q swung her tiny feet. She could dangle said feet because she was far back in her seat and shorter than most beings. Cuteness was added when she twiddled her delicate, glove-covered thumbs...

Sigh! As if they were *actually* helping. Why did their information on Odissa have to be so vague? And *who* on this god-forsaken planet didn't have a cell phone these days? It was the twenty-first century, for crying out loud! They could have tracked her if she'd only had a phone! They were very good at tracking. They were the best at it.

Jesus Christmas, they'd never find her!

"Um," came Q's mild and pusillanimous voice from the passenger seat (her voice matched what she was wearing, as always). "Didn't they tell you the license plate number, Mecca?" Of course she knew they had. She could read her Master's thoughts—though not the ones he'd accidentally forgotten.

"Yeah," Mecca grumbled. Of course she would ask that.

"Then, um, what was it? I'm trying to help you look. Don't you *want* my help?" She put a tiny hand up to her lips, hoping her offer wouldn't offend him. Her voice was a high-pitched whisper—the kind of voice that comes from the most modest and gentle women. She was a delicate thing today.

She saw his face pinch, his eyes on the road. He could hardly see over the steering wheel. She was surprised that his feet reached the pedals. Perhaps he had grown recently.

"Don't you *want* me to help you?" she asked again.

"Mecca…" he started (yes, referring to himself in third-person—and no, it wasn't baby-talk), "…can't remember the plate numbers."

"Huh? Oh, Mecca, you're *always* forgetting," she cried. "I wish you would have told me, so I could have remembered for you. Or written it down. Why did you keep me from knowing? Now we'll never know for sure if it's the right car. Especially in this poor light."

The clouds wanted to rain/sleet.

"Well, we've got her picture, don't we?" he snapped. "Mecca knows what she looks like and what her car looks like, too. That's all Mecca needs!"

"Oh, I wish you weren't so proud and would call Mother to confirm," Q half-heartedly abnegated, smoothing out the wrinkles of her frilly Rococo dress. She looked even younger in that Alice-in-Wonderland garb—complete with self-formed lace, stockings, and bonnet.

Though it was nothing to brag about, Q was *at least* a head taller than her Master, and looked—maybe—five years older. But looking older than Mecca meant an iota.

Mecca Makepeace, you should know, had a ten-year-old's body. But a frat boy's carriage. For example, every time he sent Q into a liquor store for *the goods*, it backfired; they always had to steal their supplies. This made them very practiced at thievery.

"Mother could repeat the number for us. Or—or maybe you could call Dorian?"

"Com'on now, Q. He'd make fun of us. We can't screw this up!" he scolded her; her, the doubting voice in his head manifest. "Mecca doesn't want us to look bad. Mecca can do this *on his own*." No need for even an Automaton!

"Oh, dear," she sighed, her voice cracking. Her fingers sprouted a lacey fan and began to beat the air. "No wonder they never send us out. You can't even remember a license plate number. You should have let me help you remember. You usually do. They *expected* you to."

Mecca rolled his eyes as his Automaton fretted. She worried too much sometimes. She knew darn well that he was testing himself. HE WAS THE GREASTEST. He would prove it.

To himself, at the very least.

His Automaton went on, "And it doesn't help things that you lied and said you'd found her, back there." She snapped and re-absorbed her fan.

"Mecca has to make himself look good, Q." [49]

He turned up the radio. Its volume would have disrupted any normal tender-hearted girl's train of thought, but Q did not mind Gorillaz blasting through the speakers. She folded her hands in her lap, a life-size doll. She would match any in a display case. Today, anyway. Only today. Tomorrow she'd look different.

Mecca thought about rolling his window down, but remembered Q. Her lengthy, straight hair threatened to lash out at you if the wind ever took it; it could coil round you like a whip. Plus, the air would make her cold. She wasn't *really* wearing clothes after all.

Mecca liked to keep her comfortable. He was very considerate of his second body. He paid great attention to detail. Well, *some* details.

---

[49] Long story short, the (what I like to call) "non-baby-talk baby-talk" stems from Mecca's Q-given enlightenment. So much knowledge shoved into an underdeveloped brain manifests itself in different ways, including his speech. You could say his third-person references show how a child would conceptualize being more than one person—granted, he's not *exactly* a child in this present time. This is pretty much how our Narrator explained it to me. Just FYI.

At first glance, you would have mistaken that second body, Q, for a Japanese Lolita abducted straight from the sub-cultures at Harajuku. A second glance would have you questioning whether or not the vanadium-black haired girl was really Japanese at all.

Her nickel-kissed skin gave her a suspiciously indigenous-American appearance. Had our alleged Automaton-Creator molded that flawless face to exhibit that flat nose, full brow, brisk eyes, high cheeks, thick lips, and broad chin to fit within such an ethnicity?

Of course. Why wouldn't Vulcan want his bases covered? Especially since His designs would end up in the Americas one day. Why not?

She sighed—the absolute most adorable sound—knowing it was no use arguing with her compatriot about these issues. She was only helping him test himself.

Mecca Makepeace had a delightful and amusing face—a round orb balancing on his too-skinny body. He had alert little eyes, always narrowed (to help him think of something naughty).

His wide grin always seemed more like a gnashing—flashing those baby teeth. Once you got used to it, though, you could hear the boyish giggling that managed to escape the fangs. And if he smiled enough, you would see he was missing a tooth, the spot unfilled (for almost ten years now).

Mecca's dimpled cheeks were just the right temptation to squish or push a finger in (a trademark gesture of his, which Q's perspective helped him perfect to help him better get away with shit). His mother used to pinch those cheeks all the time. Or, at least he *hoped* that's what his mother would have done, if she had lived long enough to meet him. She'd died, just when *he* started living. But he didn't miss her. How could he? He never met her. For all he knew, he never really had a mother. He had little proof and was more apt to think he just *appeared* one day. Who needs a mother, anyway? That's what he'd been given the Automaton for.

Little Makepeace, you see, was the youngest person to ever get one. Most times, Mother and the others wouldn't have given their blessing for someone his age. In fact, he hadn't gotten an "OK." He'd gotten an "If you must."[50]

These past generations haven't let Mecca grow much. Q slowed it down.

Q was a mother to him. A mother, a sister, a friend, a toy.

Someday, he'd look older than her, he would. Then she couldn't look down at him anymore. Then—then!—he could finally be the one others first noticed (he hated how everyone addressed Q over him, thinking her more mature or his babysitter—which was true, but still). She was the one who couldn't grow. Mecca could grow. He kept track.

Now, you might get the idea to compare little Mecca to, say, Peter Pan. Very well, then, I won't stop you. The homage is certainly there, I won't deny it (the Muses do know how to recycle a concept, don't they?).[51] Just as Peter never matured, Mecca did much the same. His brain has also taken its time to ripen. But perhaps that somehow makes him all the wiser, unlike the decayed and decrepit minds of old folk (no offense, of course).

However, *unlike* Peter, Mecca felt no desire to *never grow up*. In fact, he wished he might somehow speed it along (but not too much, mind you). Ah, age is wasted on the old. But don't feel sorry for this young'un. He knew normal children had terrible lives.

For example:

Had Mecca ever gone to school, he would have had to study. Had he a mother, she would have made him eat his vegetables. Had he gone to an orphanage, he would have been given proper parents. Had he real parents, he would have had a strict bed time and missed out on all those crime-filled rumpuses.

What a miserable life to imagine!

---

[50] Leeland seems to have made things more of a "must" in their decision making, I should mention. Mecca's childhood was tied to the Automata lifestyle long before he got one. Much like Odys, as you will find out.

[51] Sure, blame it on the Muses and not your lack of creativity, Narrator.

He pushed back the sleeves of his too-big black shirt that he'd stolen (or borrowed, if you were to ask him) from Dorian. Poor Dorian often found his artifacts missing or gently abused upon re-discovery. Dorian was Mecca's favorite person to steal from because Dorian had excellent taste in *things*. In fact, this car was one of Dorian's. He had a garage full of fancy cars. He wouldn't miss one.

"Are you sure you don't want me to drive, Mecca? Of all the cars to pick, you chose this monster."

He didn't respond, because he didn't have to.

The streetlights turned on; it was just cloudy enough for them to be necessary. Under each passing light, the fair coloring of Q's lace and ruffles illuminated the car in sparkling flashes. Mecca scratched his head. His hair was naught but an afterthought—a mere darker shade than the rest of his baby-soft skin. Or, at least, it would have been if we could see it under his "Ninja mask"—which is where Dorian's shirt comes in. The shirt came with the car. Those too-big *sleeves* I mentioned earlier, well, they weren't on his arms.

It wasn't really a Ninja mask. It was more or less a black t-shirt craftily folded to LOOK like a ninja mask. An assassin must make do.

The shirt tag was sticking up on his forehead like some unshaven curl, because he forgot to fold it under. He still gets points for trying.

But as I was saying, Mecca didn't have hair. Anything but a buzz officiously interfered with his cosplay (he had a vast collection of wigs and hats, you see—none of which he had time to grab before this "mission").

"LOOK!" Mecca exclaimed, pointing to the opposite lane. Q lifted her submissive eyes, just as Odissa drove by; Q could tell Odissa was (embarrassingly enough) singing and wiggling in her car seat. "Mecca *told* Q we wouldn't need numbers. Mecca is the great-EST!"

Q's mouth hung wide. "This is all too convenient. Vulcan *meant* for us to find her. I can smell it. The nose knows." She rubbed her nose, keeping her eyes on Odissa.

Mecca grumbled. He didn't want to think that maybe (just maybe) Q's nose had led him to Odissa. Q mentally assured him that she was *just now* smelling such things and that he really *was* THE GREATEST.

And of course she was right—there was never any doubt about his greatness, really.

Tongue between his lips for concentration (making his mask protrude), the little boy swerved and drove across the grass divider. It left a tire trail in the moist grass. They sped on up to catch the silver car.

ILLEGAL U TURN.

Q's nose was tickling away. They were *meant* to be following this car…

You may find it hard to believe that two kiddos wouldn't be spotted driving, or, because of their raging recklessness, be pulled over. Not to worry. These two had planned for the worst. This car had tinted windows. Mecca utilized those windows to the fullest extent and would often pick his nose without feeling guilty.

And if a cop pulled them over? No problem there. The vast assortment of handguns Q could create would get our friends out of most situations. The guns were for intimidation…mostly. Mother would positively hate it if they *actually* killed someone. And besides, Mecca would out-speed a cop before he'd pull over for one. Because he was the greatest.

They bobbed between cars and lanes.

"Do you really need that?" Q asked him, in regards to his "mask." It was slipping off his head.

Adjusting it as he steered with one hand, he looked over at Q. "Humph! Look at what you're wearing. You should change your outfit to fit the assignment. Mother never gives us work, so you should have fun with it."

"But *you* told me to wear this."

"It's messing Mecca's concentration," he barked, pounding on the steering wheel. "Q will not ruin this fun for Mecca!"

Rolling her eyes at his pout, her frilly dress sunk back into her skin, re-surfacing to be a tight cat-burglar-like costume. She looked at him through her "mask." Her voice muffled by her own outer skin, "Better?"

"Mecca's satisfied, though Mecca wanted something more…ninja."

"You do know this is a *stalking* assignment, right? Not an *assassination*."

"Mecca is ninja! When we get up to the car, Mecca will take off the mask and become a spy. That's what the sunglasses are for." He pointed to the dashboard (also a pair of Dorian's).

"Looks like she's turning left," she sighed, adjusting her mask. He was always dressing her up, like some doll or role-playing partner. "Also looks like her picture, yes," Q said, as she glanced at the driver beside them. They slowed down to tail her.

A few minutes later they would "re-confirm" spotting Odissa—Q would personally make the phone call. Gottah give those updates.

"…What did Mecca tell Q? When making a phone call, Q should wear a head-set!"

"I'm not a telemarketer! And the headset gets in the way of the real phone, you ass."

Now that she was out of the Lolita costume, she could act with less propriety.

"Then Q must think of a better costume for the occasion!"

(There was a costume for *every* occasion).

"If you can't think of one then how the hell am I supposed to?" she mumbled.

She thought about it and turned herself into a Beverly Hills-esque pre-teen: too much bling and too much sass. As she re-dialed the phone number, she said, "I can't believe we, like, actually found her. But, like, then again, I can't, like, believe half of the other things we've done either."

LIKE.

"It doesn't matter if we believe it, Q. *They're* the ones who have to."

They were very good at making people believe what they wanted them to believe.

"Oh, they will believe us. Right until Odissa walks through that door too early."

(Odys had been right to hope she'd leave as early as possible).

"Dorian's probably so bored he won't mind either way."

"Unless we walk in on him defiling yet another bathtub."

They both giggled.

Stanza: Orphans and the pathetic fallacy.

Meanwhile…

The ice cream truck screeched to a stop. Maybe at a red light? No. Bob killed the engine.

The door opened. The dim light made Maud and Odys's eyes squint. Cestus waved a hand in front of his nose. Their cigarette smoke wafted out with them.

"Did you *have* to smoke in my truck?" Bob caught Odys's deer-in-the-headlights look. "Don't look at me like I'm about to dump your body in a ditch, boy. I'm not going to kill you unless you deserve it. Besides, I don't like taking care of free Automatons once their Masters are dead. Too risky. You're not worth the post-*effort* of killing for no damn reason. Now, rule number one, don't talk about Leeland. It will make her cry. Two," Bob held up two fingers, "Don't drag this out. I've got somewhere to be. And so do you."

Odys stood up, but Bob held her hand higher, telling him to stay put, she wasn't done. "And three, Maud has to stay out here."

"Why can't she come with me?" For the first time since all *this* started, he wanted her more than anything.

"It's just standard procedure. Standard fucking procedure."

"You say 'standard' like this happens all the time. It's been—what?—over twenty years since something INTERESTING happened, right?" Maud chided as she hopped out of the truck.

Bob huffed, "She just can't go in."

"In where?" Odys stepped out of the truck, glancing around.

They were in a park. An RV park. Out in the middle of…

Jesus Christ, where was this place? Land of the abandoned, that's where. Odys never knew there was an RV park this close to them. Granted, all these trees kept the outside world pretty much invisible. Yup, this was a no-man's land. An isolated spot reserved for the junkiest of trailers, rusted cars, underfed hounds, and toothless folk.

Odys wanted to cry.

Cestus pointed to the right, to the closest trailer. It was a rusty, pill-shaped RV with pop-out sides and an extended canopy. A wicker table and chair set were neatly arranged underneath the too-huge canopy. Something told Odys the trailer hadn't originally come with all those bells and whistles—that it had been modified.

It was getting too dark and the poor streetlight in the middle of the lot did nothing to illuminate more details. Overall, Odys would have thought that people with gold-making Automatons could afford, um, something more accommodating.

There were maybe twenty or so filled spots scattered about the gravel. A few children had poked their heads out, spotting the ice cream truck but didn't approach. Even little kids could tell this rundown hunk-of-junk didn't have the good stuff.

"Cestus," Bob said as she locked up the truck up, "escort him, please."

"This way." Cestus yanked Odys from his safe-place.

Odys turned and gave Maud a weary look through his in-the-way hair. As they approached the trailer, Odys spotted a dainty tea set on the wicker table—but one saucer was missing its splendid tea cup. He heard someone take a nearby sip. Beyond the table was a boy walking from the curved nub of the RV's nose. He had obviously wished to go unnoticed until that very moment. He stepped away from the tangled brush and ungroomed trees—trees that converged with the trailer's front as if it had been purposefully pushed against the greenery to somehow make it blend in better. The trailer's oneness with the flora made a nice little niche to listen from and not be seen. He'd been waiting underneath the nose. Expecting them.

The boy held the cup in one hand, elfish fingers looped trough the tiny handle. An adult's hand could comfortably fit two. He had three—and could have squeezed in four. In his other hand, he grasped something worthy of hiding. Had it not been for the boy's relaxed face and attitude, Odys would have guessed the reason he'd been lurking was to conceal the pipe he'd been smoking—but not just any pipe. A pipe that suited him quite nicely. A kiseru pipe.

He walked up to them, sucking on the kiseru—his dainty face shameless. He held the pipe blatantly—for the entire white-trash world to see.

He was the most riveting child Odys had ever seen. But that was, of course, because this child was not a child. The boy was so striking that Odys found himself staring, making sure it wasn't an alien. Or a wee spirit.

But he was none of the above.

This Automaton was a god toting his customary symbols—the tea cup and pipe in his hands—hands that sported clean but too-long nails. They were claws—sharp points just like the tips of his side-swept bangs. The fringe-hair grew to his eyes and would have annoyed a normal person. The rest of his hair framed his face, draped over his delicate shoulders, trailed down his lower back like a veil.

Mother's Automaton blew out his pipe smoke, a purposefully indiscreet and gauche exhalation reserved for the next. He put his teacup down and crossed his arms. His wrist and fingers supported his pipe like a branch for a bird. His every graceful action achieved a purpose—what purpose?

Cestus nodded and greeted the other Automaton, "*Anselm.*"

ANSELM: Automaton of Gwendolyn Gwendy.

ANSELM: The youngest-looking Automaton.

ANSELM: The Automaton with the oldest Master.

ANSELM: Gwendolyn Gwendy's Automaton.

Chapter the twelfth,

We all wear many faces:

Do some need a face lift?

Cestus, not stopping to chat (as if Anselm wouldn't want to be bothered), led Odys to the door. Cestus was about to knock when—

Anselm was next to them in an instant, an eerie smile on his face. His grin made his jaw-line protrude. It made him look like a man, only miniature. His oblong lids flashed those expressive eyes—eyes like newly-minted dimes. Without saying a word, the boy opened the door with a self-made finger-key. He opened it slightly.

No need to knock; Mother's Automaton welcomed them.

He was wearing only a vest on top—even in this cold!—like some sophisticated ragamuffin. He didn't even shiver or hold himself for warmth. Poor Maud shivered as if naked and gripped her new shawl for warmth. Cestus even gave "burrr" sounds here or there.

"Thank you," Cestus said. The boy came just above his knee-cap and made no effort to push the door open fully.

Cestus thought Anselm's rude behavior was funny—Odys somehow missed the joke. They were fucking with him—trying to scare him—test his fight or flight.

Cestus entered after Odys. Anselm followed close behind—not shutting the door. He gave Cestus a wide-eyed look that said more than words. He'd take it from here. Cestus patted the little Automaton on his shoulder and left without words.

Maud watched it all from afar. She leaned against the ice cream truck, arms crossed. She thought about smoking a cigarette.

"Stay where we can see you," Bob grumbled at her as she walked over to the chairs under the canopy to sit. The tea was for her (Mother was always a good hostess).

Maud nodded, not going to move an inch. She was going to stand here. And wait. And prove her Master was good.

She looked up at the setting sun, then back down at Bob. She counted how many times Bob stirred her tea—one—two—three—four…

Stanza: A Prioress that is best dressed.

Odys was alone with the Automaton.

He tried to distract himself.

The trailer was a gypsy hollow—a cave, more like. The lackluster lamps cast entrancing shadows. Wooden beads hung as a door from the ceiling. Colorful-but-faded drapery covered every available surface. Hypnotic incense and candles burned, creating a sweaty and exotic aroma. Odys loved any kind of smoke; it was fire he feared.

The place was cramped—with books upon books—a large collection of Catholic works and Spanish titles. He recognized one, and only one: *Cien Años de Soledad*. He had read it in English and had taken enough Spanish classes to understand the title.

Funny, to see a book like *that* on a shelf owned by *these* people; hundreds of years had passed among the Automatons and their Masters. Perhaps only *they* could appreciate the repetitive nature and continual stream of isolation Marquez presented.

Anselm watched him reading the titles, making Odys self-conscious.

The sitting area brimmed with pillows bursting over their seats. Odys could see a welcoming, built-in bed at the butt of the trailer. Tiny potted plants decorated every crevice and surface: herbs, flowers, ferns, the like. It presented an earthy feel that contrasted with the cold weather he'd just retreated from.

Anselm set down his pipe (its smoke was dwindling) on a special stand atop a nearby ledge and went straight to the pillows, nesting himself among them. Just sitting there.

He stared at Odys like an alien examining an earthling—an amoral interest on his little face. His homogenized eyes, with slight, attractive folds underneath, made the Automaton seem wiser. He was as slender as he was tiny. His jewel-head of platinum-white hair (that Odys would have called "bleached," had he not known better) gave him a false sense of age—an old elf.

Whereas Q simply acted like a life-sized doll, Anselm *was* one. A creepy living doll.

The boy didn't blink. The boy didn't say a word. The boy didn't even breathe.

(Odys noticed this because he would have counted).

Instead, he tried to ignore Anselm and wait six seconds between each one of his own breaths. When that got old, he pretended to be interested in the dying pipe smoke. It had the most delicious flavor and lingered in his lungs. The faint etching on the pipe's tobacco-basin caught Odys's eye. Before, Anselm's long-nailed fingers had concealed it. Now, it danced behind the floating smoke. It was the symbol of the hanging snake. The snake on a pole. The bronze snake of Moses.

Or, as it was later adopted: the cross of Flamel.

The Automaton's gaze widened with delight when he noticed Odys strip his eyes from the alchemic symbol. Odys recognized it—of course Odys recognized it! This symbol was everywhere...in certain circles. Including his father's books.

This very symbol was part of what made Odys realize his "father" was infatuated with ancient myth. Myth was central to many alchemic concepts—alchemy being the precursor to the sciences. His father was obsessed with that unholy trinity—myth, alchemy, science. But now—just now—Odys realized his father's *obsession* had always been more. Odys's heart raced, mind jumping to his father—and to Mr. Augury. *More* made sense now. Too much sense.

Anselm could tell the image bothered him, so his fingertips reached out and brushed away the image, leaving a charred pipe basin behind. It was then that Odys understood Anselm had probably etched the symbol there to begin with—with those long, thin nails. *Are all Automatons obsessed?* Odys thought. *Do they make their Masters obsessed?*

Let's answer that later.

As the staffs of Asklepios and Hermes's presaged the crucified Christ, this snake-cross symbol predestined another divine shift: Mother, too, was a symbol—one for the Automaton Masters.[52]

---

[52]Fun fact: As the bronze serpent (see Numbers 21:4-9) is much like the rod of Hermes (the caduceus, with two entwined snakes) and the staff of Asclepius; the re-occurring image is further invoked by Jesus Christ (see John 3:14-15). The parallel to this story, however, would be that the cross of Nickolas Flamel, who has historical and legendary roots in alchemy, is slightly connected to the god Vulcan, who was and is seen as an alchemical and/or metallurgical god.

Because of her Automaton's mystical quality and the loyal hype, Odys expected Mother to be some wise Galadriel or *Matrix* Oracle.

However, his fanboy expectations are about to be WAY OFF.

A divider within the trailer pushed back. Odys looked to his left, into the now-exposed kitchen. At last he saw her. His eyes widened in fear, then narrowed in confusion.

Despite her attempt, she lacked a certain *mystery*.

The venerable-looking woman didn't give one glance to Odys. She walked to the window beside Anselm, her own teacup in hand. She peered through the blinds at Maud, Cestus, and Bob. One half of her lips pulled up.

Her age was ripe, though her complexion bore only smile-lines. She looked certainly old enough to be *a* mother—but not Bob's or Dorian's. She barely looked older than Bob. How did she get away with such reverence—such a title as "Mother"?

But even with apparent youthfulness, she was worn down with age. She moved as if stiff and sore from some invisible chain restricting her—an age-old chain of secrets passed down to her from previous generations. Though she could almost pass for in her late thirties, her oddities gave her away. She was old despite her youth; she was young despite her age.

She took a sip from her cup, slowly. Odys noticed her hands shake—a tremble.

Odys could barely make out Bob's figure through the blinds. Half of her body was cut off by the ledge. He did, however, notice she slipped a few jolts from a thin flask into her newly-poured tea. He smiled, though he didn't mean to. He saw Maud studying her nails. But back to Mother.

He wondered if he should say something first? Perhaps a hello? No, he didn't want to seem in a hurry.

"I suppose," Gwen finally began, "you'd like to know where you are?"

"You don't have to tell me, if it puts you in danger."

Still looking out the window, she said, "Dear boy, what makes you think we're in danger? Perhaps all this"—she waved her hand—"was to protect *you* more than me?" Odys doubted that, and hated the mind games.

"Oh, of course it isn't true. I tend to protect myself *to* protect my children." She sighed, wrapping both hands around her tea.

Odys noticed a silver wedding band on her ring finger. It made him conscious of the one on his own. He stuffed that hand in his pocket.

"Yet..." she said as she studied her tea. The steam rose to her face and she breathed it in like a priestess inhaling sacred smoke. "I do want to protect you, Odys." She adjusted her sweater. Her draping, ruffled attire gave her the dearness of a Catholic nun, though the bright colors and Mesoamerican patterns gave her all the flair of a village *bruja*.

She compressed her grape-colored lips into a thoughtful frown. Her dark lids blinked more than was natural, batting things away, keeping tears locked behind those feathery lashes. Odys wished those eyes would land.

"Ansi says you smell like smoke. Automatons have good noses." She tapped her nose. "You smoke?"

"Cigarettes, yes," Odys nodded, overly enthusiastic.

"Ansi also says you like to stare at him," a laugh behind her voice—a laugh at an inside joke. "He appreciates the attention, I assure you." She leaned to her Automaton. Anselm reached up and covered her hand with his. She continued staring out the window. "He is a very vain man, I tell you."

Man?

Dear little Ansi kept his gaze on Odys. The tiny freak still hadn't blinked. Was he working hard at sending chills down Odys's spine? For some reason, Odys got the impression Gwen wasn't *making* him do it. It just came naturally. Gwen didn't seem the type to toy with people in such drawn-out ways. Even if a ghost smiles at you, it's no less unnerving to know it's a ghost.[53]

---

[53] Or, maybe an old woman in the body of a young child is just creepy in itself.

"Anselm likes to be admired. And I like it when people admire him," Gwen added, more for herself. Though she faced one direction, her starry eyes never rested. They darted around their focus, never giving whole attention—as if parts of the foci were too bright and made her eyes water.

"And I am just as vain as he, if only in a different way. I am vain in the fact I flaunt my children—the Masters and Automatons I love. They are, perhaps, the only reason I haven't given up yet. Unlike Pepin. I'm selfish to want to stay with them. To fix this—this problem."

Which problem?

"I smoke a pipe," she confessed—her topic spurts didn't seem out of character, her speech as fluttery as her eyes. "Ansi introduced me to it. Our addictions used to be black tea with milk, warm baths, and…stew. Homemade, of course. Funny, how addictions can be replaced. I smoke only in the evenings, but I delight in it more than other habits now. My, Maud is covered more than usual. It's usually like trying to keep a hat on a cat with her and clothes. She just can't do it. It takes too much. That's how she was designed. But you like her modest, I hear?"

News got around too quickly—another reason Odys hated cell phones.

"I do hope Bob wasn't too rough with you." A subtle wrinkle appeared between her thick eyebrows. She put a hand on her chest. Skinny and far from well-endowed, Mother's flat chest made her appear younger.

She would have looked more refined with salty flecks in her great mass of fine-velvet hair; Odys suspected those lighter roots meant she dyed it. But despite her touch-ups, she was a dashing woman—gentle, reserved. Her thick hair lent the perfect equalizer to her prominent forehead and large eyes.

Let me repeat myself/paint the imagery thick:

While her overall appearance screamed loud octaves of bright Frida-Kahlo colors, she was also in tune with a symphony of muted Virgin-of-Guadalupe mildness. To be unoriginal: She was a woman who aged like wine. Yes, she could be summed up so easily—so *clichély*. It's what made her so approachable. So adored.[54]

"Dorian called before you arrived. Said Bob may have scared you. Cestus, I'm afraid, got all her tender spirit and she was left with the churning contempt. She wasn't always this way. None of us were. She's less spiteful when she's drunk, though." Mother's eyes glistened with dewy tears, about to weep. She quickly changed the subject, "Did Maud tell you how Automatons got their title? I ask because Dorian says you don't seem to know much."

"No," Odys answered, half curious and half reluctant. He put his hands deeper in his pockets. He still hadn't sat down/she still hadn't invited him to.

Mother sighed, looking up at the ceiling. She gestured to nothing. Her prayer to Vulcan a whisper, "You want me to tell him everything—the back story? You want me to do the work for You? Making him sync with Maud would be easier and quicker for everyone!"[55]

She mumbled in Spanish before sighing and accepting her duty.

"We gave them their name. Pepin and I. Calling them 'robots' or something else just didn't fit. 'Automaton' is somehow more respectful. And the term 'humanoid' makes them seem like—like aliens or scientific experiments…"

She paused to remember where she was going with this tangent—this monologue. She was putting on a play—something she'd often recited to herself. She had expected this moment. She knew exactly what she needed to say—if only she could remember.

"Hefesto—Vulcan, excuse me—had named them something else. 'Guarders.' That's what he called them—at least, in English. Though, that word itself is archaic and we'd now translate it to 'Guardians,' I guess. Even the Automatons found that title too silly for modern standards. Vulcan hasn't complained about our name

---

[54] I don't particularly find her loveable. She cries too much and talks too much and touches Anselm/herself too much (ha, ha).

[55] But we, as readers, would be so left out!

change, so he must understand language's evolution." To herself, "At least he understands *that*."

She shook her head, clearing her thoughts. "'Automaton' proved suitable. These alloyed creatures cannot wield themselves, so *Automaton* just makes more sense. You only need to wind them up once for their gears to turn on their own."

Anselm stood up, knocking over a few pillows. He didn't care to pick them up. He stepped to the other side of Gwendolyn, eyes never leaving Odys. He brought her hand to his cheek, his lips almost brushing it.

"I do wish you'd stop, Anselm. Stop looking at him; it upsets me, you know," an instantaneous response to a provoked thought. "Stop staring at him, I don't want to see his face, not yet." So hard to block Odys out. She patted Anselm's face away, but he did not budge. "Stop tempting me."

Anselm blinked and turned his head away, as if Gwen finally agreed with herself that she didn't want to see Odys. The wall would now be Anselm's focus. Mother's soul would stifle her own bipolar curiosity.

"Sometimes I can't help myself," she choked out a laugh, eyes dancing at Odys's feet. Though she laughed, she dabbed her eye. "As you may or may not know, Odys, the Automatons have an expansive memory. They knew each other from their creation. Thankfully, that's something no Master has forced any of them to forget. I assume Vulcan gave them a memory because he wanted them to recognize each other. Vulcan, who has been known to stick his nose in our affairs, created nine Automatons. Yet, nine is not the perfect number, is it?"

Though the number was *odd*, Odys actually had nothing against it. Nine divided by three equaled three. Nine minus three equaled six. Turn six over and it would be nine. Nine was just an upside-down six. It wasn't the *worst* of the odd numbers. But yes, why nine? Why was that number important?[56]

---

[56] I don't really get why it's so important that there be an even number, unless our Narrator is just as OCD as Odys or assumes Vulcan is too. Or, maybe the point is really about the "holiness" of the number nine. I don't know. I leave it up to your interpretation (one more reason to release this story upon the world—to help me better understand BLA, if it can be

"That's because there are actually ten—ten *creations*. Except the first was…"

"A failure." Anselm finished the sentence for her. His voice as haunting as his looks. Odys wasn't sure he'd really spoken.

"A god failed in their plans?" Odys asked. It sounded illogical. Impossible.

"No," Gwen corrected, "Vulcan himself didn't fail. The first *creation* failed. The very first Automaton was no Automaton at all. Granted, there have been many creations much like Automatons in the past—beings also made by Vulcan. But *these* automaton-Automatons were created for a specific reason." She gestured to Anselm. "As the Automatons will tell you, their First needed no human soul to function. And, since it needed nothing, it had free will. Vulcan created it for a purpose and *it* chose not to do it. It failed. Thus, he made nine more creations. Automatons. Beings that lacked the wind-up key."

Nine more problems, some might say.

He felt the urge to ask, "And what was the First creation's purpose?"

"To protect mankind. To be good. To…" Pause. "Well, perhaps I should no answer for de gods"—her old accent slipped through in her distress. "We still don't know whether or not Vulcan made *them* on his own volition or under higher orders. Either way, he did so willingly—he *did* it. The First's origination had no true evil intention behind it. Vulcan has always appeared—to me—to be the type to do *the will* of the Universe—to do 'good.'"

But she didn't seem at peace with Vulcan's harmony…

"The nine Automata were created to take down the First." Her eyes narrowed in thought exactly when Anselm's did too. "And the first re-cast—the first of the nine Automatons, not *the* First—was Admund—the creation you thought was your father, Odys. Vulcan designed him before the others. I want you to know this." She paused, biting her lip. "He was a first draft—the one with the most convoluted ideas behind

---

done). However, I did find in my research that every year on the island of Lemnos fires were extinguished in Hephaestus's honor and would not be reignited for nine days. It takes nine to purify, I guess? But enough of my conspiracy theories.

him. Besides the First, of course. He was not yet simplified like the other Automata. Vulcan's idea was *grand*. That is why Admund is grand."[57]

She bowed her head, sickened to make excuses for Admund and his Master. "As El Herrero—the Blacksmith—went down the line, the Automata-idea became more *practical*. Practical as a paperclip or coin. Given to humans, they served their predestined purpose. The First was greater than a single Automaton, I hear. That's why Vulcan needed nine."

"Could the god not take down his creation himself?"

Anselm's head snapped in his direction. "Did he not?"

"What he means is," translated Gwen, "didn't he *solve* the problem by creating the others?"

Maud's voice ran through Odys's head. *Hand of God, Hand of God, Hand of God.*

Gwen went on, "Who are you to question Vulcan's methods? A man has sex with a woman and creates a child, yet when the child grows up and becomes evil, can the parent simply kill their offspring? No, there are laws that bind the parent—moral and governmental. Who are we to even understand the laws that bind the gods?"

"Do we trust Vulcan blindly, then?" Odys laughed, to see how she'd react. He instantly regretted being so bold. *She didn't deserve that.*

"You are not blind, Odys Odelyn. You are yet to open your eyes." She moved away from the window to sit down on the built-in furniture. Anselm stood beside her, leaning against the seat, hand on her leg. He conducted himself like a man. He caressed her knee in a protective and almost controlling way, as if she were *his*.

"Speaking of opening eyes," Gwen went on. "When will you open yourself to Maud? According to Dorian's updates, you're suicidal."

"I'm not," he said too quickly. He took in a deep breath. "I'm not suicidal."

---

[57] Admund's inanimate form is an iron stylus. Cestus is a safety pin. Anselm's, a broken compact. Q's, a hat pin (or, "bobby" pin). I edited out mentions of this because it was so easily summed up here.

"That's good, then." She took a sip of tea. "Dorian also said you were *brown*. Is that correct?" She waited. "Ah, I've confused you. Dorian can see people's favorite colors. I assumed he would have dropped that bomb by now. Dorian says my color is a red-purple. He wasn't blind before he gained Fletcher, yes? Some say when you lose one body part the others take over or adapt. He can now see colors—auras. We think Fletcher helped such an adaptation, but the fact remains he's *always* right."

Your color doesn't mix well with others.

"How did he go blind? Don't Automatons protect us from harm?"

Mother flinched. "Did you learn nothing from Pepin's suicide, Odys?" She waved it away. "Forget I said it. Let me finish with my other historia—the history of Automata. You've not heard it, correct?"

He shook his head. "I don't know any of this. Maud hasn't told me."

"She shouldn't have to."

So Mother was testing him—testing his acceptance of Maud—as if he should know everything Maud knew by now.

"Where was I? Ah, the nine. Yes, they took down the First. And that was that. I'm sure Maud can present you with the full details if you're still curious. Verbally, of course." She frowned in his direction. "But my point is, Odys, the Automatons served their purpose. It was up to humans to decide their new one. When the first Masters left with their Automatons, fate took its course. The Masters went on with their lives. The Automatons trickled down the timeline into the present era. The Automatons were scattered."

She took in a breath, remembering. "So many lives and ages. Just because a Master can live longer does not mean life is certain. Not only have Masters killed each other before—from the beginning—but Automatons can only protect your body from so much. You can still catch a cold, you know. Sometimes it's nice to be sick. It reminds you that you're still human. Many a Master has been killed by his own body. Cancer, obesity, disease, suicide. You are not immortal if you don't want to be. Sometimes sickness is suicide."

She glanced at him—at his *direction*, not him. She wondered how he would react to her last comment. She wanted to know *how* suicidal he was.

I'm NOT suicidal, he thought at her.

She adjusted Anselm's clothing—his skin. "You'd be surprised how many Masters Automatons have had. Long life should mean few Masters for an Automaton, yes? But no. Ah, enough of death. As I said, the Automatons were scattered. Not even *they* knew the whereabouts of their brothers and sisters. It's not like we could put out an ad in the paper. We've tracked down their history, of course—we know what Automaton has been where. If they ever forget—if they are ever *forced* to forget—they can relearn it and put their history back together by talking to another. Fill in the blanks."

She sipped her tea. Her eyes had been dancing around him, absorbing everything but his face. "I wasn't always the oldest Master, you know."

"Pepin, yes," Odys stated, glad he finally related to this speech somehow.

"No," Gwen killed his hope. "Not Pepin, dear. He and I might have stumbled across each other in [some Victorian-era date year here], but that hardly made us the oldest. We were the ones to track down everyone. Or to begin to, at least. Once we started, we had the help of the others. And no, it wasn't easy convincing everyone to rearrange their lifestyle. Automatons are hard enough to accommodate…

"Yes, we found Masters older than ourselves. Of course, some died and we relocated the Automatons to suitable new Masters. Poor Cestus, when we first met him, his Master was two hundred and thirty nine years and—oh—" (her eyes went up in thought) "four months, two weeks and six days old, I believe—that's what *Ansi* believes. If that's wrong, I have the date written down somewhere, of course, but…"

She flashed her eyes in Odys's direction, quizzing him, wondering if he was doing the math (and, if he was, was he comparing it to something he *already* knew?).

How could he know? Why shouldn't he know? Why wouldn't he know?

What do you know, Odys?

Nothing, you idiot, because you haven't synced with Maud.

"But you see, when that Master had touched Cestus, he was in his eighties. He was already so old. The age we look now depends on when we first touched our Automatons. That, and several other factors." She looked at Anselm for a brief second. "There was also one Master, God bless her soul; she tuckered out when the cancer struck—well, we think the cancer was inside her before she touched her Automaton. She also caught a cold and it finished her off. We think she wanted it to. She wasn't alive when the whole group finally organized. Such a shame," she dabbed her eyes as Anselm soothed her. "Arranging Masters is emotional work. And it asks much of the Master—for they cannot *really* agree to what they're getting into. Not until they have the Automaton is it obvious what kind of burden they are. Thankfully,"—her voice cracked a little—"we don't have to do it often."

Especially when Pepin does it for you.

Gwen was staring at the floor now. "As you might have noticed, Odys, we have rules. And we're a family. Like it or not, you're figuratively married to Maud, now. And we don't like the fact it was done—how do you say it?—in Vegas."

"Shotgun wedding," Anselm whispered to her, cutting eyes at Odys.

"Yes, the worst kind of arrangements. The family wasn't there. The family didn't sanctify it—bless it."

"But I was forced to marry," Odys pleaded—as if he agreed with the allusion.

"An *arranged* marriage." Anselm nodded once in agreement. "And yet, still so much like a raping of our daughter."

Odys wondered if Anselm had ever talked so much.

Gwen shifted her legs, a physical manifestation of her mental shift. "I have decided an introduction to our founding ground-rules might be a good way to start off." So things hadn't really started, huh? "Also, your reaction to said rules will be a perfect way to judge your character, I think."

FIRST RULE ABOUT AUTOMATON CLUB.

"Rules: number one," Gwen began, as if reading from a piece of paper floating in the air. "One and only one Automaton. If you get more than one, we even you out.

You see, we'd rather not learn what would happen if all Automatons were bonded to one soul—one Master. Two heads are better than one, they say—but more than that is reserved for the divine."

A picture of a many-armed and many-headed Vishnu or Shiva or So-on shuffled through Odys's mind like a deck of Hindu cards. *That's what Leeland will be if he keeps at it*, he thought to himself with a gulp.[58]

"As I'm sure you know," Mother went on, "Leeland broke this rule but is yet to be punished. Punishment is easier said than done, yes. But remember we do have leverage on *you*. You cannot become like Leeland. We won't let you. We've learned from our mistake.

"Rule number two: Let no outsider know about us. If Odissa finds out, that is one thing. It is another for her to know *too* much and for that knowledge to pervade the world. If we can trust her, fine. But we'll only trust her with so much. If she slips— even once—she will have to be quieted. You understand?"

He didn't delight in hearing those words, and she didn't delight in speaking them. He could almost see the water-works forming; she wore her heart outwardly.

He refused to answer her.

Unable to look in his direction, she glanced at her lap. Anselm kept eye contact for her. "Just think of what would happen, Odys, if the government found out. We've had to erase many things, in the past. We take no pleasure in it, and it gets harder each time."

"Then why not let the world know?" Maybe if she had left Odissa off her list he wouldn't be so defensive but..."Wouldn't it make this world better, if you did? People would—would flock to you. Who could—could interfere with you? Wouldn't it be *easier*? What do you risk, if you're found out? You can't die. You could do so much."

---

[58] Personally, I thought of Lord Voldemort and the Horcruxes, with Leeland's soul split into so many parts.

151

Gwen helped herself to a moment's breath; she was taking time to unburden herself. "Sí, I've wondered if the world had the right to know. Perhaps it does. However, we're not the only things hiding, are we? Ah, you don't know what I mean. But someday, you will. You will learn that Vulcan himself hides."

"But Vulcan has reason to."

Anselm chuckled behind his Master.

"What reason?" Gwen smiled a curious smile.

"The same as God's?"

"So you're saying He wants people to believe with faith? Where did you get that revelation, Odys?"

"I only thought—"

"I can see why you'd think it—as if all the gods want us to believe without seeing? Ah, Odys. That's not so. Even I've seen Vulcan and need no faith to believe in him. And he doesn't want or need my faith. Some gods, I assume, don't even want to be *believed* in. For sure, they conceal themselves for many reasons, but answer this. Odys, will you—right now—step into the light and show the world what you have? Would you *really* tell them you have an Automaton, even show them what Maud can do?"

"Probably not."

"Exactly. We don't want that attention. We don't know if it's right to expose ourselves and therefore the others like us by default. Once it's done, it can't be undone. Thus, as a general rule, we won't overstep our bounds. That's merely the first reason why. Number three," she held up three fingers. "Kill no one you don't have to. Even if Odissa finds out, we may let her live. We'll take great pains to keep people alive. But if it becomes more than pangs, we mustn't die for them. The gods have entrusted us with these secrets. And we will keep them."

She opened her mouth, about to explain those statements. "When—when I first gained Anselm, it—it wasn't easy. To hide him was easy, but to keep myself hidden wasn't. I could run from my family, but they could always catch up.

They…*suspected*. You act differently when your soul's outside you—when there is *more* to you. It is not simply a matter of pretending. It's a matter of remembering which lie goes where. And sometimes you say things others don't understand. You know what your Automaton knows—things humans cannot comprehend."

Odys understood. For one, he knew that Augury was Leeland. His sister didn't know that. He understood how it'd be easy to slip up.

"The fourth rule is: spend wisely. Use fake names, cover your tracks, be seen as little as possible. Remember your every step lest it cost you later. For certain, the world would love—absolutely—your Automaton's ability to make gold, wouldn't it? Ah, to be adored for your ability to create national riches! But what would riches be, if gold became so available? What's gold, but one of the weakest metals? Even coal can be burned for warmth, but what can gold do?"

She pulled at her golden cross necklace, as if it cursed her for saying such things. "Rule number five: treat your Automaton fairly. Do not abuse them. However, I feel I needn't stress this point with you—someone who refuses to *use* your Automaton in the first place. Number six." She paused, trying to remember.

In part, these rules seemed arbitrary. This shocked Odys—and he wasn't sure why. Were they not handed down on stone tablets? Not inscribed by Vulcan himself?

"You must be ready to defend this family. We don't just sit around, enjoying long life. We sometimes meddle, when we can. Gold can go a long way, but it cannot solve this world's problems." She paused, trying to give an example. "Dorian, God bless him, walked into a burning house once—saved two children and a dog. Needless to say, everyone watching saw his face—and Fletcher's. They wished to make them heroes. Not a scratch on them, of course. When things like that happen, we try to pass as…" She blushed, as if she had just thought something religiously irreverent. "The Automatons are better at it, at passing for angels. They are so beautiful, aren't they?"

Angels? Hm. Anselm here was more like a creepy diablito.

"Angels! That brings back memories, doesn't it, Ansi?" She asked him as if he might help her remember.[59]

"For a time, I didn't accept Ansi. Though he told me what he was—*proved* his abilities—it was hard for me to believe he was also a *part* of me. He was like a genie to me. Just some slave and external facet bound to me, not my own *soul*. At first sight, I thought he was an angel, the way he reflected light..." She smiled to herself, reminiscing. "That's not to say I didn't—as we say today—*sync* with him. Oh, yes, I did that. I was much too young to realize I could choose *not* to."

Again, it seemed like she was scolding Odys.

She breathed in deeply, the fluttering gasp her prayer. "In *Nueva España*—New Spain—when I found Ansi, my family was fairly well off. For that time, we might be considered upper middle-class. We owned one of the largest ranchos in the area. My father had great plans and hoped I would help in reaching them. He wanted me to marry his—you might say—*business partner*, a man with large ties to those who would usher in the Mexican Empire. My mother just wanted me to marry *period*. Needless to say, I didn't delight in the arranged planning—I even begged to become a nun. I stole one of my father's horses and ran," she added with mirth.

Anselm watched him, making sure Maud hadn't told him any of this; Mother didn't want to re-tell old news.

"I headed north with nothing but a bag of clothes and a gun. No money. I did not get too far that night. I couldn't see a damn thing—except for an old well overrun with weeds. I found it from memory. I slept there that night. That morning, I had let down the bucket to try and draw my horse a drink and I noticed something at the bottom—under the rocks of the well's crumbling wall. The sun hit it just right, otherwise I wouldn't have seen it. There was barely any water in the well. That's why it had been abandoned. The rope was too short—it wouldn't let the bucket

---

[59] Prepare yourself, reader, you're about to get an origin story you didn't ask for. If you don't care how Gwen ended up with Anselm (because no one expects you to have a hard-on for Gwen's past like BLA), go ahead and skip to the stanza titled: BACK UP THE BACK STORY. Otherwise, my apologies for being unable to chop this obligatory info-dump out...But at least it's not a fucking flashback. We draw the line somewhere.

scrape the bottom. Someone had dropped the object there purposefully— purposefully out of reach." She was looking at it now. She was re-observing her own history. Anselm had recorded every antique detail in their brain. "I knew I would need water—for me and my horse. But I also knew I needed money. Whatever was down there was precious metal—or worth a meal, at least. At first I thought it might be a pocket watch. I tore my dress and made the rope longer. It took me hours to fish him out of the murky bottom.

"Later, Ansi would tell me his previous Master had left him there, knowing he could come back for him. He'd hidden Ansi there, away from his fellows. Those fellows had started to question the horse-breaker's surprising vitality against the horses' bucking and bruising—and also the man's astounding collection of golden-cast objects."

"The man, of course, had refused to do rocks," Anselm chided. "To do so would make others think he'd struck gold somewhere—on someone else's land. Too much attention. If his objects had a shape, they were less likely to think he'd found it from the ground. Granted, people started thinking he had stolen the objects. He also had a terrible gambling problem. I was used to repay a hefty amount of debt."

"Needless to say, he wasn't the wisest Master Ansi's ever had. Automatons can only enlighten so much. Sometimes sin clouds the light."

"He rarely let me out of his pockets. Too drunk to remember where he'd even put me, sometimes."

"That's how he'd died, by the way," Gwen added. "He'd hidden Ansi from the eyes of others, only to swear off drinking and die of liver failure two days later. That's what we assume he died of, anyway. His distance from Ansi likely worsened the impact of withdrawal. He killed himself, basically, in that way."

"He wanted to die, though," Anselm stated. "He knew he wasn't smart enough to keep up his game with me.[60] The other ranch hands had planned on killing him, in

---

[60] And an Automaton is only as smart as the Master allows. If the Master is too stupid to realize what power they hold, of course there is not much hope for him.

fact. Of course, that would not have worked. *They* couldn't have killed him. But he was in love with one of the other men on the ranch. The fact that his friend actually hated him had caused much heartbreak. He didn't have me long at all."

Mother wished to distract Odys from Anselm's emotionless explanation: "Ansi's Master before him was—"

Odys guessed she'd say a bullfighter. He quickly told himself not to be a racist like Pepin.

"Well, perhaps I should start farther back."

Anselm, she explained, had been brought over with *los conquistadores*, and sailed on the [name redacted].

A passenger had kept the pocket mirror a secret, but the secret hadn't done him much good: He had struggled to keep Anselm in his inanimate form while with his comrades—never really sleeping on the ship or on land. One night, natives attacked. Anselm's conquistador-Master took it as an opportunity to abandon the others and create his ordained city of gold. He would use Anselm to not only record his name in history, but to raise it up: The natives would worship him as a god and the Spanish Empire would honor him with a title. He had no modest plans.

But the man soon became lost. He had lost all possible contact with his fellow explorers. Glory would mean nothing if no one recognized him. The heat and loneliness drove him mad. He fell ill and died in the forest, assuming he alone survived the natives' attack. He had *let* the fever take him—suicide.

Not even an Automaton is much good in a new world; Anselm hadn't known where they were. Anselm was no help. An Automaton only knows what it has been taught, what it has observed.

Thus, Anselm, in his inanimate form, rested beside the skeleton of his former Master for many years, waiting to be touched again. The forest flora had consumed him and the decaying body.

Anselm was inanimate until a native, who had been recently banished from his Aztec city for unmentionable reasons, tripped over the remains and landed on

Anselm. The older Aztec had no real use for the gold Anselm could make, since it was the excrement of the gods. But nevertheless, he found a companion in him. Anselm had to calmly explain (in the man's own tongue) that no, he was not a god, though one made him, and so on and so forth.[61]

The man contemplated using Anselm as a weapon to re-enter his civilization by force, perhaps to even become king. However, on the long journey back to the man's homestead, he fell ill. And died.

"Most likely from previous tooth decay, poor nutrition, and a newly-touched Automaton sucking most of his energy." Anselm could remember the pain, as well as the location of the death. "He was already so pitiful—a reason he had been banished in the first place. Always complaining. Always begging. But at least he died with such new ideas and hope."

"The corn got them every time," Gwen added, mournful for those who came before her. She pointed to her teeth. "But that brings us back to square one. The horse-breaker discovered Ansi when he was running from a town he'd just robbed with his band. They were trying to make their way to Brazil—running from the law. They had hidden in the cave the Aztec had crawled into to die. The others left him behind when the horse-breaker fell ill after touching Anselm. They left him beside the Aztec's skeleton. He found his way to a Mexican rancho instead."

Anselm had terrible luck in Masters apparently.

"I had slept in that well for almost a week," Anselm went on, sitting beside Mother in the open seat, "as my Master had commanded. I waited for him to either return or call me to him. The strain of our distance *promoted* his unexpected death. Liver failure might not have been such an issue otherwise." He told his story with little sentiment.

"Thus, Ansi was mine. But I did not get past the well that day. As you know well, Odys, I fell ill instantly, my consciousness becoming aware of my soul—aware of

---

[61] An Automaton, who knows the thoughts of his or her Master, also knows their language automatically, I would assume. This is how they collect languages.

my necessary need for the thing *taken* out of me. The workers of the land I was on eventually saw my horse and discovered me. Ansi hid. My parents were soon contacted, for my family was well-known. I was taken back home. The doctor examined me. I was bedridden with 'unknown sickness.' Privately, I heard the doctor whisper to my father that it could be the stress he was putting upon me. I could hear my mother begging him to change his mind..."

She paused, gathering her thoughts. "It was in the dead of night that I learned the truth of my illness—the first time I saw my Ansi. It had taken a lot out of us, for him to journey to me."

Too weak to stay formed for long, I might add.

"He had to be quiet—unseen. I was fifteen then.[62] Ansi told me of the others out there. He told me of things I'd never been taught. He opened my mind, as Maud could do for you. His memories—what he had of them—were given to me. I became changed, enlightened. My parents did not like me talking about my new dreams—the dreams Ansi had helped me acquire. Dreams of Spaniards and Aztecs and gods. When I was well again, they locked me in my room—my punishment for trying to running away...But, of course, Ansi could help me escape. Which is what happened." Her lips parted in merry smile. "They had kept me in there for over a month. They could hear me talking in my room, to Ansi. I wanted them to hear—to let them think I was talking to the divine. In a way, I was. He was my angel."

Anselm reached out and put a hand upon Gwen's. He didn't care if Odys noticed. "But, once I was free from my family, I made a life of my own—*our* own. We never needed anything. It was easier back then to do as you pleased—to drift and wonder. You think I would have stood out, coming to the United States with Ansi. But things could be stranger back then. Ah, back then. It was so much easier to cheat and lie and be forgotten. Now we need papers, cards, licenses, codes, passwords—so many

---

[62] Math tip: I've calculated that for every 100 years a Master has an Automaton it seems to age them about 10 physically. It checks out.

things to dance around. Ay, just listen to me! I sound like a grandmother in her rocking chair."

Pause.

"Ansi convinced me to attend university. I assumed a fake name here or there. Never got a degree, of course. I moved too many times. But, oh, I tell you! To learn for the sake of learning, that's a gift. School, of course, is easy, since your Automaton can remember everything you forget. Also, to observe the evolution of the university has been a show…

Stanza: Origin stories are so unORIGINal.

"For a time, it was just Ansi and me, in the Americas. We took many travels. We never stayed in the same place for long. It was upon one of our travels, sojourning in France, that we visited a circus. Ansi had learned the new French just so we could know our way around."[63]

Or rather, you made him learn it so you didn't have to? Lazy Mother!

"It was a traveling circus. It was no grand thing, but it turned out to be a *very* special display. As we sat in the stands, Ansi noticed two Automatons—two performers in the chaotic show. In the three rings were two Masters. Turns out, an 'American' owned the circus with his fellow French comrade. The American, of course, was not really American at all. It was Pepin. Granted, he had lived in Louisiana for a time before he moved back to England—long enough to perfect an accent. See, when his wife had left him, he'd taken Maud and traveled the world. He eventually ended up in France. There, he had *also* watched a traveling circus, just like me. Except *that* circus he hadn't co-owned. From that crowd, Maud and Pepin had spotted Fletcher. And Pepin found his true calling. The circus was the perfect place for them."

---

[63] New French. Opposed to, say, Norman French, Old French, What-have-you (which, perhaps, Anselm knew before coming to the Americas) (?).

Odys pictured Maud in her tight suit, riding a horse, swinging from the trapeze, or—even better—as the bearded lady. If she could grow clothes then why not facial hair?

"Pepin and Fletcher's Master went into business together—bought out many circuses for a great sum, let the owners retire. Pepin took over magic tricks, and Maurice (the other Master), he dealt with, well, everything else. In a matter of years, though, Pepin got bored with it all, for a Master needn't work. Hobbies should never be work, yes? Eventually Maurice left, too. They gave away their circus for free, to a trusted family. However, it didn't have as much prestige when the Automatons and Masters left. No one could do their tricks or dare-devil stunts. The new owners hated that they didn't share their 'secrets.' Even our best intentions are spoiled, Odys."

She looked down at her pretty feet. She had a dignified way of rearranging them periodically. "Thus, Pepin, Maurice, and I began our travels together, finding the others. That was un circo all on its own. As Maud herself will tell you, the Automatons did most of the work. They knew the signs. They'd finally been given the proper chance to find each other. Once everyone was tracked down, that was hardly the solution to our problems. The next step was to find inheritors of our legacy, to set up a systematic order to our chaos. We decided the States would be where we'd base ourselves. After all, it's easy for those who stand out to blend in here. The melting pot of the world, America!"

And what was Vulcan melting down?

"But back to rule number six"—story time was over—"we have to relocate, when we overstep, though overstepping is not always bad in itself—as long as it does a good. Not even Jesus stayed in the world to heal all the sick. We all do what we came to do. I'm sure there are more rules, but I can't think of them now. We don't need to address them all just yet."

She flipped her wrist to glance her watch. "The rules only seem to make me tell long stories, anyway." She reached out and Anselm clutched her hand. With that simple gesture, Odys realized that, at one time, there hadn't been such a drastic physical age difference between them.

Stanza: BACK UP THE BACK STORY.[64]

"You said you had to find inheritors—earlier." Odys wanted her to clarify. *Is that what I was to Pepin?*

"We composed a list of worthy candidates, people we could trust." It sounded like an organ donor list. "Some died before we could make them one of us. Others, well, they're still alive, but might not want an Automaton if offered one, since they're so old already. We have to make hard decisions, Odys. Sometimes we are not fair." She sighed. "Others are young and don't know we have chosen them. And others, well, are like you. In by default."

"Who's on the list?"

She crossed herself, asking for forgiveness from those she could not save. "Ah, it doesn't matter. It's best not to know. Most will never get an Automaton. We will lose them as friends. Plus, Leeland would love to know those names, so I can't tell them to you."

"How does someone get on it?"

"We make them kill each other in a gladiator arena and drink the blood of virgins."

JUST KIDDING MOTHER NEVER SAID THAT JUST SEEING IF YOU WERE PAYING ATTENTION AND YOU WERE GOOD FOR YOU.[65]

"We vote on them, agree on them." She shrugged.

"And that's how Leeland got in?"

"Yes, yes. Democracy. Two wolves and a lamb deciding on what's for dinner."

Odys was confused. Was Leeland the lamb?

"At first, he *was* good." She had trouble admitting it; her eyes became glossy. "You see, Odys, he was kind, once. We all loved him. And he loved us. He loved us

---

[64] "No man chooses evil because it is evil, he only mistakes if for happiness, the good that he seeks." —Mary Wollstonecraft.
[65] Mental eye-roll. See what I have to put up with?

too much. I wished to become a nun in my frivolous youth. Ansi saved me from that choice. Leeland didn't understand this until later."

She noticed his quizzical stance. "Don't overthink it, Odys. You know exactly what I mean." She went on with her history. "For a time, there was little for us to worry about, though the First World War didn't make things easy. We kept a low profile. Pepin, though, bless him, went to fight—in *both*. When the second war came around, I kept Anselm well hidden in case they thought he was Japanese. He looks very Asian, no? It was during those wars that Leeland appeared in our lives. Pepin wrote to me about a young, orphaned Jewish boy from France he had befriended. Leeland later fought with Pepin in the second. Leeland worshiped Pepin. Such a bright boy. In a way, Leeland was Pepin's son. He let the boy ripen a bit before proposing that we give Leeland the next available Automaton. Leeland was part of the family...we liked to keep Automatons in the family. We hated hiding the truth from him."

She looked at Odys's hands, trying to say more without words.

He put those hands back in his pockets. "Will Odissa be part of the family?"

"Odys," she shook her head, "*You* aren't even part yet. But I hope you will be. It only seems fair, that she'd get an Automaton, doesn't it?" She smiled, hopeful. "It's not all up to me. I have to think of others. We don't even know how she'll react towards this."

"And you don't want another Leeland."

She bit her lip in response.

Anselm was glaring at Odys now. STOP TALKING ABOUT LEELAND. Don't make Mother/me cry.

"You must understand, Odys. Leeland was like a son to me, too. I *could* have been his mother, though that is not why I..."

Refused his advances.

"Leeland hated them, after he found out."

"Them?"

"The Automatons," she snapped. "Because of me, he hates them. Part of me hates them, too. Just look at what they've done to *your* life, Odys. In a matter of days, everything's changed for you. For us all.

"Leeland plans to eliminate all Masters so Automata won't be a problem for him—or the world—any longer. When we gave him Admund, he thought I wanted to live with him forever." From the corner of her eye, she noted Odys's reaction. "Like I said, don't overthink it."

She could see that he was, through Anselm. "Because of me, Leeland killed a Master named Rhett—Rhett Bernice Rouben. He was known as Bernice in our circles. That's how Leeland gained Coraza." She calmed herself a little. "Leeland threatened to Bernice's last surviving daughter and her family if he didn't give himself up. His daughter, middle aged at that time, already thought her father was dead. He had faked his own death to avoid explaining his agerasia. But Bernice was a good man. Of course he gave up willingly—his daughter had a family of her own. We had a mess to clean up afterwards, but it was otherwise a clean job.

"We others had a choice to make. Either give up the last remaining lives that mattered to us, or give ourselves up and let Leeland win. He had something on all of us." *Had.*

She closed her eyes and breathed in. She needed to get back on target. "When this group was founded, we agreed to certain rules—to make things fair. Even Pepin Pound agreed to them. Enforced them, also. But with you, Odys, he broke them." Her brown eyes flashed up at him.

Upon looking at him—*finally* looking at him—her eyes welled up with tears.

Oh, GAWD. Bob was gonna kill him.

What'd he do?—what'd he do?!

Mother turned her dear face away, fingers on her mouth. Anselm retrieved a handy kerchief from his pant pocket, as if this were expected. He glared at Odys.

Look what you did to me.

163

"Oh, don't keep looking at him, Ansi," Mother whimpered between hiccup sounds. "You see, I cry far too easily. That's why I can't look at you. *Ay, mi dios!* He is such a nice young man, Ansi! Do you not see his kind eyes, Ansi? Look at his fear. It makes me so angry!" She pounded her knee with a fist. "So angry this happened to *him!*"

Anselm smoothed back her hair as she tried to collect herself. She seemed more upset at the fact she couldn't control her emotions. "Yes, yes, Gwendolyn. I like him too."

Huh? He did? An how did he treat the people he *didn't* like?

Anselm lifted her chin with his long-nailed fingers. "He must be going home now, Gwen. We don't want to make him late for his sister." His face was inches from hers, too close for Odys's comfort. "Best get to it."

She nodded, stood up, dabbed her nose again, and faced Odys. Though her eyes filled with new tears, she stood her ground:

"To the final reason you're here, Odys. You must understand the situation I am in. Pepin, though not a foe, was not the closest friend either. He wasn't being a hermit for retirement. He didn't *just* want privacy for privacy's sake. You see, there was a vacant Automaton. A great bout of evidence suggests Pepin did something with it. Before we could give it to the next person we all agreed upon, we realized it was out of our reach. Though Maud may know little about it—or perhaps nothing at all—Pepin may have given the Automaton to someone else—someone like you. Or, he has hidden it so well we cannot find him—it."

Pepin was so willing to give away Maud, how much easier would it be to give away an inanimate Automaton with no Master to kill off?

"Maud's said nothing," he assured her.

"So you see our situation."

"No, not really. How could Pepin get away with something like that?"

Were they not more careful?

Mother's chest swelled. She hadn't wanted to get into this. "When we are deciding on our next choice for a Master, someone must guard the inactive Automaton. That someone was Pepin. Granted, he had it in his 'protection' for many, many years. But, he'd always done it before. We trusted him. Also, let's just say that the group takes its time in picking. We are very careful. We'd only just agreed on our next choice and tried to contact Pepin when...we realized he'd cut off all contact with us. He avoided us. He hid from us. *Years* later, when we finally tracked him down..."

Her eyes met his once more.

Oh.

"Thus, you can see why we don't trust him. Though we have no precise proof he's done anything *bad* with the missing Automaton, he never told us where it is. It's discomforting to think where our Automaton might end up—or *has* ended up. What if the Automaton is in the hands of someone who cannot handle it—who might misuse it? And did they even agree to accept the burden? They would be like you, Odys. It is so unfair what we all must suffer through. I have always wished there were some way to end our endless cycle."

She dabbed her nose and glanced at a small clock on the wall. Her eyes seemed hesitant to observe it. Time was no worry to their kind, but it also gave little comfort. She wanted him to leave now.

"Gwen?"

"Call me Mother, if you like. Everyone else does."

He fought to form the word. "Mother, then. Do you know who my real parents are? How did Leeland come to have us—my sister and I—if we aren't his? Raised by his Automaton or not, does that mean we *can't* be his children?" He already knew one of the answers.

Gwen moved her eyes from him then closed them to hold back the tears. Hadn't Bob told him not to bring up Leeland? Why couldn't he control himself?

Because he felt entitled to know. He had the right to his own past.

165

"Though there is quite a lot we do suspect, Odys, it wouldn't be right to give you the information when it isn't certain. Not from me. Besides, the fact you have Maud—who can tell you just as much as *we* suspect—makes us wonder if we should take away motivation for syncing with her. You are killing yourself, Odys Odelyn. Like rejecting food, you reject Maud."

His face fell—how dare she know so much about him.

"But we will tell you, if you end up more than just a trick."

Odys nodded. He noticed Anselm was playing with a cell phone now, the glow not helping his creepy face.

"It is time for you to go, Odys," she said, like some Ms. Havisham around her stopped clocks. "This meeting went well—better than expected. You will see me again. In the meantime, keep your sister uninformed of our secrets. For her protection as well as ours."

She showed him to the door, opening it, letting the cold air attack. Before Odys was entirely out the door, he turned. "Why didn't Dorian tell me about the missing Automaton?" The question seemed to surprise her. "Did you tell him not to tell me?"

"No." Her voice was soft yet coaxing. "But maybe if you stopped rejecting Maud and accepted her fully, you would have known without being told, Odys. If Dorian did not tell you, it was merely because it didn't matter at the time. Why does this matter now?" She narrowed her eyes, curious.

"Because..." He paused, waiting for the answer. "I don't think Maud knew about—*remembered*—the missing Automaton. She would have told me, had she known. And—and she is now upset about it." He looked to Maud at the Ice Cream truck. "She didn't remember Pepin did this. I can almost feel it."

"So you're not reading her thoughts?" Mother asked, disappointed.

"Did Pepin give you an—an alibi?" he asked, as if trying to sort out the discomfort Maud made him feel. "Any excuse or reason why he wouldn't give it back?"

Mother's eyes smiled as she spoke, proud of Odys and his cleverness. Her attention darted from Odys to Maud near the ice cream truck. "No, he did not. That's why we have mixed feelings on the matter. We had hoped that if Pepin was innocent, he would have told us who had taken it, or why he was hording it. Either he kept silent because he was the criminal, or he could not tell us because—"

"He knew something you didn't?"

She nodded slowly. "Leeland is always very—how should I say it?—perceptive. If Pepin's silence was so Leeland would not hear, then Pepin was wise. However, that means he remained silent for us as well. Why wouldn't he give us the Automaton?"

"Why would he not, at the least, tell us that he *couldn't* tell us?" Anselm reminded them as he rubbed his eyes with the tips of his fingers.

"Forgive us, Odys, but my Automaton is my skeptical nature. I am grateful he took it from me. It suits him better. He is also sleepy. He sneezes out easily when tired—because he worries for me. And that is never safe for us. We also do not want you to be late. You want to beat your sister home, don't you?"

"I was surprised they found her."

"Ah, well, Automatons are crafty things." She tapped her nose, as if he should know what the action meant.

As he left, Gwendolyn Gwendy looked out her trailer window once more, parting the blinds with the hook of her finger. "He's so ill, Ansi."

"He's not suicidal," Anselm said as he took up his pipe once more. "Dorian is wrong about that."

"He's too kind to want Maud. That's it."

Anselm nodded. "That's why he is refusing her."

"He doesn't understand that it's actually wrong to fight against the inevitable."

Lighting his newly-stuffed pipe with a match, Anselm sucked in. "But Maud isn't the winter season that he can ignore until spring."

"He has such a kind face. He must truly hate all of this."

"He'll get used to it. Or else." He continued to scroll through their phone as he smoked.

"I don't want to have to kill him, Ansi. I don't."

Anselm removed the pipe from his lips. "But I won't let him harm us, Gwendolyn. I won't let him disturb what must be done. I won't. Just pray he does what's right and we won't have to."

"I think Dorian wanted him to be suicidal for that very reason. So that we wouldn't have to."

Stanza: The immortal mortal.

When Odys had left the trailer, he'd realized just how out of breath he'd been. Like an asthmatic, each step closer to Maud was a loosening of the intangible noose around his neck—a fish plopping back into his bowl, his lungs relished Maud's relief. He didn't even notice Bob bitching about not being able to tell if mother had cried.

Odys couldn't wait to be locked back up in the ice cream truck so he could touch Maud without shame. He grabbed and held her hand to his head, repeating "Fuck, fuck, fuck," to himself as the truck started.

When he no longer felt like all the blood was rushing to his head, they sat back and had a little in-the-dark conversation I think you'll find interesting:

[...]⁶⁶

---

[66]Omitted to speed things along:

    "'Aren't you going to ask me?"

Odys kept his eyes closed and thumped the back of his head on the metal wall. "Ask you what?"

"The questions. The questions you had about Gwen and Anselm. The ones you couldn't ask Mother."

"Isn't the fact you're bringing it up some form of me asking?" he stated. He still didn't like she could read his mind—that she *was* his mind. "So, like, she's in love with—in some sort of love with—" He cleared his throat. "Herself?"

"You picked up on that did you?" Maud laughed, but it wasn't funny. "She said she wanted to be a nun, didn't she? What is the self, if not an image of God?" Another laugh.

"However she wants to justify it, I suppose." He frowned at the statement, in no position to judge. "I just don't understand how she's so forgiving of Leeland. When she talked about him, she teared up as if she felt sorry for him."

"You can't blame him for wanting to solve a problem"—Maud knew she was a problem—"I only wish he had a different solution."

"Is that what he thinks it is? That's why he's killing everyone? Because Gwen won't fuck him?"

"Masters have killed each other for far dumber reasons than that, Odys."

Stoplight; the velocity made them shift in place.

"Just what was Vulcan *thinking* when he created Automatons?"

"Well, as you now know, he made us to take down the first. We called her Alpha. Well, she wasn't *exactly* female. All Automatons are, in some way, androgynous."

"I still don't see why he had to create Automatons to stop her."

"Alpha was...different. She had no inanimate form, though she could take on any object's shape. She was, perhaps, an advanced Automaton—a rough draft so complex that she needed to be chiseled down to fit within her format. That's what Vulcan did when He created us. We were her editors—editors to a story He wrote."

"How did you stop her, then?"

"In Admund—your father—Vulcan instilled what you might call innate knowledge of Alchemic sciences—which is where Leeland, perhaps, finds his prolific knowledge and skill in many areas, taking it from his Automaton like someone downloading an application."

Sounded like jacking into the Matrix.

"Don't get me wrong, we all brought something to the table. But Admund led us. With the help of the others, Admund and his Master stripped many of Alpha's principles down. We took away the physical. Made her, in some ways, dependent on a human soul and body."

She recounted this history as if she did not remember it—and perhaps she didn't anymore—but had been told what she'd forgotten.

"A willing vessel—a young temple girl—accepted the burden of housing Alpha inside her. We trapped Alpha in human form. In all actuality, you might say we turned Alpha into a ghost-spirit. That's how we put her inside the girl. Like a demon possessing a body, she was *within*. However, unlike a demon, she couldn't leave her vessel and died with it. She also didn't *control* the girl. The girl was still aware. She still *was*. We were thankful for that." Maud paused. "Alpha's life was bound to the girl's—dependent upon it. There was nothing left of her when the girl died. Her—or *their*, rather—grave is in [somewhere in Italy], as Vulcan ordered."

"If we're the hands of Vulcan, then he should wash His hands more often. I mean, why do you *still* exist? You've served your purpose. Alpha's gone. Why do we still need you? Why can't Vulcan take you away from us?"

"What need of evil has man? Yet it exists, Odys. Doesn't man himself—at least once—contemplate his own purpose? Yes, I wish I knew what Vulcan had in mind. This is far from the best of all possible situations."

She sighed. He sighed.

"Let me illustrate my statement with something: Various cultures all have their flood myths—the one that wiped out humanity. Noah, Gilgamesh, the like. Yet the Universe,

Stanza: Chimeras of man and metal.

Since Odys (and you) got a shit-ton of backstory from Mother just now, why not a little more? This next part should've been at the very beginning of the novel (but we knew you wouldn't notice it otherwise)/Book Intermission/This is the Prologue-thing:

Narrator's (not the Editor's) preface (Gabbler wants nothing to do with this part),

Aztec gold:

What's the price of your soul?[67]

The Muses can kiss my ass. Inspiration's done too much damage already—Gabbler suspects I'm insane. Yet Gabbler's still so interested in my story. Gabbler hopes I'm joking—only putting on a show (Gabbler has always liked my eccentricities).

For sure, I'll put on a show! Right after I get off my soapbox. This "Preface" is all Gabbler allowed me in terms of my *opinion*.

(This is what the epic has become, people).

The subject I'm writing about is typically captured in verse, not prose, so I'm not so sure the Muses would even answer my call if I "invoked" Them (which is how my

---

when it recreated the world after that flood, still saved parts from the previous to re-purpose things, right? It's not uncommon for gods to use scraps. Even humans are scraps, Odys. Not just Automatons."

Scrap metal.

"We're not easily disposable. We *can* be repurposed. But you take my point. I won't go on with my questionable theodicy. There is ditheism to every god."

Driving, driving, driving.

They were silent for many miles.

"...And no, actually," Maud said, a joking chide in her tone, "I *wasn't* the Bearded Lady, thank you very much. I was the magician's Lovely Apprentice. I was also the sideshow to draw them into the tent. I had many jobs in *El Circo*."'

[67] I tried to get our Narrator to *not* include this part. But they insisted. A compromise was putting it (inconveniently) here. Overall, I suppose it will give Automata (as characters) more context as well as formally introduce ourselves.

predecessors went about things). Their silence—just like the rest of the gods'—is all the inspiration I need.

(Again, this is what the epic has become, people).

Now, you have the right to stop reading. I can't stop you from putting this book down. Even if I could, I wouldn't try. You either read or you don't. It's already been decided.

I could go into a long tangent over fate and destiny—how you were predestined to notice this book. But I won't. You wouldn't take me seriously. Gabbler doesn't take me seriously. Gabbler doesn't see things like I do, yet Gabbler loves me.

Am I being unclear? Let me start again:

Freedom. The gods want you to think you have it. Freedom enslaves you to Them. The gods use our freedoms against us. They manipulate us into thinking we have choices, that freedom has intrinsic value. But you always end up picking what They wanted you to pick. They can always use your choices for Their will. Always.

That's what happened to me. And it's happened to you.

Now, I'm sure I sound like some holier-than-thou psycho at this point, and I'll not correct you. Even Gabbler cringes when I put things so frankly. Gabbler says I should just tell the story, not convince you of anything. But then I tell Gabbler, *Shouldn't they know what the gods are doing to them?*

Now, it's not my objective to teach you life's elementary paradoxes, but someone needs to break it down for you: out of so many options, Fate's brought us together. You chose this book, yes. But why?

Your eyes follow each line accordingly. You might even turn the page—if I'm entertaining enough. Yes, yes, the gods took care of everything for me. I didn't even have to try.

And *of course* the gods would help. This story's too much fun for them—my irreverent comments included. Of course they'd let this story *happen*. They allowed you to notice this book and, for some reason, They allowed me to write it. This was

Their plan all along—even the prose format and Gabbler's footnotes and this brazenly-inserted preface.

(This is what the epic has become, people).

Now let me give some back story—best to get it over with.

Cortés and his kind shouldn't have searched for El Dorado. It had been in Europe all along—a city of gold manifest in a being—a divine tool capable of creating more gold than a ship could carry—an alchemical slave who knows its creator-god's metallurgical secrets.

An Automaton.

Of course, those Spaniards had no way of knowing what complex fortune hid on board their ship, tucked away. How *could* they know that Ponce de León's Fountain of Youth isn't a fountain? They could not. And they would not.

Not if the Automaton's human Master had a say.

It doesn't matter what ship—or where—or when. It's best for you not to know. Gabbler thinks it'd only cause trouble. You'd start to really believe me, then. And *then* I'd have your free will completely—you'd have no choice but to believe. Gabbler says that name-dropping would only hurt my purposes. Gabbler says I mustn't frighten readers away. Gabbler says that even my lies are *faithful to the spirit of truth*.

See, Gabbler wants them to be lies, and I understand. I must pretend this is just "a story." Otherwise, Gabbler becomes impatient and shifty-eyed.

But as I was saying, a Spaniard brought the first Automaton over.

The rest of the smithy-god's creations took their time in arriving to the West's west. They had nothing but time—TICK TOCK! In this *time* they drew the attention of other gods.

Not just the Greco-Roman ones, no.

The Automata were in a new land.

The humans, who use their free will, had started moving all over the world. To and fro. If humans move, then Automata move. The gods watched anxiously. The gods of one place counseled with the gods of another. The gods knew the Automata—beings enslaved to humans—could likely cause a lot of problems if not inhibited. Humans could misuse them. They *did* misuse them.

But Hephaestus-Vulcan assured the Holy Ones They need not worry—do not worry!—worry not, Universe, for Automata will help mankind carry out Our will.

Their will be done!

And it was.

That is how this story actually begins—where I, your Narrator, fit in.

As you might have guessed, I'm omnipresent (which is good for Narrators to be, I see all sides). I wasn't always so ubiquitous, though. Like Cortés (unfortunately), I am a god created out of nothing and someone history will rightfully scorn—a metamorphosis! Yes, yes, this is my apotheosis.

Really, this quasi-immortality is *the least* the gods could do, considering everything I suffered for them.

…This is why Gabbler thinks I'm mad.

You'll find out soon enough—sooner than I'd like—that I'm a character in this story. I've changed a lot since *then*, though. Divinity aside, I hardly recognize myself. Maybe that's a good thing. It's easier for Gabbler to doubt me, then.

Oh, how Gabbler doubts. Gabbler loves me too much to believe entirely. Gabbler is free from the truth. It makes me hope Gabbler's here willingly, despite knowing so much…

Dear Mortal-Gabbler didn't exactly like my participation in this story. Gabbler said I could've been a better character. Gabbler's right. Yet, Gabbler didn't disown me. Gabbler's my editor.[68]

---

[68]Among other things. I'm also part of this story's frame, apparently (though some might say I'm nothing but a footnote). I didn't have such a major role in our Narrator's first typed drafts. And yes, they are typed before I see them. The Narrator is a mute and cannot verbally tell me anything, so this is not dictation. I thank God for computers, otherwise, I'd know so little about our Narrator—god complex and all.

Gabbler says I should establish my intent—my purpose—with this story. As if I claim one! Should I claim one? Gabbler says *That's what prefaces are for.* I'm not so sure. But fine. What's one more lie? It somehow proves my point...

Thus, my intent is to make you question blind men.

Homer was blind. Milton was blind. I am mute.

What good is poetry to me if I cannot recite it? It gives me no joy. I can scarcely eat, let alone speak. Prose is further punishment for my self-inflicted sins. Only Gabbler dulls the pain.

Gabbler's blind to it, my pain.

Yet we make a poetic pair.

Gabbler thinks I secretly wish to embellish pre-established myth. So be it. After all, an epic is the least pretentious effort a writer can attempt, right? Sure. But do notice: there's more than one reason I wanted two names tacked to this story (i.e. let's move this secondary shitpile to a primary worth respecting!).[69]

Ah, what else should I mention? Words, words, words! So many to choose from, yet you only need one: Freedom. Do we have it or not?

Let that be prefatory for now, Reader. In the meantime, let's get back to the story. The twins' lives are about to change forever. And, more or less, so is mine.[70]

---

[69] As in Primary vs. Secondary Epics.

[70] **Editor's foreword(s),**
Please use your free will to choose one of the following notes (but do read both, thanks):
Which is for you?

Dear Prone to Believe,
As you can tell, this isn't my story. I'm only its Editor. My footnotes should help you tolerate the Narrator—someone very dear to me. I've changed names, locations, and facts to make the Narrator's story a treatise—a parable—an allegory—a myth. Because that's what it is to me. The Narrator has (hesitantly) allowed me to do this. See, with my overt participation, this is a story within a story—a lie within the truth. This way, no one expects you to believe it— especially the Narrator's Preface (above). But you can if you like. For sure, I don't believe Homer's version of history, but I do believe in his storytelling abilities.
—G.B. Gabbler
P.S. Someone needs to tell you not all Automata are wind-up toys. Even you are a machine.

Dear Prone to Doubt,

Stanza: Enough introduction!

Now then, that Prologue [Foreword(s) and Preface] wasn't *so* bad was it? And besides, this story wouldn't fit within its "genre" without it. Gabbler said we should sell this as an urban fantasy. Don't most have them? Was ours just as vague and mysterious? I'm nothing if not formulaic.

Oh, and by the way, I forgot to mention above that if you *do* happen to notice any plot holes or typos or whateverthehellticksyouoff in this manuscript BLAME IT ON GABBLER, NOT ME. I can hardly be held responsible for mistakes Gabbler failed to notice.[71]

Stanza: Automatons are a perfect excuse for soliloquy.

Back at the apartment:

Fletcher cleared his throat. "My legs're sore."

"Stand up, then."

He did. He faced Dorian. "I'm bored. I need something to do. And something to chew. Something new. Can I go to the gas station at the corner?"

"We shouldn't leave." Though Dorian actually liked the idea.

"But I'm bored! And you feel too ugly for me to give you a BJ."

"I can't help it if I'm bloated from all that pizza. Besides. We already had enough outdoor fun when we put on the new door for this apartment."

"Com'on! You'll be fine on your own. I'll be five minutes. You know how fast I can run."

Dorian frowned, fighting with himself. "Go make some coffee or something."

Like me, you may not take the Narrator seriously, but some parts you should admire. At the risk of sounding defensive: even Homer sang an urban fantasy for his day, and Virgil's propaganda was the first of eminent fanfiction. This "tradition" is how I tolerate my part in my lover's imagination. So if I play along, don't judge me. I have my reasons; I openly undermine my own authority—all relationships need compromise. Besides, lies make truth much more entertaining... Also, if you can't properly suspend your disbelief, then it's good this book began at Chapter One—ornate introductions like these don't help Doubters stomach the fantasy anyway (and I hate prologues just like the rest of you).
—G.B. Gabbler
P.S. *A cyborg metaphor has more to do with changing the human soul than the human body.*
[71] Sigh. You see my work is cut out for me.

Fletcher straddled Dorian and pet his hair. Dorian's soul didn't want more coffee. Not unless it was sugary and packed with calories. He begged again, "You know, if Leeland's waiting for us, then why not present him with an opportunity? It's better than just sitting here. Me leaving isn't something Leeland would expect." He leaned in to whisper, "Why would we do something so stupid?"

"Fine, then." Dorian gave into himself—that nagging Automaton. There was something recalcitrant inside Dorian. Fletcher manifested it. "But you better make this trip count."

Fletcher kissed his Master, lips still touching when he said, "As you wish!" And he flew out the door, forgetting to lock it behind him (not that the broken doorframe would do much to support a lock regardless). He'd turned out the lights, though. Dorian didn't need those.

The television cast blue waves over him.

(Cue uneasy silence).

Just as Dorian was about to zone out and start listening to the TV again, his phone distracted him.

Perfect timing.

He wished Fletcher were here to see the number. He couldn't see it. But something told him he already knew who it was. A smile spread across his lips as he answered it. It was no happy expression.

"Yes?" he said.

"Hello, Dorian," came that familiar Baroque voice—the voice that sent chills of irrational hate down Dorian's spine. No other voice could cause his laid-back back to become so tense. "I see the group is all astir. Something the matter?"

Dorian took a moment to formulate a rational response. "The gods have a way of letting you time things so *precisely*, Leeland."

"They must be on my side, then. But answer my question. Your answer will be part of my transition. You know I don't call unless there's a point. *What* has the family in such a fluster? Everyone moving—here and there. I can hardly keep tabs on you all."

"I think you know, Leeland," Dorian growled. The hairs on the back of his neck stood up. Do you see his fingers balling into a fist? I do.

"I may or may not know," Leeland agreed, satisfaction ringing through his coyness. "However, Coraza just told me Fletcher stepped outside. Her eyes are watching. You are a poor babysitter, Dorian. Your soul can't sit still for long."

Dorian said nothing, his face composed as he listened, apprehensive.

"Anyway, how's that old dog, Pepin? I haven't heard from him in a while, you know. Have you? Ah, I guess he's not talking to you lot either, then? He can be a pompous prick at times can't he? Or, should I say, *couldn't* he?" Leeland chuckled, fond of his own joke; his French accent, which he had learned to suppress, often showed itself through such forced speeches. "What? Too soon? Pepin wouldn't want us to be so serious. He'd want us to—to remember him fondly with laughter and—"

"How did you find out?"

"The nose knows, Dorian. Vulcan let Admund smell it. Admund's been watching the stars, Dorian. Don't you know they're aligning? The gods are plotting *us*, dear boy. We're the stars of their production."

"What's this call about then? If you want to kill me, come on in. Do it."

"You know that won't be necessary. Coraza is fine in her place. But by the look of things, you've practically invited her in. I'm sorry to say that I'll have to turn down the invitation. I can't give you what you want, Dorian. I can't."

"Then why bother making your Automaton watch us?" *Keep him talking, keep him talking,* Fletcher reminded Dorian.

"Because I need to know what you are up to. I must make sure everything is falling into place."

"Aren't you afraid you'll spoil the fun by telling me you're planning something, Leeland?"

"Who said I was planning anything? Can't I call to check up on things, Dori? Can't I? After all, you are babysitting my children. Well, they're not *my* children. They're my Automaton's children."

"What do I have to do to get you to show your face, Leeland? Even if it's your Coraza-face, I'd still like to see it."

"Funny you would say that, Dorian. You can't really see anything. You're blind. Don't you remember I took your sight from you?"

"You didn't take it from me. I gave it to you."

"I'm glad you put it that way. I did not enjoy accepting it, even if it did buy you more time."

"I know how you like to play fair."

"But your eyes didn't buy *enough* time, did they? They still died because you couldn't figure out how to stop me. Well, that's not to say you didn't *know* how to stop me. You could have given me what I really wanted. But I was kind enough to let you all try. Was it worth the price though? Do you still like living—living as a blind man?"

Dorian considered it for a moment, fighting to keep his calm. "Maybe, if it caused you to save the twins."

"That is not why I 'adopted' them. Just because you took out your eyes, like I asked, does not mean I felt indebted to you. Admittedly, I thought you'd demand to know who the twins *really* are—demand proof. Yes, they are *exactly* who you think they are. I know you're not stupid."

It was odd to see Dorian's normally-stoic face so shadowed with emotion. His face cringed as if about to weep, but his voice didn't mirror it. "So you really want me to believe they're *those* twins?" He rubbed his mouth, trying to rub away his expression. "I'll not fall for it."

"Well, I suppose you are right, Dorian. I need to clarify. So go on. Ask me. Don't you want to be sure? *Beg* me for proof. I could find twins anywhere. You need to be sure."

But Dorian didn't beg.

"Come now, ask. You know you can't do a DNA test on them. You weren't related by blood."

(And Leeland wasn't stupid enough to leave their real family's bodies available for such things).

Dorian remained silent.

"You won't play along? But I thought that's what this was for you, Dorian. A game. You always had such a fun time playing with others' lives—gambling your eyes away. But moving on. What I can't make out is why Pepin gave Maud to my son. Or, excuse me, my semi-adopted son, on my Automaton's side. Maybe you can help me, Dorian:

"Did Pepin give Maud to Odys because I wouldn't harm him, my quasi-child, and therefore be unable to complete my so-called 'goal' at collecting every Automaton from you purposeless Masters? That would put a lot of faith on children I forced my Automaton to raise, though. Admund—Odi Odelyn, that is—never cared much for his duties. But that only comes with being *my* Automaton—I'm not the fathering type. Yes, yes, that does make Pepin out to be stupid, doesn't it? So, either Pepin was stupid or...he was on my side. Could it be that my philosophies finally won him over? Did he become sympathetic with my plight? Pepin did, after all, love me as a son, didn't he? That's why they gave me Admund in the first place, isn't it?

"Maybe Odys will be smarter than you were, Dorian. He won't give up everything just so he can keep his cursed Automaton."

His disappointment in Dorian's choices could not be missed.

"Now, I do want you to notice that Odissa just left me and I had *every* opportunity to use her against Odys—against *all* of you, potentially—right then and there. But I didn't. I let her go. She came so willingly to me, too. Odys might do something stupid if I don't let her go next time."

The line went dead.

Dorian was too preoccupied in calming himself to turn off his phone. Once done with that, he'd think about calling Mother. Mother needed to know he had finally made contact.

Just as he had opened his mouth to call Gwen (voice activated calling, you see), he heard something out in the apartment entry hall. He paused, listening, trying not to breathe. The doorknob twisted.

The door swung open with a slow creak—its reaction to a cautious tap. The person on the other side wasn't in a hurry to enter.

But who was it?

Well.

I hate to ruin a surprise (yes, it was meant to be a surprise—meant to be dragged out and BOMB-DROPPED), but let's be sure to side-step any plot holes here and instead remember we were recently introduced to Mecca and his truth-bending ways. Yes, yes. We can therefore safely assume this is Odissa—even though we're just as blind as Dorian at the moment. But Dorian, the poor dear, cannot *assume*. That's *dramatic irony* for you, if you did not know.[72]

If you didn't, now you do. You're welcome.[73]

But, THE POINT is don't be fooled. I've shared some of my omnipotent power with you so you can just sit back and enjoy the shit about to hit Dorian's fan:

See, to Dorian it could not be Fletcher, no, because Fletcher, right then, was at the cash register, paying for his gum and worrying about what his Master had just sensed. *That* Dorian could see. It wasn't Maud or Odys, no, because Bob would call when they had arrived. *That* was standard fucking procedure. It wasn't a neighbor, either, because those people usually knocked. *That* was just common courtesy. And, of course, it couldn't be Odissa, no, because Mecca had said she was still on her way in his last update. *That* left only one relevant option.

---

[72] No, that's Mecca for you.

[73] BLA is very didactic. BLA loves to teach *me* things too. BLA can't help it. The god complex makes for one huge, patronizing issue I struggle against on a daily basis—and *I'm* the one with the graduate degree.

He was about to see one of Leeland's faces.

Yet, part of him questioned such a conclusion—but he brushed it aside. *Who else could it be? The cat? Cats can't open doors. Not even broken ones.*

The person on the other side no doubt found the unlocked door strange. Even Leeland understood the human penchant of locking doors.

Maybe Leeland was just toying with him. Leeland was fond of using psychological measures to prove his points. From the genesis, Leeland's agenda didn't include outright killing. In fact, they hadn't seen pleasure in his eyes when he took his second Automaton. To be fair, Leeland hadn't *killed* anyone. Ever. He got *others* to do it for him—he got them to give up their own lives.

Let me rephrase:

Leeland didn't *enjoy* killing people. He simply wanted them to kill themselves.

This tactic had helped level the playing field—a playing field for a holy war Leeland had discovered—a war that not only God would approve, but Vulcan too. After all, Vulcan had let things line up so perfectly for Leeland. Leeland was a finger on the Vulcan-hand of God. This was the will of the Universe. Otherwise, it would not be so.

Now, since I've decided to go into a back-story during an edgy scene, I won't interrupt it much-much more. I will only say this: Leeland was miserable. Mother had made him that way. Mother's unnatural love for her precious, disgusting Anselm-self had been the final proof needed to define Automatons as evil. If one Automaton made a single person unhappy (such as himself), they were not worth their price. Not to Leeland. Without much more reasoning than that (for what more did he need?), Leeland decided to spare all humans of their unhappiness. He took it upon himself to cleanse the world. He would take on the burden of bearing all Automatons, for he was the most logical of them (clearly).

Dorian's mind raced forward, not to and fro. Though he doubted Coraza had come in to kill him, he wondered why Leeland would change his mind. Perhaps she thought she might not be heard coming in. Perhaps she was just coming to leave something for him. Perhaps she wanted to watch him beg for a death she would not give.

The door fully opened and he heard a footstep. You would never expect a blind man to move so quickly—jumping and pinning the enterer to the wall. It was a girl, yes. That much was certain. His crushing arm felt subtle breasts. It *was* Coraza. By God, it could be no other (else there's a major plot hole a-ripping, ha, ha).[74]

Dorian had expected her to submit this easily. That was how Leeland toyed with him.

"Why're you here?" Dorian demanded as he smashed "Coraza" into the wall.

A whimper.

A pretending sound—no less! He knew Leeland's games. The craven noise gripped his heart, which began his fury. He hated when Leeland fucked with him—when Masters used their Automatons as emotional puppets. That's why he'd acted so promptly. He didn't have time to second-guess himself. Not now. "Answer me!"

A small, frightened cry.

He didn't believe the sound; it teased him. "Not even going to fight me? Too much of a saint to kill me outright? What's he going to take this time? Both hands? Both feet? Take them, then!" Dorian shouted through his teeth. He practically foamed at the mouth, his hands like steal traps clutching her clothes. He could almost see Coraza's steel-black skin, her glazed-over and Master-possessed eyes, her graceful frame, unfettered smile.

Any second now she would laugh in his face.

"Why bother coming in if you're not going to take what's yours?" (As docile as Dorian normally is, it's quite scary to see him like this. He was growling furiously—making sure to cram his opinion in swiftly. If she was going to let him be angry, then he'd take the opportunity).

"This reaction what you wanted? Wanted to make sure you can get under my skin? You win, Coraza! What do you want me to say—to do—to make us even? You

---

[74] For Dorian's small world, maybe.

coward! I'll never give you peace—I'll never take my *real* anger out on you. Why do you think you're still alive, you miserable prick? You think this is *cathartic* for me?"

Well, Dorian, that's hard to answer, since you're choking her...

He realized she tried to speak but failed. Normally, an Automaton wouldn't have such trouble—even *if* a human could have closed off their throat...

Suddenly, the clothes he gripped felt too real. Her pain seemed too real. *She* was too real.

"Please, I—I don't know what you're talking about! I—I live here! I'm—I'm *Odissa!*"

ODISSA ODELYN: The girl coming through the plot hole (neatly re-stitched).

DISLIKES: Smudges on her glasses, because she has a hard enough time seeing as it is (thanks a lot, Dorian).

SIGN: Gemini (go figure).

WORD: Nympholepsy, because it sounds dirty.

Chapter the thirteenth,

Mecca's trickery:

Wasn't that dramatic? Wasn't that ironic?

"I'm Odissa Odelyn!" Not this Coraza-person he was talking about. "Please! Please, you're—you're hurting me."

It certainly wasn't Coraza's voice.

She could see herself in his sunglasses and was left to imagine the gruesome revelation behind them.

His body relaxed but not his grip. He didn't want her to run away screaming.

"If it's money you want, I'll give it to you," the girl pleaded, though he didn't look like a robber. His confused countenance confirmed that she had no need to fear him. Much.

To get him to speak through his muddle, she went on, "I swear, I don't know what's going on—I'm not trying to trick you! I—"

But he put a hand over her mouth. Well, it was more or less where he *guessed* her mouth to be. Close enough. She went a little cross-eyed, looking at his hand.

He didn't like that this girl—the one who had the right to be affronted—was actually trying to *sympathize* with him. No need for intervention mode.

"Shh!"

Her little heart was beating like a rabbit's.

"I—I—I thought you were someone else." (Clearly). "Please don't scream or call for someone or—or talk so loudly. Can you do that?" He tried to reason with her, but he sounded more like a criminal trying to hide. It didn't help his case.

He felt her head try to nod under his hand. She'd do anything as long as you didn't accuse her of being someone else again. It was scary to be so confused—was she being robbed or murdered or kidnapped or not?

Dorian stepped back, hands raised for calm. "Are you OK?"

"I don't know."

He used his ears to detect her next movement. But she didn't move. She was too afraid to. She kept herself pressed against the wall.

As he continued to step back, he almost tripped over her stray bag. He'd forced her to drop it when he'd pounced. He smoothed out his shirt as he closed the door, clearing his throat. "Well, I'm sure this all looks bad," he said, his voice shaking.

She said nothing to reassure him.

Stupid! This is why he's always so composed. Composed, composed, composed! In the heat of emotion—ANY EMOTION!—he exploded. When void of sentiment or passion, he'd found it helped him never be so *rash*. He'd worked hard at building up his flawless reputation; stripped himself of emotional expression; suppressed any feeling.

"How badly did I hurt you?"

"Why the fuck are you in my apartment?"

Oh, that.

She went on when he didn't answer quickly enough. "D-does this have to do with—"

"Odys, yes," he answered, trying to fill the silence. He pushed his fingers into his hair, other hand on his hip.

Odissa paled. How did they know her brother's name?!

"Yes, this involves your brother."

Dorian flipped on the nearest light switch, so she could see him clearly (Fletcher, who was on his way, had reminded him to do it). Odissa became panicky at the sight of him; this man was being hesitant for a reason. He moved so slowly and deliberately.

Her voice growing higher, "What did Odys do? Does he owe you money? I have money—I can—"

"This isn't about money!" He quickly quieted that. *Jesus, you'd think her brother was a cheating drug dealer or something, the way she talks!*

"Then—then what's this about? *Why* are you in my apartment? God, I knew he'd do something. He always does." She was rambling to herself, no longer even looking at him, as if he weren't there—as if she hadn't just been attacked.

Dorian turned to the side, hand rubbing his lower face as if he might crush himself.

Odissa noticed him once more. Was this man blushing? He didn't seem the type. He seemed too repressed to express such silly emotions. Even his earlier-conveyed fury far from befitted him…She wondered why on earth he would jump *her*. One look was enough to tell she needed no more than verbal threat to make her cower. The lights might have been off before, but it wasn't as if it had been too dark to see her mousiness. Was this man blind or something? No, he seemed to see well enough…despite the fact he was wearing sunglasses in the dark.

She rubbed the back of her head; it was sore to the touch. "Why is my apartment number wrong?"

Yes, about that. "It's a long story." Please don't ask him. Please stop talking.

185

"Did Odys do it? Did he switch the apartment numbers to hide from you? The idiot!"

"Why do you think Odys would do something *stupid* like that?" He put his hands on his hips, actually curious.

Her hand dropped from her neck. She had no answer. There was no answer for the stupid things Odys did when upset. For example: the first time after "seeing" her father and Mr. Augury, she'd come home to a re-arranged apartment. Her room was then in the living room, his in the dining area, and the kitchen had held the couch. His excuse had been, "I couldn't stand it, being in the apartment alone and knowing you wouldn't be back soon. The emptiness kept reminding me of it. So I changed it." He'd consented that it didn't make *normal* sense, yes. But if part of his life was irregular, then all of it should be too, so there. Every consecutive visit after that, she'd come home to something just as weird, unfortunate, or bothersome. (Odys isn't as normal as he'd like us to believe).[75]

Now, back to the present:

Fletcher burst through the open door, saving them from each other.

He no longer had the dreads and was wearing a snazzy cop uniform he'd just assumed on his way up—or, what he hoped looked very much like one.[76] He pretended he was surprised to see Odissa. Fletcher took on a deep, respectable, and official voice. "Oh! Odissa Odelyn. You're home earlier than expected. Hello, I'm Officer Fletcher." *Fletcher, Fletcher So-and-so.* He extended a hand.

"Sorry I'm panting, those stairs wear me out." As well as running half a block. "Just went for coffee. Nothing happened, did it?" He looked between them as if he could tell (of course he could tell! He was practically THERE when it happened—listening through his Master's ears). He waited for no answer. "Sorry to surprise you, Ms. Odelyn. We, um, thought you'd be a little longer...We're from the police, sector

---

[75] Can't said I did believe it.

[76] Just to be clear: I do not think Fletcher's natural state includes dreadlocks in the first place. Just so you know.

69"—he cleared his throat, regretting his number choice—"3. Dorian, here, is on duty. Your brother should be home shortly."

Nice save, Fletcher. He even had a small cup of faux coffee in his hand. His outfit was complete with a large, quickly-formed badge on his breast. If only all uniforms looked so good. This outfit was going to cost Dorian in energy later.

Odissa found it easier to interact with Fletcher (she knew *what* he was: a cop—versus whatever Dorian claimed to be), "What is going on?"

"Dorian hasn't said yet?" Fletcher put on a frown (he was a very good thespian), "Miss, your brother was unintentionally involved in one of our cases—a suicide, two days ago. A man approached him and, well, threatened your brother before shooting himself. We have reason to believe Mr. Odelyn may be in further danger—as well as you. We've been assigned to remain with you at all times." He took a fake sip from his fake coffee.

He spun his lies with such dignity and grace Odissa wanted nothing more than to believe him. *OK, so he's done nothing wrong.*

"Your brother's coming home as we speak—from the station. Don't worry, he's fine. Though, if you forgive me," he said, hiding one side of his mouth from Dorian, "I'd say the stress has had its toll on him. He didn't take the scene very well. Threw up a little. Well, a lot actually. I mean, everywhere. He'll be a story we tell the newbies for the next decade, right Dorian? Blood and guts must upset him. He's not gotten much sleep these past few days. Clearly doesn't deal with stress well."

He could tell Odissa was starting to think things through as he rambled so he stepped up his pace, "He'll be another thirty minutes or so. If you'll just sit down at the table, here," he directed her with authority, "I'll show you the newspaper article and the file about the case. The article lists no names, for Odys's protection, but it'll prove my point." He leaned over and whispered to Dorian as Odissa walked to the table, *We should kill Mecca.* "I think you probably need to make a call or two, detective?"

187

"You know I do." Dorian slipped out. Fletcher closed the door behind him. His Master was going to make a very important phone call. (Once he stopped rage-shaking, of course).

Odissa picked up her glasses along her way to the table. Dorian had somehow managed to shake them off her little nose upon impact.

Sitting down, she rubbed her shoulder. She was bound to bruise. Worse than a nectarine in a batting cage.

"Sorry about Dorian." Fletcher was almost too apologetic, catching her curiosity. "He was expecting someone else. Did he say anything that frightened you?"

Yeah, everything. She didn't want to overtly tattle on Dorian. She wasn't sure he deserved it; and, if he was a cop like Fletcher, hadn't he just been doing his job? "I can't—can't remember. I think I scared *him*."

"This is a very serious situation, Ms. Odelyn. We all get a little antsy." He half-winked at her. Working his magic, Fletcher pulled out an official-looking manila envelope from their duffle bag. From the sheaf of important-looking papers, he showed her the article in the local section. When Dorian and Fletcher had been spying on Odys, they had clipped it out for later "scrapbooking."

It was a small, unimportant paragraph. Public suicide. Body unidentified. Many witnesses. No one else injured. Police would not disclose further details. Yada, yada. In other words, the *real* police had no idea what was going on. And nor would they.

"This is what the man looked like. You don't happen to recognize him do you?" He had pulled the picture from his "pocket." When she tried to take it from him he shook his head. "No, no. It's our only copy." *Don't touch.*

She shook her head, apologizing that she couldn't help.

Fletcher put the picture away. "Would the name Pepin Pound ring any bells?"

"Only the alliterative ones," she smiled past her nerves, scolding herself for trying to be witty at a time like this. *Maybe I have a concussion.*

"That's quite all right. We didn't expect you to recognize him, anyways."

A little bit more chatting and:

"Why, though," Odissa wondered, "do you have to stay with us, if it was a suicide? What did the man threaten?" She cleaned her glasses on her shirt compulsively. She put them back on to read the article one more time. She was glad it didn't mention names. She hated attention.

"Ms. Odelyn, this is a highly classified case. We're not allowed to talk about it, and Odys isn't necessarily allowed, either. In fact, he doesn't even know how valuable his information may be. Not even I do. I just do what I'm told," he said, trying to make it light. "We'll be staying here, until things are settled. Undercover, that sort of thing. For your safety. We'll try not to impose."

She narrowed her eyes. She disliked the thought of company. It was always a hassle to entertain or be civil. Though she had many questions (like who Dorian had thought she was) she thought it best not to ask. Her questions would likely sound stupid anyway. She didn't know a *thing* about how these situations worked. She didn't even watch cop shows, so all his bullcrap seemed believable.

"What about..." she began but stopped.

"Yes?" Fletcher said, acting concerned. Her timidity warmed his heart.

"My school and work. I have to go to them this week. I can leave the apartment, right?"

"Let's just say you have to stay here, Ms. Odelyn." He braced himself for her reaction.

With downcast eyes, a sound escaped her lips. At least she wouldn't have to go to work and pretend to like people. "This seems like the witness protection program." Her eyes flickered up. It wasn't was it?

He pursed his lips. "You will have to quit your job."

"You mean I can't go back—ever? It will take that long to sort this out?" Her voice teetered on shrill.

"We can talk about it once your brother arrives."

"But if I need to quit my job, shouldn't I do so?"

"Actually, we've arranged to have it done for you."

Gooddeal! She hated confrontation. She realized her relief and felt strange for accepting it so easily. "Can I make some coffee?"

She was asking to use her own stuff now?

"How about I make you some myself? I hear you've been driving all day." Plus, his Master still felt bad about assaulting her.

…She didn't like how comfortable they already were in her home.

Stanza: Mechanical syllogism is used.

Dorian, his fingers moving swiftly, had called up his little friend Mecca.

Dorian didn't think Mecca had shirked his duties. Mecca was too loyal for that. Little Mecca broke rules *just* enough to evade scorn. No, this little "mess up" was far from a breach in dependability; it was more targeted, most likely. And the target of his exploits? Dorian, of course, for he was easiest to hit.

Mecca did not lie (often). This was not a lie (most likely). This was his masterpiece (as was everything).

As Dorian expected, Mecca didn't pick up.

"Hello?" Q answered.

"Q!" Dorian greeted, a fake smile matching his too-merry voice, "Hand the phone to your Master there, now, please. I need to speak with the little tyke."

"Dorian, he's…he's busy at the moment."

The falter in her voice meant she'd covered for him. Not even his soul was a good liar after they'd been caught. "Busy? Doin' what exactly?"

Silence was the very answer he'd expected.

"Tell him to pick me out something to read, then, since you're both at a fucking comic book store."

He could hear Q's moan-of-dread—almost hear her guts churn. Dorian always knew where he could find his unreliable little *Pygmaeus*.[77]

---

[77] My Narrator has mentioned to me that Mecca also got his kicks out of going to the *actual* book store, finding a few hardbacks with sleeves, removing said sleeves, slipping them on upside down, and then squeezing the book back on the shelf. The simple satisfaction that the

"We—we haven't been here all day. We just arrived."

"Yes, because you are so very truthful all of the time."

"Dorian, you know we get bored. We *did* follow her, I swear. We watched her walk into the apartment too. We just didn't call. And we—we didn't *lie*. Not really. We just neglected to tell you everything. You see, after you tapped their phone line, Mother sent us as soon as Odissa left the message where she was."

"I know that."

Q was stalling. "And at first *Mother* told *us* to tell *you* to tell *Odys*"—Dorian tried to keep up—"that Odissa was actually going to be later, so Odys would come to Mother more willingly."

"We all knew that, now get to the point."

"But when Mecca actually gave his first real update, he lied to Mother about the time, because he hadn't *actually* found Odissa yet and wanted to impress you all with the short time it took to find her. He was trying to do things on his own, you see. He needed the self-motivation."

"So you *did* lie?"

"Only so he could impress you all! He gave Mother a time estimate that *could* have been true if we'd found her *right then*. But we did find her eventually, though. It's like Vulcan *meant* for it to happen!"

"I seriously doubt He meant for you to lie."[78]

She made excuses for her Master, "He can't sit still long enough to read a *real* book, that's why we're here—in this comic book store. If he hadn't made it fun for himself, we wouldn't have done the job in the first place. Mecca knows when he's nothing more than a plot device to move a main character along."[79]

What. A. Clusterfuck.

---

next browser would get upside down text was enough to fuel him for a few days. Q got the ones on the taller shelves. This was their purpose in life. Rather, one of them.

[78] ...Or did He?

[79] His real purpose in this story is to annoy other characters and he would rather not break away from that, my Narrator tells me.

Dorian had to give the guy credit. He'd managed to find a moving car all on his own—without the use of a helicopter. (Thank God no one gave him a helicopter).

"But you didn't follow procedure. You let everyone believe—multiple times— that she would be here later." All his updates were lies. LIES.

"Yes, but," Q interrupted. "It was almost as if Vulcan *meant* for us to keep lying. Vulcan knew Mecca needed this to look good. Mec deserved it. You won't tell Mother, will you? You're good for it, Dori."

"I fucking jumped her, Q! Fletcher wasn't there and—"

"Wut?" she giggled. This was better than expected. Vulcan could be so hilarious!

"So you're glad I scared the shit out of her?"

"Why the hell did you *jump* her?"

"I swear to God, Mecca!" He was talking to Mecca through her now—she was the phone. He cursed them out in Spanish. He was just grateful they didn't do anything *funny* to Odissa. Like make her crash her car or something (oh-ho, what fun!). "You could have jeopardized everything, Mecca! Do you *want* her to find out about us?"

"The fuck did you jump her for? Why wasn't Fletcher there? You should be glad we'll promise not to tell Mother you were playing with fire by letting Fletcher out. We're even now!"

Dorian held the phone down, swallowing rage. When he put the phone back to his ear Q was still talking. "…but honestly, do you always attack people coming into their homes? Were you scared, wittle Dorian?"

He was silent. He didn't want to tell Mecca about Leeland—how Leeland had called. The little bastard didn't have the right to know. So he changed the subject. Huffing, "Are the employees giving him dirty looks?"

She whispered into the cell. "Only a little, but he's already traded in a few and there's a life-size you-know-what for sale. He's bound to snatch it up. We've never been in this store before, so there's a whole new selection of collectables he's debating over. Really, he might as well buy the whole store." Dorian could tell she'd gone outside, by the sound of the cars zooming by. "He just doesn't know if he has enough storage for everything he wants."

"As long as he doesn't make you take pictures with the life size you-know-what, like he did with the *other* you-know-whats." Dorian remembered the albums upon albums Mecca had of his Automaton in unreasonable situations with all his fanboy memorabilia. Mecca forced her to assume specific costumes to fit the unholy scenes. God only knows what he really took them for. Probably sold them at high school campuses after school, though he didn't need the money. Likely passed them out for free. Maybe pasted them on telephone poles.

"He says you didn't have to look at the last ones, you know. It's not his fault you're a pedophile."

"I'M FUCKING BLIND, IT'S NOT LIKE I WAS LOOKING!" He shouted into the phone. Those pictures had scarred him through Fletcher—and had given Fletcher a nosebleed of liquid metal-blood as he tried to filter the images for Dorian, but failed. "You tell the little punk that he's going to get a spanking next time I see him."

As if she was embarrassed to say it out loud, "Mecca says that you can give me *two* spankings to make up for it, as long as he can take the pictures."

"And I'll break that fucking camera. Jesus Christ, little pervert. Anyways, Q, I've got to go. Tell Mecca this isn't over. Mother *will* hear about this."

"Yeah, sure," Q mocked him, "Go tell Mommy you let Fletcher leave the apartment. Mecca still managed to find a fucking moving car. Mecca is the greatest!"[80]

---

[80] I told our Narrator that Mecca is a very cartoonish character (not that the others aren't, but, when compared, Mecca is somewhat unrealistic in my opinion). In one second, he will be carrying on an intelligent conversation with another adult and in the next demanding something like a bratty five-year-old. He doesn't act his actual age *or* the age of his body. To this our Narrator replied: "Mecca wants to grow up, but he doesn't know what he's asking for. How could he? No one does. Yet he knows a little more than most, because he has an Automaton. However, it is that same Automaton that is slowing his brain development down too. I think poor Mecca himself is confused about how he should act." I would have told our Narrator to cut him as a character, but I learned he had a bigger role to play in the second volume, so I let this slide. He is a necessary evil. Just take my word for it.

Still spewing muffled curses (in Spanish), Dorian hung up.

It was most likely the group's fault for giving Mecca a virtually meaningless (and very dull) assignment. Mecca could smell a purposeless job a mile away. Might as well put a camera on a slug just to make sure it wouldn't recite the alphabet—that's what this job had been to him.

But then again, *they had found her.*

"Vulcan's paying attention again," he whispered to himself. He rubbed his forehead, trying to process his disbelief.

He needed to call Mother. Somebody needed to update the rest of them.

He waited for ten minutes—he even counted—before calling her. He had to make sure he was calm enough to talk about Leeland. The cold air helped freeze his emotions.

He listened to Fletcher and Odissa's awkward conversation in his head—a conversation Fletcher was managing well. *At least one of me knows what he's doing—even on autopilot.*

Counting, counting, counting. Waiting, waiting, waiting.

According to Mecca's previous (and false) calculations, Odissa would have been arriving right about…*now.*

On the phone with mother:

"He called me, Mother." Mecca was already in the back of his mind.

"…I suspected he would—that he'd call at least one of you. Oh, Dorian, I wish he'd have called someone else. I know how it affects you. I can still hear the rage in your voice."

They talked a little in Spanish—they drug it out from each other.

Mother would let him pause and she would listen to his silence. She knew he needed silence.

"Before you go, I must say I don't think Odys is suicidal. You're wrong about this one, Dorian."

"But you know I can see these things, Mother." He ran a finger along the wood panel wall. Calling Gwen "Mother" came so natural to him now. What started as a joke that they slowly let him in on now felt just as easy as calling to an Auntie or Grandma. What didn't feel right was why he didn't call her "Madre" to put his own spin on things. Albeit, it was too late to change now. "Did he make you cry?"

"Do not be silly, Dorian. I cry even when happy. But Bob, now, she's stressed because of this. I need to find something to distract her. I think I'll send her to the cabin. Should she prepare it? We need to be together. You know how these things get everyone worked up. We need a break."

"*Si, si,* yes," he rambled on in Spanish to her. When they spoke Spanish, they were being private. Sharing a private matter. I'll not intrude by jotting it down. "Ah, I have to let you go, Gwen. I'm getting another call. I think it might be Bob with Odys."

"All right. Goodnight. Keep me informed. I want texts every hour."

As he answered the phone, he could hear the ice cream truck's too-merry tune.

"Hello?"

"We're fucking ten minutes away."

That was all.

He continued to wait outside for them to come up, pacing. There were only two sets of footsteps. The mini biker gang had not come up with Odys and Maud. They'd done their job and that was it.

Though Dorian couldn't see it, Odys had allowed Maud to take his hand. Upon seeing Dorian outside his door, Odys drew it back. The anti-PDA was in his nature.

"Um, why do I have someone else's door?" Odys asked.

"Don't ask questions if you don't want to know," Dorian said. He had wanted this moment to be funnier.

Odys took off his hat Bob had given him and thrust it at Maud, tired of looking ridiculous. He made to open the door, but Dorian stopped him. "I must warn you. Your sister, she...she came earlier than expected."

195

"You lied to us, Dorian?" Maud accused. She tried to peak through the window to see what was going on in the apartment. "To make us go willingly? You know we should've been here when she arrived."

"Yes, well, believe me, it wasn't planned," he half-lied.

Maud severed her eyes, studying him. "Wait. You sent *Mecca*, didn't you?"

"I didn't. Mother did. Everyone else was tied up."

"So you aren't lying?" Odys asked, trying to work this out. *Who the hell is Mecca and why is he named after the most famous Islamic pilgrimage site?*[81]

"No. I—I'm not. In fact, when she came in I—I thought she was someone else, so I—I..." Dorian cringed. "I *frightened* her."

That's one way to put it.

Though Dorian seemed sorry, Odys was not in a forgiving mood and pushed past him. Dorian managed to grab hold of Maud and prep her. They needed to make sure their stories were straight. Maud took off her shawl and "put on" her own version of an officer-esque uniform. Sadly, she looked more like a stripper about to "arrest" someone who'd been a naughty boy.[82]

Odys walked in on Odissa sipping a cooling cup of coffee, awkwardly chatting with Fletcher about headlines in a newspaper they were sharing (Fletcher had numbed her further questions by saying things like, "But I'll save those details for when your brother gets home." And she had taken it as a hint to start up the small talk). Her head lifted when Odys burst into the room.

"Odys, they told me what happened..." she managed to get out before he'd knelt down beside her; she'd tried to stand up to greet him, but he'd gotten to her fast. He held her head and kissed her hair, as if to make sure his hands weren't deceiving him. She shied away from him. "Fletcher said you didn't know the man—"

His eyes landed on Fletcher. They'd get their lies straightened out later. Right now, let him inspect his sister. Odissa's eyes flickered to Maud, who closed the door

---

[81] Is it offensive that he assumes Mecca is a boy name? I'm not sure.
[82] A potato sack on Maud would look good.

quietly behind her. That Dorian fellow—the one out of uniform—still hadn't come back in.

Maud walked up to them, extending a hand and comforting smile. "Hello, I'm Maud. Good to meet you. I'm Odys's police escort for the time being."

Short and simple of it. She put a hand to her hip, where her formed gun rested.

"Escort" is one word for it. Odissa felt hideous with Maud in the room. She had worn her comfy traveling clothes and minimal makeup today.

Odys pressed his sister. "Dorian said he frightened you? What happened? What did he say to you?"

She found a cigarette. "I'm fine, Odys. But, God, you look like crap." She noticed he didn't want to talk about it. She changed subjects. "I almost wish I had a cell phone so I could have known what I was coming home to." She forced a laugh (she was the one who had always enforced the NO CELL PHONES rule).[83]

"We won't be in the way," Fletcher assured her. "Odissa and I were just getting to know each other, Odys. She's been very *cooperative*. Where were you again, Odissa? I know Odys told us, but I can't remember for the life of me." Fletcher asked, now drinking out of a REAL coffee mug (earlier, he had pretended to throw away the adjunct paper-like one away, very smooth-like).

Odissa shot Odys a look. "I was with my lawyer," she exhaled the smoke from her trembling lips, praying that her alibi (if she could even call it that) didn't drift off along with the exhalation. "My father's will allots us sporadic checks—which is in my purse by the way, Odys. Don't let me forget. Our lawyer, Mr. Augury, handles them. Writes in the numbers, even. I was gone to collect it." She could see Fletcher was about to ask more, so she saved him the trouble. "My father's will states we must meet at his [let's just say grave site]—an aggressive rule, but," she shrugged, "worth the money." She flicked her cigarette in the ashtray.

---

[83] If you don't have a cell phone, then it's certainly harder for Odys to stalk you when you go on a trip, for one.

"You were gone a long while just for a *visit*, though," Fletcher stated—not caring if he was unceremonious.

"Well, I'm not going to drive all the way out there and not get other stuff done," Odissa answered matter-of-factly. "I mean, not only does Augury take his time, but…" She paused, noticing Fletcher watching her brother. Odys was glaring at the table. "I also take mine."

"We tried calling him," Fletcher continued the conversation, a cop once more. "Odys didn't seem to have any of his…working numbers." Fletcher let on a light air of suspicion.

Odissa looked down at the floor beside her. She realized she was already telling them things they knew. But she would play along.

"Where is Mr. Augury's firm?" Fletcher helped her. He took out a "pen" and writing "pad" from his "back pocket," ready to "scribble down" her answers.

"Well, I don't know where he's based. In fact, he said he'd just finished with a bit of traveling." Of course he had. "He's retired, if that clarifies the situation. He was one of our father's closest friends, so Odys and I are his special case. I'm not sure what number would be best to reach him. Most times, we either stick to previously arranged dates or he—he calls me." She looked at Odys, who had taken up a chair diagonal to her. With her every word he cringed.

"What did your father do for a living again, Odys?" Fletcher asked, as if Odys mentioned it before and he'd only forgotten.

"What does our father have to do with this?" Odissa asked, hoping to avoid a long conversation. Her eyes flicked to Odys and back. He, too, didn't like where this was going. "It's not like our father was here when it happened. Neither was I."

"All information's valuable," Fletcher stated, as if it had *merely* been a question. "I know no one expects to talk about this sort of thing to strangers, but it's routine." Aw, look at Fletcher, trying to sound all legit. "Like I said, we aren't allowed to talk about the finer details of this case. What you don't say may be the very key we need.

Might as well tell us what you know, so it can be cleared." He said that last part sweetly.

Odissa sat still, averted her eyes. She gripped her coffee cup so tightly her knuckles whitened. Fletcher's eyes darted from the girl to Odys to Maud. Maud, who knew what the twins were experiencing, had turned away. She pretended to listen to the quiet television. She was only here because of protocol, don't mind her, tralalalala.

Odys's eyes flashed to Fletcher, jaw clenching. He glanced at the door, as if telling Fletcher to listen for Dorian, and listen well, because he'd only say this once. "Our father wasn't one for sharing details. We guessed that he was a doctor in another country, before he immigrated to America—and 'immigrant' may or may not be the proper term for him."

Fletcher's face pinched at Odys, reminding him to keep calm. "Where was your father from?" Fletcher wanted to know what lies Leeland had woven. He wanted to watch Odissa react to them. Her reactions could prove Odys's innocence.

Odissa shook her head. "He kept that from us."

Fletcher frowned. "You don't have a guess?"

"European."

She was playing this off as nothing. She *believed* it was nothing.

"And I'm sure," Odys went on for her, "you understand, Officer Fletcher, how licenses don't always neatly cross borders, so if he *were* a doctor, there may be no record of it here. That's what we always presumed. Even Mr. Augury handles most facts with that same *undertone*."

Odissa looked at him funny, wondering why he'd stress that point. "We've no way of proving what he was or wasn't. But he *was* in the medical profession."

"And your relationship with him wasn't on the best terms, yes?"

"Why does that matter?" Odissa cut off her brother's hostile "Yes."

Fletcher was taken aback. Odissa had said it so accusingly, as if it weren't anybody's business—even if it could solve the case of the century.

"Why bother us about *that* detail? He's tortured us enough beyond the grave. Please, let the dead rest, and let that say enough of how we feel about him."

Her eyes begged Fletcher to not provoke Odys.

Odys turned to his sister. "It won't make me mad to tell them. Besides, they may stop the questioning for now, in front of you, but when I'm alone with them, they'll push it."

Her body tensed. Was this stranger not as polite as he put on?

Fletcher stared at her, watching her wheels turn.

Something clicked behind Odissa's eyes. *This isn't some protection program. This is house arrest.* Their father had really screwed up this time.

The topic boiled up in Odys's throat, ready to come out in heated, gurgling words: "You want to know why we hate him? Why *I* hate him"—for Odys could not speak for Odissa, not entirely. "My father performed tests and…" Odys struggled for the right word. "*Experiments.*"

Fletcher screwed up his face. Why was Odys starting with this point? Granted, that *sounded* like Admund™—his brand, his mark left on a Master.

"When she was a child, well, our *father* diagnosed her with a condition. Whether or not he came to that conclusion on his own or with a second opinion, he was correct. Our current doctors verified it."

Odissa cut in, as if her brother weren't explaining it right, "But it's not any illness, so don't look so concerned. We're dealing with a pre-existing—a born-with—issue. If you even want to call it an *issue.* My father was a bored rich man needing something to fix. Our lawyer, Augury, still swears by our father's contribution to the medical field. Augury has done a lot of legal work for others in the medical profession, you see…"

Yeah, yeah. Sure he has.

To his sister, "Augury defended him only because he—" But Odys stopped himself. Gentler, "You and I both know Augury defends those others wouldn't." He looked at Fletcher, "Apparently, as Mr. Augury has before implied, Odissa's a perfect match for what one of our father's studies needed and, well, she became his favorite guinea pig." Odys's face twitched. He was staring at the table, as if he might explode if he made eye contact.

Odissa felt the need to defend her brother's dramatics. "My father came very close to finding a cure. But he ultimately failed."

"But if you're twins, then…" Fletcher pointed between them, wanting to be clear. This Dr. Frankenstein story was jumbled enough as it was.

"No, it's not like that," she answered. "I'm what he needed only because I am, well, female. It has—or had—to do with my…reproductive organs. It's not life-threatening. It never was. And it probably shouldn't have been explored to begin with. It wasn't like I got to consent to such major decisions about my own body. How can a child consent?"

Odissa half-wished the female cop, there, would do the interrogation. It would be less embarrassing, and she had such a sympathetic face. She glanced at Maud, who was realigning the candles on the windowsill as she tried to blend in with the wall— *Odys isn't the only one fidgeting,* Odissa thought.

Odys shook his head, anger still simmering, "She's putting it too delicately."

Odissa tried to watch Odys balance out this conversation, but her eyes kept moving back to Maud and the expression on her face—an expression so much like Odys's. *She agrees with Odys. She already knows. Do they all know?*

"Before she hit puberty, he began his *tests.* Overall, she was a case study— maybe one of many. Don't ask about his research. He never let *her* ask."

Doctors making house calls only because they live there.

"Your answer's not telling me anything, Mr. Odelyn. What *harm* came from your father's medical tests? Why does this cause you so much trouble?" *Tell me why you hate him so much.*

Odissa leaned forward. "Because eventually he tried to get me pregnant. Then he succeeded. All of them miscarried within"—she searched her brain for a measurement—"weeks of conception. This all happened before I was even eighteen. And like hell I got to choose who the father was."

Fletcher didn't breathe as he digested Odissa's words. He could feel the goosebumps forming on his Master's arms outside—such bumps weren't there because of the winter cold. He didn't realize Leeland would go to such great lengths—or that his plans for the twins could expand so nefariously. "But *why* would your father—Odi Odelyn—do that?"

She clarified, "There was no sex involved, if that's why you look so shocked. It was all done by artificial means. Probably some castaway sperm from the sperm bank garbage." She forced a laugh, though her hand couldn't hide her trembling lips. "Did the man who killed himself know my father?"

"Yes," Fletcher answered.

Odys's nostrils flared, disagreeing with Fletcher's choice to admit it. He could tell it got his sister to think—think *inside* the box—think things like "Maybe the man who killed himself had illegal research of his own and wanted his secrets to die with him?" *This has nothing to do with real life, Odissa!*

Odys finally looked at Fletcher. His voice low, "If you think about it, Fletcher, children—grandchildren—are a lot of *leverage*, aren't they? They're *investments*."

Odissa's head turned, wondering what that meant. She was certain now—certain that Odys knew something he couldn't tell her—something they wouldn't let him tell. *Everyone knows what this is but me.*

Fletcher remembered to breathe. "If that's the case, then I can see why you have your reasons for hating him, Mr. Odelyn."

Odissa latched on to Fletcher's discomfort. "Since our father obviously has something to do with the suicide, why not ask direct questions about him?"

Fletcher offered her the edge of his smile, liking her bitterness. "Well, your perspective on things has given me much to think about. But all right. The cat's out of the bag, I guess. Your father has *a little* something to do with this case." He crossed his legs, his arms. "If you hated your father so much, why didn't you report him? Why didn't you let the authorities—even, say, a nanny or random adult—know what he'd done to you? It clearly bothered you—even as a child. It's stuck with Odys all these years."

"There's the fact we have, in the past, feared our income would cease if we spoke too loudly about him. We're dealing with a great deal of money, here. Money we don't know the root source of. We just…" She stopped herself, waning.

"What?" Fletch coaxed. But the question was directed to Odys, as if he might allow his sister to speak more—might tell her it was alright. Was there something more to this?

"Is that not enough?" she asked Fletcher. Her expression seemed to both beg and scold him. "Don't get me wrong, I'm not ashamed of telling you the basic facts— even spurting off my medical history. But there are some things doctors simply shouldn't do. Most of all, there are things *fathers* shouldn't do."

Odys wanted to yell, HE WASN'T OUR FATHER. But he wouldn't jeopardize everything—including this innocence-test.

Fletcher bowed his head. "Your father seems just as mysterious to you as he still is to us, Odissa Odelyn."

"But he's not mysterious," Odissa said. "It's like we said before. He was a bored rich man."

"And now his lawyer is a bored rich man, isn't that right, Ms. Odelyn?" He pulled a picture of "Audell Augury" from his "pocket" and watched her reaction.

"Is this about *him* or my father?"

Fletcher sighed. "Both, really." And he put the picture away.

Dorian walked through the door. He didn't say a word.

Odys could tell these guys hadn't dealt with an outsider—a "regular" human—in a long while, at least not in this fashion. They weren't sure how to act around Odissa—a human girl they'd have to pretend around. Pretending took its toll. Maud's "outfit" was already weighing on Odys…

"Can you," Fletcher called back their attention, "possibly let us see the check you mentioned, then? For the account number."

Looking to Odys for permission, Odissa gave it to them. "It's not his name, you know. Augury doesn't put his name on them. I don't know who really signs them, though he said it goes through our father's account managers—whatever that means."

Fletcher, after studying it, passed it to Maud, who handed it to Dorian. After pretending to look at it, he stepped back outside to make a phone call about the numbers.

"Is this necessary?" Odissa asked, eyes searching Fletcher and Odys. She'd worked hard for that check, *nothing better happen to it*. "Why must you contact him? Tell me what you're looking for so I can help."

There was something too eager in that statement.

"If we knew that ourselves, we would ask, Ms. Odelyn. For the time being, there's no way to hurry this along."

"Can I have a word with Odissa, Fletcher?" Odys asked.

Odissa didn't like he had to ask.

"What about?"

"Is that a no?"

"It wouldn't be *appropriate*, Odys." He saw Odissa's stare. "This case is very important. We cannot let you endanger others by spreading what you know."

"You make it seem like *I'm* someone suspicious," Odissa said. "As if I'm a suspect that might have killed the man who shot *himself*. We have nothing valuable to hide."

"Then let's not hide, shall we?"

As they continued to wait for Dorian, Odissa grew restless. Someone needed to say something, to interrupt the clanging silence. "Where's Bulfinch?"

"Check your room," Odys suggested. The cat was always in her room. It was basically his.

Fletcher didn't protest her getting up from the table alone, so she smothered her latest cigarette and went. Flipping on the light, she noticed Bulfinch's tail sticking out from under the bed. He was never really good at hiding. "I see you've kept the room in order…" She glanced at the cluttered bed, her dresser, her shelves, her desk.

The only reason she ever used this room was for the sleek computer sitting atop it and to be alone sometimes. Odys had the laptop.

Since she was going to be stuck in here tonight, she could lock herself in and catch up on her web browsing. Yes, yes, she would have to entertain herself tonight. The computer would put her to sleep.

Staring at the computer, she noticed the modem.

Gasp!

It had been…crushed.

Smashed. Battered. *Murdered.*

"What the hell?" she whispered to herself as she rushed to examine it. Then, she saw the actual computer. It was bleeding frayed cables—gorged of circuits—drawn and quartered of all internet possibility.

She traced the cable to the landline. It looked like someone had taken scissors to it. Her outside-world connection was gone.[84]

She wasn't stupid. She knew her brother wouldn't destroy his own connection. This was something more. This had to do with the "police." But why would police destroy a computer? Internet connection was one thing. It was *another* to kill the computer.

It could all be replaced, yes. But until then, Odissa would be trapped in this room. Just as they had wanted.

She looked about. She could tell things had been touched—moved slightly. She set a picture frame back up. Someone had been snooping. *They* had been snooping. Not only had they destroyed her computer but they had invaded her privacy. That was worst of all.

---

[84] Fletcher: Helping Odissa avoid carpel tunnel, if only for one more day.

After calming herself and reasoning out what this meant, she set the modem down. As normal as could be, she waltzed toward the kitchen, passing Maud, who seemed concerned about her reaction to the room.

"Anyone want more coffee?" Odissa asked.

Fletcher watched her as she moved about the kitchen. Even Odys could tell she was acting strangely. As she fumbled in the cabinet for a new mug (though she hadn't finished her last one) she intentionally dropped it, letting it fall onto the counter. As if she had been trying to catch it, she knocked over the phone and a paper stack. The mug cracked on the counter and smashed to a million pieces on the floor.

"My God," she said, nervously apologizing. She bent down to pick up the disjointed phone, listening carefully. No dial tone.

She set the phone back in its place. Odys had rushed over to clean up the broken pieces of the mug. He sensed the fear radiating off her.

"I'll clean it, Odys," she tried to shoo him away. *Act natural, Odys!*

"Odissa, you already have a mug over there," he told her quietly.

"Oh, yes. I'm just so tired."

"It *is* getting late," Fletcher said, leaning back in his chair so he could better see what they were doing. "Maybe we should all get to bed."

He was *sending* them to bed.

"Should I make up the couch?" Odissa asked, taking the garbage basket from Odys and brushing the last of the mug's fragments into it.

"Won't be necessary," Fletcher said, standing. "We don't sleep on the job."

Dorian walked in, as if he had noticed some cue. He put the check back on the table.

To keep with their act, Maud said, "I'm calling it a night. Fletcher, show me out, please."

"Will do."

The Automatons stepped out. Dorian "watched" the twins finish cleaning up the mug. "Will the television bother you if we watch it tonight?" he asked them.

"No," Odissa answered for the both of them, studying the area they'd just cleaned. "Well, I'll go to bed then." She nodded to Odys.

The awkwardness of the "goodnight" was astounding. They never told each other goodnight. Never needed to.

She took her luggage and shut her door. The two human men in the apartment stood there. They could hear her clearing her bed. There were so many piles stacked atop it. It took her a great deal of time to tidy—maybe because she was taking her time. She had too much time. She wasn't going to sleep tonight. Not with strangers in her home.

"She's too accepting of this situation," Dorian noted, his voice hushed. Odys stared at her door. "I thought she'd have more resistance to this whole *thing*." Even Dorian didn't know what to call it.

"She suspects something," Odys told him quietly. He hoped she couldn't hear them talking. "But, since she knows this has something to do with our father, she's too defensive to break her cover. She thinks she's protecting us. She was always paranoid people would find out about him."

"Find out about him?"

"We always knew he didn't accomplish things in the most legal ways possible."

"She probably noticed what we did to her computer," Dorian noted. Even *he* thought the mug incident was weird—yet clever.

Odys guessed what he meant and picked up the phone. Listened. "Did you *have* to cut the wires?" He realized Fletcher had probably done it when he "searched the place."

Dorian stepped closer, to make sure his whisper got to him. "We can't have her doing anything rash, Odys."

"Now she *will* do something rash because she'll feel caged here," he hissed back at him. "She won't understand."

"She doesn't have to understand, Odys. That's the point."

"So you want her to find out, then? Mother would be *thrilled* if you lost control of this situation."

Dorian sunk back from the statement, considering a new thought. "Despite all the questions you both answered for us tonight, Odys, there's one that goes unanswered." Which is? "Why does your hate for your unnatural father lead you to love your sister so unnaturally? The whole Byblis thing, sure. But the other *strangeness* is so thick I could cut it with a knife."[85]

"What does that have to do with any of—of this?" He eyed the door, waiting for Fletcher to come back in with Maud so he could take her and go to bed, but Dorian clearly wanted a word—or two or three. He could see Fletcher's shadow underneath the door, waiting for Odys to answer his Master.

"Does Leeland know you fuck your sister?" He wasn't judging. He was simply wondering if Leeland ever cared to notice the two children his Automaton had raised were so symbiotic. "I mean, how could he have missed it?"

"You think he really cared enough to notice?" Odys's voice was low and sizzling. "And what if I *had* gotten her pregnant? Wouldn't more kids be like having more Bulfinches around? More *leverage?* Not that he doesn't control our lives enough already." He paused, looking back to Odissa's door. "We were finally going to be free of him, but then all of *this* happened."

"But he was hardly in your life. In fact, he had killed himself to be out of it. What more freedom do you mean?"

"Odi—I mean Leeland—Leeland's always been here—looming over. And I've watched what he's done to my sister for far too long."

"He still manipulates her. So what? She's the one that still lets *him* in her life. Or is that not what you mean? Tell me what all this horror-suspense about experiments and such actually means. We've let you build it up long enough."[86]

---

[85] Byblis, in myth, loved her twin brother.
[86] Indeed.

"There are some things more *vile* than two twins fucking, Dorian." Odys wondered if he really didn't know. Dorian seemed to know everything about him already.

"I never said you were vile." Dorian tried to keep Odys calm. "But I know there's something you're not telling me—a reason you hate Leeland more than she ever will."

"Because it's not my place to tell," Odys hissed.

Odys saw the pity in Dorian's expression. It unnerved him. Why would Dorian—out of so many emotions—choose pity? Odys didn't want his pity.

Fletcher walked back in, penny in hand. He looked left and right to make sure the coast was clear.

Odys went to retrieve Maud, but Fletcher held her over Odys's head. Leaning down, he commanded, "You best sleep with her tonight."

Odys cringed, not liking the way that sounded and praying to God Odissa hadn't heard it. "Would. You. Shut. Up?"

No, not yet.

"Hey, hey, now," he said. He raised his hand, too high for Odys to grab at. He rolled Maud over his supple fingertips—bump, bump, bump. Maud was bound to be dizzy. "She might have your soul, but you still have our property. Keep that in mind. We don't want any more of her sneezing-fits because of your self-sabotaging tendencies, m'kay? It not only puts you in danger, but all of us. Leeland called, while you were away. Your sister needs to've all the protection she can get, right? We'll all be handicapped if Maud sneezes out."

Fletcher, with the back of his thumb, tossed Maud in the air; Odys fumbled for her.

"Now off to bed with you." Fletcher shooed him away, nodding to his room like a dad.

When they heard his door lock, Fletcher turned to Dorian. "Should we tell him not to lock it? So petulant."

"We have his sister, don't we?" Dorian answered, as if it were nothing to celebrate. "He'll behave." He sat down at the table and picked up Fletcher's used coffee. He gripped it for comfort. He still felt bad about what he'd just put the girl through.

"Don't beat yourself up about it," Fletcher told, so softly Dorian could barely hear. Fletcher studied himself in a nearby wall mirror. He looked sofuckinggood in a uniform. "You can't avoid her from here on out and also do your job."

"Yes, yes, I know." Dorian was already past that.

Now his major worries were how he'd maneuver their glib charade to keep Odissa unaware of his blindness. As Fletcher had observed her, he could tell—as her eyes had followed Dorian for fleeting seconds—she didn't think Dorian fit the role of a cop. And he certainly wasn't as *aware of his surroundings* as other people.

Dorian didn't "see" as clearly when Fletcher was away. Though the surrounding's blueprint remained logged in the Automaton's mind like a file Dorian could retrieve for later use, it was much safer for him to move if the file was constantly updated.

"I don't think she's stupid," Fletcher admitted. He watched her door, as if it might open. "But I don't think she's brave enough to question authority."

"To question authority, no. But to question what is and is not authority? She fits the type."

"She's an odd little thing, you bet."

"She *is* interesting, isn't she? How she can control her brother." Dorian placed a stick of gum in his mouth. "Yet she's so gentle."

"You should stop trying to see things in them, Dorian. It only hurts you."

"Yes, but there's not much left to hurt, now, is there?"

"I wonder what her favorite color is?"

"She looks brown, like her brother," Dorian stated. "But I don't think she's brown."

"Maybe taupe?" Fletcher's lip pulled up at his guess.

"Or just grey."

"Oh. I see," Fletcher sated, his face becoming serious. "I get it."

"And what exactly do you get? What am I *allowing* you to get?" Dorian needed his soul to help him face the facts.

Fletcher sighed. Dorian could almost hear Fletcher's tall shoulders hunch over, feel his Automaton shove his long hands in his self-fabricated pockets. "The girl reminds me of her too, Dorian, but so have many other girls."

"But even Odys reminds me of her. It's not something they could fake—"

Fletcher reached out and put a hand on the back of his Master's neck, his manner shifting. Crouching over Dorian he kissed his forehead, his lips lingering to mouth, "Then maybe it really is them."

"That's exactly what Leeland would want me to think," Dorian mumbled, putting a hand on Fletcher's arm.

A few minutes later, they would go to bed—on the couch, of course. They would sleep, despite what they told Odissa. They always slept *lightly* anyway. Wakefulness was what was *heavy*.

Stanza: No man is an island, but a woman is her own continent.

Odys, after placing Maud upon his dresser, sat upon his bed, head in hands.

"At least she arrived home in one piece," Maud stated, folding her thin arms after reforming. She sat, shapely legs crossed, upon the dresser—as if still a weightless penny.

"I don't like how she's involved in this—her private life examined."

"I'm surprised they didn't press further. Take it as a sign they believe what you're telling them. They're sympathetic."

"I don't even know how I'm going to tell her that our father wasn't our father and that Mr. Augury is actually..." He squeezed his hands.

"Odys, your sister can stick up for herself. Vengeance isn't yours to take. If anyone's, it's hers. Any evil committed has been upon her."

"Anything done to her is done to me," Odys hissed. "Shouldn't you know that, by now? Shouldn't you, my *Automaton*,"—he mocked—"know that by now? Don't you know what that man has done to us? What *hell* our lives have been? And now it turns out it didn't have to be that way—it was all an—an *act*."

Odys stood up, his catharsis over. Walking over to the dresser, he pulled open the drawer below her bare toes. Rummaging for a second, he pulled out two articles.

"Here," he extended one of his shirts and shorts to her. "They're too big for you, yes, but it'll save you—or *us*—the trouble of 'concentration' tonight. No *accidents*."

Taking the outfit, she commented, "You make it sound like I'm a bed wetter."

She slipped on the clothes, bunching up the short's slack with one hand.

"You take the bed," Odys pointed.

"Take the bed? You aren't—?"

"No, I'm sleeping on the floor."

"But Odys! We're both tired. We'll be ill tomorrow, if we don't…you know."

Touch.

"Whatever. Now go to bed." He couldn't stand knowing she was right. Even now he wanted to snuggle up to her like a cold pillow.

Sticking to his original plan, he took a blanket from the bed, one of the pillows, turned off the lights, and flopped on the floor.

Maud breathed in deep. No good could come of this.

A few seconds passed as they tried to fall asleep, but Odys still had something on his mind. "Mother said Leeland has something on all of them. I want to know what their weaknesses were. They know mine."

"Yours is still alive though. Theirs was taken from them. It's no good to know them now."

"I still want to know who I'm dealing with."

Her voice almost too quiet, "For Bob he—Leeland took her husband.[87] And when that didn't work..." She paused. "He marked her body—with marks worse than scars."

"Her spots?"

"No," Maud whispered. "Those spots cover up his marks—the words he wrote on her—the words he engraved upon her skin to remind her of what he'd taken. Small words, big words. Even a few sentences."

When Odys didn't respond she went on: "Silly, isn't it? The extremes he goes to, to *avoid* killing people. It's almost comical. He wants them to agree with him—agree Automata should not exist. He wants Masters to kill themselves and surrender. He doesn't just take, he wants to feel *right*. Now each time Bob looks in the mirror, she remembers what he took from her."

She waited until his thoughts were ready to process more information.

"He hopes to continue to remind her, until she gives up hope. Until she can't bear herself any longer. But she didn't remove the marks he put. She only covered them. If she removed them then he would win. She owns her marks now. She hated tattoos—her old self is nothing like she is now. She gave her past to Cestus. That is the only way she remains strong against Leeland—she gave up her own *self* to fight him."

"No, she gave up her husband. She let him die."

Maud sighed, agreeing with him. "But not just that, Odys. It was Gwen's fault it happened to her—her 'branding.' Cestus was away on business for Gwen when Bob got her first round of marks. Leeland's done it to her more than once. Gwen feels guilty because she had sent Cestus to do the *business*—both times. They wouldn't have been able to get to Bob if Cestus had been there." She rolled over on her other side. "Leeland sent his Automatons to do it. She could not fight them on her own. She had no choice but to let them—let them go on with their *inquisition*. They beat

---

[87] I previously erased a reference to Bob's birth year. She met her husband waaay after gaining her Automaton. Born around the start of the Philippine-American war.

her up pretty bad and she woke up with the words. Apparently, she had let it slip once that she hated tattoos."[88]

"And Dorian? How did Leeland hurt him? What did his eyes have to do with his weakness?"

She didn't answer immediately. "Do you trust me enough by now to know I have your best interests at hand? You don't want to know why Dorian gave up his eyes. Every fiber of your soul is keeping me from telling you, Odys. It's part of the reason why we haven't synced yet."

Odys stared into the darkness, fists clenching. "That's what I'm afraid of. I don't want to know but they'll find a way to force it on me, won't they?"

Stanza: Adam ate the apple so he could rule Eve.

Odissa, semi-regretting the phone-stunt she'd just pulled, had finished moving all the objects from her bed. The last item was a box full of school files. She plopped it next to the basket of dirty laundry she'd just put down.

She peeled off the first layer of covers and, a few pats here and there, the dust was off.

She hadn't seen this surface in…

Months? A year? More or less.

Falling back on the bed, Bulfinch accompanied her (he happened to like the new, comfy space). "Ah, Bulfinch," she whispered while rubbing his side, "I am too nervous to get ready for bed. Perhaps in a few hours I'll peek out."

She stared at her door.

In a faint voice, "I'll tell you what I think, Bulfinch. Hey, don't move. It's rude. I'm still talking." She dangled him over her face. "There's something strange about this. Why did that one think I was Coraza?"—she said it with the same flair Dorian had given it. "I think my father might have had some unfinished business before he died. I don't think these are clean cops."

---

[88] I find it interesting that Bob didn't have her tattoos removed. Granted, she would probably have to remove them herself because she is a Master and nothing but a Master can "harm" her. It might have just been easier to blot out the words.

They aren't cops at all, Bulfinch tried to correct her.

She let him go and propped herself on her elbows. "And tell me, dear, did Odys feed you well while I was away?"

The cat rubbed against her.

"Ah, I thought not. In all this chaos, though, I can't blame him. If you had seen someone blow their head off, you'd forget about things too, I bet."

The cat was not forgiving.

She plopped back down. The cat curled up beside her, under her arm. "This is all inconvenient, isn't it, Bul?"

He threw his head back and meowed, *No more inconvenient than when you forget to clean the litter box, Odissa.*

"And by the way, my trip went fine, thanks for asking..." She trailed off in thought. She snuggled closer to him. "It's just you and me now."

Bulfinch didn't think she knew how to count.

Over his loud purring, she listened through the paper-thin walls. She could hear the TV.

Stanza: Eve offered Adam knowledge.

A few more hours passed, and, as Odys rolled over to straighten out his stiff back (the floor was unkind) he rolled atop something other than spacious floor.

His body pressed against his Automaton, who, during the night, had rolled off the bed to be near him. She didn't even stir when he'd squished her.

"Well, that worked well," he grumbled to himself. He partially understood she wasn't to blame—though neither was he. It was some magnetic attraction (literally). Odys gave in, waking her up. "Come on, we'll share the fucking bed."

Letting her tuck in, he crawled under the covers. "Back to back," Odys added, for clarification. Maud smiled as she rolled over. It was a relief.

Stanza: Adam went down with Eve.

Dorian found himself half-asleep and half-aware of what was going on. That is why, when Odissa finally got up in the middle of the night to espy the premises, she not only saw Dorian lounged awkwardly across the couch, but a Fletcher lounged awkwardly atop his Master.

And by "awkwardly" I mean "nakedly."

In Dorian's momentary drowse, he'd allowed Fletcher to function on his own…resulting in the automatic form-shift as the Automaton, too, snoozed.

Very stiffly, very quietly, and very uncomfortably, Odissa closed the door and locked it. Upon hearing the door close, Dorian started. Assuming what had happened, he punched his Automaton awake and—

Her back still pressed against the door, Odissa found her bearings and looked down at Bulfinch. "I don't think cops wear their birthday suit to work, do you, Bulfinch?"

Bulfinch, being a cat, had little problems with that attire. After all, it's what he wore most often. God knows he'd be pissed if you tried to dress him in anything else.

Stanza: Adam didn't try to stop Eve.

That morning:

Odys woke up to utter beatitude—finally, he didn't feel like his body was fighting poison.

That sickness, if only for this moment, had been dulled. No, not dulled, taken away. He knew it would come back, yes, if he moved away from Maud. But right now he was whole again. On the plus side, he was much more at ease knowing that, even though he slept next to an unsought woman (or something very much like a woman), he wouldn't open his heavy eyelids to see her naked.

No. More. Surprises.

He even hoped Maud wouldn't notice if he snuggled in a little closer, pretending to still be asleep. Even if she did notice, though, he wouldn't be too embarrassed. Why should he feel embarrassed? Just like someone hugging their arms around themselves for warmth, your arms never tattled, and neither would Maud.

"Wakey, wakey. Eggs and bakey," came a soft whisper above them. The gentle sound was just enough to echo through Odys's eternal Zen-space.

"Geezus!" Odys gasped, putting his hands up. The weapon Q held looked more like a metal Nerf gun.

Maud and Odys quickly sat upright, scooting back as far as possible—back away from the gun invading their bubble.

Odys glanced at Maud, who, to his surprise, held a pair of her own weapons, ready to shoot—she'd formed them so quickly, hair in her face.

"Good morning, Maudy!" Mecca said, his head peaking around Q's. He was dangling off her back like a giant monkey, his limbs making Q look like she had six arms. He whipped out a camera, shooting away.

"Mecca shot some really great photos of you both sleeping. This shot is *also* fantastic."

Clickclickclick.

Maud shot the camera out of his hand; the poor thing exploded and caught fire (Automaton bullets aren't so much *bullets* as they are metal bits hot with energy).[89]

Q created a second gun as her poor Master mourned his camera. "Those photos were on the *other* one!" she said, as if she had bested Maud. Mecca tucked his second camera under his arm like a football. Q shielded him like a mother.

It seemed someone as petite as Q might snap from Mecca's weight, but we're talking Automatons here, so this girl was just fine. She carried him around all the time. Mecca hated floors (his feet were too sacred for such things).

"Mind telling me what the hell's going on here?" Odys asked Maud, as if she should know.

"Odys, meet Mecca and Q. Master and Automaton."

"Mecca is here!" he proclaimed. Odys was finally getting to meet him!

"They let a *child* be a Master?" Odys said.

---

[89] A type of booger, you might even say. [Correction: my Narrator tells me to make a lava analogy here. Fine, hot-ore analogy made].

"Mecca is not a child! Mecca will use dirt on you if you don't mind your manners! Your whole graduating class will have these pictures of you and Maud in bed if you cross me again. You must obey Mecca!"

"If you put those online," Maud growled, "I'll break every single one of your little action figure dolls. The ones you had to steal from that museum in New Mexico. You hear me? The ones in the Colorado bunker. *I know about them!*"

Mecca stuck out his tongue, unafraid.

"Put down your guns, Q!" Maud said, growling.

"No. You're *our* captive now, act like one."

Play along, Maud, play along!

"And how does Dorian feel about that?" She tried to see out the open door, as if they might have had to fight Dorian over "warden rights."

"Dorian has no authority over this," Mecca said. "Mother sent us!"

"We received a call this morning," Q said. "Er, well, a call and a text and another call. Long story short, Mother wants you for brunch."

Mecca, the saggy backpack on his Automaton's shoulders, exclaimed, "Oh my God, Q, do you see what Maud's wearing? She's got on *real* clothes! Look, they're too big."

Maud made her guns disappear as she pulled the covers up. She saw Mecca itching to start up his camera to record the proof.

Dorian poked his head through the door, a sinister look upon his usually-composed face. "What'd I tell you? I told you to keep it down. There's a *normal* person in this apartment." The reprimand was muted as much as could be. "I don't want to clean up more messes."

Mecca cowered into Q, burrowing the camera further. When he'd arrived this morning, Dorian had confiscated his first one before he'd let him even come through the apartment door (good thing he'd brought his backups).

Q guarded Mecca from Dorian like a shepherdess, he her faun.

…More like rotten satyr.

"Why the hell are there little kids in here?" Odys demanded, remembering to keep his voice down mid-sentence.

"What'd I just say? Mecca's not a little kid!" Mecca pointed at the camera.

Q covered Mecca's mouth with a hand, reminding him to keep it down. Pushing her hand away, "Mecca—who is older than you!—has come to collect you—for your next appointment with Mother. She has big news. Big news you won't hear if you keep forgetting your place, young man." He narrowed his don't-fuck-with-me eyes. Q raised her gun higher.

Chewing some of the gum Mecca had brought him (a peace offering), Dorian said, "Odys, meet the reason I scared the shit out of your sister last night."

"Mecca's not the one that made Dorian jump her, or why Fletcher wasn't there to see things *straight!*" He laughed. "Straight! Get it?"

Q shook her head; let's not bring that up. There wasn't enough gum in the world.

"You said you scared her last night, not jumped her!" Odys hissed. He was almost glad they'd done it. Maybe Odissa would stay afraid of them.

"She's fine, though, isn't she?" Dorian shrugged it off, smacking his gum, trying to pretend he didn't care.

"You shouldn't let Fletcher leave the apartment," Maud admonished, taking off Odys's shorts. Odys noticed Mecca tilt his head as he watched her. As she stripped, she only revealed another layer of clothes (even so, Odys didn't like how she'd simply change in front of them!). "Why would you let him leave?" She tossed Odys's clothes at Dorian's face.

"He's sorta handsome, though, ain't he, Q?" Mecca asked Q about Odys. "You think our top girl followers will fancy him?"

"Since when do you cater to girls?" Maud asked.

"Since forever," Q said, "You should see the numbers Fletcher and Dorian have."

"The ones of them in bed get quite a few hits. Granted, they might be queer-hits, not girls."

"All right, Mec," Dorian finished this conversation. "You've done your damage." Just as he had wanted. "Get out," he ordered. "Let Odys get dressed."

"Dressed?" Odys asked as the party trickled out (Mecca glowering at Dorian). "Don't I have a say in this? Why do I have to go this early?" *Doesn't Gwen know brunch is between breakfast and lunchtime?*

"Why's the sky blue? Why's the grass green?"

"Why am I going?"

Tired of his questions, "Have you forgotten, Odys, we have you outnumbered? Right now, Fletcher's outside Odissa's door, gun ready. I have to obey Mother's orders, just as you do. By all means, I'd rather be at home letting Fletcher tickle my balls, but you and I both know this is some serious shit. No time for sleeping. Look at these bags under my eyes!"

"You're an old bag!" Q shout-whispered to his back.

Dorian took in a deep breath and closed the door.

Odys turned to Maud, eyebrows raised.

"Mother probably just wants to see *how much* you'll tolerate her. I just can't believe she'd send Mecca. Why not Bob again? Bob must be busy. Busy doing something else. Something more important. But what's more important than us right now? Makes me wonder. Mecca's actually older than Dorian, if you can believe it." She was like some personal narrator for Odys. Too bad he can't hear me. I'd do a better job. I KNOW EVERYTHING.

"That's fucked up," he said, rubbing the back of his neck. "But if he's older than Dorian, shouldn't he *look* older than, what, a nine year old?" He hunted for clean clothes, miserably tired. "I mean, immortality or not, we're not fucking vampires, right?"

He paused and waited until she shook her head. She laughed. "If anyone's most like vampires, it's the Automatons, not the Masters." She redirected, "Automatons affect each Master differently, depending on what *stage* of human the Automaton enters into. From the very inception of the Automaton bond, the human's aging is slowed. Gravity cannot pull to form wrinkles so easily; the human cells cannot die so easily. The human state is somewhat suspended from decomposition, left less damaged by time. Age is a form of death, in a way. Entropy. We shield from even that, though we can't stop it completely. We can't go against nature."

Yes, yes, it all makes sense, thanks for the early morning lesson. He half-listened while checking himself in the mirror—he needed to make sure he looked sloppy enough. He didn't have to try hard.

"I assume Dorian likes the fact Mecca will take some of your hatred. Dorian doesn't like being hated."

Not hearing her, "Will it be the ice cream truck again?"

"Definitely not," she sighed. "Not if Mecca's driving."

Once Odys was ready, he stuck his head out the door. The coast was clear. Well, clear of any twin sister. Fletcher really was at her door, holding a handgun to get the message across. And to stop Odissa if she were to try to come out before Odys left.

Mecca was still in his Automaton's arms, tongue out as he went through the pictures saved on his camera. They were in the doorway, letting in the cold morning air. Q had her huge gun resting on her shoulder, observing reality for her Master while he curated his fantasies.

Odys was about to ask if he could tell Odissa he'd be back soon, but Fletcher shook his head as he pointed for them to go on. Maud gave him the finger as they redirected to the door. This wasn't fair.

As Q started out, she nodded her farewell, "Fletcher, Dorian." Her gun disappeared back into her skin.

They walked through the parking lot (to God only knew what kind of vehicle). Mecca bobbed up and down between Q's every step. He said, "Mecca wants to tell you that your sister's in good hands. Excellent hands. Mecca knows you're worried, yes. Mecca knows all about you. Mecca thinks he might like you a lot because Mecca got Big Mama to tell Mecca everything."

"By Big Mama, does he mean Mother?" Odys asked Maud.

"No," Q answered for her. "That's Cestus."

"Mecca names things whatever he wants to," Maud added, clarifying what Q had just clarified. "And changes them to suit his mood."

"Yeah, Big Mama said he liked you," Mecca went on, sticking out his scrawny legs and arms behind his Automaton like a double pair of wings. "Big Mama said you're a real nice boy, even though you look like a street beggar. And if Big Mama thinks so, that means Bobmation thinks so too."

Odys assumed: Bob + Dalmation - Dal = Bobmation.[90]

He figured it was nicer that the B-word.

Mecca continued his logic, "And if Bobmation thinks so, then you've passed level one. And if you pass level one, that means level two must be cleared. Level two would be Mecca and Q, here. Mecca and Q will let you know your score by the day's end. If you pass, then you'll move on to level three. That should be the final level. That's Mother's level, that is."

Odys looked around for the car. "Which one are we getting into?"

As if Odys should already know, "Mecca will let you pick." Mecca and Q grinned wickedly. "Mecca never drives the same car twice."

"Are you joking?"

"Mecca does joke sometimes, but Mecca's not joking right now, because stealing a car is a very serious crime."

"He's telling the truth," Q stated, as if her word was Mecca-law.

"They're not joking," Maud confirmed. "However," she said to them, a bit crossly, "to keep with your record, Mecca, how about you drive Odissa's car down there, and we drive it back? After all, if we're driving it back, that means Mother's let us *come* back, right?"

Mecca and Q looked at each other. Odys could almost see the inner conversation shooting out their eyes like laser beams. Sticking out his tongue in thought, Mecca

---

[90] Bob needs a Bobmation plantation, where all of her can roam (I need to shut up; we don't have Disney money). But deargod if I have to buffer one more cutesy Mecca quirk, I'm gonna barf.

made Q answer them, "Mecca says that, for you, Maud, we'll make the exception. But only if you let us take a picture of you in your cop uniform."

Rolling her eyes, she agreed.

Mecca whipped out his camera, and Maud, like some natural pin-up, struck a pose.

"Fucking hell, can we go now?" she barked after the flash.

Stanza: Eve knew God was hiding something.

From the window, Fletcher had watched them leaving the apartment parking lot. Until they were out of sight, he and his Master waited patiently.

"All clear."

They sprang into action.

Dorian started pacing, hand upon chin (to help his thinking).

"You *know* we need to get this over with," Fletcher reasoned with him. "We have to or we'll go mad."

"Do it," Dorian nodded to her door. Fletcher had Odissa's door knob off in an instant. He dropped it as he turned into a paperclip. Dorian scooped him up and clipped him to his coat pocket. His eyes on his chest.

He swam into the room. "Good morning, Ms. Odelyn. Rise and shine."

But she was already awake, eyes wide. "You—you broke my door!"

"You and I suffer a lot of broken doors, don't we? Yes, I *should* have knocked. I should do a lot of things society tells me to do. But I don't. Now, what're you reading?"

"Can't you fucking see? What if I had been dressing? Jesus Christ, you can't just barge in here and—"

"No, actually, I can't see."

She jerked back. "What? You have eye problems or something?" She hoped he couldn't see, indeed; see her ratty hair, smudged face, wrinkled clothes. She pulled the blanket toward her chin.

She was usually very clean and proper. She never showed her bed-face to anyone except Odys. Never.

"Bingo," Dorian said. "I can't see *as well as most*."

"Then why do you have this job, if you can't see?" Is that why he'd attacked her last night? But he had seemed quite coordinated—even now, he…

"I see well enough." He knew that wasn't satisfying. "I'll not pretend otherwise, I'm not an *official* cop. But I do my work for them—a liaison. A freelancer. Auxiliary. Whatever. Fletcher's official, though, isn't he?"—as if he wanted her opinion. "So, what are you reading?"

"The dictionary," Odissa said, aghast. She tossed her book down. It wasn't really the dictionary, but she felt the need to lie—to test his sight.

He nodded and stuffed his hands in his pockets. Then, he pretended to glance around. Odissa wished she could see behind his reflective lenses. For a while, they both said nothing.

"You realize it's rude to be in here, don't you?"

"Oh, yes, no doubt about that." He sat in her desk chair. He nudged a box that had once cluttered her bed. "But I also think it's rude you're being such a bad hostess."

"Do you know how early it is?"

"I was hoping that, since your brother's gone, we might have a little chat."

"He's gone?" there was slight panic in her voice. He knew she heard him talking out there—but she never thought he'd leave her.

"Gone back to the station."

"Station 69?" she mocked.

"The very one."

"You realize you're making me uncomfortable in my own home, don't you?"

"And I attacked you in your own home as well, don't forget that. How are you by the way? Bruises?" He gestured to his own neck area.

She ignored his question. "What was your name again?" Though she remembered. She remembered because she'd liked his name. She just wanted to make sure it hadn't changed overnight.

"Dorian."

"Like Dorian Gray," she mused. On top of it, he was the perfect manifestation of Oscar Wildean ideals. That was his historical parallel. Odissa liked historical context. Odissa had decided it befit him. Odissa was never wrong in her decisions. It was her natural ability. Yet she couldn't historically place Fletcher or Maud—those other two. She found it impossible. It bothered her.

He chuckled at the irony. "Yes. Though, if my last name were his, I'd spell it with an 'e' instead of an 'a.' Sounds more achromatic."

"...I don't think the color spectrum depends on spelling."

"You'd be surprised. Grey happens to be my favorite color." He paused, waiting for her to say "I never would have guessed!" as most people did (based on his *gay rainbow* appearance). But she didn't. "If I had to guess, I'd say you had a particular fondness for that color?"[91] He lifted a lone shoe out of one of her many boxes. He loved shoes.

Narrowing her eyes, "Why'd you say that?"

Did she have a diary she didn't know about—a diary he'd read?

She watched him shrug. "Fate has a way of being clever, doesn't it?"

She ignored her goose bumps and said, "It's silver, actually." She swallowed. "How'd you know?"

"Well, I didn't, obviously. You like silver. Not *grey*."

"What's your last name then?" She needed it for future reference.

"Dandor. Dorian Dandor's the name. Babysitting's the game."

"Dador? As in, means 'giver'?"

"No, no, *Dan*dor. But how wonderful! You know Spanish."

---

[91] Is grey even a real color?

"Not enough to know what you and that other cop were talking about late last night."

He grinned at her standoffishness. "Would you like some breakfast? Cup of tea? Coffee? To come out of the bedroom?"

"I'd rather take a shower, please."

"And close another door?" He gestured to the one he'd just broken.

"I have a feeling you aren't supposed to be breaking doors, Mr. Dandor."

"Dorian, please. What are you going to do, tattle on me?"

"Why are you really talking to me?"

"I need some company."

She moved her feet off the bed. "No one should have company this early. Where's your other half—Fletcher—if you're so bored?"

"He's out at the car, checking the grounds." Lie. "That's his job for now. Just you and me in here. All alone. No one to stop me from breaking doors. Tell, Odissa, are you always this reclusive? Don't you want something to eat?"

"It's too early for breakfast. I just woke up."

"Don't lie, Odissa. You've been awake. Trying to eavesdrop. Haven't you?"

She wanted control of the conversation. "You have a paperclip on your pocket."

"My lucky charm." He patted it. He tried to smile—such a half-assed action.

She reached across the bed to the floor, for her purse. She pulled out a cigarette. Maybe it would make him leave her alone. SMOKE HIM OUT.

"So early?" he asked, frowning.

"Want one?"

"Not unless it's a bubble gum one."

Her lips half-smiled around the cigarette as she lit it. "This whole thing isn't for our protection is it?" she asked, blowing out a lung full of air-ash. "You're not really cops—none of you. Maybe you're dirty cops?"

He said nothing, merely smiled. This was exactly what he wanted. She could see it. "Your friends don't act like cops—or anything in between. You're all pretending in front of me. But you almost don't care if I notice or not."

"People notice things all the time. Doesn't mean they really know what's going on."

"Was someone else over this morning—a little kid? I heard a knock at the door."

"No need to worry about that."

"Who said I was worried? I was just curious." She was trying to sound confident.

"Sometimes curiosity can kill. Just ask the cat."

Deciding she wanted to test his limits, "Can I take a shower now?"

"I wasn't aware you had to ask."

"I wasn't aware I didn't have to."

"Well, if that's the case then, no. You may not take a shower." His smile was wider than we've ever seen it. She amused him.

He pushed up his incognito glasses. She pushed up her own. Mimicry.

Wanting to throw her off guard, "Did you ever want children?" He crossed his arms, as if her reply might take a while.

His partner Fletcher must have explained "it" clearly to him, so she quickly unfurrowed her brows. "You don't have to ask so politely. It's not a touchy subject for me. And the answer is no. Not really."

He itched his nose. "And do you have a boyfriend we should consider? No one poking their nose in to check up on you?"

"Why? Would you attack them too?"

"Probably. We need a clear coast, that's all. But seriously, is there anything you'd like to inform me about—when your brother isn't around?"

"And what about you? That Fletcher, last night. You two were working on the job. Real professional."

He didn't even blush. In fact, his grin grew wider. Wider and wilder. Wilde.

What an Oscar!

She wondered if she could cash in on this glee. "Odys knows what this is really about, doesn't he?" she pressed. "Did he try to find something out about my father? Did he get into trouble because of it?"

"Let's say that Odys didn't *have* to try to find information on your father. It found him."

"*Are* they dirty cops, then? Maud and Fletcher?"

"Very. Very dirty. Very naughty."

"Was it really a suicide? Or did Odys see something he wasn't supposed to see?"

"Yes and yes."

"Did Odys also do something he shouldn't have? Does he owe you something?"

"Yes and yes."

Stanza: Adam didn't have the balls to bite first.

Driving.

In the back of Odissa's car, Maud and Odys sat stiffly. Mecca and Q occupied the front seats. They didn't wear their seat belts.

Odys prayed Mecca knew what he was doing. Maud seemed at ease with his driving—even though he could hardly see over the wheel or reach the pedals—but Odys couldn't shake the fact a cop might see a little kid zooming past. Odys looked like the only adult in the car.

As Mecca sped down the highway, tongue sticking out, Odys asked, "Just wondering: why are you letting me have windows to see where we're going?"

"Mother has selected a meeting spot for brunch. A public place," Q responded over her shoulder. "Of course she's already moved from the last location. Mother can't be too cautious, since you could've calculated the turns and speed. Maud's very smart, we know. It's not even because we don't trust you. But someone could get the info out of you. No doubt we're being watched." She turned to Maud, "Leeland called Dorian. Just thought you should know. We just found out about it."

Maud asked, "So where are we meeting Mother?"

"It's a surprise."

To fill the silence, Q and Mecca rolled down their windows and proceeded to scream at anyone jogging, walking, sitting, jaywalking and so on in the chill morning air. The onlooker's faces were priceless, trying to find the scream's source as they whizzed by.

DOPPLER EFFECT.

Maud rolled her eyes. They always did this.

But soon—very soon, thankfully—their throats could not take the cold, and they found the radio a warmer entertainment.

Odys gazed out his window, not seeing.

"You think Odissa will be all right?" he asked Maud.

"Why wouldn't she be?" Maud replied.

He looked at her. She was already turned to face him, expecting him to turn his head. Her eyes widened, like a flash bulb going off. Her expression seemed to say: *But I do think she has the right to know—eventually—that Odi Odelyn wasn't your real father—whether or not they want you to mention it.*

Scratch that. It didn't *seem* like she was saying it. It was—WAS!—Maud saying it.

In his head.

Or, maybe it was in *her* head and *he* was just tapping into *it*.

But, still, he had HEARD it.

Without even trying.

She put a stabilizing hand on his arm, smiling, proud of him—delighted he had finally read her thoughts. Did this mean he wasn't fighting "it" anymore?

Nope. When her fingers touched his bare skin, he felt relief. Their non-verbal communication had drained them. This big step forward had cost him—in fact, it was an *over*step. He was panting.

Q turned the radio up, the undulating noise a wall of privacy. However, privacy was unnecessary. They were done talking, for now. He felt his pockets for his cigarettes. But Maud already held an open carton. "They were in your other jacket. I knew you'd forgotten."

"Thanks." He took the pack hesitantly, like some expensive gift he wasn't sure he should accept.

She touched the end of the cigarette to light it before he could even reach for a lighter. He held the cigarette limply between his lips, not sure what just happened. His chin jutted out to steady it. But still it wavered just like his decision to start smoking it.

"Mecca wouldn't mind one as well, thank you very much," the little Master said over his shoulder, extending his little fingers.

Maud, speaking for Odys, "We don't give out smokes to minors."

"Mecca is no minor!"

"Minor in age, no; minor character, yes."[92]

"Gasp!" Q said, putting a hand over her mouth. "We take offense."

Maud scoffed. "The 'little man syndrome' is so overdone. Even 'little pervert.' Act normal for once."

"Bah!" Mecca said. "Mecca has worked years to perfect his image—qualities clichéd and new! Don't belittle Mecca's art."

"Pornography, more like," Odys said to himself. He wasn't sure why he'd said it, but he liked the bitter laughs the other pair gave.

Q turned down the radio, glad they were all conversing now. "Mother told you the extra Automaton's still missing, right? They say you don't know what Pepin did with it." Her bright eyes hoped for a secret or two. *You can trust me.*

"She doesn't remember."

"You mean *you* don't remember." Q's eyes danced. "Did Maud tell you how ironic it is, though?"

"How ironic what is?" Odys was supposed to guess, apparently.

---

[92] See? Even the other characters feel the same way about Mecca as I do.

"The missing Automaton is a twin, too. He and Maud are made from the same casting and materials. They're both coins—both pennies. The only two Automatons with dates on them. No need for carbon dating. They're very *specific* objects, compared to us others. In a way, Vulcan made them to be a pair, didn't he? They're his two cents. He first gave the twin-Automatons to a brother and sister. He made them to match each other."

Q's eyes cut to Odys, to see how curious he was about her little tangent. She turned in her seat, her little butt in the air. Her tiny hand clutched the headrest. "You didn't explain it, Maud? Oh, geez. I *do* think it's funny—that the *twin* would gain a *twin* Automaton. Don't you, Mecca?"

Of course he did.

Q giggled. "Perhaps the gods had something to do with this? Makes you wonder if Vulcan isn't laughing at the irony himself. Like two handguns, they were designed to work together—" she shot the air with her fingers "—but are still quite useful when apart, of course."

Odys looked at his Automaton, a tinge of fear flashing in his sepia eyes (the kind of eerie fear that makes your skin prickle—prickle at a plot that twists too much together). He wasn't sure why it unnerved him, but the stars had lined up too well for this. He didn't like being part of the line.

"It's not as dramatic as she makes it sound," Maud waved her away—though her eyes were wide. She'd been too preoccupied lately to ever realize the congruity.

Q went on despite Maud, "I think it's a good sign, Odys Odelyn. You're supposed to have Maud. It's a clear sign. We paired ones *see* the signs. And smell them too." She squished her nose. "That's why we're so interested in you—why we haven't killed you yet."

"One of the reasons," Mecca clarified himself.

As the car stopped (they'd barely driven as far as Odys thought they might), Odys didn't care to notice where they were parking. He was too busy feeling like the gods' pawn.

"You really don't remember what Pepin did with your brother, Maud?" Q pressed. "Not even a guess?"

Maud to Q, "I don't even remember if Pepin had him at all, at the end. I don't know what Pepin did with *Madus*."[93]

Q: Automaton of Mecca Makepeace, at your fan service!

WHAT NOT TO DO: Mock her Master by asking him if he's grown recently. Besides, he'll let you KNOW if he's grown. You'll never stop hearing about it.

CUTEST OUTFIT: A maid outfit.

FAVORITE POSE: Moe pose!

Chapter the fourteenth,

Internal corruption:

Which devices have malfunctioned?

Odissa wondered what was stopping her from dashing out of the room—out of the apartment. He admitted he was blind, didn't he? Well, partially.

Whatever that meant.

But then again, he had moved pretty fast last night, when he'd pounced on her. She decided to stay put. "I can offer you money…if it will make you leave us alone."

He chuckled. She was too cute. "You may take your shower now."

She couldn't help but wane. He was done with her. He'd wadded her up and thrown her away. He just sat there, in her room, watching her collect clean clothes for after. Didn't say a word.

As she closed the swollen door to her bathroom, she saw his grooming bags—the ones he'd shoved in the huge duffle bag he'd brought. Locking the door behind her, she told herself it would be safe to peek.

---

[93] Yes, I'll admit that I couldn't really come up with a good "M" name replacement for Madus and so I just rearranged the letters of Maud's name and added an "S." All the other Automata names have interesting meanings or connotations. Poor Madus's doesn't.

He used more products than she did. Or, maybe it was some of Fletcher's stuff too (she didn't know Automata needed no beauty products). She noticed a polka-dotted straightening iron.

She frowned. What had she expected to find—drugs?

She turned on the shower.

She looked over her shoulder at the bathroom's locked door. Surely, two *gay* men wouldn't care to see her naked. She was safe.

Stanza: *Dorian Gray* and his picture.

Dorian removed the paperclip perched on his pocket and let him fall to the ground.

"*Jesus Christos*," Fletcher whistled. He appeared beside Dorian, wearing his cop uniform in case Odissa came out. A smile lit his face as he glanced around for his Master. "You sure know how to carry a conversation."

"Yes, well, I wanted her to talk—talk more about Leeland."

"Then why didn't you try harder?"

"Because I think I already know why Leeland 'adopted' these twins."

"Psh. You knew that from the beginning."

"Yes, but." He stopped.

Fletcher finished for him. "Now we know why he was able to hide it from us. He liked having them believe he was in the mob or…whatever." He waved his hand. "Even this seems normal to her. Makes you wonder who Lee's been socializing with these past years, doesn't it? We're not the worst she's seen," he snorted.

Obeying Dorian's thoughts, he pulled out his Master's phone and punched in some numbers.

As it rang, he handed it to Dorian. "Ah, Dorian!" Mother's voice sounded from the phone. "I was just about to call you. I just saw Mecca's car, but there's still a little time. You call for something?"

"Yes, Gwen. It'll be done soon. She's up and everything. Taking a shower now. I'll call you when it's done."

"Ah, *bien, bien.* You didn't have to start so soon. I told you I'd call when we needed her out."

"I thought I'd let her take one good shower before doing it."

"Ah, that is very kind. And early means we have more wiggle room."

"Also, I…"

"Yes?"

"Um." He sighed, not knowing what to say. "Er—fair warning, Mecca's picture-happy today. He has more than one camera."

"Nothing new," she mumbled in Spanish. "Oh, and Dorian—"

"Sí?"

"I know you think you know for sure, Dori. Even I do. But—but Leeland is clever. Don't get too attached. Leeland's been planning to do something with these twins for a long while now. It might not be them."

The line went dead.

The bitch has us tapped Dorian laughed, calmly putting away the phone. He patted it with his hand. Mother was always listening.

"She should trust us more," Fletcher said, watching his Master.

"No, it's comforting to know we scare her a little." Dorian smiled. "I don't blame her. She's right. She's always right." He put his hand on his hip. "They may not even *be* twins. Odissa looks younger, anyway. Leeland could have found two children who looked alike and—"

"But why'd he go to that trouble?"

Dorian sat down beside his Automaton. "Why'd he go to the trouble of raising two children at all?"

"These rhetorical questions aren't settling anything." Fletcher leaned into his Master's hair, to whisper in his ear. "Maybe we should believe and fall into the trap. We'll let it close in on us this time." Fletcher put a hand on his Master's arm. "Maybe if we play along, Leeland'll take me away from you. And you'll be free from needing answers."

"My thoughts sound scary when said aloud." Dorian rolled away.

"All the better to make Mother worry. She needs to listen. We can't be doing anything stupid now, can we?"

Stanza: The self-made man.

Fletcher and Dorian had hovered like vultures waiting to swoop—floating in this and that room, hardly lighting. Odissa took long showers, indeed. At least now she was blow-drying her hair. They could hear it.

Dorian walked to Odissa's bookcase. Fletcher turned his head in the bookcase's direction, so Dorian could better inspect. Dorian ran his fingers along the spines, as if they could read the titles.

"You think Pepin could have died for *me*, Fletcher? You think Pepin was trying to lessen the leverage Leeland potentially has on me?"

"I don't know about *lessen*. Now you and Odys share the same leverage, don't you? A leverage you didn't even know still existed until recently."

"If correct, Pepin had a lot riding on how much I'd care about Odissa. I mean, I let her die once already. Along with her brother and parents."

Fletcher sighed. He assured him once again, "You didn't know she existed back then, though. You thought Leeland was lying to you. And even then you gave up your eyes to buy time—time to try and verify if Dory[94] really did have twins..." Fletcher stopped himself, looking past his Master. He could remember Coraza off in the distance, verifying for Leeland that Dorian had ruined his eyes. That was the first thing he saw for Dorian—the first thing his Master could not see himself.

"But it didn't buy enough time." He pushed up his glasses. "I just hoped it'd be that simple—why Pepin died."

"Pepin wasn't simple."

"I want to tell the twins who I think they are." Dorian pulled out one of Odissa's books. He put it back in the wrong place, wondering if she'd notice when she came back in. "Be a dear and step closer, I want to see these titles properly."

---

[94] That's Dory with a "Y," not an "I." Not to be confused with Dorian's nickname of "Dori."

"It might confuse them, if you told them." Fletcher put a hand on his Master's lower back. His Master was tired. Best to stay close. "Besides, Odys will eventually sync with Maud and there'll be no more hiding it."

"Exactly. Why not fess up to it now? I don't want them to hate me even more."

"The only reason Maud hasn't told him yet is (likely) because she knows we did the right thing; Odys doesn't want to hate you yet. He's trying to make a way to accept you and what you did. And even so, not even *Maud* can verify if Odys is or is not of the right set of twins, so we might want their forgiveness for nothing." He frowned. "Well, not *nothing*, but at least not *everything*. And can I just say that I don't think it's wise for Mecca to be handling the cat?" He narrowed his eyes at Bulfinch, who was watching with headlight eyes from under the bed.

"At least we don't have to do it. Bulfinch hates us. He's on to us. Besides," Dorian went on. "Mecca could use something other than Q to play with."

"He does play with himself a lot, doesn't he?"

They both sniggered. Dorian said, "We're going to have to teach him a lesson, for what he did last night. I think some of his storage units might need to burn down. The ones in Arkansas, too."

"The film props? That's an assault to history, though! Those things are priceless."

"Perhaps you're right. It wasn't *entirely* his fault I jumped her. Maybe just sell everything in them. At the lowest price. Call [name redacted]'s bar friend." Dorian snapped his fingers. "What's-his-name."

Fletcher nodded. He'd get to it later. "Odd titles, aren't they?" Fletcher asked once their grins had become straight lines again.

"She's well-read. Too well-read, almost."

"It's eerie, Dorian. It's too eerie—even for genetics—that their reading tastes should be—"

"So alike? Yes, I agree. Fate has a way of being obvious, no? I miss reading. Though, it's easier now that you've done—and do—it for me."

Fletcher had a plethora of editions stored up before Dorian got him. "I made you smarter, I did." He tapped his head.

Dorian dusted off a book's cover. "No quicker way to read than to 'download' it from your Automaton."

"I wouldn't say *download*."

"No, I wouldn't; not in public. Ah, *The Wizard of Oz*. Like I said, fate, right? My, my. This is an old copy."

"The American version of *Alice in Wonderland*. Geez, I remember when this first came out. And *Alice*, for that matter."

"And the movies."

"Makes me feel old."

"We *are* old."

Fletcher's ears perked, but his eyes remained focused on what Dorian was "looking" at.

"Did you find anything incriminating?" Odissa asked from the doorway. She'd finally come out. She was clean, done up, dressed.

"For someone who works at a library, shouldn't you believe in borrowing books?" Dorian stated, gesturing with the book to her unmanageable collection.

She glared. "Well, they come in handy when the internet's down."

"I wouldn't unpack, dear." She had opened a suitcase. "Fletcher and I have somewhere to go, and you must *come with*."

"I thought I couldn't leave the apartment?"

"This is standard procedure." Dorian cleared the clot in his throat, hating that he sounded like Bob.

"Will Odys know I'm leaving?"

"He'll know." Eventually.

Panic in her voice, "How long will it take? He'd like to know where I am."

Dorian took out another piece of gum. "Or is it that *you'd* like him to know?" he said, feeding the gum in like a vending machine dollar slot.

"Where are we going?"

"It's a surprise."

"You really want me out of this room, don't you?"

The boys just grinned at her. It made her skin prickle.

"Please, let me call him."

"Please? As if I wouldn't let you?"

"Would you, then?"

"Well, since I have the choice, then, no. Get your coat, Ms. Odelyn. We're going down the yellow brick road." He tossed the *Oz* book on her bed and led her out.

Fletcher tapped his nose at the book as he left. He could *smell* what Vulcan was up to.

Stanza: A triplet of twins.

Mecca had parked the car in a large, empty lot. A few quiet buildings lined it.

"Where are we going?" Odys had said before opening his door

"That pub there," Q had pointed. "But first, that pawn shop, just up the way."

Mecca nodded. "Best in this area. Haven't hit it for a few months now. Mecca needs cash."

"We aren't driving there?" Odys squeaked, in no health condition to walk.

"Walking is safer. We won't have to steal another car after. Mecca has his rules."

"Can't you go there on your own time?"

"And waste gas to drive up there when we're so close?"

"It's not your gas, is it?"

Mecca shrugged. "Mecca is green."

Stealing cars = environmentally friendly.

"Not how that works."

"Stop whining, Mr. Beans!" Mecca shouted downhill to them as Q picked up her pace.

Odys turned to Maud, aghast at his nickname. She cringed. "My translation is because they're associating you with coffee beans. They *were* just in your apartment..."

Odys huffed. "Has no one ever taught him manners?"

"You'd think they'd come preloaded in an Automaton. Wouldn't need to be taught." Maud pushed him into a starting pace to catch up with them.

The pawn shop was, however, not entirely just "up the way." In fact, it was almost five blocks later when they finally reached it.

"Where the hell were they pointing to?" Odys was exasperated. He was jealous of the man relaxing on the metal bench outside the shop—a man very interested in why four youngsters were entering the underground market—er, I mean *pawn* shop.

Q set Mecca on his feet (pretending that he had become too heavy for her). He looked strange on the ground—a baby gazelle taking first steps.

"You sure this is a pawn shop?" Maud asked Q. The sign was written in another language.

"Yes. The owner is Hmong. That's why the sign," Q answered.

Maud explained to Odys, "It doesn't even say 'Pawn Shop' in Hmong! How was I to know?"—as if Odys were judging her foreign language abilities.

"Come on," Mecca ordered. "You both have to come in, too."

Inside, the small shop with garage-sale flair had posters with Asian faces, advertisements in Asian words (both calligraphy and typeface), and heavenly high-pitched music playing overhead. A man came from the back, pushing past the curtain of red wooden beads. He remembered Mecca and Q (who could forget them?). Q began to speak (in what I can tell you is a Hmong dialect), gesturing to Mecca. He retrieved a few objects from his cargo pockets: a golden doorknob (that had once been brass), a golden ring (that had once been plastic), a golden clothes pin (that had once been wood).

The man smiled.

Mecca took the first price he offered, though it wasn't a high number. But what was money to Mecca when he'd gotten these objects for free? At least he hadn't stolen them—never mind, he *might* have. He had to find some way to make it "fun."

Q thanked the man and they left, passing by the man on the outside bench again (he shuffled his papers at them).

Mecca counted out the money. He licked his thumb more than once to help him count. He handed Odys some cash. "Here. Mother wants you to have a safety net."

"What? What for?"

Maud nodded. *Take it, Odys*. He took it.

Mecca tossed Odys the keys on their way back to the pub. "Q will blow up your car if you try to leave before Mother dismisses you," Mecca warned him.

They finally arrived at Splinky's so-called tavern. Odys reached for Maud's hand, feeling sick from all the walking. Too woozy to be apologetic about it.

The pub was a shabby little excuse for a drinking spot but cheery nonetheless.

"Bob knows the owners. Technically helped them start up the place," Q informed them, their tour guide. "The couple was pretty much destitute when she found them. It's only open evenings. We can't go in then when there's people. And when the owners might see us."

She saw Odys's confusion.

"The owners don't know where they got the money from, but Bob earns it back. They think it's an angel. An angel of whiskey!"

"Like hell they do," Maud said. "They probably think it's a drug lord they don't want to piss off, especially since they're doing so well."

Q rambled on, "So they don't call the cops whenever they know she's been in. Funny, isn't it, how near we've always been to you, Odys? Your campus is only twenty miles that way. Granted, we stay in many places. But it's strange you were going to school where we do a lot of our *business*. Vulcan's been playing plot-twister, we're sure." Q stopped outside the door. "Maud must stay out here. With me."

Q handed Mecca to Odys. Take the baby, Odys.

Through the backdoor, Odys and Mecca made their way into the main lounge; complete with table, chairs, and plethora of available alcohol.

"They turned off the power so the cameras go out. That's why the candles," Mecca explained. Enough light seeped through the windows that candles were slightly unnecessary.

Bob was sitting at the table, booted feet crossed and resting atop it. Her fingers comforted a shot-glass, wetted. Her eyes—or eye, rather (the other behind that huge glob of curled bangs)—stared at the table as if it were saying the most frightening things.

Her free hand flicked the antique-looking compact on the table. "They're here, tell her," she ordered it, as if it was some walky-talky or baby monitor.

The antique compact sprang to life, stretching out into a boy figure. The metal rippled and stretched outward, taking its time. Slowly, it formed a place for facial features. For a brief second it reflected Odys's face like a mirror. Then, losing some of its sheen, it became less chrome-like. Anselm sat cross-legged on the table, dense once more, staring at Odys. The table his lotus bloom. He opened his translucent eyes.

Mecca (in his best Irish brogue), "Oy, Bob, pissed yet?" He giggled to himself, proud at his cleverness as he slid down Odys's body and dashed behind the bar.

Bob paid no more mind to them, her duty done. Instead, she poured herself another drink. Downing it, she sucked air through her teeth.

Anselm looked down upon her, his white hair sliding over his shoulder. "Gwen said she is coming. And to be hospitable."

Pouring another drink, Bob chortled. For Bob, that meant not doing a damn thing.

"No need to get up," Mecca stated, as if Bob had offered him a drink. "Mecca can help himself." And help himself he did. He found a paper bag and began filling it like a shopping cart.

"Please," Anselm said to Odys. "Sit down." He gestured to the seat across from Bob. Though Odys would rather have stood than come near Bob and the creepy child-thing, he obeyed. Anselm watched him—continued to stare at him. "Bob?"

"What?" she barked at the Automaton.

Anselm said, "When's Cestus going to arrive?"

"Well, since he can't fucking grow wings and fucking fly, however long it takes to drive here."

"Perhaps you should go outside and wait for him. And leave the bottle behind." He grabbed it before she finished reaching.

Plopping her feet down, she wobbled up. "Thought you'd never let me leave." Was she being held hostage? As she passed by Mecca she pointed at him. "What's my rule?" she barked. He took a few steps back, crooked smile on his lips. He obeyed the five-foot rule (Bob had a measurable circumference).

Mecca waddled his heavy bag beside Odys with a clank. Bottle-toasting Anselm with an unopened whiskey, "Sesshōmaru."[95]

Anselm cut his eyes as Mecca snatched Bob's remaining bottle—no need to waste it.

Anselm leaned forward, elbows on his knees. To Odys, "And how is Maud?"

"Fine."

"He slept with her," Mecca stated. "I have pictures, want to see?"

Odys winced.

"No, that's all right, Mecca." Anselm to Odys, "Willingly?"

"Yep," Mecca answered, trying to stuff a smaller bottle in his coat pocket to make room.

"Let him answer, Mecca," the Automaton scolded, lifting a long-nailed finger. "We need to know his progress. It isn't progress if we do everything for him."

"I did," Odys replied, hoping to abolish this conversation.

---

[95] Name of a white-haired character in the anime and manga *Inuyasha*. This is probably only funny to Mecca. Or our geeky Narrator.

"Well," Anselm said. "You do look better today. Not perfect, but better. Dorian thinks so, too. He sends us updates on you, you know."

"I know."

Mother walked through the storage door—what had she been doing behind a storage door? Odys was surprised to see her in a pantsuit, not some pollera or Puebla dress. It seemed topsy-turvy to even imagine her in something so modernized. Her hair, however, was the one thing modern custom hadn't tamed. It was plaited down in a mass of rolling, twisted, softly-entwined braids over braids—some thick, some thin. Had she not been in her neutral pantsuit, she'd have been a dark lady fortune teller, Anselm her crystal ball.

Her kind eyes smiled as they found Odys. "Hello, Odys. Forgive me, but I was chatting on the phone." With Dorian. With others.

"He slept with Maud," Mecca repeated; he liked telling everyone Odys's business.

"As you've said, Mecca. And do not need to say yet again." She took Bob's seat after rubbing Mecca's bare head. Anselm took himself off the table, to rest an arm on the back of Gwen's chair. He was watching Mecca now, as if Gwen had taken over the responsibility of watching Odys.

"I haven't *not* slept with her," Odys said. "I was too sick before to know I was even doing it."

"Well, I'm glad you did. It's the only reason you're still alive, Odys. Look, your energy wavers as we speak. So pale. Your lips are blue. But it will ameliorate—once you finally decide to sync with her. How's your sister?"

"Fine."

"So I hear." Mother tore her eyes away, something happy in her tone. "I have also heard *other* things recently."

Mecca picked up his sack, taking the hint. "Help me carry this!" He shouted for Q to meet him half way—as if he needed to shout. His bag was about to rip by the time Q took it from him. He still insisted on being held along with their alcohol.

"He never sits still, that one," Gwen mused, staring at the door they'd just slammed. "But then again, I don't blame him. He knows a bit of what I plan to talk about."

Odys wished Anselm would leave, too. It would be easier to go through this without some supernatural creeper distracting him. Anselm moved around his Master and reached for the bottle Mecca had left behind. He swished around the liquid, observing the lively air bubbles. He lifted his hand and a translucent glass formed between his budded fingertips. He poured the contents of the bottle into himself, to drink properly.

"Now, Odys," Mother said. "I know I disturbed your sleep. But I have important news. Something's come up. This isn't how I wanted our relationships to begin, but then again, we both never asked for this in the first place."

Anselm finished his drink, though not all of the contents had been drunk. Instead, the self-formed glass closed its lips inward and absorbed the liquid into his skin. Anselm was merely enjoying the act itself, not the drink. Did Automata even enjoy consuming things like humans did?

When the Automaton reopened his fist, a circular object had replaced the shrinking glass. He let it fall to the ground, attached to thread-like chord—a nerve, a vein, a hair for the yo-yo to coil about. Up and down. Up and down. Up and down.

Up.

And down.

"As you know," Mother went on, as if her Automaton wasn't being a terrible distraction, "Leeland adopted you for a reason. You know we probably know that reason—or we have a guess. I will tell you that guess—after you do something for me first."

At the mention of Leeland's name, Anselm snapped up the yo-yo. His palm crushed it back into himself. The Automaton's fun didn't distract Mother. Anselm did the fidgeting for her. Busying her from crying.

Why isn't she bursting into tears right now like last time? Odys stared at Gwen. Brown eyes meeting brown eyes.

Brown eyes so much like his…

"I met you here because there are other shops around—with employees opening and customers shopping. The people tend to ward off Leeland. He doesn't want to make a scene. Scenes are last resorts for him."

There was a loud boom outside.

"But not a last resort for us, apparently," Mother grimaced—as if the explosion had been louder than expected. Odys looked out the cloudy window. His car had just exploded. Q was putting down her arm just as Maud was bursting in. Bob was pointing, ordering Q to follow "that bitch" Maud. Bob had given the order for Mecca to murder the car.

"What the hell is going on?" Maud shouted at Mother.

Odys stood up, as if he might run out—but he knew better.

Q, Mecca, Bob, and Anselm were all pointing guns at Odys. The message was clear. Maud held up a hand—stay put, Odys.

Mother sat back in her chair. "We can't have you running away after what I'm about to tell you, Odys. Granted, there are other cars out there for the taking, but you've never stolen a car and I think you'll behave once I remind you we have your sister, Odys." She looked at Anselm's gun. "He doesn't have to really form this thing to shoot something at you. But, God, how it reminds us humans what they're capable of, no?" She pursed her lips, to stop them from trembling. She stood back, seeing Maud glow red-hot.

"You kill her, they kill Odissa," Anselm reminded Maud as he reabsorbed his gun. He tilted his head toward Odys. Mother paced to the door, closer to her followers, Anselm her bright shadow.

Anselm's hands were behind his back. Mother, too, kept her appendages close, rubbing her fingers as she fretted. She continued, "I'm surprised how trusting you were of me—to obey me to come here. I am sorry for it. So sorry. Odys, as we speak, Dorian is taking Odissa out of the apartment."

"*Kidnapping* her?" Maud shouted, stepping to the door as if Odys should too.

"DON'T!" Bob shouted, gesturing at Odys with her weapon.

"You can't stop Dorian," Anselm said to Maud. "You know as well as anyone how pointless that thought is. You don't know where they're taking her." He noticed Maud glared at the others—as if they might tell her if she *forced* them to. "And *they* don't know, either."

Odys didn't like how Maud relented. But he heard her whisper, "I could find them if Vulcan let me smell them out."

"But he didn't let you smell *this* out, did he? He didn't warn you we would do this," Anselm reminded her.

Mother didn't like the tension, so she soothed it, "I lied to you yesterday, Odys. Which leads me to my big news. Madus isn't lost." Her lowered lids begged for forgiveness.

Mecca and Q's eyes grew wide, as shocked as Odys. Bob, however, seemed unaffected by the news. It was clear she knew something Mecca didn't.

"I lied because I was testing you."

Mecca and Q's eyes narrowed, contemplating why they, too, had needed to be tested.

"I know where the Automaton is. We just learned of its location—very recently. And you, Odys, will recover it for us."

"He will?" Mecca said. If anyone should be recovering the Automaton it should be someone loyal to Mother. Someone great. Someone like Mecca.

"Mecca," Anselm said tersely, "You know what needs to be done. You may go now. Hurry."

Mecca lowered his gun hesitantly and, crawling up on Q's back (her gun still raised), backed out of the room. They would steal a car in the adjacent lot.

"What's he doing? Where's he going?" Maud demanded, panicked. But she could see it on their faces—she'd been through *this* before—or, she'd seen it done to others. Perhaps she'd even *done* it to others. "I know what this is. We don't need to live like you! Leeland already knows where they live. Why cover their tracks? Why ruin their lives more? You know we have a cat in that apartment!"

"He will save Bulfinch!" Anselm shouted back. "Calm yourself. You know this has to be done, Maud. You're only reacting this way because of *his* foolish denial to how things have to be."

"*What* has to be done?" Odys cried, so confused.

"They're erasing you," Maud said, her voice cracking.

"More like just blowing up your apartment," Bob laughed. "Don't be so damn dramatic, Maud."

"Odys," Mother pleaded. "You know we are good people. Otherwise you would have fought against us by now." She gestured to Maud, who hadn't even bothered to form a threatening gun. "We're your only means of survival now. You depend on us. This *has* to be done." She went over to the bar, where a manila envelope rested. She picked it up, hand wavering for a heartbeat. "You do this for me, and you are one of us. Officially."

She placed the heavy envelope on the table—a parcel she'd prepared ahead of time. She rubbed her hand on her sleeve, as if the package had left residue on her fingers. "That, there, contains a cell phone, cards, fake passport, and instructions." As she stared at the envelope, her face contorted. "I lied to you about Pepin. And now I've stolen your sister to get you to do what I want. You might never trust me again because of this, but I have no choice."

"No choice?" Odys asked, confused.

Her eyes met his for a half-second, as if it hadn't been the truth. For sure, Mother knew there were other, less effective ways her little errand might be done.

"It's the only option, Gwen," Bob assured Mother. "The only way. You don't *need* Odys to trust you."

She shook her head. "He needs someone to trust. I wanted to be that person. I really did. But the stars have aligned too perfectly for me to be kind." She dabbed her cheeks.

"He will learn to trust you, once he realizes *why* you lied. The others understand this. He'll be no different. But, if he is…"

"But I've never lied like this before."

"There's a first for everything. This has to be done, Gwen—for his own good."

Maud realized Bob had put her gun down. Bob was trying to maintain her serious composure. Bob no longer cared about Maud or Odys. Bob's focus was on Mother and her hesitant authority.

Mother straightened, as if Bob had reminded her of her power.

"Odys," Anselm said, trying to stay on target. "Leeland knows where Madus is as well. That is because *one of us* told him."

"Who?" Maud demanded, shocked at Mother's lack of control over the group. Her eyes darted to Bob, as if Bob had already foreshadowed everything leading up to this point—this point about Mother's crumbling empire.

"Who?" Mother said. "Who do you think, Maud? The only one of us you haven't seen yet."

Yes, yes, count on your fingers, Reader. How many Masters and Automata are you aware of? How many have you officially met?[96]

Her voice low, "Wasn't it strange that she wouldn't be here to welcome you after all these years, Maud? It's because she's ashamed of what she's about to do—what she's been planning to do for Leeland."

Maud could barely say it, "*Rosemund?*"

ROSEMUND: Caffar's Master (because you wouldn't know, unless I told you).

---

[96] Part of the answer is that there are nine Automatons: 1) Maud 2) Fletcher 3) Admund 4) Cestus 5) Anslem 6) Quarrel 7) Coraza 8) Madus 9) Caffar.

QUICK BACKSTORY: When she was six years old and trying to figure out how an electrical outlet worked: They didn't make the child-proof crap back then. She slapped on some gloves and went to experiment. Upon realizing that sticking a fork into the socket led to sparks, electrical shock, and the fork melting to the wall (causing more sparks), it was no surprise that her parent's apartment caught fire. Rosemund was very proud of her conclusions—she learned something new every day! Not only did the entire slum-building burn down, but the flames licked off half her skin. From then on, she hated fire. But she loved the power of electricity that could cause it. Rosemund told her parents to blame fire, *not* electricity, for their homelessness. They blamed neither.

QUIRK: If you asked Dorian, he'd say her brain was fried one too many times, making her senses senseless—her common sense too common.

RANDOM FACT GENERATOR: She has red hair, which she thinks is more suitable for a pyromaniac. But she can see where "G-d" might have made the mistake. Needless to say, she can't wait till her head turns white. But with an Automaton, that might be a while. Or never.

Chapter the fifteenth,

A rose is a rose is a rose:

But what is it by any other name?

"But why would Rosemund defect?"—Rosemund was one of them!—"How does *she* know where Madus is?" Maud's questions made Odys swallow hard—how had Mother lost her loyalist?

"Because Pepin sent Madus to her—before he died!" Anselm shouted, as if Maud wasn't paying attention to the real matter: "Who knows or cares *why* he did it—or what he wanted *her* to do with it. Rosemund is willing to give Madus to Leeland—freely. Seems she doesn't want another Master to suffer and eventually surrender their Automaton in death. Seems she thinks Leeland will end up with all the Automatons anyway."

Odys laughed. "And you think I can stop her?" Odys mocked.

"Not stop her, no." Anselm shook his head, his eyes clouded in thought. "But you could change her mind. She freely admitted to us what she was about to do. She knows we see her reasoning, and she is too much one of us to hide the truth. But she would not let *us* explain *our* reasoning on why she shouldn't give up Madus."

"As if it would ever be a good idea to give another Automaton to Leeland?" Maud said. "Oh my god. You don't think it's a bad idea, do you? You stupid woman!"

Anselm's lips twitched. A shadow fell over his inimical face. He took a step forward. Maud did the same, two cast statues confronting each other. The Automata's figures seemed to harden and glimmer like layered armor, their faces blazing with molten anger. Their expressions were emotionless, except for their flickering eyes—radiating—locked in mutual threatening.

"You will lie and tell her Odissa needs the Automaton," Mother said loudly, to calm the entire room.

"Lie? As in Odissa *won't* get to have Madus if I do succeed?" Odys shouted. He was already coming to the conclusion that *if* he ever got his hands on an inanimate Automaton, he would give it to Odissa—whether or not she wanted one.

Anselm noticed Odys's wheels turning. "Even if you do convince Rosemund, she won't be so stupid as to let you near the inanimate Automaton, boy."

"So it's completely out of the question?" Maud asked, studying the envelope with curious eyes.

"I cannot guarantee anything at this time," Mother side-stepped.

"Just like you can't guarantee you know who I really am?" Odys asked. "You *know* who my parents are—maybe *you're* even my mother?"

Bob rolled her eye, not even attempting to hide her huff.

"Any one of us—the Masters—*could* be your parent, yes. Maybe even Mecca. Your accusation is valid only in the light of our youth. But of our history? None of us parented you, Odys. I'm not your mother. Not in that way." She covered her mouth, as if to stop what she was about to say, "Maybe if you synced with Maud—

maybe if you stopped telling her to keep quiet—you would be able to connect the dots—connect as many as *we* have connected. But you haven't earned the right to know our secrets yet—secrets we thought had died along with your poor parents when Leeland killed them."

Odys didn't like the way Maud looked confused—as if Pepin had erased a portion of her memory that caused her current glitch; she was busy connecting dots—but would he ever allow her to show him their completed picture?

Gwen to Odys: "Will you do this for me?"

"What will you do to Odissa if I don't?"

"I rather hoped you wouldn't make us come up with ideas, Odys."

Stanza: I'm getting my planets mixed up with my gods.

Let's fast forward. About an hour later, back at that so-called pawn shop, this will happen:

A woman walked through the door. The bell above her rang.

The fluorescent lights reflected in her black sunglass lenses—lenses mere shades darker than her charcoal-black skin. Like the rainbows in crow feathers or the vibrant shine in oil, the flickering lights played off her form. Had you been there, in that grimy shop, you would have blinked. Several times.

The first round of blinking would settle your eyes—to persuade yourself that her skin was perhaps moist with fresh, glossy sweat or lotion—that her silky makeup gave her that ebon polish. Or that maybe its tone, like a polished mirror, was simply so dark it couldn't help but shine.

The second round of eye-fluttering would be to pretend your eyes hadn't lingered on her physicality. This newcomer was worth staring at.

Her angular features elaborated her gaunt-oval head—a bare head, without hat or hair. Her nose peaked brusquely from her trenchant profile. Her face found its beauty in length rather than the width. The protruding cheekbones of her otherworldly-face framed broad lips. Those broad lips detailed her face with elegance.

Finally, we meet a face of Leeland.

Ignoring the entranced human eyes, she walked to the store corner where the man who'd been pretending to read the newspaper on the bench was now looking at the silver collection. She stood stiff on the tile floor. Her stonewall posture mimicked her down-to-business countenance. Her focus was unbroken. The man at the *Silverware and Etc.* didn't know what to make of her. Her splendor and purpose made him shift in place.

"What happened?" Her voice was like steel—smooth, hard, cold. Her bursting lips formed the words as if they needn't move to articulate the resounding question.

"They were with a boy—a young man. A white young man with brown hair. He played with it a lot, the tips."

Coraza smiled. She knew Odys and Odissa fiddled with their long hair when their fingers had no cigarette to play with. That was one trait that made them identical.

"And a woman—a young girl was with him."

"Yes, but what *happened?*"

"I can't remember all the names. I—I didn't hear them very well." He pretended to be shopping still.

"What did they sell?"

"Odd objects. The little black boy gave the white one money, after."

"Which direction did they go?"

He told her. "I watched the youngest girl use a bomb or something on the car that's still on fire, there," he pointed out the window beside them, where cops and a fire truck were now, around Odys's old car—though their presence hadn't been needed. The fire was dwindling. "I didn't believe my eyes—but I swear it looked like it was coming from her hand, not a bomb. No one else even noticed here—only after the fact." He saw she wasn't interested in his vision. "After that, the people inside the pub started to disperse. Then, the white kid that was with the younger ones—he took a car with that fine lookin' Muslim girl—the young girl. It was over with quickly."

She didn't seem interested in the car fire or anything about Splinky's Tavern. "Did the kids say anything peculiar when they were here?"

"Look, lady, you told me to watch them, not listen. Mind my own business, like. What did you expect, with instructions like what you gave? I have nothing else for you."

Coraza's Nefertiti-profile pulled up in smile. She crossed her long arms and leaned forward. Her beautiful skin hypnotized his eyes. She was letting it shine for that purpose. "Are you so sure you *didn't* hear more?"

She had noticed the ear plug dangling from his pocket—an ear plug to a listening device small as an MP3 player. He likely heard everything, then. Everything. She mentally complimented him on being prepared. He was worth the money. She pulled on the bud. The cord tugged up its device. It was no iPod. "What did you hear?"

"Look, I don't know what this is about, but—but those kids said some really weird shit. I don't know what you think I normally do, but this ain't like no job I've ever done before—kids involved. *Kids*. The fact that they were saying such things out loud—even that little boy—talking about it in *public*. If they're smart enough to thieve then they should be smart enough to not admit their crimes out loud." He laughed, as if so wise and mature about these illegal matters.

Coraza's obsidian lips twitched, almost smiling. "What makes you think they didn't *know* you were listening?"

His eyes widened. This poor man had gotten more than he'd bargained for when he accepted a thousand now, a thousand once the job was done. "Which family *are* you working for again? The Qiblas? Lakotas? I swear, I'm a freelancer, I have no ties."

"Ah, don't be so afraid, Mr. Menes."

He didn't obey. All he could do was be afraid.

"I know the man you spoke with on the phone didn't brief you properly over who you'd be spying on today. Don't worry. Those you spied on won't be interested in what you overheard."

"Funny, if I don't believe you." His voice wavered. When he'd accepted this job, he'd gotten goosebumps. They'd never gone away. There was something strange about *these* people. Something unholy holy. Something not human. He didn't like people who would hunt children—even if they weren't the law-abiding kind. *Maybe they weren't kids at all.*

"I promise you, they won't care what you overheard. In fact, we had hoped they'd use you to deliver a *message* or two to us. Not that they didn't. But we had hoped they'd be more overt. They have been, in the past. They've let our spies hear *things*. You did a fine job, Mr. Menes. At the end of the day, they just needed to know they were being watched. Here, here's your sum." She pulled out an envelope from her tight-jacket pocket. "You may go now, Mr. Menes. Don't worry, we'll not be calling you again, especially since this seems to have disturbed you."

Was his fear so obvious?

She could smell it on him. "We appreciate your work."

Menes took his money. Didn't bother to count it—or to watch Coraza hand yet another envelope to the Hmong man behind the counter—*You didn't see anything.*

Menes couldn't get away fast enough. Too bad that, after Mr. Menes finally made it out alive, he didn't make it *in*:

He opened his car door—but before he'd even slammed it shut—

The bomb went off.

His left leg was still dangling out the door.

Leeland doesn't kill people. They kill themselves. They triggered their own fate.[97]

(Semantics can be so forgiving).

Coraza left when she heard the screaming, dashing behind the building to lay low—inanimately—for a while until this whole thing blew over.

---

[97] This whole "Leeland doesn't kill people" thing made me have a conversation once with our Narrator you may find funny: I said, "He's essentially claiming he's a peanut and everyone has a peanut allergy." Our mute Narrator snorted and typed out, "Put that in a fucking footnote!" So I did.

On concrete as a bent nail—the kind that had been hammered and struck off-aim, the head warped, the point dulled—she could hear her Master's self-comforting thoughts: *Menes chose his fate; he chose to open the car door that third time* [the third time sets it off], *just as he'd chosen his job.*

Stanza: Finding a purpose purposefully.

A bit before Odys had stolen his first car, Odissa had walked through the apartment complex's parking lot, between Fletcher and Dorian. Fletcher led the way. It had just started sprinkling. The cement was spotted. It would stop momentarily.

As they walked through the rows of parked cars, Odissa stopped mid-step. Dorian almost bumped into her (and would have, had Fletcher not turned around). "My car's gone."

"Mecca," Fletcher told Dorian briskly.

"Your brother must have taken your car," Dorian explained, "No need to worry."

He gestured for her to keep moving, putting a hand on her lower back. Though it wasn't a directive push, he kept his fingertips there so he'd not risk running her over her again. He could feel her spine stiffen. He liked the feeling. Better to have her diverted than clear-minded. The last thing they needed was for her to catch every detail.

"Just where did you park?" It was cold; she was already freezing.

"We didn't. The cab's coming to pick us up."

"You called a cab?" She was expecting a cop car—which the lot lacked.

"And there he is. Poor man, he's been driving around since morning when Mother sent for him," Fletcher stated. They had wanted him to be ready for them—in case anything happened.

"Mother?" Odissa asked, confused about their family tree. Were these men brothers now? They looked nothing alike. And they slept naked together!

…But let's not go *there,* Odissa.

"Never mind that," Dorian shushed her.

The cab driver pulled up, some old fellow with a checkered cap. "Been drivin' round for hours," he shouted as his window rolled down. "The lady said to be lookin' for a tall redheaded fellow alongside a man and girl. I'sume that's you? Hope you know how much she said you'd pay. I set the timer, y'know. It's been going since five this morning. Ya'll already have a bill."

"Yes, yes," Dorian assured the driver, wide smile on his face. He opened the door for Odissa. Fletcher went to the other side. "Just be glad we're actually leaving early, mate. Otherwise you'd be bored shitless for another half hour."

Odissa didn't like this. No, not at all. The expression on the cab driver's face told her even *he* was suspicious—he didn't know what he was getting into. His eyes darted between Dorian and Fletcher, then to Odissa as he turned on and off his windshield wiper. She looked away when their eyes met; his seemed concerned for her. This all looked very bad, indeed (ahem). Sex trafficking? Drug trafficking? Mafia escort? All of the above?

Odissa was starting to realize this had *everything* to do with her father.

Fletcher was still in his cop outfit, which made this situation even stranger. Why did a cop need a taxi?

Dorian reached in his coat pocket, pulled out his wallet, leaned over the front seat. "Here. This is for so far—to prove we're honest customers, all right?"

The man's eyes widened. Yeah, yeah. Honest. He took the money. "Still going to the dentist office, am I?"

"Yes," Dorian answered, tapping the seat. "And please, no more saying aloud where we plan on going."

Odissa cut her eyes. Why not? And why on earth the dentist?

The driver was wise, and stayed quiet…all the way to the dentist's.

Odissa's heart fluttered. This was *her* dentist. When they pulled into the parking garage, she could no longer hope otherwise.

As Fletcher unbuckled his seatbelt, she looked to him. Was she getting out too?

"No," Dorian answered, putting a hand on her arm. "You're staying here."

Her skin prickled. Why hadn't Fletcher answered her? Hadn't her eyes asked *him?* How did Dorian know her question?

Fletcher shut the car door. The cab driver's eyes watched this procession in his mirrors. He wouldn't say a word. If you knew little, you'd be blamed for little.

Dorian broke the awkward silence. "Tell me, Odissa, how many cars are on this level?"

What was this? Some poorly-timed version of I-Spy? "Pardon?"

"Count the cars, Odissa." It was gentle command but a command nonetheless. When she didn't obey he reminded her, "Don't make me ask you a third time, Odissa. Don't you want to see your brother again?"

"One, two…five…ten, eleven, fourteen. Yes, Fourteen."

He put his head back. "And how many gold cars are there?"

It was dark in the garage. Not easy to tell. "Four?"

"No, five," the cab driver corrected her, "One just pulled in."

The color of the car didn't actually matter. It was more or less an exercise to get Odissa prepared for the real test.

"Wonderful," Dorian false-complimented. "Now, how many blue?"

"None."

"White?"

"Three?"

"Good." He nodded to himself. Leaning towards her, he whispered, "Now, if anything looks odd to you, I want you to tell me—right? Remember I can't see very well."

Hesitantly, "All right."

"*Does* anything look out of place? Anything?"

She took a moment, trying to find something interesting—something to interrupt the silence. "In the **handicap** parking spot, there's an abandoned **walking cane**."

Dorian suppressed a grin. The real test had begun! "What are the words?"

"Words?" she regurgitated. Her heart was racing. He was starting to scare her.

"The words—anywhere, on anything. What do they say? Read to me, Odissa. Read!"

She doubted he really expected her to go so far as to read car tags. She ran her eyes around the lot. They stumbled upon a commercial vehicle, the kind with crappy advertising pasted on the side. "Professional **Welding** School," she said aloud, "Night classes, call—"

But Dorian cut her off. "That's good. Anything else?"

Odissa huffed. He was being demanding—making the driver nervous. She didn't know if Dorian was serious. Was he mocking her gullibility in some way?

She looked up when something fluttered past. She thought it was a bird, but it turned out to be a flier. "Local **heavy metal** festival—last weekend," she summarized. The winter wind had forced it against a car's tire.

"Splendid. Now, that's all I needed, thank you."

Good seeing-eye dog!

A few minutes later, Fletcher was back in the cab. As Fletcher situated himself, Odissa noticed his eyes checking for everything she had verified to Dorian—the cane, the commercial vehicle advertisement, the already-blown-away flier. He sniffed the air like a hound picking up a scent—the nose knows. "Let's go," he told the cab driver, thump-thumping the seat.

As he was empty handed, Odissa wondered what he'd done back at the dentist office. Surely he hadn't had an appointment. That was too fast.

(NO DUH).

Out of the parking garage, they drove up the street a little ways. Taking a right, they went up a tapering hill and turned into a church parking lot, some hideous white-painted building with "Kirk" in the name. The huge parking lot was vacant—it wasn't a Sunday.

Dorian handed the driver another cash wad. "Out," he ordered Odissa. The driver left them in the lot. "What time is it, Fletcher?" Dorian asked as he strutted to nowhere in particular.

"The perfect time. Not a car in the lot. The maintenance folks don't come in for another hour and a half. We can go in unnoticed. Cestus was right."

"That's right."

They walked through the lot, up the concrete stairs and around to a back door. Fletcher added, "By the way, kudos on your six-year run of no cavities."

He'd said it just so he could see Odissa's eyes widen. He'd snuck in, yes. Whipped the dentistry hard-drive clean, corrupted their networks, grabbed the "Odelyn, Odissa" file from the cabinet, thumbed through it quickly, tossed a few papers in *this* and *that* trashcan.[98]

Mecca and Q would take care of her previous dentist's dental records on their way into town, though most information had been transferred when Odissa had switched dentists.

No dental history means no dental identification.

Before coming up to the church door, Fletcher peaked under the lid of a black trashcan. He pulled out a huge bag stowed away among the trash sacks. "Ah, this is one of Cestus's, I'm positive. I thought Anselm would've done the actual delivery." He shook out the bodybag, sniffing it again. Cestus always found the nicest ones, the kind with the dark black tarp that melted quite well—like rubber.

Odissa's jaw dropped, "What the hell?"

"Don't worry, Ms. Odelyn," Dorian said, pushing her onward. "It's not for you. Well, not for the *real* you, anyways." He didn't lead her to the door, but behind one of the building's modernized buttresses.

"I'll be right back," Fletcher said.

"Make it quick, dear," Dorian said as Fletcher kicked in the door effortlessly. Dorian crossed his arms—*muy impaciente.*

She could hear the alarm sounding. "What the fuck are you guys doing?" Odissa demanded. "The cops will be here any minute—what the hell was that bag for?"

---

[98] I'm not sure why Fletcher didn't also grab Odys's folder. But I do know that if both went missing it might make authorities suspicious. Plus, they are "getting rid" of Odys a different way.

"The *cops* are already here, remember?" Dorian said, grabbing at her arm in case she tried to step away. Odissa saw him flounder for her appendage. His blindness seemed to come in waves. "Don't worry. There's no cameras. Or, there won't be."

"That's not what I—"

"Watch for the cars, Odissa. Watch for them." He pulled her back against the buttress, next to him. When he felt she wouldn't do anything stupid, he loosened his grip.

"There's a funeral tomorrow, you see. The church partners with the memorial service across the street. There was a young girl who was in a car accident a few days ago. She was about your height, yes. Closed casket service. Practically unidentifiable. I'm sure Fletcher can rip her jaw right out"—he pop-clicked his tongue, gesturing—"No teeth, see? We [as in Q] had to go through a lot of obituaries to find one suitable for you. Seems Fate wanted you erased from the mainstream, Odissa. The gods made this work out too perfectly. Well, not for the dead girl, though. But her family'll never know she's been removed. They'll not want to see that body again."

His hand tightened as Odissa tried to step away. Horrified, she prayed—PRAYED—the police would be here quickly—quickly now! She'd scream, thrash, fight. And then, when the cops saw her struggle, she'd tell them what freaks these supposed cops were.

Fletcher came out, the bodybag full and over his shoulder. The corpse weightless—merely a sash. Into the bushes she went, to be picked back up later.

Dorian dragged Odissa back down the concrete steps, her thrashing and reprimands didn't affect him. The alarm was screaming in the background, but they seemed in no hurry to leave.

"Let go of me! Are you fucking insane?"

"Fletcher, handle this, please," Dorian said as they waited for the first cop car to pull into the lot. Fletcher had her hands behind her back before she even knew Dorian had let go. Click, click.

"What the fuck?" she spat, over her shoulder. Where'd he pull those cuffs from? If it hadn't happened behind her back, she would have seen his fingers sprout the shiny metal cop-chains. He held her there, in place; chained to him.

As the second cop car drove up, the first car emptied its officer.

"Hello, officer," Dorian said, raising his hands. "In my coat pocket, you'll find my badge and papers. This is a classified case; please do your homework. This girl here was just trying to hide, that's why the alarm."

Fletcher also let one of his hands leave Odissa's back and flashed them his "badge." Dorian stepped to the side of the cop car, as if he were helping them get at his pocket—hands still up. As a cop came to Fletcher, Fletcher flashed his "badge" again. When the officer reached for it, Fletcher's hand switched to a gun so fast the officer died with that honorable insignia as his last sight.

As Odissa screamed, the second cop went down.

Now, because this had all happened behind her back, she had no (positive) clue what she had just witnessed. The cops had been killed, yes, but how? What had Fletcher shot them with? Fletcher threw her to Dorian, who quickly brought her down to the ground and covered her eyes with the inside of his jacket. She struggled a little, but was also afraid she might lose her life too if she got in the crossfire.

She would not see Fletcher blow up one cop car, enter the remaining one and disable its recording equipment and tracking systems, then go over to the dead officers and take apart their radios and cell phones. When done, he reached inside his "pockets," digging for supplies. Dorian uncovered her face just in time to show Fletcher scattering some money and pill bottles in the corner of the parking lot— right where the pavement met the trees.[99]

They'd think this was a failed drug bust, hopefully. As seen on TV. Kirk on the Pill.

"Get in the car," Dorian ordered Odissa. She was too much in shock to scream again. How had they been able to do this—all of *this*—in under a minute? Why did

---

[99] It's funny to me how Fletcher keeps cash and random drugs stored inside him.

the cops look more burned than shot—their wounds sizzling? She couldn't stop staring.

Fletcher retrieved his dead body from behind the bushes, placed it in the trunk, and crawled into the driver's seat. Dorian accompanied Odissa in the back.

"You killed them," she said eventually. "They did nothing wrong." She realized there were little flicks of blood on her shirt. They were turning brown—they looked more like food stains.

"It was either you or them, Odissa. I happen to care more about you," Dorian smiled. It was no happy sight. "Besides, it will distract from the fact that things went on *inside* that church."

Dorian laid his head back against the seat, slouching downward, as if to sleep. Odissa noticed Fletcher's eyes flickering to her in the mirror, every once in a while.

"I'm hungry, Fletcher," Dorian stated. He took off his blood-splattered coat and looked positively clean.

"I could eat something," his Automaton agreed.

"How do you feel about a pit stop, Odissa? There's bound to be a gas station somewhere by the river."

They were going to the river. To dump the body.

"I'm not hungry," she said as Fletcher turned on the cop lights so they could speed.

"Ah, that's right. You and your brother sustain yourselves on air pollution and soggy dirt—or, excuse me, cigs and coffee. But if you don't mind, we normal people need food."

Yes, normal. Very normal.

Stanza: Snail mail is the best mail.

Odys and Maud were less than five minutes from the apartment, depending on those traffic lights that Odys wasn't paying attention to.

Odys was yet to leave for his Super-Dangerous-(That'sWhyMotherDidn'tWantToDoIt) Mission, though he had every intention on going to Canada (yes, that's where Mother was sending him). But, before he obeyed Mother, there was something he needed to do.

O Canada!

Maud leaned her head upon the cold window, her coppery curls scrunching against the glass. The grey clouds had decided to shake out a little bit of snow. She looked at the car's side mirror, watching as it started to collect like lint along the edge of the road. *The weather's giving us a little bit of everything today—so unpredictable.* The snow would not last long, for the ground was too warm. "She's not going to be there, Odys. They took her. Bulfinch won't be there either."

His hands gripped the steering wheel of his first stolen car. "I just want to see it." He wanted to see what they'd done to his apartment. "I just want to see it."

Maud held her tongue. She knew her Master had to see for himself. Maybe then he would start to believe what she told him. "They've erased you, Odys." She had told him again and again as they had driven.

"In such a short amount of time?"

"Don't underestimate Mecca. He loves to blow things up."

"I could stop him."

"Don't get caught. The cops will be looking for you. Odissa won't be there—"

But he had told her, "I don't care. I'm going to see it."

And they drove by—far enough that the neighbors standing outside of Odys's burnt apartment building couldn't see him but close enough that he could see Mecca had released a very controlled fire where Odys used to live. "Someone could have gotten hurt," Odys mumbled.

"But no one did." She watched the cleanup crew work away. "They don't fake peoples' deaths that often."

"Really? Because they seem really good at it."

"You're dead now, Odys. They've given you a gift, really. It shows they have faith in you."

He scoffed at her forced words.

"You should check your mail," Maud said. "One last time."

"But the people—" Odys said. He studied the firemen cleaning up the area and keeping people calm. "The cameras, too." He pointed at the news crew about to start a second report on "the situation."

But Maud shook her head, telling him to think through what she'd just said. "I'll go. I'll go check your mail." And she was out of the car, running down the sidewalk before Odys could reconsider. He saw her dash around the corner of a building to the mailboxes.

He pulled over to the curb, waiting. But just as he had sighed—telling himself that he should never have driven by here—her door opened again. "You have a letter."

Maud was beaming.

"I do?"

"Your mail runs early," she smiled as she closed her door behind her. "I *knew* this would happen." She smelled the envelope, pushing it to her nose. *The nose knows.* She looked up at him, nodding. "Pepin, Odys!" She pushed it into Odys's hands. "He always knew when to keep in touch."

"And when to vacate." He took the envelope from her. No return address. "Why do I feel like I *knew* this was going to happen?"

She shrugged. "I'm your intuition. And no, I didn't know for sure I'd find this. But we *did* have a suspicion that Pepin knew when to send a letter. Or, *I* had one."

"I don't like that Pepin is still in your head," he frowned.

"Do you *know*, Odys, when's the best time to send a letter?" she mused. "When Mother thinks she's destroyed the address." She gestured to the charred building behind her. "Pepin must have known she'd kick you off the grid."

But he didn't open the letter. He tucked it into his coat and began to drive away.

"But Odys!" Maud scolded. "It's from Pepin. I know it."

"Not here." Odys said. He glared at Maud, wondering why she had been so happy. Was *he* also happy and he just didn't know it?

He tucked away the thought. He had to get out of here.

Maud leaned forward in her seat, inconspicuously shielding any view someone might have of his face.

"It seems too perfect," Odys whispered as they blended back into traffic. "Too coincidental. To be sent a letter!"

*Post*humously.

"You're not going to open it."

He frowned at her. "Of course not. To open it would mean there *are* reasons. I'm not sure I want to know what they are."

I REJECT YOU AND YOUR REASONS, PEPIN J. POUND.

"Don't reject the reasons like you're rejecting me," she said quietly, looking into his purple-mooned eyes. Hers didn't look much better. For every brief moment of relief they exchanged, they took two steps back. They weren't getting anywhere.

"I'm afraid there might be reasons I won't like. Or worse, I just might like them and have to respect the bastard for what he's done."

He turned on his blinker, about to turn right—heading toward their little *mission* Mother had given him—the mission in the manila envelope. The mission Maud would later burn and drop into the bus station's bathroom sink.

Odys's heart was pounding—pounding next to that letter in his coat's breast pocket. Maud could hear it. She could feel it.

"I already don't *like* this situation," Odys continued to justify his actions. "That means I won't *like* his reasons."

"You don't know if it's from him," she said, playing devil's advocate.

"You and I both know it's from him, Maud. It's like—what's the word?" He snapped his fingers, "—*Cryptomnesia*. He made you forget he sent that fucking letter and now you're remembering it." He refused to look at her. "This has all been arranged. My whole fucking *life* has been arranged, Maud. And anything the letter says can't be too helpful, right? He *meant* for me to be clueless. Otherwise Pepin would've told me everything in the first place. This is just to dangle his plan in front of me. To give me hope that this is going somewhere. I'll not be Pepin's puppet on a string. I'll not let him pull those strings only to cut them later. That's what my so-called *father* did—is *doing*. And I'm fucking tired of it."

She looked away from him, knowing he was right. This letter deserved to be rejected with the same neurosis he gave everything else. Rejecting this wasn't out of his character.

But then she realized something.

She suck-clicked her tongue, eyebrows lifting. "But you still *have* a letter, Odys. You have something the others don't."

He glanced at her for a brief second. She was right.

Stanza: God in the machine.

In the crappiest gas/rest station that they could find: Fletcher had popped out *another* cardboard drink holder. He'd already made himself four sugary drinks. He was on his fifth. "Aren't you getting anything?" He asked Odissa. "Don't make us guess what you want."

"Pick out anything. Otherwise I'm going to have to buy one of each," Dorian warned. "You have to tell me what you want."

Odissa couldn't even find the courage to look directly at them. Not after what they'd just done. Keeping her pale face averted, her eyes darted to and fro. She was only being compliant in order to save other poor souls from getting murdered. She felt responsible for what had happened to those cops.

Dorian began to pick up one of everything from the racks. "Just tell me when to stop," he said, trying to get a reaction from her. He was showing off.

The too-young cashier was very interested in Fletcher. She'd actually put down her magazine to stare at him. It wasn't so much *sexual* attraction as it was the self-same curiosity people have when slowing down to glimpse a car wreck.

"No, don't get the chips. Get the pastries!" Fletcher whined, putting a lid on one of his drinks. He licked his fingers clean. He popped open another drink holder.

Fletcher leaned forward to Odissa. "Don't look so glum. We look suspicious." His eyes gestured to the cashier.

Odissa glared at him. "Obviously not suspicious enough," she mumbled. Before leaving the car they'd warned her not to say a word. Now they expected her to play along? Why did they even let her out? To make is seem like they were good guys? What? "Besides, you're doing it just fine on your own. Just look at all this liquid."

Fletcher made the fountain squirt out sweet tea. Tasted it. It needed more sugar. "Get me some packets. No, more." Taking the six sugar packets from her, he ripped them all at once. Pouring, he said, "You should tell him to stop now. He's trying to hold everything."

Dorian was still gathering items.

"Stop, please." Odissa said. Whatever she ate she'd just wash down with a pack of cigarettes. "Dorian, stop it!" Dorian didn't seem to hear her. The gum selection distracted him.

The cashier wasn't sure they were serious when Dorian dumped everything on the counter. "Sweet tooth," he said, proud of his destined diabetes. "Fletcher, dear, cover this and I'll go to the shithouse. Can I have a key, Madame?" He pointed to the restroom keys behind her.

"Do be careful," Fletcher wished, taking out Dorian's wallet. He'd never been in that bathroom before, though he'd been sure to remember where it was when they'd walked in, as well as the rest of the place. He knew when his Master had to piss.

Dorian reached into his jacket pocket. "I'm prepared," he said, taking out his folded white cane. It confused Odissa just a little. Why suddenly so blind?

The poor girl at the register had to ring up each item. Someone new walked in. All they wanted were some cigarettes and lotto ticket, but they had to wait because of Dorian and Fletcher. Fletcher pointed at Odissa, as if to apologize for their wait. "She's hungry."

He paid, making Odissa take the sacks while he carried the drinks.

She couldn't stop herself, "Why didn't we stop at a gas station *after* we dumped the body?" They stood outside in the cold, waiting for Dorian. It had stopped snowing and the sun was actually trying to crawl out from the clouds.

"Why don't you say it a little louder, so everyone can hear?" Fletcher was very hard to talk with. There was something haunting about him, as if multiple beings were peering through those black eyes—more than one agenda. On top of that, his odd attractiveness made him intimidating. Too impossible to be real.

"I could scream, you know. I could have told the girl back there to call the cops and tell them you have a dead body in the trunk."

He set down one of his drink holders and picked out a soda. "Yes, but, you didn't," he explained, the straw between his teeth. "You have to comply, don't you? Don't you want to see your brother again?" He downed the drink. Picked up another.

"You're going to disgorge."

"I don't think so, babe." He sucked it dry. Tossed it in the bin beside him.

"Do you two always work together?"

"Yes." It was one of those automatic answers.

He continued to stare in the direction of the bathroom. He slouched against the building.

"Is that your *natural* hair color?"

"You want to make small talk now? That what this is?"

"You can tell me what's going on. I won't do anything stupid. Not if will hurt my brother."

Fletcher said nothing.

"I've seen worse—worse than what you did, back there. I'm not afraid of you."

"You think we want you to be?"

"Just tell me what's going on!"

"What if our lips are sealed to protect you?"

"That the truth?"

He shrugged. "You're no damsel in distress. That's the truth."

Though she was glad to break stereotypes: "But isn't this so Odys will rescue me—so he'll *do* something for you?"

Fletcher's lips twitched. "You're safer than he is right now, babe. He's the one in distress."

"What's that supposed to mean?"

But the subject was fleeting. Fletcher whipped his head around, panicked expression on his face—as if he'd just seen someone he recognized. But his eyes were too distant to be seeing. "Shut up, be quiet!" The straw poked his face, missing his lips. He watched the far-off bathroom door. "I knew it!" he shouted, ignoring the stares of those trying to enter the store.

"Um, knew what?" Odissa squeaked.

Knew he *smelled* something.

He stretched out a hand and plopped it on her face—a giant sea-star latched to her features. "Didn't I say shut up? I'm listening!" Mumbling, "I have to help him remember—he's letting me listen—he needs me—shut up."

Odissa lurched back.

Fletcher laugh-talked. "Oh-ho! I *knew* I smelled him. I could smell that ashy smoke miles away."

Stanza: The bright bring none.[100]

Dorian had walked around the building, unfolding his stick. He'd effortlessly made the corner, passed the truckers filling up their tanks. When he'd opened the door, however, the mental-images went blank, and the walking stick went down; Fletcher hadn't seen into this room. He put the key in his back pocket, the lanyard-tag dangling out.

A smile had been on his face as he had listened to Fletcher and Odissa chat. Then he remembered he had to pee, and he tapped his way to the urinals.

---

[100] A reference to John Bunyan's Author's Apology in the *Pilgrim's Progress*: "Dark Clouds bring Waters, when the bright bring none."

"Right in front of you, my man," a husky voice directed. Another good guy having a piss.

"Thank you, sir," Dorian said, his stick running into the spare spot.

"Don't 'sir' me, Dorian," the man said. Dorian heard him zip up his pants. "Sir's too informal. I much prefer 'Your Highness' or 'Your Majesty.'"

"Don't be such a queen, *Vulcan*."

VULCAN: Has suddenly taken notice.

DORIAN IS: One of the first in a long line of visits he'll be making.

DORIAN IS: Blind but can still read the signs.

DORIAN IS: About to be tampered with.

Chapter the sixteenth,

Not even:

Uneven?

Dorian tucked his stick under his arm and unzipped. "How did I know you'd be in here?"

"Because I *told* you. Besides. The water closet is where I was raised. Flushed out of Olympus, I was." Or flung out, whichever.

"True, true," Dorian said. He'd been expecting this—Fletcher's nose had been picking up the scent—a scent someone purposefully leaves behind like piss; it wafted through Fletcher's nostrils and into Dorian's brain. *The nose knows.*

Dorian heard Vulcan go over to wash his hands and noted the sinks' location. He could hear one of the god's feet dragging as he made his way—a limp, for sure.

"You do that on purpose, I think. You make your composite selves just as distorted as myth would depict."

Too bad we can't see Vulcan, either. But don't worry; he'll just be different next time anyway. The gods never stay the same. Why would they be so dull?

"Yes, I could fix this lame leg—this lame leg known by all. But it takes more effort than I desire. It's how I was *fashioned*, and it got me where I am. It's one of my *characteristics*. Those aren't overturned overnight. How are you to know it's me, if I don't give you *some* sort of sign?"

"As if other gods can't fake a limp?"

"As if other gods would bother to talk to you."

Dorian chuckled, zipping up. "Dear god, please help me to the sink so that I might gain clean hands." He held up his palms, walking stick still underarm.

"You'll not wash your hands of this yet, Dori."

The god turned the water on and Dorian followed the sound.

"I know you're not on my side of things but…If I ask, will you tell me who they are?"

"What, the twins?"

"Who else?" Dorian answered.

"I can't do everything for you, Dori." He led Dorian's hand to the soap dispenser. "Though I can't keep you from asking."

As Dorian lathered up, he frowned. Quietly, "Who are they, then?"

"They're Odys and Odissa. That's who they are. And that's who *they* think they are."

"Why won't you tell me—for sure?"

"Humans see things they want to see, Dorian. Who am I to tamper with that?"

"I want to see, *period*." Dorian rinsed his hands. He was handed a wad of paper towels.

"Yes, yes. Everybody wants something. I'm glad my job's gotten less demanding, in this modern age. Don't have to tolerate as many prayers. Though, some gods see that as a negative. But I see prayers as giving man false power. If you want to empower a human—to give him real potential—you teach him the Arts. You give him power he can control. Like Alchemy. People've forgotten my hand in Alchemy. Now they always relate me to volcanos and blacksmiths. I'm more." He took the towels from Dorian, to toss them. "Am I not an Arch-chemic, Dori?"

Dorian put his stick down. "I don't see you taking your own advice much, V. Even Automatons have limited knowledge of your so-called Alchemy. But they're good at making gold, I'll give you that. Artisanal junk."

The god chuckled. "I always liked you, Dorian. Every time we speak, you try to press my buttons."

"But you haven't killed me yet." He paused. "Yet you *did* let me gouge out my eyes."

"Like I said, I'm not answering prayers."

"Clearly."

"And don't exaggerate. You didn't *gouge* your eyes out. They're still in there."

"Might as well not be."

He heard the Smithy-god inhale, wanting to change the subject. "Odissa's not like other girls, is she? With her every word, she looks as if she might whimper *and* growl. Much like Wisdom. I tried to fuck Wisdom, once. She didn't appreciate it."[101]

Dorian didn't *appreciate* this conversation.

"But that was a long time ago, and we both aren't what we used to be—she and I. Anyways, you, my Oedipus, will be fucking her soon, your '*Wisdom.*'"

"Cómo?"

"You heard me. I know you're not as deaf as you are blind." That one-liner was getting old. "She's yours, that Odissa. Might as well obey it. Don't avoid the oracle. You can't escape fate, Dori. In fact, be grateful. It's rare humans ever find their truest soul-mate, let alone have them pointed out. Though, this all depends on what you call a 'soul-mate.' There's bound to be different kinds, you know. Well, perhaps you don't."

"And I should just believe your prophecy because?"

"I'm married to the goddess of love, aren't I?"

"Are you? I can never keep up with you lot." He actually knew too much about gods. "I thought that marriage was officially over by now."

---

[101] Most likely a reference to when Hephaestus tried to rape Athena. She escaped him.

"Hey, now, even my hammer is an expression of beating love," the god chuckled. "But yes, a god-marriage isn't easily undone. Our divorces are...messier. Consort, wife, lover. Never mind the definitions of them all. Once the bond is made you're forever associated. But I know where you're coming from—we are a confusing sort. Also, it all depends on what Face of mine you're talking to. Sometimes I love my wife. Sometimes I hate her. Different wife for each Face."[102]

Dorian knew all about Faces.

"As I was saying, my wife-lover-consort—*They*—have investments in my work as well."

"Investments?"

"When I score, she scores. She's taken an interest and has fine-tuned some of my blueprints. I may not like how she went about it, but hey. Happy wife, happy life. That's why you'll fall in love with Odissa. My wife informs me there's no point in Us tweaking Odissa's interests—because she's already *interested*. Besides, Jostaca couldn't escape her role in the prophecy, either."

"I don't like the way you're paralleling this situation to such a *complex*, thank you very much. That story had no happy ending."

"But, geez, it was sure cathartic, wasn't it?"[103]

"I'd rather be purged another way."

"Yes, Dori. I know. But even if the twins are who you think they are, this was always going to happen. Even if I didn't want it to. You see, *all* the gods are suddenly envious of my toys. But I'm willing to share. Dori, the gods are paying attention to me now. Don't disappoint."

"So you thought I was going to fight my fate, did you?"

---

[102] Faces are like forms for gods. Look into Platonics if you want to get all "philosophical." This is a point to be elaborated later. You could even parallel this to the *Hand of God* Maud was talking about earlier, if you feel like it. / On His wife: different versions of the Vulcan/Hephaestus myth list varying wives/consorts. I would argue that for this story you are supposed to assume They are (sometimes) representative of the same being, or He had many "wives." Either way.

[103] He's still talking about *Oedipus Rex*.

"Don't ask questions. Questions only lead to truth. You already have the truth."

"I prefer boys, you know. Though I don't mind making females swoon, I've an image to uphold. I don't think this'll work."

"Yes, but preference doesn't mean always. Like Dionysus, it's time to stop playing dress-up."

"Dionysus? Really? That's the best you could come up with? I prefer to be called, like, oh I don't know, Tiresias or something. You're changing my sexuality."

"You still have a dick you want to keep, though, don't you?"

"I suppose you're right, yeah."

This was a transformation of Woolfian proportions. *And Orlando herself showed no surprise at it,* Dorian thought.[104]

"Dorian, you may be a woman trapped in a man's body, but my wife wants to make you a trapped *lesbian*. Don't worry, though, I tried to stop her. I said to her, 'You're stealing one of the good ones from the gay community. Curse you, Aphrodite!!!' You can't see it, but I'm shaking my fist for you."

Not liking being mocked, "And what did She say to that?"

"She shrugged and said she probably just fulfilled every fag hag's wet dream, so what's one curse among so many devoted? Besides, Odissa'll be better than using Fletcher to masturbate, right?"

"At least I'm not trying to rape a goddess." Vulcan's simmering silence was reaction enough for Dorian. So he moved on. "And what will Odissa think when she finds out I'm under a love spell? It's not very fair to her, is it? It won't be real."

"You and I both know that 'real' is relative. I'm a fucking god, Dorian. I decide what's real."

"You can decide only if the other gods let you. Even if you are a Face of the same Universe, you're nothing without Them. Tell me, V. Do They *all* know what you're up to? Lately Fletcher's nose has been tickling. He smells the Others—and

---

[104] Direct quote from *Orlando*. (Dorian is Orlando in this quote. When Orlando is transformed, he/she doesn't seem bothered by it).

they smell *ashy*. You're cooking something in the oven. And it involves the whole Universe—including Those who aren't willing to let you recast things? Why this sudden interest in your kids?"

"Better that you leave, Dorian. Fletcher's making Odissa nervous. You shouldn't have let him drop into this conversation. Your soul's too curious."

"I wish you'd tell your Wife to be more kind, V. Remember what happened to my last romance? Remember what Leeland did to him? Don't you care?"

"Romance? Please! Dorian, the only person you've ever loved is yourself. Odissa will be a great beard to show otherwise, though. And you'll be hers as well. She needs to get away from her brother. *He* needs to get away from *her*. They've never been apart. This is a lesson I need them to learn. Odys is one of my concerns now."

"So if we all fucked our siblings, you'd care about us?"

"Exactly why I care about you. You really screwed your own sister over, didn't you, Dorian?"

A gruff hand pushed him out of the bathroom.

Stanza: The Yellow Brick Road is symbolic and will only lead to more metaphors.

Odissa remained silent as they drove to the river. She didn't open her mouth. Words couldn't help her.

She'd remained silent when Dorian had come back from the bathroom. She'd remained silent as the two men stuffed their faces with sweets in the cop car. She'd remained silent when they'd arrived at the river front.

"Might I see your purse, Odissa?" Dorian asked, putting out his hand.

"What? Why?" she stammered, thrown off. Her fingers fell from the strand of hair she had been twirling.

"Let me see your purse. Please."

She scooted it to him. She watched as he dove into the bottomless thing. What did his fingers search for? He pulled out her cigarettes. "Here, you need one of these." He retrieved one, as well as her lighter.

With trembling hands, she smoked.

"No need to fret, dear," Dorian said. He turned his face to the window, as if he could see out of it. "We have to do this."

"What—what *exactly* are we doing?" the smoke trailed from her lips brokenly, just like her voice. "Why are you doing this to me?"

"We're saving your life by killing you off."

"Does Odys know this?"

"By now? Probably," he said, taking her wallet out. He'd pass it to Fletcher later, to plant at the "crime scene" they were about to half-ass.

The river was shallow, with little pebble island-patches. They'd been in want of a good rain. Fletcher had opened Dorian's door for him, in case he needed out. The back cop car doors don't open from the inside, you see. There weren't even handles to try.

Fletcher closed the trunk and walked into the wooded thicket, the body bag over his shoulder. A carton of the cop's for-emergencies gasoline swung at his side. They'd filled it before leaving the gas station.

Dorian propped his foot upon the door's bottom frame, resting his arm on his knee. You shall not pass, Odissa. Don't even think about it.

She finished her cigarette. "Can you toss this out, for me?" she asked. "It's my cigarette."

She placed it gently between his willing fingers.

She scolded herself after she passed it to him. She should have used it to burn him, distract him. Maybe she could have squeezed passed him. But she wasn't that creative or courageous.

Not knowing what came over her (but perhaps wanting to distract herself from what Fletcher was doing to the corpse in the woods), "So, are you two, like, together?"

"Together?"

"You and—and Fletcher."

"What makes you think so?"

"Well, I'm not so sure I think it at all, that's why I'm asking," there was a nervous quaver to her voice that tried to pass as wittiness. "Though it's not every day a man sleeps on top of another naked if they're not together."

"Ah, that's right. You did see that, didn't you?" He nodded to himself, but said no more.

"Well?"

"Well what?"

"Are you?"

"Am I what?"

"With him?"

"What would it matter to you?"

She built up all the meanness she could, and stated, "He sure fancied that female cop, last night. Kept staring at her. And the fact that you would fool around on a job—"

"Any other discrepancies in our sexuality you'd like to address?" Dorian said through his undaunted smirk.

"Are you gay or not?"

"I've sucked enough cocks to know it's not a simple yes or no, dear."

"Why's it such a hard question?"

He shrugged. "For a kiss, you can find out."

Her face turned paper-white. Perhaps she'd gone too far. "Excuse me?"

"Was it not a good enough offer? Well then, perhaps I'll make it worth your while." He scratched his chin, considering something outlandish. "How about a ten second head start, out the door? Real-time. For a kiss, we can see how far you get in this cop car when I step out to blindly chase you and *you* step back in to drive away. Notice, Fletcher left the keys."

Her eyes saw them.

"Yes, this is a set-up. You don't know what I'm planning when I give you this option. Will you even be safer in your own hands? Will we do something to your brother if you leave? What? I'll outright admit it. Maybe I've started to feel sorry for you, Odissa. Maybe I want you to get away. But, like my sexuality, you won't know until you kiss me, right?"

No response. Odissa was horrified, frozen like a rabbit.

"Ah, hard to make up your mind, is it? Well, like my head start, my offer also has a ten-second expiration. One. Two. Three…"

Odissa snatched up her purse, scooted closer to him, put a hand on the chain wall blocking the front from the back seat, and paused.

"…Six."

He put his knee and arm higher, blocking her from the open door. She knew he was playing with her, but she was willing to let him believe she was stupid—maybe then they'd relax and slip up. Testing his rules, she began to climb over him.

He grabbed her arm and pulled her back down. He'd not simply let her go. PAY THE TROLL TOLL. He smiled, "Eight."

Sucking in a bracing breath, she forced her face into his. He stopped counting. He lowered his leg as she continued crawl over him in his seat, but he wouldn't release her. She tried to draw her mouth away from the bubble-gum flavored lips, but he dragged her back to him. He didn't fight for dominance—only for her to stay put.

She had half her body out of the car, one foot touched the ground—

With his other hand, he grabbed her neck—she was pushing against him now. He stood up with her when she was finally out of the car, grabbing her other arm—he was doing the kissing now. She dropped her purse as she tried to pull away—she didn't need it anyway.

He closed the car door with his foot gracelessly and led her backwards to the car. She pressed herself against it, to get away from him. He took the sides of her face, as if to kiss her again. But he didn't. He merely held her face before releasing her. He shrugged. "I'd let you fuck me." Before he stepped back, she gave him a good slap, to go along with that kiss. It knocked his glasses off.

"Fucking weirdo!"

Holding his face, eyes closed, he started counting. "One! Two!"

She dashed away and went to the driver's door, slamming it behind her. She started the car—cursing under her breath. She slammed on the gas to get away—but to where? She hadn't planned on getting this far. She thought Dorian would have wrapped up this game by now. But no, she was *winning*.

The tires screeched as the dirt flew up behind her. She was just yards away from the main road before—WAH-WHAM.

Something hit her diagonally—something that had pushed the car's nose into a nearby tree. And that something had been Fletcher.

Not sure if she believed her own eyes, the only thing she could reasonably assume was… She had hit Fletcher.

But how was he alive?!

She crawled out of the crumpled car, panting as heavily as Fletcher. He'd rushed from the woods just to stop her. In the blink of an eye, he had her wrist and was dragging her back to Dorian. Dorian was kicking rocks around with his foot, humming. Very pleased with himself.

Fletcher set the girl down on a camper's log (the area was a favorite public outdoor site). Odissa obeyed, studying Fletcher. She shook from shock, not from the cold. Had she, or had she not, just hit him with a car?

"What the fuck were you thinking?" the Automaton confronted his Master. "You had me run all the goddamn way for this?" He pointed at Odissa.

"Ah! You know very well I was *not* thinking."

"Obviously!"

"Yes, yes, Fletcher. It was certainly spur-of-the-moment, but how are they to find out? Do they even *have* to know that I slipped up accidentally?"

"*Accidentally?*" Fletcher repeated, hands on his non-existent hips. "What're we going to do? What if they ask how she found out about me?"

"Well, look on the bright side. Now she knows, and we don't have to pretend anymore. At least, not as much. But please, continue to scold me. It's helping us work out this scenario."

(It really was, actually. That's why Fletcher was doing it).

"Jesus Christ, Dorian, Mother's going to be pissed. She'll know we did it on purpose. She probably heard the whole thing on your phone!"

"Yes, yes—if she's not busy right now with Mr. Messyhair. *Pero*, even so, you must admit it was pretty cute." He walked over to Odissa, still wide-eyed with shock.

Bending down to her he said, "You won't tell anyone I gave you the idea now, will you? It was all *your* idea, right? You tried to get out when I offended you—nay, *scared* you, if anyone asks. And as I held you back, you assaulted me, you distracted me—with that kiss. That yummy kiss. That clear?"

Odissa didn't know if she nodded or not. She certainly didn't say anything aloud.

"By God, if you want to see your brother again, it should be. Now come here, you're on lock down." He presented his hand—so sweetly Odissa thought him bipolar.

She lurched back from it. "What the fuck are you people? Some type government experiments or something?" Is *that* why they'd been interested in her father's work?

It was now that she noticed Dorian's breath was turning to fog in the cold and Fletcher's wasn't.

"Fletcher, go finish up the job and then see if the car will still run. If not, maybe you can fix it." Dorian put his hands in his jacket pockets, chewing his gum.

"Are you—you some sort of mutant?" She felt so stupid asking it.

Mutant? Superhero? Alien?

Almost any answer would have satisfied, really—anything to make her feel less crazy.

"No," Dorian snorted. "I'm just the love-struck girl who wants to have your children, apparently."

"Stop playing with me. What does my brother have to do with you?"

"The better question is what do *you*—not your brother—have to do with me?" He let that sink in. "Perhaps I don't give a fuck about your brother?"

Dorian barely gave any fucks.

Fletcher eventually pulled up the accordion-nosed car. Only one headlight worked. It blazed through the cloudy day.

Dorian opened the door for her. "I'm going to state it plainly. A god—Vulcan himself—has given you to me. You're mine. That is who you are, Odissa. You read the signs yourself."

…What, was she dealing with two *demigods* now?

"You're mine and I have a mind to make you like it. We're going to be happy together. Now, if you don't mind,"—he gestured to the inside of the crumpled car— "Follow the yellow brick road, my *Dorothy*."

DORIC DIMITRI: Twin of Dorothy (their mother originally spelt it 'Dorothie') Dimitri.

PARENTS: Dory and Dominic (his father spelt it 'Dominick') Dimitri.

HIS MOTHER, DORY: At one time her last name was Dandor (spelt 'Dander' by many a school teacher).

HIS UNCLE WHO DIDN'T KNOW HIS STEP-SISTER HAD RECENTLY GIVEN BIRTH TO TWINS WHEN HE LET LEELAND KILL HER: Dorian Dandor (he spells it no other way).[105]

Chapter the seventeenth,

Wonkier windings:

Just another brick in the road?

Time for some much-needed voiceover in this story:

---

[105] Step-sister. Whew. That's a relief. Was beginning to think our Narrator was completely obsessed with incestuous relationships and that was starting to make me worry…Not that I'm really comfortable with the whole thing, but still.

Dorian just called Odissa "Dorothy," yes. But, despite the fact we're now filming this novel in color, it has little to do with *The Wizard of Oz*...[106]

Stanza: Stockholm Syndrome; this is how it works.

"Don't call her that." Fletcher marched toward his side of the cop car. Fletcher had "pulled" a "gun" out from himself and pointed it at Odissa to coax her back into the car—otherwise she wouldn't have budged. "Don't confuse her more."

He slammed the door behind her and crawled into the driver's seat. He glanced at her once in the mirror.

Odissa didn't have the slightest idea what they were rambling about. Most of all, she didn't care. Goose bumps formed on her arms as she wavered between curiosity and fear about these supernatural *whatevers*.

"Ah, just look at her. Her expression's perfect. This, Fletcher, is the kind of babysitting I enjoy—the kind where you get to be nanny and the boogieman at the same time."

"She looks like she's having a heart attack," Fletcher mumbled.

"That's reality for you. Real as a stroke."

"Tell me what you are," she demanded, pressing herself against the closed car door. "And don't you dare say vampire, or I'll punch you in your face."

God knows she hated tweenage vampire novels, and her life was *not* about to be like that shit.[107]

Fletcher snorted at that one. "Don't expect to *know* what we are even if we do end up telling you. Besides, we're not *really* the same thing anyways." He pointed between himself and his Master.

"Not the same thing?" What the fuck did that mean?

Stanza: But enough of me spraying apprehension in the air…(squirt, squirt).

So, I may have glazed over a few facts previously. Let me mention those "facts" now: Right after Odys and Maud had left the others at the pub way back in chapter

---

[106] Well that wasn't a lot of voiceover…

[107] It's amazing how much vampire culture is showing up in this novel. Please forgive.

fifteen, Maud had ripped open the manila envelope, scanned its contents, and known exactly what to do. Digging in Odys's coat pocket for a lighter, she had explained, "To burn the unimportant contents later."

"What does it say?" he had asked her as they had sped away to his apartment.

Tell him what to do, Maud! Tell him what! Tell him!

"It doesn't matter just now, does it? Because you have a quick plan of your own. You're going to stop by your apartment and see what they've done. You're going to make sure they're not liars. That they mean business. But I tell you, Odys, they do."

"I don't care."

And so they had driven by. And gotten the mail. And then Odys had said, "Now what?" as they had sped away from the scene.

"You already know, Odys," Maud had said as she watched him turn on the blinker one more time. "You've been driving there this entire time."

He had swallowed hard, a panic in him fizzing up as goose bumps on his arms. He had been thinking so much about his sister and his apartment and that stupidfucking letter that he hadn't even realized it. "Then give me all of it." *Give me all you know, Maud. Don't leave me in the dark. Tell me what we're doing.*

In an exchange no words could even describe, his thoughts were imbibed within hers. The anxiety forced their minds to connect. Or, at least, connect more than they ever had before. In a matter of seconds, it was as if he'd read the entire novella-length directives—well, more like a Sparknotes version.

With annotations *a la* Maud.

As Odys had tried not to black out, Maud helped him steer. "Fucking pull over for a second."

"No, I'm fine."

He was not. It felt like someone punched him in the balls.

Maud tucked the two plane tickets and other important papers into her "bra" and started tinkering with the burner phone Mother had also supplied. She pointed to a little square near the battery. "She's listening," she had whispered. And she put the phone back together.

Let her hear, then. Odys had grumbled in his mind.

But Maud put the phone inside herself deeply—to muffle any sound.

They ditched their car outside the airport. They were on the plane to Canada within an hour and a half. He placed Maud in the metal-detector tray with his new cell phone and keys. He retrieved her. "For good luck," he had said to the TSA agent who noticed the strange looking coin. Luckily, they were more concerned with his sweaty sick-face than his oversized pocket change. *What is she, a fucking numismatist?*

Once Odys was seated, buckled in, the plane preparing for takeoff...

The in-flight movie started to play. His mind organized the thoughts Maud had given him. And with those thoughts, he suddenly realized the prominence of what they'd just done—the massive exchange of information overloading his brain. The mere thought gave him a headache.

He reached for the vomit bag, not feeling well as the cabin pressure squeezed him. But he hadn't eaten anything, so there was no point.

"What if the contents of that letter contain something that can stop Rosemund from feeling she needs to turn her back on us?" Maud pressed. She was in his mind. He hit his chest pocket, where she was, grumbling at her to "Shuddup." The person sitting next to him watched him nervously.

He thought back at her (it was a struggle): *"If he was dumb enough to send her Madus, I seriously doubt he planned for the need to stop her from misusing him."*

...

"I can't figure it out, Odys. What would make Rosemund do this? I almost wonder if we're not part of a distraction for something—something else they plan for Rosemund."

"Well, whatever I am, I know I have no choice. As soon as she sees me begging for Madus—the twin for my twin—she's supposed to submit? I doubt her heart's so caring at this point."

"What other angle have they got?"

"For one, why don't they just fucking kill her? Why send me to draw things out? She's broken the rules. They should punish her."

"She hasn't broken the rules."

"She's willing to help Leeland break them."

"You don't know what I know, Odys. Rosemund is good. Too much so to kill her."

He sighed, resting his head back. He dug her out of his pocket and held her for comfort. He was beginning to appreciate her and what she could give. Hell, if she could scan Mother's 20-something pages of a honey-do list (that Anselm had typed out in a matter of minutes) and later store it like some USB port able to jack into his brain, he'd have Maud read the entire internet. He'd be the most fucking intelligent being in the world.

…But what good would any of that knowledge be if he was a nobody—if he was dead to the world and couldn't share it with anyone?

"I don't think I want Odissa to have him, your 'twin'—even if we can collect him." Even if Mother would let Odissa have him.

"You don't mean that. Stop fussing. Odissa will grow old without him. She'll need protection too. She will die before you. You cannot be one. You must be two. Always even—"

"The fact they're holding her as bait means they don't trust me still. I could have done this without ultimatum."

"Could have? Yes. But would have? No."

"They'll never know now, will they?"

"Let's get this over with and then we can decide if we even want Odissa to be a part of this—in that way."

"Yes. Let's just stick to the plan. And if that fails, I've got my letter to tempt them."

Speaking of the plan, Odys kept running it through his mind as if counting:

Land in Canada. Take a cab to the bus station. Take a bus to such-and-such a place, where Rosemund had been tracked. Beg for Madus. Simple.

"What if I fail at this?"

"We'll be fine. She probably doesn't think anyone will come after her. After all, they're sending you—not someone she knows. Then again, if Rosemund's mad enough to do this, I wonder what else she'll do."

"That's not comforting."

"You know what would make you feel better?" Maud asked him. *"If you COMPLETELY synced with me. There is so much you would know—and be able to do—if only you'd—"*

"If it's anything like what I just did with you—you flooding my brain—I don't know if I could handle it."

"It only hurts because you only allowed a slight portion. You can't open the door just a crack and expect the world to fit through."

"I'll take only what I need from you," he said aloud, forgetting himself.

He got a few head turns with that one.

Stanza: More cracks in the foundation.

After a few hours of driving, Fletcher parked the smashed-up cop car in a no-parking fire-lane (it would make it back to its owners more quickly if illegally parked). Dorian woke up from his nap as the car stopped. It was then that Odissa stopped watching him and remembered herself.

Fletcher emerged from his seat, junk food wrappers clinging to him and flying away with the chill wind before he could stuff them back into the car. "Damn static!" he hissed, cursing the dryness of winter. (Static is much worse if you are an Automaton, it is safe to assume).

Opening the car door for his Master and Odissa, Fletcher's eyes scanned the premises. The street lights had just come on—the too-early moon was trying to free herself from the grey clouds and invade what was left of the day. Odissa followed Fletcher's eyes and could tell they were about to walk across the street into a shoddy motel.

Dorian stretched his arms and cracked his back while Fletcher made sure no one was watching.

"This is one of our safe zones," Dorian informed, as if giving her a tour. "We have them all over the country."

There were a total of five cars in the parking lot. The concrete was cracked, and there were several pot holes they had to avoid.

"You own this place?"

"Own?" Dorian repeated, as if that were silly. "This shithole? No. However, we do have room 25B all to ourselves tonight; we always keep it rented."

As Fletcher walked up to the door, he hesitated, wondering if he should do *it* in front of her. "Might as well," Dorian said as Fletcher looked over his shoulder.

Odissa gasped as Fletcher's body mutated. Sinking into himself—through his clothes and into his chest—his hand rummaged as if searching through a deep pocket. He hadn't used the key in quite some time, so he wasn't sure where he had stowed it away. But he was sure it was *somewhere* in his chest—where he didn't need to get at often. Soon enough, he pulled out the hotel keycard.

"I can't do that," Dorian stated, as if explaining the new rules for some board game they were starting to play. Taking her by the arm, "Only Fletcher can. He's the Automaton, *I'm* the human."

Dorian pulled Odissa over the threshold and Fletcher flipped on the light.

"If hungry, please tell," Dorian said. Fletcher put the snack sacks in the fridge. "We can have something brought. Delivery and the like. Anything you please. Aren't you getting hungry?"

Odissa lingered by the door as Dorian closed it behind her, releasing her arm. He made sure to bolt it—no more door problems, please.

Stanza: As one door closes, another is busted open.

Around this time, Bob had found Mecca outside the comic book store. The only reason he'd confessed his location was because she'd wanted him to track Dorian's phone. She could do it herself—through Cestus—if she really cared to. But she'd needed the excuse. "You can do it so much damn faster anyway. You already have it set up and everything."

Mecca had eyed her suspiciously as Q typed away on his laptop. Q had passed Mecca, the large baby, to Cestus. He climbed up Cestus like a tree, to perch on his shoulders. He pulled at Cestus's long mustache like someone holding bike handlebars.

"Veroom!" He made sure everyone acknowledged his joke before settling down. He put his cheek on Cestus's head, resting.

"We were just about to spy on Odys," Q admitted as she clicked *here* and *there*. "I'm glad Mother finally updated us on her plans for him, but geez. She could have done it a lot sooner. It would have made our tapping less slapdash. Could have planned things better."

"You know she couldn't tell you what she was up to. It would have ruined the surprise."

"As if we couldn't play along?" Q said, offended (they were excellent at playing along). "*You* did, didn't you? You played along."

Bob didn't comment.

Q went on clicking and typing, "You want to stick around for the big show? Odys's plane just landed. We have his phone tapped—if Maud hasn't tampered with it. *Will Odys live or die? Find out tonight!*"

"I'm good, thanks."

"But look at this; this is a picture of what we did to his apartment. They'll never figure out what happened." Q gestured to her screen—a picture of Odys's meticulously controlled apartment fire. "The body we planted—"

"Don't want to know," Bob said. She'd had enough of dead bodies for a lifetime. For two lifetimes. "Get back to finding Dorian."

"Why you suspicious of Dorian, Bob?" Mecca asked.

"He's not where he's supposed to be, that's all."

"How do you know he's not? Where's he supposed to be?" Q studied her face as she showed her the screen in Mecca's newly-stolen car.

Bob leaned on the open door, squinting her old eyes. "Certainly not there. Why the hell does he have her in our southeast hotel room?"

"Mother didn't tell him not to," Q shrugged. Why was this important to Bob?

Cestus stuck his finger though Bulfinch's pet crate. The cat rubbed against it, as if he didn't mind him (yet he had put up quite the fight against Q and Mecca). "He just wants out," Cestus said, catching Mecca's jealousy.

"Well, kids," Bob huffed. "Now we know where Dorian's at. If Mother asks, tell her." She turned to leave.

"Why wouldn't she just ask you? You're her hunting dog, Bobmation!"

Cestus put Mecca back in Q's arms. "Stay safe now." He patted Mecca's head.

But the others didn't understand. "Why does this matter, Bob?" Mecca pressed.

"Dorian didn't have to take her that far out." Bob reinforced. "He's putting distance between us. He's planning something. These twins change everything."

"What makes you say that?"

"Someone told me."

"Who?"

"Can't you smell Him on me? Worse than Odys's damn apartment, the ash." She was turning to leave—to go back to her motorcycle.

"He came to you?" Q yelled after them. "What else did He tell you?" She could see it on Bob's passing face that there was more. "Does Mother know He came to you?"

But Bob merely raised her hand in goodbye—didn't even bother to wave it.

"She knows something we don't know," Q said over the motorcycle's roar.

"Why would Vulcan visit her and not us? We're the important ones," Mecca said back.

Bulfinch watched them watching Bob. *No, I'm the important one.*

Stanza: But they soon remembered they could spy on Odys.

Let me fill you in on what you missed while we were observing Bob and Mecca, over there:

The plane landed. Odys (and Maud) took a shuttle and a taxi to Somewhereoranother, Canada. There, they waited for the next bus to take them a few mumble-mumble miles thisaway.

And so they sat and sat and sat at the waiting station in Canada. Maud had purchased the tickets with one of the credit cards left in the envelope (anything to avoid stealing). She even used the sleek smart-phone to text Mother—as the instructions had requested—to give her an update.

"She won't respond, but you can be sure she got it," Maud sighed, putting the phone away.

When they had arrived at the station via taxi, Odys had gone to the restroom and let Maud form up. They'd gotten a few stares when they'd both come out of the men's room. Of course it looked scandalous.

The chairs at the station were shaped like melting half-eggs. Not the most comfortable things to sit in. The place smelled like freshly-poured bleach, but other than that, it was quite respectable. There were twenty or so riders waiting on buses. The room wasn't small, so they didn't have to sit next to anyone. They could whisper quietly in their private row, over the old-school background music…if only that old guy hadn't sat right across from them.

Maud watched with heated curiosity, leaning into Odys. Her hands were like the metal rails leading up outdoor steps, both cold and jolting as they helped you keep your bearings. She had previously assumed a tight pea-jacket to blend in, but was still as cold as her surroundings.

She studied the newcomer, the one sitting too close to them. Odys's eyes flickered once to him, but he was otherwise unconcerned. Sure, this guy had about forty other egg-seats to choose from, but perhaps he just liked this spot. Maud certainly gave it a view.

Odys was more concerned with how *concerned* Maud was. She glared at the older man, the man who had used a cane to aid his slightly unbalanced gait.[108]

It was a fancy cane, at that. The arch ended in flourish-of-a-knob.

Maud's nose itched. Something was in the air. Something like ash.

The man had a short beard that covered his weathered skin. Though his clothes were clean, and he (on first glance) seemed well-groomed, they couldn't help but notice his grimy fingernails, his blistered hands. The man caught her staring out of the corner of his eye and smiled. Almost every tooth was lined in a frame of gold.

Nice grill.

Her eyes started to dance around the room, looking for the signs. The silent big-screen TV behind the man was showing the news. The closed captions read, "Hawaiian volcano shows slight signs of activity."

Some otaku kid sitting next to his mom was wearing a *Fullmetal Alchemist: Brotherhood* t-shirt.

His little brother, who had been blabbering on about Star Trek, mimicked the fanboy's live-long-and-prosper sign.[109]

"No need to look for more goddamn signs, Maud, dear," the man said. He put his bad leg across his knee—the manly sort of leg-cross. "It's me." He tucked his cane into the crevice of the egg-chairs, out of the way.

---

[108] Clue.
[109] So many clues it's now evidence.

Odys's eyes slid to Maud. What'd he miss?

Only the lining up of the Alchemical universe, that's all.

"You could have come sooner, you know," Maud said.

The man rolled his shoulders. "Is that any way to speak to your father?"

"Father," Maud snorted, rolling her eyes. But if so funny, why was she gripping Odys's arm like she might pull him under her protection? And, why was he allowing her?

"I admit it's been a damn-long while. Nevertheless, aren't you going to be a good girl and introduce me to your new Master, goddamnit?"

She scrunched her nose.

"Who is he?" Odys whispered. But he had a feeling he already knew.

"Odys, this is—this is my maker. Vulcan."

Stanza: The Goddamnit Face of Vulcan breaks the Maya.

Odys's spine stiffened, his eyes widening in awe. It was like spider webs had landed upon them, making Odys cringe—no, poor analogy. It was as if ash and soot were falling on them—making Odys dance from their tickling heat.

As if formal introductions were a bother, Vulcan glanced down and brushed forming ash from the fold of his shirt. As he lifted his head, his eyes glowed as if hot coals, flickering between Odys and Maud like sulfur reacting to elements.

"Don't overdo it, V," Maud huffed at his exhibition.

Odys wondered if he should run, because, let's face it, when you look divinity itself in the face you can no longer deny the divine exist.

Odys wanted to deny.

Odys wanted to reject.

Odys wanted to do as Odys does.

"*Maker*, Maud?" Vulcan said, frowning at his shirt, the ashes refused to leave the fabric's fibers. "Though, I suppose the goddamn word got the job done, right? Right. Of course I'm right. I'm a bloody god, for Christ's sake, goddamnit. I'm always right. Now, down to business—I wouldn't be here if it wasn't important. It's not like I can be *entirely* everywhere at once. I'm not the biggest god on the block, you know. That's not to say I didn't plan this goddamn part out, so don't think it sloppy. I do have my reasons.

"Oh, speaking of reasons, there's a process to this." He coughed out a breath like smoke. "I'm supposed to tell you to not be afraid—fear not—and all that jazz, to keep you from running with your tail between your legs. Your goddamn Miranda rights. So, don't be so uptight, son. I'm not here to smite you. That's not my job. Relax a little, goddamnit, you're making a scene. Yeah, I've got dirt on you—but it's not my style to use it.

"Oho, what I know, though! But I'm no Automaton, am I? Nope. You can't keep my mouth shut, can you? Ah, not that I open it much. I'm not fond of playing with men. Or speaking with them. Granted, not many of Us speak anymore, goddamnit. But it's even worse with me. I don't get out much. When I do, I always dress for the part—I can't help myself," he wiggled his dirty, gout-ridden fingers as he gestured to his cane. "It's not because I *have* to, but because, well, I feel the *need* to. It's my signature, certain traits. My Maker's Mark. My trademark. Limp and all, I'm not ashamed of what I am, or what I look like *manifest*. But anyways, I'll say what I've come to say—"

"Verily." Maud got a word in edge-wise!

Something told Odys that Vulcan was a man of many masks. Or various bodies, that is. The fact Maud took her time in recognizing him made him realize this.

Odys tried not to tremble—he wasn't sure what trembling would mean. Would he be trembling out of fear or awe? Or would that be the same thing, really?

Vulcan settled into himself once more, lacing his fingers across his distended belly. "Ah, Maud, dear, you've always had better fashion-sense than me. I don't know where you got it, but you did come out the perfect, hard-boiled vixen. I wonder which Muse inspired me to shape you. Not a one has yet claimed to be your mother.[110]

---

[110] Not to say Maud has a mother. He means solely the inspiration for her.

"Not that I blame them of course, goddamnit. We're all very much concerned with our own fates at the moment, rather than our spawns'. But I'm not like them. I invest in my children's future. Ah, this is fun, making him squirm, Maud. They always squirm at first, don't they? Later, when I'm gone, they wish I was here all the time, to hold their hand. Maud will tell you, Odys—just ask her—won't you, Maud?"

She didn't respond.

"Maud. You hate that name don't you, Odys? It was all the rage in London there for a while, though, wasn't it? I knew it would be, goddamnit. That's why I gave it to her. I knew you'd grow into it someday. Any of you got a light?"

He pulled out a pipe, from a non-existent pocket.

"You don't need a lighter," Maud said. "Besides, you can't smoke in here."

"I can if I want, goddamnit! Besides, it's not like they can see me. Well, they *can*, some of them. But the others won't remember a single aspect of me. Not at all. It's all been arranged." He waved it off as his pipe began to smoke—on its own.

Odys stared at the pipe as if he'd just witnessed a miracle.

"Yes, I'm a god of fire too—not just smiths and limps—because that's what's going on in the back of your mind, right? You're trying to classify me, and modernize me, and pin me down. Howsoever, you shouldn't, goddamnit. Depending on who and what you're talking to, I'm the god of many things. It's not like all gods can't have overlapping areas, goddamnit. We're always changing. That's how things work. Give and take. Everybody—even you, Odelyn—give and take." He pointed to Maud. "Some creations take more than others. Those that take too much will incur quite a bit of debt to society. That's how my first *model* ended up.[111]

"Sure, I'd made Automaton-esque things before. But I went with a new design, that time. And the rough draft—Maud's oldest 'sister,' if you will—was just that. Rough. That one—the Monster, as they call her—I named her Alpha. A good name, though it didn't fit her, really. Not that there's much to goddamn names anyways."

---

[111] He's talking about Alpha, the being he made before the nine Automatons.

He gestured to Maud. "*Maud.* No one's named Maud now. But the name fit once. It had a time and place. Everything has a time and a place, Odys Odelyn."

He tapped his pipe on the side of his seat. "That reminds me of a story, goddamnit. A really good one. I think you'll like it, Odys." He pointed to him with his pipe. "Once upon a time," he mused, staring off into bygone-space, "there were two wind-up toys that needed a good, goddamn winding. The toy maker, you see, usually saw to that sort of thing. And they—the toys—were happy. But one day, they took the key the toy maker used to wind them, so that they could wind themselves. And so the toy maker learned that his toys did not love *him*, but only what he could *give* them. His creations were willing to *steal* from him. His purpose in making the toys in the first place was so that he might be able to give—give all that he had. He wanted to give and to be cheerful in doing so. So he turned the wind-up toys into marionettes. They could keep their precious key, yes, yes. But now there were *strings* attached."

He chuckled at his parable, as if it applied to their situation here and now.

"I can tell you worked hard on that story, so I'll not tell you what a load of shit it is," Maud said.

Odys cringed, appalled she would insult a god like that. But Maud was suddenly much more comfortable around her maker since it didn't seem like he wanted something from them.

"Thank you, I came up with it just now. It's my current philosophy on creations, goddamnit. The puppets will always need *some* strings. That's the point. The hinges, the joints, the bolts that you can't control, however, can't be blamed on the maker when you hand free will over to them. There are bad eggs in every carton, but how's that the goddamn chicken's fault? A scientist does many a failed experiment before coming up with the finished product."

He gestured to Maud. *The finished product.*

"You need not go on," Maud sighed. "We get the point."

"We do?" Odys noticed the clock overhead. They'd have to be leaving soon.

295

"Don't worry," Vulcan assured them. "You'll get there safe and sound. I know how important it is to you that you go. Your sister's fate depends on it. *Or so they say.*"

"So you know what's going on?" Odys asked him.

"Know? Dear boy, why wouldn't I *know?*"

"Will they hurt her if I fail?"

"If you fail, that means you'll be dead. Mother'll have no use for your sister, then, goddamnit. If I were you, I'd be asking about your own life-thread, boy. Rosemund's an insane motherfucker." He laughed. "Well, she'd *like* to be, anyways, goddamnit!"

When Maud frowned he went on (the closest thing to acknowledgment of his inside joke).

"Let me give you an example of what I mean: I was chatting with Rosemund just this morning and we were revisiting her latest accidental explosion. Nearly took out an entire block. Only fourteen were severely injured, thank *me*. They'll be out of hospital in a couple of months. Except one little snot who visited Rome last year with his parents. He took a leak on one of my friend's favorite resting spots. I simply can't forgive that. He won't recover so nicely. He could have held it in."

"You mean you were there, with Rosemund, and you didn't take the extra Automaton away from her? You didn't do anything to stop her?" Odys questioned.

"Whoa, whoa, now. Before you start telling me when to blink, I'll stop you right there. You should be glad you're not worse off now, as is, goddamnit. I could have teleported her ass right in front of you and dealt her the upper hand. Where's the gratitude for that?"

"So you're on Leeland's side, then?" Odys was beginning to lose heart—no, *faith*.

"Hey, what makes you think I pick sides at all, goddamnit? Who says this is even good versus evil, eh?[112] Just take a look at yourself, friend. You're no saint. I mean, have you ever stopped for a minute and asked yourself *why* they're so anti-Leeland? Do they even really hate him? If they wanted to be rid of him, they could have done it a long time ago—even you've thought that.

"You most of all, Odys, know what a sick fuck he is. Hell, Leeland—Augury— virtually *was* your father, just masked. My oh my, what else does Leeland have his hands in?" The god wiggled his fingers. "If he can direct the lives of two twins by extension, who else is under his sway? And riddle me this: they're *just now* finding out about you? Honestly, Pepin had to off himself before they realized you existed— let alone that you're Leeland's Automaton's kids. It makes it seem like they didn't know because they didn't *want* to know. They didn't *want to know* about all the freakish things he's doing—all the freakish things he's done. And why don't they want to know? Well, I think I've said enough—just enough to evade the Higher Up's reprimanding. Thus, before you start making me pick sides, you'd best make sure you're on the right one, bucko."

Odys realized Vulcan had been leaning forward—into them—when the god finally sat back. With a sigh he did away with his pipe; it disappeared into his jacket pocket, still smoking.

"Also, there's a reason I never told them—Mother—you existed, Odys. There are reasons I keep certain secrets. There's a reason I've kept your *father's* secrets. In fact, I particularly like Leeland, the goddamn bastard."

"Why would you keep his secrets?" Odys growled. "You could solve all of this— fix everything! Why don't you?"

"Honestly, can you believe this boy, Maud? Tells me what I should do! These goddamn humans. They can't figure out their own lives, but they can *sure* tell the gods how to act."

---

[112] "...eh?" This is funny because they're in Canada right now. You have permission to laugh (please laugh).

"Maybe if you acted at all…"

Ignoring Maud, his lava-hot eyes flashed to Odys. With his thumb, he gestured in Maud's direction. "You know, I'm surprised you haven't fucked her brains out yet."

The statement was so profanely ribald Odys didn't catch on.

"Ah. Not that you let her use them anyways, her brains. Truthfully, most men would've found it justified ages ago. Even Pepin did, a few times. He made her forget that, though."

"You're lying. Trying to test him."

"He was ashamed. I can't blame him, no. She breaks down even the most chaste. I purposefully designed her as the prettiest of the species, a perfect vessel to tangibly exhibit my flirtatious qualities."

Was this a conversation with Pygmalion or what?

"I put part of myself in her, as all creators do to their best pieces. They're a type of homunculus—a form of me. Maud's the paragon of my—Well, just look at her. She doesn't even have to be *trying*, for her body to *scream* desirability—among other things. Ah, but what can I say? I did it unconsciously."

"Did you make Alpha unconsciously too?" Maud reprimanded him—the one who also made *the mistake*.

"Hubris is never acceptable, boy, even in the guise of your Automaton. Don't think I can't see you in her. I know the means and measures of my creations. You may not have your hand up her ass, but you still make the puppet talk. She's not just a fancy toy. Gods know you lot don't deserve them. But here I am,"—he tapped his chest—"the instruction manual, son. Mark my words: just because you're a rare case, Odys Odelyn, doesn't mean you are special. You goddamn, self-righteous prick. Yes, yes, you haven't fucked her yet. Not all of them do, but you haven't even wanted to look at her from the start. It's your whole *twincest* thing, I guess." He turned to stare out the window.

A cold sleet-spit was pattering.

"If you think about it, it would be an entirely less disturbing relationship than the one with your sister. No offense."

Hostilely: "None taken."

Their bus number was called. Maud forced Odys to stand with her.

"You really should get to know yourself, Odys," Vulcan said as the number was repeated. He looked up at them. "You're even without Odissa now. You're two."

Odys glared at him—almost snarling. "No. I'm odd now. Uneven. Because of you and your games. I'm three." *And I will not forgive you for it.*

"One more thing before you go, dears. I have an announcement to make—a foreshadowing sort-of-thing. It's in my contracts to get the memo out. We're making a comeback, We gods. Can't you see the excitement on my face? I do have a spring in my limp, don't I? My dull complexion is brighter. Exactly, Maud, exactly. I'm finally getting some recognition—a role where I'm on top, goddamnit! You might call it a promotion."

"And?" Maud said, impatient.

"I'm just letting you know there's a big project in the works, and I've been elected as head-honcho. They like my ideas, upstairs," he pointed with a wink, "We've struck gold this time, Maud, baby. Gold."

"We? You mean you're going to involve us?"

Vulcan stood, taking up his cane. "You know, I've noticed a new fad—everyone on earth seems to be 'going green.' Have you noticed? It's a sort of salvaging of the goddamn planet, I guess. I suppose you might say the same for We transcendent beings. Fair warning: the gods are very interested in my resources. We're starting a recycling gig. It's going to make human efforts seem like baby steps."

The end.

No more chitchat.

Now, you might think he would have just disappeared, which would have been the *stylistic* thing to do. Also, it would have allowed them to catch their bus and make it to their destination on time. However, that is *not* how it happened.

Instead of the Smithy-god leaving…

They were the ones who disappeared.

In the blink of an eye, they were standing on a street corner—no wheels-on-the-bus necessary. With a heavy sigh, Maud said, "This is so like him, to be more malicious in play than helpful. He's not always so frank, though." She took in their surroundings, factoring in their exact location like some well-endowed GPS. "He has many Faces. This one wasn't comforting. He was too—too—pleased with himself."

"Yeah. If I'd known he'd do this, we wouldn't have had to buy these *goddamned* tickets."

Stanza: No tickets to paradise.

After they had ditched their car (for it was time to steal a new one), Gwen and Anselm had walked hand in hand down the street, the yellow street lights haloing them here and there as they passed. Anselm kept looking over his shoulder.

Anselm and Gwendolyn made sure to walk very slowly, to take their time. Every few steps they would pause and look around. Or sit on a bench. Or backtrack to look at some peculiar whatnot. They were killing time. Time was all they had left.

Gwen put one of her phones away. "Shall we get some coffee, then, Ansi? We won't be sleeping tonight."

"I'd like to be warmer, yes."

When there: "I'll have a [such and such] with an extra shot of espresso, and…"

Anselm: "The same."

The elderly barista-lady smiled down at him. "A bit young, aren't we, for coffee?" She made small talk as she punched in the buttons. "And so late at night!"

She waited for Gwen to tell him no and to pick something else.

Anselm donned his best shy-baby face and snuggled closer to Gwen.

"Yes, but just this once," Gwen insisted, handing her the cash. She wasn't a bad mother. *Don't tell me how to raise my kid.*

They stood to the side as they waited for their expensive, earth-friendly beverages. Anselm glared at the barista as she made the drinks, but each time she felt his wicked glare and looked up, he'd flash a wide grin to make up for it.

"You two related?" she asked, a sweet chit-chat baby-talk undertone in her high voice. Just being friendly.

"Y-yes," Gwen replied, off guard. She'd been watching the young flirting couple at the corner. Yes, yes. This was her son. Adopted. Whatever. Just make the coffee, if you don't mind.

"The youth are so hip these days. Even your little guy here has the crazy hair. Did your mom put up a fight, for that hair?" She winked at him while snapping on their coffee lids.

"Yes," Gwen said, rolling her eyes as if her son's (clearly bleached-white) hair was some sort of thing she had to put up with. Gwen pretended very well.

An elderly couple walked in. Anselm eyed them—how they acted, how they saw him, how they saw Gwen.

"I'll be with you in a moment," the barista said to them, her countenance suddenly rushed. Handing Gwen their coffee, "Ah, at least it's just hair, right? That's what I told myself when my grandson shaved his head. You'll get through it too, though—us grandmothers have to stick together, right?"

Grandmothers.

Gwen's heart sank.

The lady quickly turned to the new customers, not seeing Gwen's reaction. "Right," Gwen replied, taking the cups. Handing Anselm his, they turned to go. They weren't staying to drink them after all.

As they turned, Anselm flashed his brimstone eyes at the sleepy toddler who had been staring, making it cry from fear. It was enough of a distraction to make everyone forget about the strange old woman with the white-haired youth...

Gwendolyn found a bus-stop bench to sit on. Hands shaking, she gripped her coffee. Anselm put a hand on her knee.

She bit her lip as she straightened her back. "I never thought the day would come when they thought I was your *grandmother*."

People were usually kind enough to assume he was adopted. Even old ladies can adopt, see. People would at least beat around the bush. Even when he adjusted his skin tone and facial features to look more like her, there was still something that people would stare at them for (of course there was); and then they would brush it off as *he's not really hers, that's why I keep staring*. Usually it was so simple for Gwen to avoid the truth.

"This is the south—full of hillbillies, Gwen," Anselm said, standing up and facing her. He set his coffee on the pavement. "They have children when they're fifteen and are grandmothers by thirty. You know that. It was only one person."

"It was only one person when they started thinking I was your *mother*, Ansi. But that number grew."

A winter-chill swept over them, whipping Anselm's hair out from his face like sprouting icicles. His voice sharp and clear, "And so what if that number grows? Do you think numbers matter to me? Will they make me love you any less? *Have* they made me love you less?"

Could Automatons love at all, would be the better question.

Leaning into her, his white hair falling past those child-sized shoulders, he took her delicate chin. He forced her mascara-smudged eyes to look into his polished pools. He shook his head. He could see her thoughts, they were his own. She was thinking about how wonderful it would be if she could never grow old, if he could grow old.

At this rate, when would she become Anselm's great-grandmother? Great-great-grandmother? Was just a matter of time. There was never enough time. Even when you had so much of it.

Mother closed her eyes. "Of course the Fates would make this happen at a time like now. They know my hate for Vulcan and so the Fates provoke me. They mean to make me emotional!" She was angry-crying now. They were usually sadder tears.

"Don't," he ordered her. He looked about before putting his forehead upon hers. "Don't waver now. There'll be plenty of tears when this is all over. We've others to save them for. Come, Gwen," he whispered in her ear, "don't cry for us."

Stanza: Should you make yourself accept yourself?

For a few minutes, Maud and Odys had stood on the street corner, letting Maud take in her surroundings. She paced to and fro, heals clicking on the sidewalk.

"I know where we are," she finally said.

"You do?" Odys asked, surprised. Vulcan had transported them without so much as a commentary on *why* or *where*.

"Yes. This way."

He took her hand, because he was cold. Not that her touch warmed, but it did help him focus. "Where are we going?"

"That's the thing, isn't Odys? You don't know. But you *could*." There was something bitter in her voice. She was panicked—just as much as he.

He was showing up in her.

"This is going to take a lot out of us, for us to find them. And by us, I mean *me*. I might sneeze out, Odys, and then I'll be no help to you. We haven't eaten well in a while—or slept well. If Odissa is depending on us..." She huffed as they walked across the street, her eyes darting here and there, searching for something. "Well, *we* can't even depend on *us*."

When they stepped up on the curb, Odys pulled her back. He was sure the party standing on the deck of that snazzy nightclub thought they were a couple. But at this point he didn't care. He only cared about getting this over. "Do it, then. I mean, *let's* do it."

Maud sighed, impatient. "If you were willing, then it would have happened already. You have to accept the reality of this situation. It's not some switch I can flip. Not when I'm the switch."

He stared at her for a moment. She was no help. Cursing under his breath, he wrenched himself away. A grubby trash bin felt the wrath of his foot. One, two, three, four, five, six times. He didn't know how to let go of his control—after all, that's what he WAS. Control.

Panting a little, he looked back at her—back at *Maud*. Maud, with her cruel stare, a stare he was making her give, *Maud*. Maud, the voice of reason he was finally letting speak, *Maud*. Maud, the thing he wanted most to touch yet recoiled from, *Maud*.

Maud, Maud, Maud.

"Fine," he growled.

He stepped toward her. He was going to do it. He was going to let go.

He came at her, grabbing her up by the arm and dragging her in front of storefront window. Had anyone been watching, they would have thought Maud should look afraid, as if she'd just angered some jealous lover who was about to beat the living shit out of her. But her subtle grin said otherwise.

See, Odys was nothing to fear. Not only because he didn't intend to hurt her, but because he toppled over at her feet. "You really needed that running start huh? You should have seen yourself. You looked ridiculous."

"I know—" he moaned as he fought back his stomach juices.

Looking down at him with a this-was-expected glance, Maud crossed her arms. This could take a second.

Her nose scrunched at him. "Ah, geez, really? But you didn't eat anything! You *never* eat anything! The hell's that coming from?"

Heaving while resting his shaky hands on his shaky knees, Odys held back a second up-chuck. She danced around his slimy vomit with her pretty feet.

"Go on, let it all out." Finally, pity in her voice. She patted his back.

"Holy fuck," he managed to utter through his heaving spasms, as if he'd just run a marathon. His palsied face looked almost as bad as when he'd first touched her. "Holyfuckingshit. I thought this was supposed to make us feel *better*."

He squeezed his eyes shut. His brain threatened to pour out his eyes. The world wouldn't stop spinning.

"Best keep that mouth closed, babe," she said as more came up. "Geez, that slimy shit must be coffee. You'll be okay, just wait for your equilibrium to settle back down." She looked about, making sure no one was offended by his sidewalk decorating.

"Give me your hand, goddamnit," he cursed—not at her, but at the world.

Gathering him up, she leaned him against the store window. She cleaned him up with the cuff of her skin-coat. Then, she leaned into him, tucked her head under his chin. She leaned into him as if finally free, finally free to relax. Unstiffen. No more holding back. She breathed in with him. They flowed as a charged, syncretic unity.

"Gah, it feels better, doesn't it, to get it all *out*—get it all *in*?" She held him up by his coat collar as he started to slip. "Revelation does this to people—unsteadies them."

He still wasn't fond of the scene they were making, but he had never felt more aware of its necessity in his life. He *understood*. He understood what it was to *be* her. He *was* her. And he could no longer be ashamed of it.

He held the back of her head and pressed her to his chest, gasping. His hot breath steamed in the cold air. He could still smell his stomach-juices beside them.

"You now know what I know, Odys Odelyn. We're finally one."

Bleary-eyed, he looked down at her. "We know too much."

Maud laughed, though he hadn't been joking—not really. Her laugh made him smile. To catch your own cleverness!

"I particularly like the part where Pepin made you read every encyclopedia edition at his favorite library. I never have to Google a big word again."

"Yeah, well, the thing about encyclopedias is they become outdated."

"Geez, George," the old lady of an elderly couple said as they walked back into their car. They were just leaving the diner across the street, "Prostitutes everywhere. I told you not to take me here."

Maud flipped them off.

Stanza: As the sun sets, something rises.

"I wasn't aware we weren't going back to the apartment," Odissa finally forced herself to say, though it was a lie. She knew this was a kidnapping (of some sort).

"Don't worry," Fletcher muttered, sitting on the bed—the *one* bed—the *only one bed*, "Bulfinch will be taken care of."

"Taken care of?" she cried.

"He means looked after."

Fletcher chuckled as he found the remote. He'd *meant* to sound menacing. He liked making people fret. That was Dorian in him.

Odissa remembered to exhale. "But I need my things—"

"Believe me, you'll be taken care of too."

"Just to clarify," Odissa swallowed hard, "This *is* a kidnapping, right? I mean, *why* did you have to fake my death? I still don't understand—" As if logic could excuse Dorian for killing two innocent cops.

Dorian waved that off. "If anything, we're protecting you."

"Protecting you from your father's sins."

Odissa sat down in the sole chair. She clutched her purse, her only comfort.

"Oh look, we're scaring her, Fletcher," Dorian reared back.

"What do you mean, my father's sins?"

"Should we tell her, Fletch?"

"Don't ask me, it's not as if I have a say in what we're doing," Fletcher grumbled.

Dorian sighed. "We could, perhaps, let her know she's adopted."

"What?" she gasped.

"Oh, how smooth," Fletcher said, no emotion in his voice.

"I know! Did it on purpose," Dorian grinned, gum flashing. "Odissa, dear, the man you know as your father wasn't your father. In fact, *no es un hombre*—he wasn't even *a man*."

"What was he then? One of *you?*" She pointed gracelessly.

Dorian's lips spread into toothy grin—smacked his gum. "He's what Fletcher is, yes."

"And, for godsake, what *is* he?" She pointed to *it*—Fletcher.

"I already told you. An Automaton. Don't you know the definition of the word? Can't you guess the connotations?"

"An Automaton?" What a ridiculous word. "So, a *toy*? A *robot*?" Somebody bring her a dictionary!

"No, no. Not in a literal sense, girl!" Fletcher said, turning the channel. "Is an Eagle Scout really an eagle? No. It's *titular*. We're really called Guarders."

"Don't confuse her. Words never do you justice anyways."

"Fuck you."

"I stand corrected." Dorian grin-giggled.

"You make that joke a lot, don't you?"

Dorian knelt down beside her. She scooted back, wondering what he might do. He was too smart, too clever.

"Your father was an Automaton controlled by a Master who was human—like me. He's not dead."

Her eyes narrowed in suspicion, brows coming together. "Alive?"

"Fletcher's immortal. He can't die. Neither could your so-called father," Dorian tried to assure her.

"I've seen my birth certificate!" She was starting to panic.

Dorian licked his bottom lip. "Don't kid yourself. You saw what Fletcher did to your car. Automatons aren't human. They can't have children. But they can fake papers."

"Best not to tell her that Odys is now one of you."

"Hush you!" But Dorian had meant him to say it. She could tell by that stupid smile.

"Like you." Odissa reinforced.

"He has an Automaton now, sí."

"But maybe not for long," Fletcher finished.

"Quieres to become un paperclip?" Dorian threatened. He was enjoying his show—his act for her. He liked spilling beans at more than one angle.

"Better twisted metal in your pocket than a humanoid who has to suffer watching you ruin everything Mother's built up. Even Odys would be pissed! Just because Vulcan tells you she's your soulmate in some gross bathroom does *not* mean you should tell her the secrets of our universe. But I congratulate you, my friend, on yet another perfect segue."

"Couldn't have done it without you, dear. Now, Odissa, this is a perfect chance to ask me about Vulcan, since I set it up so nicely. Don't let me down, dear, I worked very hard on it—this build-up."

"Vulcan? As—as in the Greek god?" *You've got to be kidding me.*

"Roman, too, technically," he corrected.

"You're serious?"

"So serious I'm breaking rules for you," Dorian said with half-energy. "Right, Fletcher?" But Fletcher was asleep, smoothly snoring. "That's right."

"Is he all right?"

"Agh, yes, he's fine," Dorian waved a hand. "He's only somewhat narcoleptic. We haven't gotten a good night's sleep in a while. He's not well. At least it's not a sneezing fit." He walked over to his Automaton.

"A fit?"

"Well, it's better than crashing, I mean. He's just bored. He's just about the only Automaton that can do this—go into sleep mode so easily. Vulcan designed him that way. That, or I make the most use of that function." He patted his Automaton like a car. "He knows when he's a third wheel. This is him saving energy. I'm bored with trying to lead you on, you see. This is me telling myself outright and doing something productive."

Like listening to a schizophrenic ramble, she nodded.

"Plus, he's pissed at me. I'm pissed *at myself.* This was probably one of our bigger screw ups, telling you what we are. But we'll suffer the consequences."

Dorian walked over to the smoke alarm on the wall. Taking it down, he removed the battery. "This thing goes off for the slightest bit of smoke. Believe me, I know." Anselm had been in here with his pipe once. The beeping was outrageous. "Now you can smoke carefree, m'dear."

It was like he was *ordering* her to smoke. She complied with his expectations and pulled one out.

Though she wasn't sure this was even real, her hands still shook. She blew out the smoke in shaky puffs, each one a prayer that this was some elaborate joke.

Dorian leaned against the wooden television stand.

Several seconds passed before she realized Dorian wasn't listening to the TV—he was listening to *her.* The equivalent of staring at her. "What?" she demanded, perhaps too rudely.

"I need to use the restroom."

"Um...OK?" Thanks for the update.

"No, you misunderstand. I'm not about to leave you out here, unsupervised, with Fletcher."

"As if you can 'watch' me any better? I'm starting to think that he's your eyes."

"How astute of you. Most don't usually notice it."

"Or could it be you wanted me to notice, like everything else?"

"Oh, that's likely too. But, as I was saying, I'm going to need you to follow me in here, thanks."

"What, to watch you piss?"

"You can close your eyes." What is it with Dorian and the *restroom*? Did he have a weak bladder? "Please don't make me force you. Because I *will* do it. Don't make me wake up Fletcher. He needs his sleep. Think of someone other than yourself."

She understood the need to keep her close. She was, after all, half-considering running away (only half). "I promise I won't try to run. I know what Fletcher can do."

"And I promise I won't do anything to you in the bathroom. Not even to the image of you in my head. But I *will* do something to you *here* if you don't do as I ask." He smiled and presented the bathroom.

She left her purse beside her, taking only her cigarette. Funny, though, when she came in, he told her to shut the door as he set the toilet lid down. "Have a sit."

"I—I thought you had to go?"

"No, I said '*use* the restroom.' The tub is in the restroom, isn't it?"

Technicality.

Dorian hadn't bathed in days (he'd been too busy babysitting).

She took a seat. But she quickly stood back up. "What the hell?"

He had turned off the lights. "Not like I need them anyways. Besides, you don't want to get embarrassed, do you? So please, sit down."

Even though the lights were off, she closed her eyes. Then, crossed her arms, crossed her legs, crossed the fine line between discomfort and comfort zone. She could feel her cigarette's ash fall to her lap. The darkness didn't make this any easier.

A discarded article of clothing brushed against her dangling foot, startling her. The light that streamed under the door showed where it landed. She could hear him take of his glasses, the ear-rests clicked together.

As he ran the water she could hear him fumbling, his hands brushing over the knob and the shower wall. She observed her cigarette's glowing tip. It illuminated her fingers, little else.

"Sorry to put you through this," he added, stepping in—no honesty in his statement.

"I'm sure you are." She watched as her cigarette burned out. Nothing more but a filter left.

"I know I'm being speedy. I guess you could say I'm making up for lost time."

"Do you want me to ask what *that* means, just so you can tell me?"

"I'll go on ahead, thank you. I'm very old, you see. Not as old as Fletcher, who is immortal, but I'm well past my mid-twenties."[113]

"Again, if you say you're a vampire, I'll punch you."

"Didn't I tell you I was human, though?"

"Vampires were humans once, too."

"I get your reasoning, but no. I swear, I won't even say that word." He sank into the tub, the spout-water still spilling. "Fletcher rubs off on me, you see. That's why I'm quasi-immortal."

"Like pixie dust?"

"No, not really."

. . .

"Aren't you going to add to that?"

"Nope."

"Why not? Why are you holding back now? I thought you wanted me to know everything."

"Eventually, yes. But I also want to keep the mystery alive, Odissa. Don't want you to like me just because I've got my hand in divine matters and the like. I also have dashing good looks, money, and excellent taste."

He turned off the water.

She could hear the shallow water rippling off him. She could also tell he'd placed his hand on the side of the tub, his rings clanked against it. Over a minute passed in dead silence. Odissa's butt was getting numb. She had to hunch over on the stiff seat. "How much longer are you going to sit there? Are you even using the soap?"

"I don't know where it is, can't see it."

"Did you even try to find it?"

"Who says I'm taking a bath to wash? Don't some just like to soak?"

"What would you do if I just walked out and sat in the main room?"

---

[113] He's robbing the cradle.

"Probably tackle you. However, I'd be wet. And naked. And I would enjoy it more. I encourage you to do it. It would be fun."

"I'm uncomfortable."

"Well, you asked the question."

"No, I mean, this seat. I need to move. Can I—can I stand?"

"Sure. So long as I don't hear that knob."

"I won't," she said, standing and stretching.

"Of course, you could always sit here, in the tub, with me. Help me find the soap."

"Wow," she said, stretching her legs. "That was the cheesiest of the queso right there."

Dorian chuckled. "Prepare for more, until you use your chip to dip."

She'd taken a few back steps to the door. She remembered her cigarette butt. "I'm going to put my cigarette out in the sink, okay?"—but it had died long ago—"That's what you'll hear."

"I think I can tell what a running faucet sounds like, and all the sounds therein."

"I'm sure," she said, fondling the area. Making sure to knock over the extra complimentary stack of paper cups and—oh, there they were—bath soaps, she slowly turned the faucet knobs…and flicked on the light switch nearby.

She was careful—her hand flat on the wall—to use her other fingers to stifle the noise.

She turned the faucet off, her scared eyes still looking down.

It was when she heard him sink back down—into the clear water—that she looked at him. She'd wanted to see his face. All of it.

His eyes were grey. Grey eyes. Cloudy eyes—once brown, maybe. They were ringed with pink-red scars as if said clouds had eclipsed two burning suns. Those eyes were painfully private, as well as the nothingness they saw. But let's leave these soul-windows, lest they become overwritten.

Suddenly, he shot higher in the tub. "You're clumsy," he stated, letting the drain up, the water swirling downward. "Now we can't use those cups. They're dirty." He rose from the water, as if a four-minute bath were all that was necessary.

Cringing and panicking, she turned from his nakedness to face the door. She realized she had gasped—but quickly turned it into a clearing-of-the-throat. "You just wasted water."

She heard him reach for the towels neatly folded above the toilet "Nah, it wasn't a waste if I got to be naked in front of you."

Her hand reached for the light, but she was afraid he'd hear the click.

"You like baths, Odissa?"

"Sometimes," she said over her shoulder. "But only to relax." She had answered too rapidly. She could hear him getting dressed—putting on the same clothes.

"Ah, same here. I don't find bathing in your own filth to be very clean." He seemed disappointed. Had he really expected something *romantic* to happen?

"Me too." Nervousness radiated within her statement. Her fingers waited for the next time he would speak so she could flip off the light without him hearing. She had to time it right; she could sense he was suspicious.

But a hand reached past her. And turned it off for her.

She had been too caught up to realize he'd stepped so close. She whipped around, willing to push him away, if need be.

"You think I couldn't hear the light's buzzing?"

She heard the I'm-not-so-stupid smile in his voice. She slowly inched backwards to the door. Her heel was upon it.

"For someone so scared, you do very brave things, Odissa. Why were you so curious? You wanted to see me without the glasses? Why didn't you just ask?"

"Who says it was the eyes?"

He leaned forward—a drip from his hair-tips fell on her arm. "When you kissed me, there was fear. Fear that I might do something to you. Not inflict pain or bodily harm or death but something metaphysical. A psychological reaction. But—you liked the kiss, yet you were afraid. Why was that?"

If he could hear the light buzzing, she wondered if she could hear the angry stroke her heart was having. "I don't trust you."

"It was if you expected no less from me; though, that thought wasn't just directed towards *me*, but what I *am* in general. And what am I? A male." He paused, for effect. "Even now, you freeze up. This morning you were sharp and somewhat enjoyed my pestering. Now you're defensive."

"Can—can you blame me?" she struggled to keep up with his smartness. "This morning you hadn't stolen a dead girl's body, killed two cops, or—"

"Taken a bath in front of you?" He laughed. "You're not in control, here—not even a little. You're vulnerable. Why not take control?"

He moved one electric-inch closer, a serene snake that could taste her fear; or, a gardener who wanted a smell so he might recognize the flower.

The doorknob jabbed into her spine, preventing her from becoming one with the wood. As she squirmed forward from the cold knob, it allowed him to brush noses with her.

"What control can I take, when *you* have it?" she snapped at him.

He took a step back. He could feel her relax. In a very *serious* tone (a *grey* sound uncharacteristic of his normal rainbow-vomit), "I think you misunderstand me, Odissa. I'm not in control here."

She saw his outline kneel down, the light from under the door making him clearer. He reached for her pants button.

"What are you doing?" She snapped at him, pushing his hand away.

He did not persist. "This—you and me—certainly isn't how I thought things would play out," He said up to her. "I was just doing a job, but then *you* came into the picture. You have more control than you think. And here I am, losing all of it." He let that settle in.

She tried to turn the knob but he fortified it with his arm.

"Tell me, Odissa, why your brother really hated your father—*still* hates your father."

"Is that why you're making fun of me? You just want to know more about my father?"

"You think I'm making fun of you? Jesus, do I really seem that fake?"

"Yes! You're fucking *gay*. You know so much about me already, Mr. Dorian. What more could I add?"

"That's probably true, but I still want you to *talk* to me."

"You tell *me* more and I'll tell *you* more."

"Ah! Getting to know each other!" He said, popping back up to her level. "Like a first date." His voice was once more the monotonous, spinning disco-ball. He leaned against the sink, making his body a diagonal blockade, the space just tight enough so she couldn't open the door.

"Usually there's no taking baths together on the first date," she mumbled.

"Together? That was in no way *together*. I may have been out of the dating scene for a few decades, but I know the difference. I can show you what *together* is like."

She said nothing.

"Well, I suppose we've done a few things most couples wouldn't *think* of doing on first dates. Chatting in a lightless bathroom one of them."

"I wouldn't know. I've never dated." She had hoped that would stop this conversation's flow—bring his elated tone down a notch. But it didn't. Only made him worse.

"Well, then! We'll have to amend that, my señorita."

She gave a little jolt, his excitement unexpected

"How about tomorrow? We can spend the day together. The whole day."—as if that wasn't the plan already. "Your literal blind date."

"Didn't we already do that?"

"So we'll call it date number two. No matter. Now, I suppose it's bedtime for you? It is for me, since I haven't gotten a proper rest in days. I know you didn't sleep so well last night either. Especially since you were so busy watching me and Fletcher, you little pervert, you. What must you do to get ready?"

"Since I don't have any of my things, I guess I'm *already* ready for bed."

Her main issue was where she was supposed to sleep.

"Ah, me too."

She heard him pick up his glasses. "I'll not wear these then, if I don't have to. You already know what my eyes look like. I'd say the same goes for my pants, but if you wear them so will I. I'm nothing if not fair."

"You do know I wear glasses, technically, right?"

"You can open the door now, if you want."

She did.

"Where did he go?" she asked, looking for Fletcher.

"What do you mean?" Dorian asked, though it wasn't a question at all. "He's right here." Dorian picked him up and pinned him on his unbuttoned shirt collar. "He'll take up less bed-space, this way."

Realizing what he meant, "But—but—but that paperclip isn't even the same *mass* as Fletcher."

"Ah, look at you, trying to bring science into religion." He pulled back the covers.

"Is he your eyes?" Odissa asked. He arranged the pillows more evenly. "Even as a paperclip?"

Dorian plopped himself on the bed and wiggled his toes. "I swear, I needn't tell you anything more, because you'd figure it all out on your own. But yes. He's my eyes—even when his eyes are shut, sometimes. Granted, he still has to be paying *attention*—which is often a challenge for us both."

He sat up, his smile dimming. "The main thing you need to know is that he *is* me. An extension *of* me. Now, enough of this chatter. Bed time." He patted the space beside him.

But he knew it wouldn't be so effortless. That's what made this so enjoyable.

Odissa sat down in the chair—her main method of rebellion.

"You think you're going to sleep there?"

"Give me a blanket."

"No. And, on top of it, I'll turn off the heater and freeze you out. We'll be snuggling in a matter of minutes."

She pulled out another cigarette. "Do it," she said, holding it between her lips.

"I *can* break the chair."

"Do it," dangling her cigarette-arm off the chair and blowing smoke out her mouth's corner.

"And I don't mind the floor either, if you decide to stretch out."

"Then. Do. It."

Dorian's countenance turned somber. With a sigh, he rolled out of bed. Turning the droning television off, he said, "I didn't think I'd have to pull it out, but..." He drew out a tiny little hand gun from his pants. It looked more like a toy than a real weapon. She froze in her chair as he pointed it at her. "Come, Odissa. In the bed." He sloppily gestured with it.

Odissa got over the gun very quickly and suppressed a smile. "You won't shoot me."

"I won't?"

"You just said I was your—your 'soul-mate' less than thirty minutes ago. Now you're willing to kill me?"

"Who said I'd shoot to kill?"

She grew very still.

"After all," Dorian shrugged, "I'm willing to steal dead bodies to make it look like you've died. I'm the one who made Fletcher kill those cops. And, what's more, I clearly have a fucking gun pointed at you. What makes you so sure you know *anything* that I'd do, Odissa?"

"Then do it already."

"I just might." For a few seconds there, he let the silence build up and raised his gun a little higher. "Plus, I'm blind, so I might not *mean* to kill you, but miss my target. Best not to make me so much as *demonstrate* it's loaded. I do, however, know you're somewhere about...*here*." He waved the gun in a circular motion about the vicinity.

"They'll hear you—they'll hear it go off."

"What? The people in the motel? Oh, Odissa, they've heard *many* things before—many of my loud noises, believe me. That's why we pay them so much. Now, in the bed, please."

With his other hand, he presented it.

"I won't."

He half cocked it.

Nothing.

He cocked it all the way.

Nothing.

He raised it higher.

Nothing.

He let gravity take the nose, the trigger guard swinging around his finger. "This, dear Odissa, is a metaphor for my dick." Limp. "And oh, how it goes off for you." He let out a series of *hee, hee, hees*—very pleased with himself.

Her skin prickled when he laughed—his *true* laughter. He was usually so void of true expression and had to pretend normal emotions. She could tell the sound also startled him—felt unnatural to his throat.

He walked over to her, put the gun on the table. "I give you the dick." He scooted it to her. "You're the man now."

She eyed it but knew better. All his talk about being *immortal* had ruined any hope that she could hurt them. His bravery enforced this.

"For Christ's sake, you're full of shit." She jabbed out her cigarette on a complimentary plastic coaster. "I'd crawl into bed just so you'd shut up."

His ears perked. "Really?"

"Yeahno," she spat.

"Fine then, have it for yourself. You win. You've limped the dick." He gestured to his own. "Fletch and I have to keep watch anyway."

"I can't sleep if I know you'll be *watching*."

Dorian's face went uber-stoic once more. "Here." He raised the paperclip up in demonstration and tucked him under her purse on the table. "Now I can't see a thing. I'll trade you places." He pointed at her chair.

She stood up. "Leave the lights on," she commanded just as he reached for the nearby switch. As she took the bed, "So I can see you."

Giving a promissory bow, he lighted the chair, next to the gun.

She faced Dorian. He stared at nothing with his vacant eyes. For a brief moment, she wanted to slap the strange grin off his face—the triumphant grin.

Because of the gauche arrangement, she felt like she was actually lying on the floor, so uncomfortable! She was so uptight she didn't even remove her glasses, though they put pressure on her nose and ears.

Dorian's hair was still damp. He smoothed it back while resting his head. She watched him put his legs on the table. An hour ticked by. He kept his eyes closed, though:

"I know you're not asleep," she said eventually.

He lifted his head. "Look, I promise I won't move from this spot. Please get some sleep, Odissa. Please." He was begging her. "Don't waste a good bed. You might not get one tomorrow."

After a few minutes of silence, she stuck her tongue out at him—waved her arm—gave him the finger. When he didn't react she knew *for sure* he couldn't see her.

Despite her best efforts, she dozed—but was startled awake when Fletcher knocked over her purse as he reformed. The noise didn't disturb Dorian, though, who was just as sleepy as Fletcher. Fletcher, in all his nude glory, sleepwalked onto

Dorian's lap. Dorian shifted his position to prop up Fletcher like a giant baby—as if he knew Fletcher was coming. Together they made a perfect pietà.

Odissa watched with wide eyes. It was in this moment she realized they needed to touch—to be near. *This is what happened last night.*

Fletcher wove his fingers through his Master's hair and nestled in. His toes reached the carpet. Dorian rested his head upon Fletcher's chest as if it were a pillow. Fletcher's leg eventually slid off and exposed his junk to Odissa—rather, what there was of it. She tried not to stare, but failed. He lacked nothing but testicles. He had no use for those. His dick could harden through sheer will.

Something told Odissa that Fletcher's genital situation was a statement on his reproductive ability rather than his gender(?).[114] Her eyes darted to their faces. They looked so uncomfortable it made her feel bad for hogging the bed—but only for a brief moment. Her eyes peeled from them and landed on the far door, trying to avoid any further thoughts about them and their body parts.

As if her eyes had predicted it, the motel door shook.

She gasped, waking the boys. Fletcher's puffy eyes noted hers and he whipped his head in the door's direction. Odissa saw—*saw!*—the bottom of the door lift as if it were a flimsy curtain—just enough for someone to slide a letter under it.

Dorian sighed, knowing what Fletcher and Odissa were seeing. "Put some clothes on, Fletcher." He slapped his Automaton's thigh as Fletcher slid off him. "Don't want to show Odissa the goods just yet."

Odissa was panting—concerned that they were *un*concerned about what they had just seen.

"Speaking of perverts," Fletcher muttered as he approached the letter. He gave a morning stretch as he looked down upon the letter. He sniffed the air before touching it. "You smell that, Dori? That's not Daddy."

"That's his Wife."

---

[114] "Sex" didn't seem the right word, here.

Fletcher ripped open the letter, a small key sliding out. He read the parchment, "'Dear Dorian-Fletcher: My husband has made me aware you're having trouble getting Odissa on your good side. I know what it's like to be trapped in a relationship, but that's no excuse for *her*. Since my husband won't allow me to tweak Odissa's interests as I've done to yours, I hope this helps. Please use this key to go to [Such-and-such a mall] to take her shopping. You girls could use a shopping trip. It's small—no security guards at this hour. You'll find all alarms and cameras disabled. This will get you through the doors. If I'm going to make you want her, I can at least help you get what you want.' Signed 'V.'"—Fletcher looked up—"And that doesn't mean Vulcan."

Odissa drew herself further into the corner. Gods really *were* involved.

Dorian stood up. "Get ready Odissa, we're going shopping."

Fletcher gathered their scattered things (including Odissa's). "I'll go start the car."

"Car? What car?" Odissa said, remembering the cop car. *Surely not that car!*

"Whichever one you like."

"Go on ahead, you two. I've a phone call to make and some shoes to put on." Dorian pushed back his hair.

They left, but Dorian didn't make a phone call. Instead, he just held the phone in his hand. Why was he so hesitant to tell Mother what he was up to?—not that he wanted to hide from her. It was impossible to do that anyway. But for the first time in a long while he wanted privacy.

Stanza: Gods in the machines—plurals.

Fletcher led Odissa out to the parking lot, his hand on the back of her neck. She was too dazed to disagree with its placement.

"Who does he have to call?" she asked—her voice too curious and excited. "Is it about Aphrodite? The gods don't normally poke their noses in your business, do they? That's why he's scared?"

"The gods are the least of his worries. Now, which car shall we take?"

"You mean you were serious?" Odissa stopped her pace.

"If you aren't going to pick, I'll do it for you."

"But why can't we call a cab?"

"Because they don't accept gold, and we haven't much cash on us."

"What?"

He touched her purse and it fell to the ground with a clanking *thud*. "Gold," he repeated himself. "Now tell me which car."

But she simply stared at her golden purse she had struggled to pick up. "All my stuff—"

"Never mind. I like this one," he pointed to the jalopy far from the parking lot lights, "Nice and crappy—and probably doesn't have a car alarm." He circled the car and slipped his mutating fingers down the thin window slot to pop the door open. Opening it for her, "Mademoiselle," he said. She watched as he shifted his attire, putting on his best chauffer suit and cap.

She cautiously curled into the car, eyes wondering if anyone else saw his costume change. It was so dark though even *she* doubted her eyes. "It looks so real, your clothes."

"That's the point," he said, noticing her hand draw back. She had wanted to touch him.

Dorian climbed into the back with Odissa. "Out of all the cars, you picked this one?"

Odissa didn't reply.

Leaning forward to his Automaton. "How's it coming, darling?"

The car started, and Fletcher responded, "Fine, dear, just fine."

WIRED.

"Then let's get going!"

"We're really going shopping because a god told us to?" Fletcher grumbled as he backed out of their spot.

"They have a game plan. And we are the chesspeices."

Fletcher rolled his eyes. "You Masters are His Automatons."

Dorian waved himself off. "Besides, what else is there to do?" To Odissa, "Are you hungry yet? Would you like some coffee, Odissa?"

"I'm fine."

"Indeed you are, but I was asking if you wanted some coffee."

With a mental eye-roll, Odissa turned away from him to stare at the fast-moving night. She could hardly remember her name, let alone keep up with his chattiness. She rested her head on the window.

Driving, driving, driving.

"Is Vulcan going to be at the mall?" She really, really hoped not. Her brain had handled enough for one night. She was in no state to visit a god.

"Why would you think that, Odissa?" Dorian asked.

"Well, did you expect Venus to show up at the hotel?"

"She has a point," Fletcher mumbled.

"No one should ever expect anything from a god."

Stanza: Meanwhile...

Bobmation had sniffed Dorian out. But she wasn't quick enough to catch him.

Bob parked her motorcycle and Cestus squeezed himself out of the sidecar, pulling up faux-goggles that disappeared back into his skull. No one with normal eyes would have noticed the goggles vanish as they passed under the awning.

Ignoring the DO NOT DISTURB sign Fletcher had left behind, Cestus rooted for his own copy of the key card. Bob unzipped her leather jacket upon entering. She placed her helmet on the table as Cestus bolted the door behind them.

"They *were* here," he said, tossing a pillow back on the messy bed. "How did they know we were coming? Wait. You smell that?"

Bob frowned away as she studied the room with her one eye. "Cigarettes."

Cestus snorted at the smell. "Venus. She's been here. She must have warned them we were coming. Didn't Vulcan tell us His plans wouldn't be disrupted? She's helping Him!"

"But why would They think we'd mess up Their plans?"

"We wanted to see Odissa, didn't we? We wanted to see her before things went"—he chose his words carefully—"bad. Maybe They knew we'd spread secrets—secrets They don't want them to know yet. Hell, we already have. We told Mecca about Vulcan."

"But it was the least They could do for us!" Bob huffed. "I only wanted to see her with my own eyes. I promised Him I'd go along with the plan, didn't I? I gave Vulcan my word. I only wanted a *glimpse*. I wanted to know what I'd be dying for." She found her flask as she peaked into the bathroom. She saw Odissa's cigarette butt in the sink and frowned at it. Under her breath, "Dorian and his damn baths!"

"You already know *what* you're dying for, Bob."

"Yes, I know *what*. But poor Gwen will think it's for—for other reasons." She stared at the wall as if reading her thoughts from it. "Not selfish ones. I know more than she does; I know what Vulcan plans to do—what he plans to do with her plans. Vulcan flat out told me, didn't he? The bastard. But I'm not dying for Gwen. I'm dying for myself. But cheers to me if I can help Gwen out while doing it." She raised her flask.

"What if Vulcan's lying? Lying about what Mother's secretly up to? What if He only wants you out of the picture—period."

"Either way, I don't want myself in this goddamned picture. And like you disbelieve Him! You saw Mecca's reaction back at the pub this morning. I'm the only one Gwen had told about the little *Madus* mission—and even then you know she was lying about it to cover something else. She only tells us her plans *after* stage one has begun. I wouldn't know that at all if Vulcan hadn't showed me—proven it to me. And why would Vulcan lie? He's never lied before. If He wants me dead, might as well not fight it. Not as if I could. He at least respects me enough to let me do it on my own terms. Not that natural events could kill me otherwise. He kind of has to respect me, doesn't he? He can't just wave his goddamn arm and BOOM I'm dead.

He's got to play by his own rules. Automata are his rules. He has to show the Others that he's in control. And he fucking is. Nah, I won't fucking fight it."

She opened the mini fridge, delighted when she found they were quite stocked up—not just with Dorian's leftover snacks. The sweets tumbled out as she reached for the mini alcoholic drinks.

"Speaking of not fighting it…" Cestus gestured to the room, the motion hesitant. She looked up at him, her bangs falling back and showing her second eye.

Her brows came together as she studied her Automaton's panicked face. Her voice breaking, "You don't think…"

But no, she *did* think. "The gods did this on purpose. They want me to do it here—now." She stood up. "Why else would They arrange this private room? Vulcan's not going to *give* me a chance to mess this up is he?" She laughed in disbelief.

She found herself sitting on the bed because her legs trembled. Cestus sat beside her. She downed the tiny bottle.

"He could have let me say goodbye to everyone."

"You and I both know you aren't good at goodbyes."

"I'm too much of a coward to say goodbye. That's why I'm about to kill myself, isn't it?" she spat.

She looked up at the ceiling fan above them. Then at the sash on the curtains. These would be useful. She sighed. "My suicide in this room will leave quite the message for Dorian. Vulcan probably means for it to. Death follows in his path." She gestured as if she could see the writing on the wall. She chuckled to herself, witty even on her deathbed.

Cestus took something out of his jacket—out of himself. "But how sad, you won't get to give her the scarf."

"I'm giving her so much more than that." She scoffed, wishing her flask wasn't half empty. Not about to get all sentimental, she swished her drink around. "Text them, then. Tell them what I'm about to do. We don't want a poor little cleaning maid to touch you first."

Stanza: Great expectations…

The mall building was antiquated—filled with dying businesses. Each store had an outside and inside entrance. They waltzed up to the front. Dorian didn't even bother to be subtle with a back door. As they opened the entrance with the key…no alarm went off.

This proved the goddess's narrative.

Dorian walked up to the nearest store. Fletcher used his own "key" to open the trellis-bar gate. Again, no alarms.

"But the camera's—" Odissa started to say as she looked up.

"Have a bit more faith, Odissa," Dorian assured her. "It's not every day a goddess tells you to go shopping. YOUR WILL BE DONE, VENUS!" He shouted it into the building.

"Venus has outdone herself this time," Fletcher mumbled, crossing his arms. "The gods really want you two together. Just have sex already and be done with it."

Odissa glared at him.

They found themselves in a department store—one trying to get rid of unwanted Halloween costumes. ALL COSTUMES ON SALE!

Dorian and Fletcher darted about. "Take anything you might need, Odissa," Dorian said. "A new purse—socks—undies. Here's your chance." He'd already picked up a purse and was stuffing things into it.

Even Fletcher had on a scarf—a scarf he (an Automaton) didn't need.

"Why are we in the costume section, again?" She felt like she was sleepwalking.

"Oh, look. She's so tired she can't remember I've already told her three times. You need something to wear for our date."

"Yes, that. But seriously."

"I *am* serious! This is a very serious occasion, our first real date. I'm thinking something with frills, aren't you, Fletcher?" He gestured to a sloppily-made Victorian dress.

Fletcher shrugged. Dorian spared little energy for him and he was fading fast. "I wish this place had a home interiors department. So that I could find a bed. Don't care if it's the small kind."

"He just doesn't understand, really," Dorian explained to Odissa. "He can wear whatever he wants. It's not often humans get to change their character." (To Dorian, clothes were character). "How about a Marie Antoinette costume?" he said pointing to a far rack. "We'd go out for *cake*."

"I'm not putting these on," Odissa said. She crossed her arms for emphasis.

"At least pick out a hat."

"Can we go if I do? I don't like this, Dorian. What if the cops show up?"

"You're forgetting our last run-in with the cops? Didn't we handle that nicely enough? What do you have to worry about?" He took a bright pink feather boa from Fletcher and draped it around his neck. "Here, if you don't put on these cat ears, I'll dress in drag."

"You say it like a threat—as if I'd care." But she found herself putting them on anyway. *I will not face the fact I want to see him in a dress. No, not today.*

"Good, now we just need to find the matching tail..." he ripped open a nearby package.

"I thought it was just the ears!"

"Oh, com'on—have some fun!" he said as Fletcher plopped a huge leopard-print pimp hat on him. He was starting to look more and more like Elton John.

She grabbed the tail from him to put it on herself. She didn't want him near her ass. "I'd have more fun if I wasn't having a god—as they say—*pimp* me out." She pointed to his hat, for effect.

Dorian giggled.

She picked up a package of feathery fake eyelashes and lost herself in their shimmery glitter—glitter that would probably flake off into her eyes and were too long to wear with glasses. When she put down the box and looked back up at him, Fletcher was gone. "Where'd he go?"

"He's going to keep watch. Just enjoy the date."

"This isn't a date."

"Well, dahling" he said, flipping the dangling boa over his shoulder, "Call it whatever you like."

Stanza: No need for a note when Automata record the whole moment perfectly.

The parking lot lights leaked through the blinds and cast eerie bars on Cestus's profile—as if trapped—trapped in thought—trapped in Bob's thoughts. So Noir.

"It worries me to see you doing the worrying for us."

He walked over and sat next to her on the bed once more, keeping his arms firmly crossed, head low. "They haven't responded to our texts."

"Not as if they don't have a lot on their plate right now," Bob adjusted the "rope" she'd made out of the curtains. She tugged on it to make sure the fan wouldn't come down. "Besides. We've been dramatic before, haven't we? Plus, it will take them a little while to figure out where we are."

Cestus said nothing.

"Vulcan approved this. He said he'd make use of my death. He *assured* us." Vulcan had, indeed, come to them. As a dwarf, small as Ptah, he had made himself known at the bar of Bob's choosing—shared a drink with her. "He gave us peace about it. Accept the peace, Cest. What else can we do? We're here—in this empty room—everything's been pre-programmed to result in this exact moment. I'm done questioning it."

"He knew we would do it anyway. With or without his divine blessing." Cestus rubbed his eyes with his huge fingers. "Eventually."

She ignored his comment. She sighed and her leather-covered body creaked. "You know, I really liked that hot cocoa you made, before we left this morning. Would have been a good recipe to take to the cabin."

"Finally perfected it, yeah. But you poured enough vodka in it to inebriate a horse."

"Well, I promise you, after tonight, I'll never drink again!" she raised her flask in the air in toast. Her leather coat sleeve pulled with the action. It showed her wrist spots. She downed the last of her drink—it was all gone.

"That's some promise. Too easy to keep."

An unnatural smile spread across Bob's face, the irony conflicting her. "I'll stop trying to pump myself up."

"We were never the funny ones anyway."

"I guess I should be more prepared for this," Bob said. She screwed the cap back on her flask and tossed it on the floor. "Jesus Christ, I thought I was. No, I *am*. I've got nothing left. I'm just anxious about how much this will hurt. It's not fair—how long it'll take. I mean, Pepin used a real gun. And just look at the mess he made. I can't imagine what an Automaton's handgun would do. No, this is the cleanest way."

She eventually stepped up on the chair and put the noose around her neck. She reached out to Cestus, in the last minute. "I want you to know, Cestus, that you've done my soul wonders."

He kicked the chair out from under her. Her force pulled the fan, cracking the ceiling and exposing wires like an uprooted tree. He waited inanimately for her to struggle to death—though it wasn't much of a struggle. Not when you're willing to go.

Her last thoughts to Cestus—the last words she inscribed upon him—were meant for his new taker: *Promise me you won't erase the memories I gave him. You can have him, but just let me live on through him.*

And just like that, there was no more Bob.

Stanza: (Nobody kills Bob until she says so).

It was exactly one hour later that the bolted motel room door cracked open—prying the bolt right off. The newcomer cast shadows over Bob's dangling body. His shadow reached up like tentacles—snatching, grabbing, smothering. Of course you can't see his face. Not at first. So, let me tell you who it is:

Admund—Automaton of Leeland—finally showed up. Leeland himself was too busy driving (no, I'll not tell you to where). Admund was closest at the time.

Bob had expected one of Leeland's faces to come, just as Vulcan said he would. This was all part of His plan. Bob had surrendered to it.

As he drove, Leeland's lips moved; and, many miles away, so did Admund's. Their speech so synchronized:

"What made you do it?" Admund said up to her, he stroked his beard in Leeland's churning thought. "And with such timing, too. How did you know this would help so much? What will your Mother say?"

But Admund could smell it in the air—the reason Bob knew. So many smells! "The gods told you what we are up to?" He looked around the room, turning his dignified head. Leeland watched and spoke through him, "You wanted to finally help me? Or is it because you know I'm finally catching Gwen's attention? Helping me is helping Gwen. Yes, yes. You knew something." He shook his finger at her, then stuffed his hands in his "pockets."

He bit his lip.

He could not know that Vulcan had told her (in slight detail) He would make use of *all* their plans—including Leeland's. But only enough to get her to submit to His will (for a human could never understand, without getting a little upset, that the gods could never really please them all).

He sat on the corner of the bed, watching the still-Cestus. "In this wake, I will confess that letting your husband die was one of the hardest things I ever did. Your spots as well made me feel so cruel—crueler than when I forced Dorian to take out his own eyes. You were always so much *harder* to disturb, Robyn. But how can a father instruct without a rod? Fathers cannot be gentle. Your Mother is finally learning this as well."

Admund took a plastic bag out from himself and put his hand inside. Through the plastic, he picked up Cestus—for later usage. He zipped the bag and folded the lips over—tucked it away inside his Automaton body. Never touching it.

He dug Bob's cell phone out of her pocket and read her messages. He deleted the texts to his Master. The others could never know the conversation. But he left the phone so they could later track it back to this room...

He was about to leave, but had one last confession stored inside him. "Since I have you here, all to myself, I might as well say something that has always weighed on me, Robyn." He wanted to push back that veil of hair in front of her eye and tuck it behind her ear—to make her like she used to be. But he didn't. He could only touch her foot for one second.

He put a hand on his chest, to steady himself. "I want you to know I wasn't playing favorites when I didn't stop you from killing your husband and yet saved Dorian's niece and nephew. You both selfishly let your loved ones die to keep your Automata. Granted, Dorian didn't know his step-sister had recently given birth. So tragic of them, that they had wanted to surprise him with the news. But that's the cost when you choose an Automaton. You lose touch with your past life and are constantly surprised it goes on without you. That's what makes Automata so vile."

He waved his hand. "But you know that story well." And his Master hated to relive it—relive that day Admund had "shared" a taxi with Mr. and Mrs. Dimitri and their new twins.

"Dorian didn't know—not for sure—what he was letting die. But you did, Robyn. You knew who you were giving up for Cestus. But I want you to know I only saved the twins because I saw a way to get at you all. And so far, the twins have been the perfect bridge to you, haven't they? They *would* have been perfect, anyway, if things—" He shook off the thought. "No matter. I'm nothing if not adaptable. Hell, I have more than one body—I can fit into any situation."

331

He pulled at the sides of his face and forced a heavy chuckle, jutting out his chin in thought for his Master. "No, Robyn. I wasn't playing favorites. In fact, I really only wanted to save one of them—one of the twins." He scratched his nose and sniffed. Venus's perfume clogged his large nostrils. "I only wanted Odissa. But you likely knew I wanted her to have a child—to make me (or Admund, really) a 'grandfather' and therefore give you lot more reasons to *reconsider* your existence. It would have made all this,"—he gestured to their inherent situation—"so much easier."

He sighed. "Would have given me more to work with. I'm barely scraping by as it is. I could have convinced you all so *quickly*, with her children involved—you and Gwen hate to see children suffer, especially. But maybe my children are why you've done this? Do you feel guilty after all these years, finally?"

He shook his head, as if that didn't make sense.

"Speaking of guilt," he sighed. "Had I known at the time how infertile Odissa would be, well…" He put up his hands. "No, I still would have saved her. There was always the possibility I could have fixed her.[115] She's still paying off, despite it. Though I saw a use for her, I knew—no, *understood*—that she would need leverage to be controlled, at least until she was grown. See, I knew leverage needs leverage sometimes. And her *leverage* turned out to be more useful than I first imagined. He's kept her out of my everyday affairs in his obsessive attempts to avoid me. That's the only reason I saved and kept *Odys*."[116]

ADMUND: The undead father.

HIS MASTER: Didn't look at all like the twins.

THE PERSONA ODI ODELYN: Left specific instructions in his will.

INSTRUCTIONS: It wasn't just about visiting a grave site. More respects must be paid.

Chapter the eighteenth,

---

[115] I'm offended he thought Odissa was broken.
[116] Notice he didn't say "let Odys live." Then again, it would have thrown off the Proper Noun ending our Narrator is so attached to.

Deus ex machina:

But which machine?

"Come, Odissa, let's browse the next stop in our *costumes*," Dorian gestured to the exit, extending an open hand.

She ignored the hand. "I'd hardly call them costumes."

"Well, we must use our imagination then, my kitty. Please, take my hand. I really can't see."

"Will Fletcher know where we're going?"

"Of course, he's already opened the next place we're going."

"And where's that?"

"The inside dollar theater just down the strip—one that's apparently been closed for some time."

"I don't want to watch a movie."

"Who said anything about a movie? I'm hoping we'll be too busy to pay attention to anything like that."

And so she found herself in a dimly lit theater before a huge and tattered screen, in a row with vandalized seats, beside a wanna-be Elton John.

Oh, and for some reason, she had a suspicion that Fletcher was watching from above in the projector stand—probably chugging away at some drink he'd stolen. She knew he was watching from somewhere—Dorian was too *aware* of his surroundings.

"Isn't this nice?" Dorian said, putting his feet on the back of the seats.

"Sure," Odissa lied. She eyed the flickering exit sign. Below it, the door was boarded up. No escape.

"I wonder if they've left a popcorn machine behind? Should I send Fletcher to look for one? Granted, he might not find any popcorn to go with it—"

"I don't really like popcorn." She adjusted her tail. It was very uncomfortable to sit with.

"So, what movie is playing?"

"There isn't one."

"Imagination, Odissa. Use it."

"I feel like I'm in someone else's movie right now. Aphrodite's."

"Well, let's not talk through the movie then. Let's play our part." Dorian laughed. "You want the gods to get their money's worth."

She hated that she wanted to laugh, so changed the subject. "It feels shallow—the fact you're in love with me because a goddess forced you. It undermines the real thing, doesn't it?"

"Does it now? Define 'real love.' I doubt everyone has the same definition. I've learned to accept fate. It takes less effort if you know the gods will handle everything. Even if I have no control, I'm still enjoying myself."

"It seems you've enjoyed a lot of things in your life time—on both ends of the spectrum."

"Believe it or not, I've always gone both ways. Well, okay, maybe more bisexual with a heavy emphasis on the male form. But there is a *minor* attraction to a select few women…"

"Sounds like a college degree."

"Ah, but I'm not the one with a complicated love life, am I? You think I can't see it?" He retrieved a fresh pack of gum. He must have stolen a new one when she wasn't looking. He tossed the wrapper behind him. "Why do you share his bed? I mean, it wouldn't be so obvious if we hadn't *seen* your bed—a bed you didn't use. Otherwise, you hide the fact well, I'm sure. You shut everyone else out because you don't need them. Why would you when you've an opposite reflection of yourself?"

"You think everyone wants to fuck themselves, is that it?"

He shrugged. "I've fucked Fletcher. Plenty of times. Most times he opens his eyes when I do it, so it's like I'm seeing myself as I fuck him. It's wonderful."

"I don't know how to respond to that."

"That's what's great about this, isn't it? We don't *need* to respond. We just understand each other. That's the key to a good relationship. Ours will be perfect."

She snorted. "It will, will it?"

"Excuse me, not *will be*, but *is*. Already."

She felt the need to defend herself. "Just because we share a bed doesn't mean anything's happening."

"No, I guess it doesn't," he passively agreed. "But at least you admit you share his bed."

"We just…always have." She found herself crossing her arms.

"Why?"

"When growing up, I'd cry without him. I was afraid of the dark and being alone. Our father…"—she paused and started up again—"He—he let us have our way, if it would shut us up. So would the nannies. Ah, look, I've finally shut you up."

"Odissa," he turned to her, leaning on the chair arm, miscalculating the direction of her face by a hair (Fletcher wasn't paying enough attention)—"*have* you fucked him? I don't want secrets between us. I need you to admit it to me."

She laughed—laughed because there was nothing else to do.

"Why not just tell me you haven't, if you haven't?"

"Because why should I?"

"So you aren't even going to *lie* about it anymore? You're just going to keep the truth from me?"

Exhausted, "Yes, exactly."

"All right, all right. We can change the subject."

"Why don't we change company while we're at it?"

"Are you saying you don't like me?"

"Exactly."

"Ah, so you *love* me," he stated, proud of his cleverness.

"Why would I do that?"

"Why *wouldn't* you?"

She said nothing.

"What else should we talk about, then?" He tilted his head, slouching in his seat. "Haven't been on one in a while, but isn't this what couples do on dates, talk about their past love lives?"

"This isn't a date."

He gripped his knees—knees attached to those legs perched on the back of the seats. "What would you call it then?"

"A fucking kidnapping."

"Awww. Because I stole your heart? That's so sentimental, darling." He let his laughter settle. "So, since we're on a date—"

"Not a date—"

"—I need to know how many sexual partners you've had. I need to know what to expect in the STD range, you know? I can still catch those things, even with an Automaton."

"This isn't romantic conversation, just to let you know." She'd move down a seat if she knew he wouldn't follow her.

"Sure, I'd rather stop the chit-chat too and get right down to business, but I don't think we've come that far yet."

Before she could comment, his phone rang.

"Aren't you going to answer that?"

"Ah," he said tapping his coat's breast pocket, apparently where he'd put his phone. "Too bad Fletcher's eyes aren't here to tell me who's calling."

"I can tell you," she offered.

"Don't insult me. Just because I'm a girl doesn't mean you have to open doors for me and the jam jar too."

"Then make Fletcher come down and read them."

"No. I liked where our conversation was going. But where were we again? Oh, yes. *How* many relationships have you been in?"

"I told you I've never dated."

"I know. But dating and fucking are not the same thing."

She stared at his phone. Its screen lighted the fabric as it rang again.

"Just answer it."

"If you insist." He picked up. "Hello? Oh? Oh, really? I see. Okay. That was quicker than we expected—Oh, yes, I guess it's hard to plan these sort of things—Of course I want to hear what you recorded from his phone. Fletcher's bored out of my wits, send it over! Oh? Mm. Yeah, we can be there, in the morning. *Sí,* puedo. [More rambling in Spanish too fast for Odissa to keep up with]. No, I wasn't aware. Yes, I'm keeping her *entertained*." He smiled in Odissa's direction, wanting her to hear. "Oh, well, that's wonderful. Oh, all right then. *Sí, sí.* Buh-bye."

"Who was it?"

"Mother."

"Your mother?"

"No, not my *real* mother. Everyone just calls her that. Apparently your brother passed—a lot quicker than expected."

"Passed?"

"He did what we wanted him to." To himself, "And so quickly too."

"So you'll leave us alone now?"

He frowned at the hope in her voice. "No, no, dear. I'm sorry but this is your life now. Your brother's no free man. None of us are."

"What does that mean?'

"You're not stupid, Odissa. You met Maud. You know what she is. We can't let Odys just do as he likes with her now that he's one of us. Don't sigh like that. It shows your worry."

"How can I not worry? Why do you even have to test him? The gods can set up a *date* for you but not make you—you and your *mother*—trust my brother? Is that it?"

"Gods might meddle in our affairs, but they aren't going to solve our problems. They're *our* problems, after all. There's no need to worry about your brother. Not when he's on our good side...I thought he'd try and track me down and take you away from me. But he did things the right way. He's such an honest boy." *He will complicate things.*

"What?"

"Let's just get back to our date."

"No, not back to our date. This *isn't* a date, Dorian. I'm not here because I want to be."

"What'd make you *want* to be?"

"I need to know the—the truth. The facts."

"Facts?"

"Like the fact you have a fucking—what do you call him?"

"Fletcher?"

"No, what *is* he again?"

"Oh, an *Automaton*."

"Right. So hard to remember. How'd you even get one? How the hell did *Odys* get one?"

"I can't tell you that."

"Maybe if you'd talk more freely with *me*, I'd talk more freely with *you*."

"I need you to trust even when I *don't* tell you, Odissa. I'm risking a lot by telling you what Fletcher is to begin with."

She looked down at her feet, not liking his real face—a face that wasn't so pretend-happy. "I don't see how it can be that complicated."

"Oh it *is* complicated. However, Odissa,"—he sunk even lower in his seat, as if about to snooze—"what *isn't* complicated is the fact we're in this complication together." He sounded like a Facebook relationship status.

"You think that's all a relationship takes? Just being in the same room with someone?"

"I do," he flirted, resting his head in his hand, leaning away from her. "If two people are in the right place at the right time, then why not?" He lifted his hand. "And it might be easier for me to give information to you if only you'd realize that I do, indeed, have a phone. That phone can make calls to get you information. Granted, it has its price. I'm a payphone."

She watched him play with his rings. "And how much does it cost, this payphone? What's a dime worth to you?"

"I'm not going to do all the research for you, Odissa. You're going to have to find out."

For a long while she was silent.

How could he be so calm, when asking her to do this? She noticed one lone, expectant eyebrow rose above his glasses, expecting an answer.

"We can take it slow, you know. The first month can be free, with a contract, of course."

"How do I sign this phone contract?" She asked it mostly to fill the silence—to give her more time to process her decision.

"Well, as long as it's a long-term contract, it's simple. The terms and conditions apply, though. I'm most definitely the girl in this relationship. I think I'll just sit right here and take it." He put his hands behind his head.

Her skin prickled—prickled because even his blunt vulgarity charmed her. "Just tell me one thing," she said.

"Anything."

"Are we going to be OK? Is my *brother* going to be OK?"

Dorian inhaled deeply, knowing her angle. "Maybe if you tell me not to hurt him—maybe if you make it so I *can't* hurt him—you'll get what you want. *Take* what you want, Odissa."

"I won't let you hurt him," she said.

"Try and stop me then. Keep me in line. This isn't about using a phone. It's about using me. You can use me, Odissa. I'm vulnerable, impressionable. I just need attention. Don't you want to give me attention? Aren't I pretty? Won't you touch me? Dial the right buttons?" His fingers wiggled and landed on her warm leg.

"If this 'phone call' gets me nowhere, I'll stop being so complacent. I *will* start trying to run away. I *will* start screaming. I *will* start telling people you're not really cops."

"I promise I'll be a good girl. I promise." He presented his hand at her side.

She picked it up. It was no gentle action. She held on to it as she stood up—as if to let him know she wasn't about to make a dash for it.

"You know," she said down to him, "It's kind of sexist that you think being a female means being the dominated one. Not all females act like that."

"Then prove it."

He lowered his legs, the only mutual response to her first move. As she pushed them apart to stand between them, she considered how *this* was going to work (he offered no advice for the situation, so she was forced to improvise). Lifting the adjustable arms of the theater seats, she placed herself in his lap—facing him. He waited patiently for her to situate and smiled when he heard her take off her glasses. He let her remove his own—as well as the felt pimp hat. She tossed it far away so that he wouldn't be able to pick it up again.

With his eyes exposed, she felt safer to lean into him. He was more vulnerable. He suppressed a grin as she touched his face. He was enjoying this too much—as if proud his sales pitch had worked. After settling into his face, she let her lips brush his, but he didn't kiss back. He just sat there like a limp doll—a doll wanting to be played with.

Slightly offended, she held the sides of his neck as her body pressed down into him. His lack of *response* impressed her—never mind, there it was. *Took him long enough.*

But she felt him cringe a little, hesitant to proceed. "Odissa," he muttered as her hands pulled at her shirt.

"Yeah?" she said, pulling away.

"What are you doing?"

"I'm seducing you. If you couldn't tell."

"Don't you *want* this phone contract?"

"I was wondering the same for you."

"I mean, don't get me wrong, you're doing great for a new customer. But don't you want to enjoy the phone call itself? How can you enjoy dialing when you refuse to press the buttons with *purpose?*"

"Fuck you. I haven't even started. Besides, I've never been"—her voice only mouthed the words—"on top. This is strange."

"Be a man," he quietly commanded—as if such a statement were ridiculous. "You're in charge."

That's what scared her. She stiffened. "Have you ever fucked a girl before?"

"Is it really so obvious that I'm gay?" *That I still am despite wanting you?*

"So, no?"

He breathed in deep. Avoiding the true answer, he laughed and said, "I let Fletcher fuck a girl once. I watched it all through him. I didn't particularly enjoy it. But she sure did. She kept stalking him afterwards. Kept asking around for him. Couldn't let him form up from his inanimate form for weeks."

Angry he had just gone into full story-time mode, "But he doesn't have any balls. I saw him."

"I knew you were looking!"

Blushing, "You lying to me?"

"No. I'm serious. He can form them like clothes. He didn't freak her out, if that's what you're worried about." He frowned. "You like him more than me? Is that what this is?"

"No. I'm just not sure you can—"

"Stay hard? Well fuck, if you keep me jabbering on like this how *could* I make it last? Honestly." He pulled at her thighs, showing her how she should move them once more.

She ruined his smile with her own lips and he finally kissed her back. He kept his eyes open, as if he wanted to see her. She kept soft-humping him and kissing him,

341

waiting for him to finally take himself out but it never happened. Her hands went to do it for him, but, for once, he guided them elsewhere as he leaned back into his seat. "It's okay, Odissa. Stop." He tried to hide the fact he was winded and his dick was still tight.

"What?"

"Not tonight." (He seems to have forgotten it was actually morning, technically).

"What? Why?" She had worked so hard! She felt used. Was this some joke to him?

"So you're saying you want to?" There was something sly in his voice.

"I thought that's what we were doing."

"Honestly, Odissa, the way you treat me!" He threw the back of his hand on his forehead—like the queen he was. "I don't sleep with people on the first date. No one would marry me if they could have the milk for free."

"I think I'm lactose intolerant now." She tried to play along but it came out too mean.

He chuckled. "Don't be such a dick." He sighed, enjoying her—even though he couldn't see her. "Your willingness to fuck a complete stranger amazes me—even if you *do* like me."

"You know why I did it." She tried to get her hands out of his grip. "I want to see my brother again."

He waited for her to calm down and he set her wrists free. The shadow-of-seriousness took him once more. "At first glance, Odissa, you're nothing but a bookworm in the corner hoping no one looks at her. That's what I thought at first. But then you slowly realize that this girl is fucking her brother for a reason, and it's probably a good one." He found her wrists again. He knew she would slap him around—she'd done it before. "I wonder what man made you retreat into your brother's arms?"

The ghost of a laugh escaped her. "You call it *retreat?* I don't call it that. I'm not escaping from misuse. You sound like him."

"You admit it? If not misuse then use; who uses you?"

She pulled back from him, but he kept her on his lap. Her frogged legs tried to stand.

He kept his face down, his grey eyes never blinking. "Who, Odissa?"

A chill trickled down her spine as his unseeing eyes then looked directly into hers, as if knowing where hers were. Timid once more, hers fluttered away. As she blushed, she noticed Fletcher standing a few rows from them near the entrance, watching them. Watching her. He loomed over the situation like a duplicate of Dorian—she was outnumbered.

"Stop looking at me," she hissed at Dorian, though looking at Fletcher. "Stop pretending you can see my face. I don't need you to look at me, Dorian. If you don't want me to lie to you, stop lying to me. I don't need it. You're the one lying—*pretending*."

Lowering his gaze, a sliver-of-a-grin haunted his lips. "Fine. It takes a lot of concentration anyways to locate your face." He put a hand on her thigh. "I won't pretend if you won't pretend. Now tell me who else you've been fucking. Does Odys know this has been going on?"

She tried to slide off him and stand up, but he wouldn't let her go—not until she answered. "Only one other. Besides Odys."

"Who?"

She paused her struggle, confused he would ask. "Who the fuck do you think?" she spat.

"I don't follow."

"My husband, you idiot." *How dare that you mention it!*

His head shot back. "You're—you're married?"

"You mean you didn't know?" Odissa said, her suspicion ringing. "But you know everything about me—"

A redness took his grey eyes and a shock took his throat. "Your last name's Odelyn!"

"I *kept* my name. That wasn't what I wanted from him." *Like he doesn't already know.*

He shook his head. "We'd know about something like this. We found no marriage license when we checked up on you. Don't lie to me, Odissa. This isn't a game. It's not funny." *Please, no.*

"*I* don't even have a copy of the license. It's not something I'm proud of. I don't go around telling people." She suddenly felt the need to comfort him. "You really didn't know?" She wondered if Dorian was only pretending—toying with her again.

"Pero—Cómo—?" He wasn't sure how to ask it.

"You never thought to ask Odys why he wears a wedding ring? One just like mine?" She tried to show him her ring. "It's for him to pretend mine isn't real." And maybe it *wasn't* real—not all of it. In her heart it wasn't.

"Why didn't you *tell* us?" Dorian spat. "How the hell did you hide this from us?"—but he wasn't talking to her. He was cursing someone else...

The spell of Venus's harmony was broken. It was tainted. Not only did Vulcan give him Odys's sloppy seconds, but some Helen-of-Troy? MARRIED! He was more pissed at Vulcan than anything else—he could almost picture the god and His Wife chuckling.

"Why didn't you tell me from the beginning you were married, Odissa?" His voice revealed how hurt he was.

"Isn't it fucking obvious? Why do you think we hate our father so much? Didn't Odys tell you? I thought that's why you didn't ask me about it in the first place. He'd go into a rage!"

When she pulled her wrist from him he realized he'd been hurting her. "My God," he said, taking her face. "That's why he didn't want Odys to visit him—only you. He never wanted Odys. Maybe that's why Pepin gave him Maud? He knew Odys isn't as safe. Odys was never the reason, that's why Pepin chose him. It was always *you*—that's why Odys had to be involved."

"I don't understand." But oh, yes, she did. She was catching on.

"Odys is the leverage. The leverage of the leverage."

She wanted to remind him she was still there, "I'm the leverage?"

"And he knew just how to leverage you, because you're married to him. You're married to *Leeland.*"

ODI ODELYN: The 'father' who made arrangements for his arrangements.

ARRANGEMENTS: Arranged a marriage with Mr. Augury (quite easily too).

ARRANGED: Because Mr. Augury needed a wife to complete what he'd arranged (cough, cough).

ARRANGES: A win-win. The twins get their inheritance and Leeland gets a pawn for spawn...if only it had worked out more fertilely.

Chapter the nineteenth,

The conclusion:

To what, nothing at all?

"Not to Leeland. To Audell Augury," She corrected him.

"That's the same person!" he barked, fuming. He latched on to her as if she might run away—as if she might realize the potential of her *leverage.* "Why the fuck would you *marry* him?"

"Because he—he threatened to ruin us, Dorian—me and Odys. To cut us off. It was the only way we could get our inheritance." She paused, done defending herself. "You know so much about him, why didn't you *know* this? I thought that's why you were kidnapping me!"

(Well, *part* of the reason why).

"Don't act as if I'm not making sense. You're the one not making sense! He *can't* be married to you, he's—he's—"

"In love with someone else? You know, do you? Of course you do. You do know everything!" She studied his reaction. "I know he loves someone else. He's made sure to tell me every time he fucks me—every time! Sometimes I think he told my father to make me marry him so that he could get back at the woman he's in love with. You know, don't you?" She leaned into him, gripping his clothes. She was so close to the truth!

He turned his head away.

She pulled back. "You of all people can't hate me for having secrets, Dorian."

"You know why I'm hiding mine. I'm not fucking normal."

"I didn't realize I was hiding mine!" She calmed herself. Her voice a whisper, "I *tried* to get out of actually marrying him. But he's too *moral* for that. Why aren't you talking? Say something. *What did I do wrong?*"

"Leeland took everything away from me. He did this to hurt me, not Gwen."

"Gwen?" *Oh, the other woman.*

"Put your shirt back on. The mall will be opening soon and we need to make sure we can get out of here." He let her off his lap and stood up, straightening his clothes. Dorian started talking to himself as Fletcher approached: "He wanted her to get pregnant and he wanted control over the child—all would mean more control over *me.*" If Dorian had had the space, he would be pacing. He settled for heavy breathing and pushing back his hair. "Marrying you meant what though? That he felt guilty for trying to impregnate you—virtually raping you?"

"What are you talking about? He never—"

"Your father was his Automaton! His Automaton was *him* trying to impregnate you." He started pacing again. "Of course being married to you kept Odys hating him, right? Meant Odys had to share you. Is that it? Kept Odys away and yet there. That's part of it too, isn't it?"

"That and the fact he wanted to fuck her to piss you off," Fletcher mumbled.

"Don't fucking say it out loud!" Dorian shouted at himself, putting a hand over his own mouth to hide his rage.

Odissa shrunk back from him. She felt the need to assure them, "I was going to ask for a divorce, once I graduated. I *never* loved him."

"That's exactly what scares us, Odissa," Fletcher added, hopping over the back of a theater seat to get a closer view. "The things you've done for money."

"Only to give us a life that would eventually free us of it!"

Instantly, the old Dorian snapped back. "Free you of it?" That earth-shattering smirk on his face miffed her. "You want a life that's free of him? Well, it looks like you've been given one." He gestured to the room. He meant himself.

"Why don't I feel like I'm free of him, then? *You're* not free of him. He seems to be the only reason we met!"

Fletcher put his head in his hand, watching them as if viewing a movie. He would have formed a self-made popcorn prop if the moment hadn't required *some* seriousness. Dorian was moving past his shock.

"I'll never be free of him," Dorian agreed. "But I can damn well make sure you are. You're my baggage now, do you understand that? Just to be clear, you better *act* like my baggage—not Odys's. Mine. If you want things to go peacefully, you'd best understand this. Odys has an Automaton and he's synced with her and that means he can no longer deny what your father did to you—or what you *let* your father do to you. He knows he is only alive because of you and you are only alive because of me. Odys can't help you now."—Quieter—"He's never been able to help you, really. You're the only reason he's still alive and, if you know what's good for the both of you, you'll remember that. I choose if Odys lives and dies because of *you*. Now, be a good boyfriend and give me back my gum."

As his lips came in, she was hesitant to kiss back. He did not kiss her nicely, but willfully—too determined—crazy psycho bitch with man strength. She took the sides of his face to restrain him.

Though her eyes were closed, her eyelids noticed a flash of red—like the flash of a camera when it catches you blinking. Pulling away, her eyebrows knit together.

Blinking past blindness, "Bulfinch?"

Fletcher was already watching the cat (who was quite fuzzed out, clinging to the back of a theater seat). Mecca popped up from behind that same seat. "Costumes! Had no idea you liked *pussies*, Dorian." (Har, har). He took a few more photos on the run.

Fletcher, who had smelled Mecca and Q seconds ago, had been waiting for them to show themselves. He lunged at Mecca (as Mecca lunged for the runaway cat). "Can't you call first?" the Automaton scolded as they dashed away.

"WHAT are you doing here Mecca?" Dorian shouted.

Q, scooping up Bulfinch, answered, "We got bored. Were you seriously just making out with a girl, Dorian?" There was something concerned in her voice, as if this wasn't how things were supposed to be.

Fletcher redirected them, "You got bored?"

"Mecca doesn't think Bulfinch is very fun. Bulfinch doesn't like to be dressed up as various things."

Snatching her cat from Q, Odissa exclaimed, "Why the fuck do they have my cat?" Bulfinch was very frizzed; she had to hold him by the scruff. She stared at Dorian, whose head turned away from her—giving no answer. This hadn't been how he wanted to tell her.

Odissa's heart raced—fast as Bulfinch's. She clutched him to her chest and steadied herself on the arch of a seat. But she didn't have time to panic about her home—

Mecca hopped up over to the seat next to her. "Mecca has decided to like you, Odissa. Mecca has decided that you shall tuck him in tonight when Mecca goes to bed."

"Like hell she will," Fletcher snapped, glowing with fury.

"Who is Mecca?" Odissa asked, turning to Fletcher, a confused arch to her brows.

"That little dingle berry right there," Fletcher pointed, frowning. (The third person always confuses people when said aloud—Mecca looks better on paper).

"At least Mecca's not a big one like you," Mecca mocked as Q picked him up.

"Why are you here, Mecca?" Dorian pressed, yet again.

"Mecca's here to follow you to the next spot."

"Were those *Mother's* orders?" Dorian doubted.

"Did Mother give you the okay to *molest* the captive?" he retorted. "Bob warned us we should keep an eye on you. This what she meant?"

"She's not a captive," Dorian defended himself. He was embarrassed he'd been caught. "And since when do you listen to that bitch? Tell Bob to keep her nose out of my ass!"

Mecca looked up to Q, ignoring Dorian. "Mecca's thinking a Princess Leia look would suit her. Dorian is Jaba. We'll photoshop those pics!"

"That's funny," Q whispered, "because she's a twin."

"Mecca is Han, come to rescue her from her own twincest!" He made his eyebrows jump, waiting for Odissa to react.

Fletcher explained, "His adolescent brain is kind of stuck in maturity limbo."

"Dorian, we brought some of the *stuff*," Q said, looking very serious, "in case you didn't have any. Mother, for sure, won't want her seeing the route to the cabin."

"Ah, you're right," Dorian said, putting a hand to his chin. "I completely forgot we'd need precautions."

Mecca laughed, leaning over the back of a theater seat. "Mecca would too, if Meca had boobs in front of Mecca's face." He pointed at Odissa. Well, more at her boobs than anything.

"This kid's a pervert," Odissa observed unnecessarily.

Mecca nodded, "But Mecca can't help it."

Fletcher rolled his eyes, thumbing at Q. "What are those, if not tits?"

"Who wants to play with your own, though? Never as much fun," Mecca said.

Odissa was slightly appalled Q just let the little boy squeeze and jiggle her tiny boob. She cradled Bulfinch away from the child.

Q handed Fletcher something in a small disposable box she'd dug from her bag.

"Are you serious?" Odissa said as Fletcher took out the LARGEST needle she'd ever seen. "What the fuck?"

Fletcher stuck it in the vial. She hated how he knew what he was doing, as if a nurse!

"You want to see your brother don't you?" he asked, squirting a little from the needle's tip. "There should be no side effects. We've used this hundreds of times. Funny, this drug was your father's recommendation, even—a long time ago. He's probably used it on you plenty, so chance has it you'll have no reaction to it." He gave a bitter smile. "Just sit back."

She saw Dorian step forward, as if he might restrain her if necessary.

"No, I'll let you." She gave Bulfinch back to Q, whose outstretched arm offered to take him.

As Fletcher gave her the dosage, he said, "We should have used some of this last night. Then we both could have gotten a good night's sleep."

She glared at Dorian as he finished. "Be nice to my cat."

"We saved him in the first place, didn't we?" he soothed, tucking her hair behind her ear.

She was asleep in a matter of seconds.

"Sooo," Mecca filled the silence. "You wanna feel her up while you got the chance?"

"Finally want to know what boobs feel like, Dorian?" Q chimed. "I would have let you feel mine."

Dorian raised one of Odissa's eyelids for Fletcher to see. "It's actually good you showed up when you did, Mec. You saved me from being too heteronormative just then. I was being too 'stereotypical masculine,' if you will. I was scaring her. And myself. Odissa isn't like other girls."

Q raised a brow. "And you're not like other boys, which is why we're still confused."

Dorian thought to Fletcher, *I almost couldn't control my anger.*

She wasn't afraid of you, though.

Fletcher carried Odissa out to the car, sitting her nearly in his Master's lap and crawling in after. Dorian cradled her as Mecca started the car.

"I think this will work out, Dorian," Fletcher said as he adjusted Odissa's cat ears. He let his too-long fingers trail down her hair, arranging it into place.

Q looked over the backseat. "Stop molesting her, Fletcher!"

Fletcher ignored her as she giggled. He merely said, "She's the one, Q. Just look how happy my Master is." He patted Dorian's sleepy face.

"But if that's a good thing, who knows?" Q baby-talked. "You smell a bit different, Dorian. Everyone does these days." She turned back around, assuming the outfit of a cat as well, to match Odissa. "I like cats, too," she assured Bulfinch (who was in her lap). He braced himself as the car moved, his eyes dizzy as the world whizzed by.

As they drove, Dorian and Fletcher didn't touch. They normally would have. They would have held hands and nestled in together. Instead, Fletcher placed his willowy hand on Odissa's knee and watched the sleeping girl for his Master. There was no need to touch Dorian. She was the conduit. "It's nice to be taken care of, isn't it, Fletcher?" Dorian kissed the top of Odissa's head before he leaned his own back.

In private thought, the two exchanged Dorian's personal plans: *Will we give Odissa an Automaton? Yes, I cannot live without her. Whether or not she wants one? Yes, whether or not she wants one—we can't lose her again. We will give her Madus. It just seems right, doesn't it? Even when we kill Leeland—oho, the plans we have for him!—we will not give her an Automaton of that man. He has tarnished her enough already. No, she will never have Admund or Coraza.*

CORAZA: The third face of Leeland.

WAS: Sometimes a nurse or nanny to the twins, though they can barely remember her.

IS: Not used very often, for Leeland is not sure how he feels about being so *feminine*.

WILL BE: A match for the screw, Caffar.

Endnote/Chapter the twentieth (depending on what you'd rather call it),
To be continued:

Who doesn't love a good cliffhanger?[117]

This story nears its end. I've been told to keep it short and sweet—not that I followed those directions (word count is such a bitch).

Read book #2 (if there *is* a book number two, publishers willing) to find out what awful things Odys had to go through on his little Mission Impossible; to find out why Vulcan wanted Bob out of the picture; to find out what Leeland plans on doing with Cestus; to find out how Dorian will avenge Odissa; etc., etc., etc. I need not go on.

But, while we're still pushing past 100,000+ words, let's analyze what this fast-approaching, half-assed ending means.

Even if this novel *was* tied up with a pretty bow, let's not kid ourselves. We all knew this was going to be a "series"—this story's self-awareness didn't exactly promise you something stand-alone in the first place.

No, this closing isn't even a real cliffhanger and it's not trying to be. This is my biggest twist. Most novels, even in a series, can stand alone. This one can't. No Epic can stand alone without the context of the others. Isn't that right, Gabbler?[118]

Do remember, even Homer got more than one volume (and *how* did he end his first tale again? Exactly. You have no right to be pissed at me. This unfinished finish is the art!). At the least, this non-ending will give you something to complain about to your friends.[119]

The worst of you will actually try to decipher this part as if it really has some meaning. *What does it mean?!* It means pick up the next damn volume. Need I convince you?

Fine. Here it goes.

Ahem.

I mean, I guess I *could* just give you a teaser for Volume 2? Say something along the lines of *"Vulcan will admit the Masters are all part of his major plan to make the*

---

[117]Me.

[118] Well, yes, all of the Epic poets kind of influenced each other by default. They were, after all, working in the same genre.

[119] See, Reader, you've gotten your money's worth. *Cringes*

gods notice his handiworks and skills—humans are just beta testers for something much more sinister." But I won't. That's not enough of a cliff to hang. That's more like a window ledge. A clear view of the street. A street that leads somewhere. The possibility of the earth to catch us if we decide to jump.

No, I need the river rushing down below. Perhaps we won't die if we fall. But where does the river lead? The rock is crumbling under our fingers. There's no one to catch us.

So, instead, I'll tell you who I am—the character who I am/will be in this story—give you a reason to hang on tight because, good lord, are those alligators?!

(Drum roll, please).

Stanza: The end ends a mystery.

They say that cats have nine lives. I've used up quite a few.

See, I used to be a cat—in a past life.[120]

I'm not anymore. Vulcan made me change all that.

What? Don't believe me? Well. You just read a whole story about how inanimate objects can become humanoid. How much easier to believe an organic creature can become a human, then?

Yes, yes. A cat becomes human.[121]

Vulcan's divine plan—to be enacted in the next volume(s)—created heavenly cyborgs of more than just humans. All animals must bow to the machine (as I, the cat, did). This book was the thesis for my own humanity. The next will be the body and conclusion to that divine claim.

Ovid and Kafka wrote of metamorphosis, but I merely mention it in passing. Just how did I become a human? Well, that's for another time—later I'll detail how Bulfinch became *me*.[122]

---

[120] I am looking at our Narrator now and can promise you they are no such animal. Completely human. As you can tell, our Narrator has quite the imagination.
[121] Or vice versa, depending on your need to work out some issues through writing this story, Narrator. But, at least there's a little more of that *dramatic irony* for you.

ME: Anonymous.

ME: Divine in my own right.

ME: A perfect example of the Author-as-God.

ME: Yet nothing without Gabbler.

End

---

[122] And now you know why we wanted two names supporting this story. Or, rather, just my name.

Learn more at:

www.circodelherreroseries.com

This book is indie.
Help spread the word about it.
Lend it to someone who might like it.